About th

C000125356

Sharon started writing as a c
proved far too short a read, and she decided to continue
stories herself, rather than waiting a whole week to find out
what happened next. This resulted in a hundred-page novel,
complete with illustrations, about a boarding school for girls
who wanted to be ballerinas. As she had never been to
boarding school and didn't know the first thing about ballet, it's
fortunate that no copies of this masterpiece exist.

She now writes contemporary romance with plenty of
humour—much to her mother's dismay, as she was convinced
Sharon was destined to be the next Catherine Cookson.

Sharon lives in East Yorkshire with her husband and German
Shepherd dog, and fits writing in around her job with the NHS,
five grown-up children and hordes of grandchildren. She is a
member of the Romantic Novelists' Association, one tenth of
The Write Romantics, and is shamefully prone to all-
consuming crushes on fictional heroes.

Find out more about Sharon on her website:
www.sharonboothwriter.com

By the same author:

There Must Be an Angel
A Kiss from a Rose
Once Upon a Long Ago
This Other Eden
Baxter's Christmas Wish

SHARON BOOTH

Resisting Mr Rochester

Fabrian Books

Published in Great Britain in 2017 by:

FABRIAN BOOKS
Kent, England
www.fabrianbooks.com

Copyright © 2017 Sharon Booth.

The moral rights of the author have been asserted.
This book is a work of fiction. Names, characters, businesses, organisations, places and events other than those clearly in the public domain, are either the product of the author's imagination or are used fictitiously. Any resemblances to actual persons, living or dead, is entirely coincidental.

Cover design by Berni Stevens.
www.bernistevensdesign.com

All rights reserved. No part of this publication may be reproduced, stored in any retrieval system, or transmitted in any form, or by any means electronic, mechanical, photocopying, recording or otherwise, without the prior written permission of the publishers.

For Tracey and Richard ~
my companions through life.
With much love always.
xxxx

Chapter One

There was no chance of taking a walk that day. It was, as my dad would say, siling down, and as I hadn't brought an umbrella, it seemed wiser to go straight home, as unappealing as that thought was.

"I don't suppose you'll be going to the park today, then." It wasn't a question. Jilly patted me on the shoulder, as I stood gazing out of the window, watching the rain bounce off the school playground. "Though, I suppose park is a bit of an exaggeration, whatever the council calls it."

I took her point, but if you ignored the broken roundabout and the graffiti scrawled all over the slide, and concentrated on the grassy area beyond, edged with trees, you could almost pretend that you weren't in the centre of Oddborough, a grim north-east city, overlooked by the concrete towers of high-rise flats.

I liked to walk to the park every day after work, sit on one of the swings, face the greenery, and daydream. Jilly, who ran the nursery school where I worked, thought I was bonkers, but then she lived in a rather pleasant suburb with her dentist husband, and had a large garden, and wide, tree-lined grass verges down her road, and therefore didn't have to grab her slice of nature with both hands, wherever she could find it.

1

"I suppose I won't," I agreed.

"Good. Come to the pub with me. We should celebrate. Not every day a girl turns thirty."

"I don't think I can be classified as a girl any longer," I said gloomily. "I'm positively geriatric."

"Geriatric? At thirty? Give over." She laughed and nudged me. "Still a spring chicken! Are you doing anything special tonight?"

I gave her a look that clearly spoke volumes, and she sighed.

"At least let me give you a lift home. I don't like to think of you standing at a bus stop in this weather."

"You live in the opposite direction to me," I reminded her with a smile.

"So? A small detour won't harm me."

"Quite a long detour, actually," I said. "Thanks, Jilly. That's really kind of you, but I'll be fine. I'm in no hurry to get home."

She pulled a face. "Trouble in paradise again? What's happened?"

"Nothing. I think that's the problem."

"You know, you really do deserve better," she told me. "You're wasting your life away, Cara Truelove. It's time you took some control back. Oh, well, if you're sure you don't want a lift, I'll see you tomorrow."

We said our goodbyes, and as she climbed into her car and began the journey home to domestic bliss in suburbia, I dashed down the street, dodging puddles and ducking umbrellas.

I reached the bus stop just as the bus arrived. Jumping on, I bought a ticket and sank onto the nearest seat, gazing unseeingly out of the dirty, rain-streaked window, my heart sinking ever lower as the bus carried me mercilessly to the Feldane estate.

"You're early tonight," Seth called from the kitchen, as I pushed open the front door of our tenth-floor flat.

My heart—foolish thing—lifted momentarily, at the fleeting hope that maybe he was making our tea, but when he strolled into the hallway, carrying a mug of coffee, my heart landed with a thud where it seemed to nestle permanently those days—in my boots.

He leaned over and planted a kiss on my cheek. "Had a good day? I've missed you." He didn't offer to pour me a drink, but carried his own into the living room.

Scowling, I hung my coat on the hook, then headed into the kitchen to make my own. At least the kettle had just boiled. With a cup of tea in hand—we didn't even share a preference for hot drinks—I followed him into the room.

It wasn't that I particularly wanted to spend the next few hours watching Seth's favourite programmes, but unless I wanted to stand in the kitchen, sit on the loo, or spend the evening in our bedroom, there wasn't much of a choice. The flat had been described by the council as compact. I could think of other descriptions.

The one good thing about the place was the view. Being on the tenth floor, I could see for miles from every window. Luckily for me, the location of our building meant that the view from our living room balcony was amazing. In the distance, I could see fields and trees—the promise of countryside. In dry weather, I would spend as much time as possible sitting on that balcony, staring into the distance and daydreaming. Years of practice had given me the ability to completely ignore the broken-down cars, piles of rubbish, and gangs of yobs congregating in the area immediately around the block of flats. My focus was all on the horizon, where there was beauty and hope.

Seth yawned.

"Tiring day?" I asked, screwing up my nose, as he put down his coffee and stretched, breaking wind as he did so. Where, I wondered, had my hunky, romantic boyfriend gone?

Evidently, sarcasm went over Seth's head. "Yeah. Been really busy," he agreed. "I've written three poems."

"Wonderful." *Well, that must have taken up fifteen minutes of his time. Bet he hasn't done the washing, though. Lazy swine.*

"Naomi popped by," he said. "She's had another row with Dad."

I tutted into my cup so he wouldn't hear me. What was new? His sister was always rowing with her dad, because he had some weird idea that people should actually go out and earn a living. Neither of his children seemed to agree with that strange philosophy. Mind you, they didn't seem to object to other people earning a living on their behalf. Naomi was twenty-six and still living at home, sponging off her father. Seth, meanwhile, had me.

"Oh, and Redmond called. Told him you were at work and you'd call him back."

"Redmond called?" Not like him. He'd already sent me a birthday card, with a twenty-pound note slotted inside. It'd been a massive relief, as it meant I had enough money for my bus fares to work until that blessed day at the end of the month, when my wages would finally go into the bank. "Did he say what he wanted?"

Seth gave me one of his looks. Once upon a time, I'd have melted at one of those looks. He used to seem

4

smouldering and sexy when he lowered his head and peered up at me with those unusual grey eyes. Lately, he just looked cross-eyed and stoned. Which he probably was, judging by the sickly-sweet smell that lingered in the air. "You know your brother," he said. "Never tells me anything. Terribly disapproving. I'm far too much of a free spirit, and he just can't handle it."

"Hmm." I fished my mobile phone out of my bag and went through the contacts list looking for Redmond's number, but when I called, I only got the engaged tone and hung up.

Tapping into the Facebook app instead, I scrolled down through my feed, wondering if anyone had posted birthday wishes to me. Jilly had, which was lovely. Redmond wasn't on Facebook, as he was far too busy being an academic genius and earning shedloads of money from his work at a university. Tamsin had posted a photograph of a vast bunch of flowers on my timeline and wished me a lovely day. She'd sent me a beautiful bouquet through the post, which had really touched me, as no one ever bought me flowers. Although, I had panicked a bit, as I didn't possess a vase. An old Pyrex jug had served the purpose. I appreciated her kind gesture, but still tutted as I caught a glimpse of another of her impossibly jolly updates.

Lovely sunny day! Off to Pilates! Feeling happy!

Trust Tamsin. Even the sun was on her side. I could just picture my sister living her perfect life in her perfect five-bedroomed detached new-build, while I was stuck in a dingy council flat with the rain pouring down outside.

My own fault, I reminded myself. *You got what you deserved.*

5

The telephone was ringing. Snapping out of my self-pitying mood, I picked up the receiver, pretty certain it would be Redmond. He was the only person I knew who used a landline rather than a mobile whenever possible. He was infuriatingly—and rather endearingly—old-fashioned,

"Evening, Cara." My brother's voice, with his broad Yorkshire accent, sounded comfortingly familiar. It reminded me of home and put a lump in my throat. "Mum asked me to call you," he said, without preamble. "It's Granny Reed. She's gone."

"Gone where?" I had visions of her escaping the nursing home and roaming the streets of Newarth, the village where she'd lived all her life. Worse, maybe she'd got as far as the moors. Maybe, even now, she was stumbling through the bracken, confused and alone. "Is it raining there? Did she take a coat?"

There was a moment's silence, then Redmond said, "No, Cara, I don't think you understand. She's gone. Kaput. Brown bread. You know. The candle has been snuffed out."

"You mean, she's dead?" Well, what else could he mean? But I didn't believe it. Even after she'd been dragged, protesting all the way, from her terraced house to the nursing home, after trying to fry chips in a pan of lime cordial—an easy mistake to make, in my opinion—and, last Christmas, attempting to pay for a twenty-pound frozen turkey in the supermarket with a bag of chocolate coins pinched from its own shelves, she'd seemed indestructible. "But she can't be."

"Why on earth not? She must have been ninety, at the very least," Redmond said without a trace of sentiment.

"Anyway, the funeral's a week on Friday, if you think you can make it. Our Lady of Lourdes Church, eleven o'clock."

"I'll try," I said, dazed. "I'll have to ask for time off work."

"I'm sure it won't be a problem—not for a family funeral. Anyway, Mum and Dad said you can sleep over at their place, if you like. Are you—I mean, will you be bringing—"

"I doubt it," I said. "Funerals aren't his thing."

Seth looked up and raised an eyebrow. I shook my head, and he went back to composing poetry in his mind. At least, that was what I assumed he was doing. It was his stock answer whenever I used to query what he was thinking about. I only had his word for that, of course. He could have been thinking about the latest episode of *The Simpsons*, or daydreaming about Jennifer Lawrence, or wondering what I was planning for tea, for all I knew. It was more likely than composing poetry, when I came to think about it, given that the stuff he came up with was so bad, it surely couldn't have taken more than five minutes to create.

To think, I used to believe he was an undiscovered literary genius.

"No, I suppose not," Redmond said. "Well, if you're there, I'll see you at the church. Have to go. We've got Susan's boss coming here for dinner. Again."

"Lucky you," I said. "Aren't you the favoured one?"

He made a sort of mumbling noise that may, or may not, have included the word bloody in it, and added, "I've told Tamsin, by the way. She's going. Surprised she can fit it in with such a hectic lifestyle, but there you go. See you there, Cara."

Seth glanced at me as I replaced the receiver. "What was that about?"

"Granny Reed," I said, feeling bewildered. "She's dead."

"Oh, right. Well, she was pretty ancient. Had a good innings."

"Did you want to go to the funeral with me?" I asked, not sure how I wanted him to respond. Part of me wanted the support, but the other half dreaded the thought of playing referee between him and my family. I knew he'd be rude and condescending towards them, yet would take immediate offence if they said anything remotely unfavourable in return. I'd be on eggshells the entire time.

He shuddered. "You're joking. I won't go anywhere near any church, and Catholic funerals go on forever. Besides, my poetry collection is at an exciting stage. I don't want to disrupt the creative process."

He took a slurp of his coffee and closed his eyes, and I clicked the Facebook icon and found Tamsin's page, spotting a later post with a very different tone.

RIP Great Grandmother Reed. My heart is truly broken. #bereft.

It was slotted between the Pilates post and another one, in which she trilled about the unexpected delights of a kale and spinach smoothie. No wonder I hadn't noticed it.

"What's for tea?" Seth queried, not bothering to open his eyes.

In my mind, I composed my own status.

Crappy rainy day! Idle boyfriend! Dead granny! Feeling pissed off! #HappyBirthdayToMe

8

Chapter Two

Granny Reed was, in fact, my great-grandmother, and Mum's granny, and she'd managed to outlive both her daughter, son-in-law, and husband, which my mum said had changed her personality completely, and not for the better. Not surprising, really. I couldn't imagine how she'd borne such terrible loss.

For all her married life, she'd lived in a two-bedroomed terraced house off Newarth's main street, and I didn't know what she was like before such tragedy marred her life, but when I was a child, she wasn't the most welcoming, or warm, person. Even so, a trip to visit her had always been something to look forward to, because it meant going back to the village I loved.

I'd lived there myself until I was seven years old, and I still considered it home, even though we'd moved to Beverley, in East Yorkshire, when Dad got a new job. The only time I got to visit the village, after that, was our monthly visit to Granny Reed.

While I seriously doubted she'd fit anyone's image of a doting granny, as I sat there in church on the day of her funeral, watching the priest sprinkle holy water over her coffin, and listening as he chanted lots of strange Latin phrases, I felt a real and genuine sadness at her loss. She had tried to make something of me, all through my childhood. She'd always been convinced that I had some talent in me somewhere and, unlike everyone else—myself included—seemed determined not to give up hope of finding it. What a shame she hadn't succeeded before she'd finally turned her back on me.

As a devout Catholic, Granny Reed had never got over the fact that her own daughter had married a protestant and turned her back on the *true religion,* so her face when she discovered that Seth's father was a Church of England vicar was a right picture. As if his long hair and lack of employment weren't enough to make her despise Seth already. She had pretty much washed her hands of me from the day I moved in with him, telling me I'd thrown away my life for a wastrel. At the time, I'd dismissed her words as the rantings of a religious, pious old nut.

Well, I was sixteen. How was I supposed to know she was spot on?

Our Lady of Lourdes Church was in the market town of Coppering, a few miles from Newarth. Catholic churches were few and far between on the Yorkshire Moors. I'd never been in a Catholic church before, and it was certainly different to the laid-back, let's-all-be-friends-play-the-guitar-and-hug-each-other atmosphere of the Anglican church. Not that I had much experience of those, either. Mum didn't believe in God, but celebrated Christmas and Easter 'just in case', while Dad was convinced that we were all computer simulations, and since he'd never found any support for his theory in the Bible, he pretty much dismissed the whole thing as a fairy tale. And Seth, he avoided the church at all costs—more to annoy his father, I suspected, than because of any real aversion to the religion.

10

I didn't think any of us really had a clue what was happening during the service. Dad yawned, and Mum nudged him. I wasn't surprised he yawned. He looked exhausted. In fact, when I'd set eyes on him for the first time in ages, earlier that day, I'd been shocked at the sight of him.

"What's wrong with Dad?" I'd demanded, the moment I could get Mum away from him.

She'd seemed flustered. "In what way?"

"In what way? How do you think? He looks shocking. He's lost so much weight, and he looks like he's aged ten years. What's happened to him? Is he ill?"

"It's retirement," she said briskly. "He's had a rough time adjusting. Felt a bit useless. Lost his appetite and couldn't sleep, but he's picking up now."

"You mean he's depressed?"

"Well, maybe a bit. At least, he was, but he's on the road to recovery now. Honestly, Cara, don't worry."

"But I can't help it," I'd said, horrified. "You should have told me. Why didn't you tell me?"

She said nothing, and I reddened, realising I hadn't exactly made any enquiries. Dad's decision to take early retirement had astonished me, frankly, given his strong work ethic. I hadn't even realised they could afford for him to retire, but Tamsin told me the company was in trouble, and they were asking for people to take voluntary redundancy. Dad had been one of the people who offered, and he had no intention of looking for another job. It had all sounded quite unlike him to me, but Tamsin didn't seem to see anything strange in his decision.

Looking at him then, I realised I should have rang him. I should have checked to see how his new life of

11

leisure was suiting him. Clearly, it wasn't suiting him, at all. He looked like an old man.

Mum tutted, then put her arm around me. "If you'd seen him a month, or two, ago, you'd have had every right to be worried, but he's improving in leaps and bounds now. I swear to you, Cara, he's fine. Got his appetite back, too. Don't worry."

Watching him sitting there, one hand stifling another yawn, I thought I was quite glad that I hadn't seen him a couple of months before. If he'd looked worse than that I'd have been terrified.

I cast a glance at Redmond, only to find him texting on his phone, which I thought rather rude. I was surprised his wife, Susan, hadn't taken it off him. She liked to do things the *proper* way. Although, she was clearly too intent on following the proceedings, pretending to be actually interested in what was happening and, more importantly, that she understood it, to notice.

I glanced over my shoulder at my sister, and Tamsin gave me a weird fake smile, as if someone had just pulled a string and forced her mouth into position. She looked even thinner than usual. Not surprising, considering how many exercise classes she attended. Beside her, her husband, Brad, glanced at his watch and looked irritated. I was amazed he'd taken time off work to attend. He was a workaholic, as Tamsin had informed us many times, with a note of pride in her voice, as if being obsessed with a job was a good thing. I had to admit, though, I'd quite like Seth to become obsessed with a job for a while—any job would do. He seriously believed that he was a professional poet, even though the only piece of writing he'd ever been paid for was a letter he'd written to a television magazine,

12

bemoaning the fact that *Torchwood* had gone 'All American'. He'd earned a whole twenty quid for that. I could have had a break from cooking and ordered a takeaway for once, if he hadn't immediately spent it on dope and a giant bar of chocolate to celebrate his staggering literary success.

Years ago, when we'd first got together, he'd had several poems published in an online magazine, which had caused us both a great deal of excitement and unfounded optimism. He hadn't received payment for them, but we'd been sure it was just the start. I'd been so wrong about that, and it seemed that Seth's failure to build on that promising beginning caused me more sadness and frustration than it did him.

As the church service ended, we all filed dutifully into the churchyard and stood solemnly as Great Granny Reed was laid to rest. Susan dabbed a tear from her eye with a proper lace hanky, not a manky old tissue from her pocket, which is what I'd have had to use if I'd been crying. I wasn't crying at all, though. I felt frozen, and it wasn't all down to the cold February air, even though that was bitter enough to strip the top layer of skin from all our faces—except for Tamsin's, who was so well insulated with such a thick layer of foundation and powder, it no doubt offered more protection than a balaclava.

"Right." Dad hooked an arm over Mum's shoulder and beamed at us all, once the priest had finally left us after politely turning down Mum's offer that he come back to Newarth with us and join us for *a drink and a bit of something to eat.* "The Cock and Bull it is."

Brad grimaced. "Really?" He glanced at his watch again, then turned appealingly to Tamsin. "Is that strictly necessary?"

"We've laid on ever such a nice spread," Mum reassured him. "Besides, it will be nice to have all my family around me for once. We never get together these days. I'm so glad you could all make it."

There was no mention of Seth. They'd never included him in anything, something for which I'd blamed them for years, until it had occurred to me that maybe he was as much at fault, if not more so. He'd despised them from the first, and had worked quite steadily and thoroughly to isolate me from them.

I had to own up to the fact that I'd allowed that to happen, though. I'd been young, and madly in love. As long as I had Seth, I hadn't needed anyone else. My family didn't understand him.

Where they saw a lazy, unemployed layabout with no respect and no future, I saw a wild, gifted romantic, with the soul of a poet and bags of potential. We were Cathy and Heathcliff, destined to be together, no matter who opposed us. We were twin souls. Children of the moors, who belonged to each other for all eternity.

I blamed Kate Bush. It was her glorious song, *Wuthering Heights*, that'd introduced me to the novel when I was at an impressionable age, which in turn convinced me that, to be happy, I simply had to find a rugged man, who didn't play by the rules of society, and who loved me, in spite of my disapproving family. Seth had fitted the bill perfectly, and when I discovered his father was a vicar, I was beside myself with joy. A vicar was the same thing as a parson, wasn't it? Seth's father was a parson, just like Emily Brontë's father! It'd appealed to my ridiculously romantic nature and overactive imagination. To me, it was

14

a sign that we were destined to be together.

How I would've loved to be able to go back in time, meet that teenage version of myself, and shake some common sense into her.

Newarth was a pretty village, perched on the edge of the North Yorkshire Moors. It had one main street, built on a gently sloping cobbled hill, a long row of interesting, independent shops, and a pub, The Cock and Bull. Apart from that, there wasn't a great deal to say about it, but I loved it, as I loved the moors beyond.

I'd desperately wanted to move back there after I left home to be with Seth, but he wasn't keen. My Heathcliff, apparently, wasn't enamoured of the moors, preferring instead the concrete comforts of city life. I wasn't sure how he managed to persuade me that we'd be better off living in a high rise flat on that gloomy estate, but then again, I couldn't figure out how he persuaded me to leave home at all.

He was nineteen when we met—gorgeous, and completely different to the boys in school, with shoulder-length brown hair, and an intensity in his expression that turned my knees to water.

I was sixteen, naive, and way too innocent.

I'd met him one fateful Saturday afternoon in the book shop, as he perused a slim volume of Romantic poetry, while I was browsing the shelves for a replacement copy of *Agnes Grey*, since my own copy had fallen to pieces. I didn't know modern men read poetry. Dad tended to stick to the sports pages of the newspapers, while Redmond seemed to have no time for anything other than reference books. As for the boys at school, they thought poetry was for girls. Their reading material tended to be mostly photographic and elicited lots of jeers and nudges and cries of *phwoar* in the school playground. I'd never met a man who read poetry for pleasure before. It was the turning point of my life. And I took the wrong turning.

"You've done her proud, love." Dad patted Mum's shoulder, then grabbed a plate and began to pile it up with sandwiches, sausage rolls and vol-au-vents, totally ignoring the salad, as usual.

Clearly, Mum was right. There was nothing wrong with his appetite. I felt a huge relief as he bit into a sausage roll and beamed with pleasure.

Predictably, Tamsin filled her own plate with nothing but lettuce leaves, tomatoes, cucumber, and the teeniest piece of chicken. Redmond and Susan looked dismayed by the spread, and I heard mutterings about the lack of couscous, olives, or hummus, while across the room, Brad lurked in a corner, his mobile phone glued to his ear.

After waiting for a crowd of Granny's friends from church to fill their plates, I grabbed a couple of cheese sandwiches and a piece of pork pie and headed over to a corner of the pub. Sliding into a seat, I wondered if I could risk sneaking out soon to take a walk. It would be a crime to come all the way up to Newarth and not walk. The moors were practically in touching distance. I wasn't bothered about the weather. The sad fact was, this might be my last visit back to my home town, and I wanted to make the most of it.

I looked up, startled, as Tamsin dropped down beside me.

"Hello, stranger." She peered at my plate, probably mentally totting up the calories, and frowned. "Been ages since I saw you. Have you forgotten me?"

"You can talk," I said. "You know where I live."

She shuddered. "Yes, I do."

Charming.

My phone beeped and I tapped on the message. It was from Seth.

What time will you be home tomorrow? You do realise we've run out of coffee? What am I supposed to do now?

I put my phone back in my bag, hardly able to suppress a sigh.

"Was that lover boy?" Tamsin prodded a tomato with her fork and eyed it suspiciously, as if it was really a calorie-laden chocolate truffle posing as something healthy. "How come he's not here?"

I was about to defend him, as I always did, telling her that he was far too busy to attend, but some spark of boldness flared up, taking even me by surprise, and I heard myself saying, "Because he's a selfish, lazy git who couldn't care less that I've just lost my great-gran. That's why."

Tamsin almost choked. "Hell, Cara! What's got into you? Don't tell me Heathcliff has finally lost his charm?"

My face heated until it was probably redder than her tomato. She didn't have to remind me of my passionate teenage pleas with her to understand how much he meant to me—that he was my very own gypsy boy, and I was his very own Cathy. I'd rather hoped she'd forgotten that. Clearly, she hadn't. Embarrassed, I picked up my pork pie and bit into it with some defiance.

"Ugh. You really shouldn't eat that stuff," she informed me. "I'm so careful about things like that. I eat ultra-healthy these days, and I've really built up my fitness,

17

too."

"I know," I said. "I'm friends with you on Facebook, remember? Though I find it hard to believe that anyone's as permanently cheerful as you are."

"I can't think what you mean," she said. "Why would I lie about it?"

I supposed she had a point, and anyway, why wouldn't she be cheerful? Her house was fabulous, judging by the photos she'd sent me when they moved in, and the ones she sometimes posted online. I'd never actually seen it for myself, but then I'd never been invited. Her husband, although far too serious for my liking, was decent enough, and certainly earned enough money to support the family. Tamsin didn't have to do anything as tiresome as work for a living. She was, as she constantly pointed out, a full-time mother to two little blonde girls who were as perfect as she was.

Alice and Robyn were ten and eight, and even though they were my nieces, I'd only met them a few times. I realised I didn't feel any real connection to them, at all, which was sad.

Feeling a sudden lump in my throat, I put the pork pie down. What was happening to me? Why were all these weird feelings of guilt, and sadness, and anger—anger! Me!—unexpectedly appearing?

Was it, I wondered, because of *that* birthday? Turning thirty had undeniably depressed me, and it had also started a panic inside me. I'd done nothing with my life. I'd not even got started. I was nowhere. A nobody.

At an ominous prickling in my eyes, I blinked furiously. I didn't do crying. I hadn't cried for at least three years. I remembered the last time quite clearly. I'd sobbed for hours, but afterwards, I'd dried my eyes and vowed *no more*. Nothing would ever touch me like that again, and I'd stuck to that. So why was I suddenly feeling such an awful churning of emotions? And, more importantly, what was I supposed to do with them?

Redmond and Susan appeared. "Do you know about the will?" They sat down beside us, forcing Tamsin and I to move even closer together, which was a rather unnerving experience.

Tamsin's face took on an eager expression. "Ooh, no! Has she left us anything?"

Susan tutted. "Really, Tamsin. Don't be so mercenary."

"Well, you brought it up," Tamsin said. "Don't tell me you haven't thought the same. Everyone knows she had a bit of money put by. We're her only relatives, aren't we? We must be in line for something."

"Not as much as you might suppose, I'd guess," Redmond informed her, in his usual pompous tone. "Most of her savings were dwindled away on that dratted nursing home. It cost a fortune to keep her there. There'd have been a lot more in her account, if she'd managed to stay in her own house."

"How inconsiderate of her," I said.

Mum and Dad came over. "There you all are. Have you had enough to eat? There's loads left, even though your granny's friends seem to have fairly substantial appetites. Tamsin, please tell me you've eaten something," Mum said, eyeing my sister's thin frame with concern.

Tamsin changed the subject. "Redmond says Granny left hardly anything in her will."

"Bloody hell, Redmond," Dad said, "let the poor old

stick go cold before you start worrying about that."

Mum nudged Susan up and sat next to her, so Dad did the same to Redmond, which meant Tamsin and I were practically stapled together. "They may as well know," Mum said. "The fact is, there's hardly anything left of any value. The nursing home fees were extortionate, in my opinion, but there you go. It's the way of the world."

"But you'll be selling her house?" Tamsin said. "That must be worth something?"

Mum and Dad exchanged puzzled glances. "Selling it? Of course not. It was rented. Didn't you know?"

It hadn't even occurred to me, and judging by the horrified expressions on my siblings' faces, it hadn't occurred to them, either. I almost laughed. So much for their expectations.

"She left me three thousand pounds," Mum admitted. "Of course, I'll give you all a little something."

"How little?" Redmond asked.

"I'll send you all a cheque for five hundred pounds," Mum promised. "I need the rest. Your dad's redundancy money paid off the mortgage, and the car finance, and all our other debts, but it hasn't left us anything to enjoy, so we're going to make the most of this little windfall. Me and your dad are going abroad. Your Auntie Sylvia's been asking us to stay with her in her house in Spain for ages, but we've never had the money to spend, really, and we didn't want to go over there and sponge off her, did we? We haven't had a holiday in ever such a long time, and we're making the most of it. It will do your dad the world of good. And then, when we get back, we're having a new carpet in the lounge."

"Well, I can't say you don't need it," Tamsin said.

"The carpet, I mean. That tatty old thing you have now is so embarrassing."

"And you deserve a holiday," I told them, thinking anything that put a bit of meat on Dad's bones and some colour in his face was fine by me. Anyway, I had *five hundred pounds*! I felt quite rich.

"Great," Redmond said. "And I lost a day's work for this."

"Oh, Redmond," Susan said mournfully. "We had such plans."

"*You* had such plans!" exclaimed Tamsin. "We were hoping to visit Disneyworld in Florida this year. The girls need to go. They're practically the only ones in their class who haven't been. They're socially deprived."

"Bloody hell," I muttered.

"Of course," Tamsin continued hastily, "we can still go. I mean, obviously, we can afford it. But it would have been a nice cushion. Extra spending money."

"What a drag," I said. "Isn't five hundred pounds a big enough cushion?"

"You've clearly never been to Florida," Tamsin said.

She wasn't wrong there. I'd never even been to London.

"The nice thing is, though," Mum continued, "she named every single one of us in her will. She's left us all a little something to remember her by. Something personal."

"Really? Like what?" Redmond sounded suspicious, as if he couldn't imagine Granny Reed having anything that he'd want, which was probably true.

Mum looked a bit nervous. "Well, for a start, she's left you her books."

"Books!" Redmond pulled a face. "Why would I want her books? Cara's the bookworm," he added scornfully, nodding in my direction. "Are you sure she didn't leave them to her?"

"No, most definitely not. She knew Cara's taste in books was more for the, er, romantic. As you know, Granny didn't hold much with romance, or any sort of fiction, for that matter. She knew how much you loved to learn, so she's left you her collection of reference books."

"Oh, God," Redmond said wearily. "You mean her collection of Bibles, don't you?"

"Not just Bibles," Mum assured him. "She has lots of books about the Holy Land, and the Catholic religion, and the lives of the saints, and—"

"Thought you said she didn't read fiction?" Susan's nose wrinkled in distaste. "I don't want all those things cluttering up my bookshelves. What would my boss say, Redmond?" She leaned forward and murmured, "Between ourselves, he's paid to have himself cryogenically frozen after death, so I hardly think he'd approve of that sort of reading material."

"Jesus," said Tamsin.

"Quite," Susan said primly.

Tamsin blinked. "Well, anyway, what about me?"

Mum beamed at her. "She left you her Rosary beads, and her treasured painting of Pope John Paul II. I told her all about your posh new house. She must have thought it would look lovely on your living room wall."

Unfortunately, Brad had just made his way to our table, and caught the gist of the conversation. "You can forget that," he told Tamsin. "No way am I having that monstrosity on my wall."

"Pope John Paul wasn't a monstrosity," Mum said, horrified. "He was a lovely man. As Popes go, anyway. They made him a saint, you know."

"I don't give a monkey's," Brad said. "I'm not dissing the subject, I'm dissing the artist. Whoever painted that picture clearly flunked art GCSE. The poor fella looks cross-eyed, and he's got orange skin."

"We're into modern art," Tamsin explained hastily. "And we don't really think it will complement the rest of our furniture."

Dad shrugged. "Something else for the skip," he said. "Oh, well. At least we can get rid of everything now. Sick of it cluttering my garage."

"What about Cara?" Susan said. "What has she got?"

They all looked at me, and I waited, thinking Granny had probably left me nothing. She had washed her hands of me, after all.

"Ah, well, Cara got the jackpot," Mum said, sounding anxious. "She left you the most valuable thing of all."

I stared at her, waiting.

"I don't know how big your flat is," Mum admitted, sounding rather ashamed, as well she should have, given that she'd never visited my home once in the whole eight years I'd lived there, "but you'll need to clear some space, love. She's left you her piano."

#

"Five hundred pounds," Tamsin said, as we left The Cock and Bull and headed up Main Street. When I'd announced I needed a walk, she'd hopped up to come with me. "Honestly, I thought she was loaded. Just shows you."

"Well, five hundred pounds is better than nothing,

and more than I expected," I said. "Thanks for lending me the train fare here, by the way. I'll be able to pay you back sooner now."

She tutted. "Don't be daft. I don't want it back. I'm quite sure I'm not that desperate for money."

So, why keep banging on about only being left five hundred pounds, then? "That's really kind of you. I've never had five hundred pounds before. I can't believe it."

She gave me a pitying look. "Just make sure Seth doesn't get his paws on it." She clapped her hands together and shivered. "Bloody hell, it's freezing. We must be mad. Still, it's good to get some exercise. Need to burn off the calories from that buffet."

I'd have thought she'd have done that just by breathing, but I decided not to say anything. She *had* lent me the train fare, after all.

"Where do you want to walk to?" she asked.

I didn't really have a plan, but as we walked, my legs seemed to carry me of their own accord down Hutson Road, where Granny Reed's house was situated.

We pulled up short when we realised someone had stuck a *To Let* sign outside.

"They didn't waste much time, did they?" Tamsin said.

"She'd been in a home for nearly a year," I pointed out. "They've probably already had another tenant in there since then. Clearly, they didn't want to stay."

"Would you?" she said, staring distastefully at the narrow, terraced house. Its front door stood right on the street. No front gardens down that road. "All damp, and musty, and gloomy. Mind you," she conceded, "they've put new windows in. That's something."

So they had. The old sash windows with the yellowing

24

net curtains had gone, replaced with uPVC frames, double glazing, and vertical blinds. Granny would have been furious.

"Remember the biscuits?" I said.

Tamsin's face cracked into a smile, disturbing her makeup. "God, do I! Always soggy. She kept them in that mouldy old pantry. Riddled with damp, wasn't it? We used to shove them in Mum's handbag, remember?"

I giggled at the memory. "And the glasses, all coated in dust."

"Ugh, that horrible cheap orange squash she used to give us, with fluff floating on the top. I don't know why we had to visit every month. It was awful. She was such a dragon."

"I don't know how you can say that," I said. "She thought you were wonderful. *Such a pretty girl,*" I said, imitating Granny's voice. "*Like a little angel.*"

"Redmond was her favourite," Tamsin argued. "He was clever, academic, top of the class."

"And captain of all the sports teams," I added. "Don't forget that."

"How could I? He reminded us enough times. Granny thought he was wonderful. Mind you, he was Mum's favourite, too. Still is."

"And you're Dad's." It was a fact, and one I'd accepted a long time ago.

"Don't be daft," she said, but didn't meet my eyes. She knew as well as I did that it was true. She was everyone's favourite, really. She'd always been so pretty, and at school she'd practically had her own fan club. Other girls had followed her around, hanging on her every word, wanting to look like her, wear their hair the way she wore hers,

25

nagging their parents to buy the same shoes as hers. Boys, meanwhile, gazed at her adoringly and fought over her—literally, on two memorable occasions. I wondered if Robert Jones and Luke Whitaker still had the scars.

"It was a long time ago," she said finally.

Quiet for a moment, we stood on the pavement, staring up at the house that held so many memories.

"Why did you do it?" she asked suddenly.

I started. "Do what?"

"You know what. Leave home. For him."

Where on earth had that come from? "I loved him," I said. "At least, I thought I did."

"Mum warned you he was going nowhere," she said. "Why didn't you listen? Why on earth would you run off with someone with so few prospects? How could you leave a decent home to live in a squat with someone like Seth?"

"He said he loved me. He said I was beautiful. He was the first person to make me believe it." I drew in a long breath and let it out again. I'd had a lot of time to think about it, having asked myself the same question many times recently. "I thought we were soulmates, and that I was the most important person in the world to him."

She stared at me. "And that's all it took?"

"You wouldn't understand," I said.

"You're right. I don't." She sighed. "And what about now? Do you still feel the same way about him?"

"No." It felt odd to admit it, and I had a pang of guilt as soon as I had. I'd never been disloyal to him before. What was happening to me?

"So, why don't you leave him?"

I shrugged. Where would I go? And what would be

26

the point, really? I may as well stay where I was. It wasn't great, but if I left, would things be any better? Better the devil you know, right?

Seth wasn't my soulmate, I'd grown sure of that, but I no longer believed in soulmates. Sadly, I no longer believed in true love, either, which was a bit ironic, given my surname. "Nowhere to go, and I couldn't afford to leave, anyway."

"You could go home. I'm sure Mum and Dad would have you."

I grinned. "What, even with the piano? Dad's relieved it's going at last. It's been stuck in their dining room since Granny moved into the home."

She laughed. "I'd take it off your hands," she lied, "but I really haven't got the room. Besides," she admitted, "it's terribly ugly, isn't it? I mean, if it was a baby grand, I might consider it, but it's such an old-fashioned mahogany upright. And mahogany just wouldn't go with my oak."

"Well, obviously." I smiled at her. "I don't mind. It'll go in my spare bedroom."

She blinked. "You're going to keep it?"

"Why not? It's all I have of her, and I'd like some keepsake."

"But the piano, of all things. I mean, you hated it!"

I leaned back, resting my elbows on the window ledge. She was right. I had hated it. For a long time, that piano had been the heavy price I'd had to pay to visit Newarth—ever since that fateful visit, one Sunday, when I was eight. I remembered it all too clearly.

We'd been ushered, as usual, into Granny's back 'parlour', a small room which'd led onto her kitchen. The parlour was dark and gloomy, looking out over an equally dark and gloomy, and rather overgrown, garden. There'd been a fake coal fire in her old tiled fireplace, and a large crucifix on the wall above it. A big, dark table took up most of the wall opposite the fireplace, while a two-seater sofa was pushed against the back wall, and an armchair stood under the window. The armchair was Granny's. Mum and Dad got the sofa, while we three children sat on the floor, nodding politely, though reluctantly, when Granny offered us orange squash.

"How are the children doing at school?" Granny enquired, as she'd shuffled into the kitchen to make the drinks.

"Oh, very well," Mum called, looking flustered. "Redmond's just been made captain of the school football team."

"Of course he has," Granny said, as she entered the room again, and handed the little prince his orange squash. As she shuffled back into the kitchen, she added, "And what about the girls?"

Mum and Dad glanced at each other. "Tamsin's just been cast in the school play. She's playing a princess."

Granny returned, carrying a glass in each hand, and bestowed a beaming smile on my sister, who looked suitably modest. "What else would she play? Look at that face, and all that beautiful fair hair."

We took our drinks from her and shook our heads furiously when she offered us a biscuit. Then came the words we all dreaded.

"And what about Cara?"

As Granny Reed turned away, Mum surreptitiously reached over and brushed the dust off the rim of Tamsin's glass. "Oh, she's not doing too badly," she said, a note of desperation in her voice. "She's very good at reading, isn't she, Ray?"

"Oh, she is," Dad agreed.

Granny tutted as she eased herself into her chair. Not that 'eased' was a word I'd connect with that high-backed, firm-cushioned piece of furniture. Clearly, Granny didn't believe in comfort. "Reading's all very well if it informs the mind. What does she read?"

Mum looked at me anxiously. I stared back at her, puzzled. Mum was the one who took me to the library. She must remember, surely? When her mouth opened and closed again without her uttering a word, I decided to take matters into my own hands.

"*Matilda*," I said eagerly. "And *Malory Towers*, and *Charlotte's Web*, and *The Railway Children*, and..."

Granny rolled her eyes. "Thought as much." She gave a big sigh.

Clearly, I'd disappointed her yet again.

Mum and Dad exchanged glances. Dad cleared his throat. "She's learning the recorder, isn't she, Sally?"

Mum looked relieved. "Oh, yes. She's learning the recorder. Doing ever so well. She can play *London's Burning* all by herself." She gave me an encouraging nod.

Granny didn't look too impressed. She shook her head. "The recorder, eh? Proper squeaky din they make." She brightened suddenly. "So, you like music?"

"Mm, yes," I said doubtfully. Did I? Well, I liked listening to music on Tamsin's radio, that was for sure. And I quite enjoyed my recorder lessons. Not so much for the music, though. More for the fact that we had the lessons in the only spare room available at that time—the staffroom. It was cosy and cheerful, with lots of comfy chairs, and a sink unit and a fridge, making it seem homelier than the classrooms. Best of all, it had French doors that opened out onto a small garden, with neat flowerbeds, which, right then, were a colourful mass of golden daffodils and scarlet tulips. The recent warm weather meant that the doors were opened during the recorder lessons, and it was proving quite difficult for me to concentrate on the teacher, when I wanted to turn the other way and gaze at the garden.

Granny startled me by hauling herself to her feet and holding out her hand. "That's it!" she proclaimed, with more excitement than I'd ever heard her use before—to me, at least.

"Er, that's what?" said Dad, as I reluctantly accepted Granny's hand. It felt dry and bony, and made me cringe inside.

"Music! Clearly, her talent lies with music. Tamsin got the looks and the personality, Redmond is academically gifted, as well as being a great sportsman. Cara's talent is obviously music."

My parents looked as doubtful as I felt. "Really?" Mum said faintly.

"Of course! We must nurture this gift." She began leading me towards the door.

I cast a fearful look over my shoulder, to see Dad looking quite anxious, and Tamsin sitting with her mouth open. Redmond sniggered, and Mum nudged him, quite fiercely.

As we left the room, I heard Redmond call, "Can we put the telly on now, Granny?"

Granny waved a hand. "If you must." The door closed behind us, and I was alone with her. She led me down the hall and stopped outside another door. I looked up at her, alarmed. The white room! It was Granny Reed's front room, and I had never been allowed inside before.

I'd heard Mum and Dad talking about her sacred white room, though. Mum had said it gave her the creeps. 'Honestly, it's like a bloody shrine. I'm surprised she hasn't rolled a stone in front of the entrance instead of having a door.'

What had she meant? What was in there?

Granny pushed the door open and ushered me in. I stepped inside and stood, trembling. The room was painted white, and there was a somewhat dingy grey carpet on the floor. A thick layer of dust covered every surface. It seemed Granny hadn't been in there much recently, either.

A rather unpleasant musty smell pervaded the room. I felt uncomfortable and wanted to leave. I never imagined I'd think fondly of Granny Reed's parlour, but it seemed positively cosy in comparison. There were two pale grey chairs either side of a fireplace, and pale grey curtains hanging at the window, along with a rather yellowing net curtain. There was a dark, hideously ugly sideboard against one wall. On it stood some faded black and white photographs, and a large clock, with a threatening tick. Other than that, the only thing in the room was a piano.

A piano!

I stared at the instrument in fascination. I'd only ever seen a piano in the school hall before. It wasn't the sort of thing I'd ever imagined a normal person would have. Then again, it was Granny Reed we were talking about.

Granny went to the fireplace and picked up a box of matches. Given how damp the room felt, I was amazed they still worked, but they must have been industrial strength, because she struck one and, after three attempts, it caught. Solemnly, she lit a white candle that'd been set beneath a huge painting dominating the chimney breast. It was of an old man in a white dress and a little white cap— a bit like the one my cousin Katy had worn when she was a bridesmaid at a wedding the previous summer.

I stared up at him, curious.

"Do you know who that is?" Granny asked me.

I swallowed hard. Was it some kind of test? "Er, God?"

I didn't think that was a bad guess, considering all the other pictures in the room. After all, there were paintings on every wall of Jesus and Mary. I knew about *them*, of course, from school. There was Jesus holding a lamb under his arm. Jesus knocking at a door, a lamp in hand. Jesus sitting at a table, surrounded by men who seemed to be having quite a party. Jesus hanging on a cross. I didn't like that picture. It was cruel and made me feel sick. Then there was Mary, who was Jesus's mum. She had a heart glowing in the middle of her chest on almost every painting. In one, she was dressed all in white, with a crown of stars around her head. In another, she wore blue, and nursed a golden-haired child on her knee. In the final one, she stood in the clouds, surrounded by baby angels. That was a particularly weird one. If Jesus and his mother were in the other pictures, it stood to reason that his father was the subject of one in the white room, surely? And everyone knew that God was Jesus's father.

Granny stared at me with evident sorrow. "It's a disgrace," she muttered. "An absolute disgrace." She leaned towards me, her eyes piercing. "This, Cara

Truelove, is His Holiness, the Pope. Does that mean anything to you?"

I considered the matter, but had to admit, it meant nothing.

Granny went quite pale. She seemed very upset about something. "The Pope," she informed me, "is the father of our church. He is God's representative on Earth. Every word he utters is a commandment from God."

I gaped at her. "What, every word?"

She nodded. "Every word. He speaks with God's voice." She gazed up at the portrait, clearly awestruck.

I examined the Pope's face. How strange it must have been not to have your own voice, I thought. Imagine opening your mouth and having that booming sound exploding from you every time. Not that I knew what God's voice sounded like, but I thought I'd quite like to hear the Pope talk so I could find out. We stood, not speaking, for a moment. The clock ticked loudly.

Then she turned to me, suddenly quite business-like. "The piano."

My eyes widened. "I can play the piano?"

That, I thought, would be fun. Mrs Hambleton played the piano at school, and no one else was allowed near it. Even Tamsin and Redmond had never played the piano.

She shuffled over to the piano stool and lifted the seat. I peered inside. The stool was also a hiding place for lots of papers. Granny flicked through them, then drew out a sheet of paper, a bit like the ones we were given in the recorder lessons, but old and yellowing.

"This will do to start with," she informed me. She placed the sheet on a stand on the front of the piano, then patted the seat. "Sit down."

33

I climbed onto the stool and stared at the sheet. Despite the recorder lessons, I still couldn't read music, but I could read the title all right. "That's *The First Noel*," I told her with a frown.

"What of it?"

"But it's April," I said. "That's a Christmas carol. You can't play Christmas carols in April."

"Nonsense. We can celebrate the birth of our Lord at any time," she said briskly. "Now, let's begin."

I'd thought the piano lesson would be fun, but it turned out to be dull and difficult. I couldn't understand anything she was saying about the marks on the music sheet, but I managed to copy her movements as she played the first line of the carol, over and over again. After half an hour, though, I was bored and rather annoyed. In between playing, over the ticking of the clock, I could just about hear the sound of the television coming from the next room, and imagined my family sitting in there, watching a programme, laughing, talking to each other, feeling relaxed and happy, while I sat there, a prisoner of Granny Reed.

On top of that, I could feel the man with God's voice staring down at me. I half expected his booming God voice to shout at me when I made a mistake. The back of my neck prickled with unease, the dust made my nose twitch, and the musky, damp smell made me feel nauseous.

"Needs tuning," Granny said, finally closing the lid of the piano, to my enormous relief. "I'll get someone in before your next visit." She went over to the fireplace and blew out the candle.

I remembered the churning feeling in my stomach at

her words. Was it to be a regular thing, then? Were my visits to Granny Reed always going to involve that sort of torture?

I'd glanced across at Mary, as she hovered in the clouds. She gazed serenely back at me. The piano lessons were probably my punishment for not being pretty like Tamsin, or clever like Redmond. I sighed. I had an awful feeling it was going to be a very long time before I mastered *The First Noel*. Christmas carols would never give me the same pleasure again.

From the next room came the sound of laughter, as my family clearly found something amusing on the television.

Right there and then, in the White Room, was the moment I knew for sure what the difference was between me and my siblings. They were good enough, and I wasn't. They were accepted and loved, just for being themselves. They were already perfect, and just what other people wanted.

I, on the other hand, was not. I wasn't pretty and popular like Tamsin. I wasn't clever and sporty like Redmond. I was small, plain, and of average intelligence, at best. If I wanted people to like me, I had to do something extraordinary, be something better than I already was.

And I didn't have a clue how to go about it.

"You want to know why I can't leave Seth?" I said, as Tamsin and I headed back toward The Cock and Bull. "Really?"

"Of course." She fastened the top button of her coat and shivered in the icy wind.

"Because no one ever wanted me, just as I was, before

him, and no one ever will again. And I can't be any better than this. This," I said, waving a hand over my duffle-coat clad form, "is as good as it gets. So Seth is as good as I can expect."

I waited for her to protest, to argue that I was being ridiculous, defeatist, negative. Instead, she stuck her hands in her pockets and began to run. "Come on. It's freezing out here. Time for a brandy!"

I guess that said it all.

Chapter Three

"Seth," I said, sitting beside him on the sofa, something I hadn't done for quite a while, "why are you here?"

He tilted his head, and I could practically hear the cogs whirring in his brain.

I sighed, knowing what he was thinking. "I don't mean in an existential way. I'm not looking to start some deep and meaningful philosophical argument. I mean, why are you here, *with me*? After all this time?"

He frowned. "What a peculiar question. I'm here because I love you. Why else would I be here?"

"But do you?" I just didn't know anymore. It seemed to me that the burning passion between us had long since dampened down until there was barely a flicker of flame left. The bonfire of our romance was in danger of becoming a pile of ashes. If it hadn't already. "Are you sure, or is it just something you say, without thinking?"

He studied my face, as if checking for signs of madness. I waited for him to say something studied and profound—or at least mildly reassuring. "Is your period due?" he enquired.

Frowning, I stood up. "I'll make the tea."

As I wandered into the kitchen, he called after me, "Have you had a bad day at work?"

"Just the usual," I replied, which must have satisfied him, because he went back to watching his favourite quiz show, *Pointless*, on the television.

Had I had a bad day at work? Well, no worse than usual. Most of the children were okay. Some, however, were little monsters, who lashed out and swore when they couldn't get their own way. Not their fault. Jilly and I had long since realised that those children were merely copying their parents. Our theories had been proven correct each time we had meetings with parents to discuss their offspring's worrying behaviour, and we were told, in no uncertain terms, that there was nothing wrong with the kids, and it was clearly down to our crappy teaching, and we'd better watch what we were saying, or there'd be trouble.

Some of the children, however, were absolute darlings, and there were a couple who were so funny and sweet and lovable, they made my insides contract with longing for my own child.

While I fried some mince and diced onions in a pan, I brooded on my childless future. I'd never really thought much about having kids when I was younger. I hadn't even played with dolls, unlike Tamsin. She'd gone through the whole pretend motherhood thing with her dolls. She used to comb their hair, and dress them up, and stick a plastic baby bottle in their mouths, then push them around in her miniature Silver Cross pram. She took it all very seriously, much as she did real motherhood. As soon as Alice arrived, she'd given up work to stay at home and look after her, and she devoted her life to making sure they ate properly, did their homework, and attended so many out-of-school activities, it was a wonder they were ever at home.

I thought about her Facebook status on Saturday

38

morning.

Happy weekend, people! Just back from shopping. Have treated myself to another gorgeous Jenny Kingston handbag! A girl can never have too many handbags, whatever the husband says! Taking child one to dance class, then later, child two to a party! Busy, busy, busy!

I supposed I could always have updated my own status.

Evening, people! Just back from a hard day at work! Have treated myself to a bag of salt and vinegar crisps. A girl can never have too many calories, whatever the scales say! Now making shepherd's pie while unemployed boyfriend watches television quiz! Pointless!

And that was how it all felt, really. Pointless. I supposed it was a good thing that we didn't have kids. I couldn't imagine Seth taking care of them. He was far too absorbed in his own life, and how could I afford to take time off work to be a full-time mother?

Luckily, Seth had made it very clear that he didn't want children, because they would only tie him down. He hadn't wanted to get married either, because marriage would only tie him down, too. It was also the reason he gave for not getting a job. Seth clearly didn't like being 'tied down', at all—apart from in the bedroom, which, frankly, was tough luck on him.

When he complained about my lack of adventure in that department, I explained that his refusal to be tied down meant that I had to work hard enough to support the pair of us, and that left me too tired to tie him down, which was ironic, if you like. He could hardly complain about that, could he, so he shut up, just in case the argument escalated and I brought up the subject of him finding a job again.

So, all in all, I couldn't imagine that I'd ever be a mother. I was *thirty*, after all. The biological clock was ticking. Maybe it was for the best. Let's face it, with our combined genes, no child of ours would have much of a start in life. Knowing our luck, it would have my looks and Seth's work ethic, which would doom it to a truly gloomy future.

With the shepherd's pie in the oven, I made him a coffee and myself a tea, and carried the drinks into the living room, wrinkling my nose at the smell of marijuana. The pungent aroma had hit me the moment I got home from work, and the Mars wrappers had been a dead giveaway, too. Dope always gave him the munchies. I wondered how he'd got the money that time.

"Have you had company today?" I asked, handing him the mug of coffee and sitting on the chair opposite him.

He nodded. "Naomi and Isolde came over."

I'd guessed as much. His sister smoked dope on a regular basis, as did her friend. Isolde was another sponger, though in her case, her parents never minded. They were loaded and had set her up in her own flat, and paid her a generous monthly allowance. They didn't really care what she did, so long as she didn't bother them. To be fair to Isolde, with parents like that, I wasn't surprised she'd turned out the way she had. Though, what Seth's and Naomi's excuse was, I couldn't imagine, since their father was a decent, hardworking and thoroughly moral man, who quite despaired of his children's lifestyle and was always very kind to me on the rare occasions we met.

"Naomi's had another massive row with Dad."

"Oh, for goodness sake! Every time you see her, she's had a row with him. Don't you get bored listening to her moaning on every day?"

He looked quite surprised at the thought. "Of course I don't. She's my sister."

"And he's your father! And he's a nice bloke. I don't understand your problem with him." To be honest, I never had, although I'd sort of pretended that I did, when Seth and I first got together. After all, I wanted Seth to believe I was on his side, no matter what. I was very good at hiding my own opinions.

"How can you say that? You know he's done nothing but try to suppress us all our lives. If Mother had lived, it would have been different. She would have let us have our creative freedom, and she'd never have forced us to go to that awful school."

That awful school, I'd eventually discovered, was only considered awful because they'd required that Seth and Naomi make the effort to learn something, which they both agreed was an infringement of their human rights and would delay the blossoming of their artistic talents—a trauma from which they considered they were still suffering.

I couldn't be bothered to get into another argument about it all, though. I was tired, hungry, and faintly nauseous from the sweet, sickly smell of the marijuana.

"Anyway," Seth continued, "there won't be any more arguments. Naomi's moving out."

"Moving out?" I was grudgingly impressed. "You mean she's actually going to get off her backside and support herself?"

He looked quite offended. "She's moving in with Isolde. It'll work out for the best. She can write her songs and play her guitar without him complaining about the noise all the time. She's happy to doss down there."

I snorted in disgust. "Doss down! Isolde has a luxurious three-bedroomed penthouse apartment! She's hardly going to be sleeping on the floor and eating beans out of a can, is she? God, talk about landing on your feet."

He seemed alarmed by my bitterness. "What on earth's wrong with you today? I really don't like this side of you, Cara. It's quite off-putting, to be honest."

"Well, I'm very sorry, I'm sure," I said, not feeling sorry, at all. "Maybe I'm just tired of being the only mug who actually works for a living around here. Maybe I'm fed up with going out to that nursery every day, to be ignored by naughty children and threatened by loutish parents. Maybe I'm sick of having to catch that bus every day, to sit with people who clearly don't know what a bar of soap looks like. Especially given the fact that you and your friends seem to do nothing but sit on your arses all day and smoke that crap, which, by the way, absolutely stinks. You know I hate it! Can't you, just for once, think about me?"

I'd never verbally complained before about Naomi and Isolde visiting him so often, though I'd long resented it. They rarely came round when they knew I'd be home, but would plonk themselves on my sofa the minute I'd headed off to work, and while I slaved away all day to earn money, they sat in my flat, smoking, and eating me out of house and home. They were bad for Seth, because they provided him with free joints, and told him how wonderful he was, and generally pandered to his ego all day.

Isolde, thin and pale with spiky blue hair, a pierced nose, and an eclectic assortment of tattoos, had once told me I'd ruined Seth's life, which I thought was a bit rich.

'You've spoilt him,' she told me. 'You let him walk all over you, and you pampered him and crushed his creativity. An artist needs to be lean and hungry, and full of anger. You're making him soft. How can he compose poetry, when you're dosing him up on sausage casserole and chocolate digestives?'

'Better than dosing him up on cannabis,' I'd retorted, stung by her cheek.

Did she think I went out to work and supported him for the fun of it? I was supporting myself. The fact that I was also putting a roof over his head and food in his stomach was an unfortunate by-product of that.

'At least cannabis helps him to connect with his soul,' she'd said darkly. 'You have no idea about art, clearly.'

'And you have no idea about rent and electricity bills, and finding bus fares to get to work at the end of the month,' I said. 'We all have our weaknesses.'

She'd given me a look of disgust and gone back into the living room to fawn over Seth.

Naomi told me once that I had no need to fear Isolde's obvious lust for him. 'He only has eyes for you,' she'd told me. 'You're his soulmate.'

'I was his soulmate when he shagged your other mate, Gina,' I pointed out. 'Didn't stop him, though, did it?'

She'd tutted. 'That was just *physical,*' she said scornfully, as if it meant nothing. 'There was no *spiritual* connection, whatsoever.' She said it as though it should've been obvious, and I was being deliberately dim.

I supposed I was, but not in the way she meant.

Seth was quiet for a moment, as if trying to digest the fact that I'd broken out of my cage and actually told him what I thought. In truth, I was quite surprised myself. I mean, I'd thought all those things for ages, but I'd never actually said them. I couldn't believe I'd had the nerve.

"Sorry," I heard myself say. "I'll check on the shepherd's pie."

As I stood up, he caught my hand. "Things will get better," he told me, his expression earnest. "I've put a plan into action. I'm going to be bringing in some money very soon, and then maybe you and I can have a holiday together. You could do with a break."

I stared at him. "You mean, you've got a job?"

He smiled. "Sort of. You'll see. All in good time."

My heart lifted, and I smiled back. "That's wonderful. I'll warm up that apple crumble for afters to celebrate, then you can tell me all about it."

He loved apple crumble, I thought, rushing into the kitchen and checking on the progress of the shepherd's pie. A few minutes more, I decided, before opening the fridge door to take out the crumble.

It wasn't there. The dish it had been in was still there, but there was nothing left in it, except a few crumbs and a large spoon. I clearly hadn't noticed earlier when I'd taken out the mince.

My heart sank, and I tried to push down the resentment I felt. No doubt the three of them had finished it off that afternoon. Brilliant. And they hadn't even had the decency to wash the dish after them.

Forcing myself to stay calm, I focused on the fact that, at last, I wouldn't be the only breadwinner in the family. A holiday! Where would we go, I wondered? Neither of us had a passport, so probably not abroad, as paying for passports would just be an added expense. And I couldn't imagine that the job would pay much. Seth had no experience and no qualifications, but nevertheless, it was a job, and a new start. There was hope. Maybe life would start to improve at last. Maybe, I thought, tearfully, Granny Reed was up there somewhere, looking out for me. Perhaps she'd forgiven me for being selfish and stupid and irresponsible, and for running off with a vicar's son.

I hoped so, anyway.

Thinking of Granny, I wandered toward the spare bedroom where Granny's piano had taken up residence. I'd taken to running my hand over it every day, though I wasn't sure why. It had arrived a week ago, much to Seth's dismay, and looked quite elegant, actually. Mum had polished it until it gleamed, and Dad had paid for a professional piano tuner to 'knock it into shape', as he put it. I wished I could find room for it in the living room, rather than hiding it away in the spare bedroom. I was even considering having lessons, if I could ever put enough money by to pay for them. Wasn't like I could use the five hundred pounds. That was safely in my bank account, in case of an unexpectedly high bill, or a broken washing machine, or some other such catastrophe.

I stopped dead as soon as I entered the room, my heart thudding with dread.

Where the piano had stood was an empty space. Apart from a box of Seth's old vinyl albums, and a pile of magazines which I'd never dared examine too closely, the bedroom was bare.

I stormed into the living room. "The piano! Where is it?"

Seth beamed at me. "Gone."

"Gone? Gone where?"

He seemed to sense that I wasn't too happy about the fact, and his smile dropped. "What's wrong with you? Thought you'd be pleased."

"Pleased about what? What have you done with it?"

"I sold it."

I dropped onto the sofa, overwhelmed with feelings I couldn't put a name to. "Sold it?"

He looked a bit uncertain. "Isolde put it on Facebook for us. Some friend of hers snapped it up. Came to pick it up today. Two hundred and fifty pounds!"

Something scarily unfamiliar began burning inside me. Something so huge, it seemed to be rendering me unable to speak. With enormous effort, I managed, "How dare you?"

He blinked. "What do you mean? I've done you a favour. It was just stuck there in that room, and you said yourself you always hated having to play the damn thing when you went to see the old woman."

"It was my piano!" My voice sounded very strange. "Nothing to do with you. Nothing to do with Isolde. What the hell gave you the right to sell it behind my back?"

He shifted uneasily. "It wasn't behind your back, exactly. It was meant to be a surprise. Two hundred and fifty pounds, Cara!"

I shook my head, dazed. "And that's the money you were talking about? I thought you were getting a job."

He smiled again, suddenly looking more sure of himself. "Ah, but it's even better than that. Isolde and I are going into business. I'm going to use the two hundred and fifty pounds as an investment. We're going to make a fortune."

I wanted to slap him. "And what business is this? It must be something amazing, if you're planning to spend *my* money on it."

He didn't seem to hear the emphasis on *my*. Obviously too enthralled in his own wonderful plans. "Isolde knows someone who knows someone who's got all the equipment, and is willing to sell it cheap. She'll be putting up most of the money, but I'll be a partner. I reckon, in that spare bedroom, we could grow quite a lot of it, and the profit from that would be fantastic. I mean, there would be expenses, obviously. We'd need to keep the heating on full all the time, for a start, but when you think what it costs just to buy enough for a few joints, we could make a fortune. I reckon we could—"

"That's your plan?" A lump of concrete seemed to be sitting in my chest, making it hard for me to breathe. "You're going to become a drug dealer?"

He glanced around like we were being watched, and glared at me. "Don't say it like that! You make it sound as if I'm one of those sordid men who push heroin on schoolchildren. This is just cannabis. Everyone smokes it."

"I don't."

"No, well. You're—you."

"Meaning?"

"Well, you're so bloody honourable, aren't you? I mean, you never do anything exciting, or edgy. Everything's by the book with you. I'm all for honesty, but you're ridiculous. It's quite boring, to be honest. Can't you just turn a blind eye? It's easy money, for God's sake."

Turn a blind eye. Oh, I was so good at that, wasn't I?

"Thanks very much."

"Well, honestly, you're so innocent. It's time you grew up. You're no fun anymore, Cara. I'm struggling to stay positive around you. I didn't like to say, but you're having a negative effect on my poetic output. I'm barely managing ten poems a week these days."

"You used to admire my innocence," I murmured. "You used to say it was refreshing."

"Yeah, well, maybe it was, when you were young. But you're thirty now, and you still don't understand the way the world works. It can be very wearing."

Something seemed to be happening inside me. Like all my feelings had been encased in a giant egg shell, and over the last few months, a tiny crack had appeared, through which some of them had managed to peep through. Suddenly, though, I could feel the shell splitting open. I stared at him in wonder. He stared back.

"What's up with you?"

I didn't answer him, just shook my head and rushed into the kitchen, where I dished out the shepherd's pie. I couldn't believe it, but my overwhelming feeling was joy.

Joy!

How extraordinarily unexpected was that?

I forced myself to sit with him as we consumed the shepherd's pie in silence, then I left him watching some programme about Coleridge and went to bed.

I couldn't sleep. I knew I wouldn't, and that was fine. I didn't want to sleep. I lay there in the darkness, thinking about Seth's little speech. Clearly, I'd been fooling myself that he loved me just the way I was. I was boring, ridiculous, unexciting. To win his approval, I would have to compromise yet again, and I was tired of compromising. I'd turned a blind eye to so many things during the fourteen years we'd been together. I'd ignored the pain those compromises had cost me, just to keep the peace, to keep him happy. I'd convinced myself that I didn't really mind living in the flat, in the city, working in a nursery on a sink estate. What did it matter where we lived, as long as we had each other? I'd told myself that it wasn't an issue that I had to earn the money, while Seth stayed at home, pretending to write poetry, even though I hadn't seen any evidence of his efforts for a couple of years. I'd persuaded myself that it was okay that he didn't want to get married, because, after all, Cathy and Heathcliff never married each other, did they? No one could deny that they were meant to be together, and they didn't need a licence and a ring to prove it. It hurt that there were no children, but maybe Seth was right. The world was overpopulated already, and it would be irresponsible to bring more into the world. Besides, children put so many restrictions on your life. We didn't want those restrictions, did we?

As I stared up into the blackness, an excitement built inside me. What was I doing? What had I been doing all those years? How had I fallen for all his—*bullshit?*

Well, I'd finally seen our relationship for what it was, and I knew, without doubt, that I couldn't un-see it.

Seth fell into bed around half-past eleven, and I waited a good half hour until his breathing was deep and regular, telling me he was asleep. As quietly as I could, I crept into the living room, switched on the lamp, and went straight to the old biscuit tin he kept by the side of the sofa. I knew he kept his joints in there, so the chances were, he would have put the piano money inside, too.

Opening the lid, I discovered a roll of twenty pound notes.

Four hundred pounds in twenties, to be exact, not two hundred and fifty.

Lying swine.

Underneath them was a piece of paper. It was a sketch of Seth, and it was an extremely flattering one. Whoever had drawn it was certainly looking through rose-tinted glasses.

I shook my head, not caring anymore. There was no signature on the paper, but as Isolde had spent two years at art school, for no reason I could fathom, unless it was to kill some time without actually doing any work, she was the most likely candidate. Maybe he'd already slept with her. Maybe he'd been sleeping with her all along, ever since the last one. He'd told me, three years ago, that his affair with Gina had been meaningless to him. That it was just sex, and sex was just another way to express the creative urge.

'I love you,' he'd assured me. 'Only you. You're my other half. My world. Infidelity means nothing.'

Well, maybe it had meant nothing to him, but his betrayal had almost destroyed me, and to survive it, I'd had to lock some part of me away, where no one could reach it. Maybe that was when my love for him had started to die, when I'd started to see him for what he really was.

I wasn't sure, and it didn't matter. All that mattered was that now I saw *everything*, and I was free.

At least, I would be, once I'd organised things.

Maybe Granny Reed had given me the greatest gift, after all.

Chapter Four

Tamsin, unsurprisingly, looked astounded, when she opened the door and found me standing on her doorstep. "What the heck are you doing here?"

"Oh, good. You're in." I pushed past her and dumped my suitcase in her hallway, then leaned against the wall in relief. "I was worried you wouldn't be back yet."

She seemed a bit nervous. "What do you mean? How do you know I was out?"

I tapped the screen of my phone a couple of times, then handed it to her. It was open on her Facebook page. *New hula-hoop class started in town! Exhausting but fun! Hope I can keep up!*

"Oh," she said, handing the phone back to me. "Well, I got back a couple of hours ago."

"And did you keep up?" I asked.

She stared at me. "Does it matter?"

Taking that to mean *no*, I smirked.

She looked almost scared. "What on earth are you doing here?" she demanded again.

"I've come to stay. It's just until tomorrow, when my new accommodation is ready," I added hastily.

She opened her mouth, then closed it again. After a moment's awkward silence, she shook her head slightly. "You'd better come through to the kitchen. I'll make you a drink."

Sitting at Tamsin's table a few minutes later, sipping tea from one of her china cups, I glanced around the kitchen admiringly. It was amazing. Very contemporary, with grey units and granite worktops, and lots of stainless steel. Several large flower displays had been dotted around. Tamsin loved flowers and was always buying them. Good job I didn't suffer from hay fever. Against one wall was a huge fridge almost as big as the kitchen in my flat. Bet she stored more interesting and tasty things in there than mince, milk, and value margarine.

From the kitchen, I studied my sister. Free of makeup, she pulled her blonde hair into a ponytail. I guessed she'd showered after her hula hoop session, and hadn't yet bothered to tart herself up again. There was no way she'd have gone into town without her war-paint. The skinny jeans and ribbed top she wore showed that she hadn't an inch of spare fat on her, and even without the makeup, she was attractive, but I noticed suddenly that there was a tired expression in her eyes, and she didn't appear to be exactly glowing with health, despite the diet and exercise programme.

"Stop staring at me," she said grumpily, "and tell me what you're doing here."

"I told you. I've come to stay. You don't mind, do you?"

"Have you left Seth?" Her eyes widened. "I don't believe you. You haven't got it in you."

"Clearly, I have." I hadn't thought myself capable of it, either, but it just showed you.

"So, why have you come here?" she asked, adding hastily, "Not that I mind, of course. Just, I would have thought you'd have gone to Mum and Dad's."

"You were closer," I said, which was partly true. It was quicker and cheaper to get to York than Beverley from Oddborough, and meant just one train, rather than two.

"Even so," she said. "And what did you mean by your new accommodation?"

I smiled. "I've booked a caravan. I can move in tomorrow. So, you see, it really is just for one night."

"A caravan? In this weather? Where abouts?"

"On the moors," I said vaguely. "It's in a field on a farm. The farmer rents it out to make extra money. I've booked it for three weeks."

"You'll be freezing! You must be mad. And what are you going to do after that? Are you going back to Seth?"

I shook my head. If there was one thing I was sure about, it was that I wasn't going back to Seth.

She waited, and when I didn't give any verbal response, she reached over and took my hand. "Seriously, Cara, what's happened?"

What had happened? I supposed I'd finally realised that Seth didn't love me the way I thought he did, and that had set me free.

It occurred to me that I just wasn't the sort of person that people loved. Not unless I was doing something they wanted, behaving the way they needed me to behave. It was always conditional, and I wasn't playing that game anymore. Love and passion had led me away from who I really was. Trying to please Seth, live a life that suited him, had forced me to compromise for the last fourteen years. And it wasn't just Seth. Looking back, I could see that I'd always done the same thing.

Even as a child, I'd always been easily persuaded into

doing things I would never have done in a million years by myself. Upon leaving school, I'd had no idea what to do for a living, but then I met Seth in that bookshop in Newarth, and that was that. He'd been spending the week in a holiday cottage on the moors with his family, and I was visiting Granny Reed, but within six weeks, he'd convinced me to move into his friend's grotty flat with him, just a couple of miles from the vicarage in Oddborough, and I wasted a year practically glued to Seth's side, totally besotted and happy to do whatever he wanted.

During that time, Seth grew increasingly irritated by the job centre's determination that he should find a job. Clearly, they didn't understand that he needed to be at home to write his poetry, and I'd totally sympathised with him, so I'd sought advice from them and ended up getting a placement at a nursery, going to college part-time to take my exams in childcare. From then on, I'd become the breadwinner, and for a long time, that was okay. We'd moved into a bedsit in the city centre, which was so bad I think the landlord should have paid us to live there, and after a few years, the council gave us the high-rise flat, which, initially, had seemed like heaven, because we had our own bathroom at last, if nothing else.

If the flat wasn't exactly a beautiful home, if Oddborough wasn't exactly my ideal location, if nursery nursing wasn't exactly my dream career choice, it didn't matter, because Seth was the man I loved, and so much better than I imagined I deserved.

The delusion I'd cocooned myself in became threatened when I realised he was sleeping with Gina, but somehow, I'd bottled up my feelings and stumbled through the last three years, closed off and numb. Until then.

I wasn't entirely sure what had changed. I couldn't pinpoint a moment when I'd started to *feel* things again. I only knew that when I did, those feelings weren't positive. And after his little speech the previous night, I'd finally realised that Seth didn't love me. He needed me. I was his protection against the world. With me in his life, he didn't have to find a job, earn money, be a grownup.

All those thoughts ran through my mind, but out loud I only said, "I'd just had enough."

"Well, about time," Tamsin said. "But how are you going to manage? What about your job?"

"I've walked out," I said, wrestling another pang of guilt. "I had no choice. If I didn't leave there and then, I might never have done it."

Jilly had been wonderful. I'd called her early that morning to tell her I wouldn't be in. That I wouldn't be in ever again. She'd been sad to hear that I was leaving, but all the same, she was glad, for my sake, that I was finally going. She'd assured me that she and the other nursery nurses would cope until they got a replacement, and wished me luck, begging me to keep in touch, which was much kinder of her than I deserved.

Tamsin stared at me, anxiety in her eyes. "He must have done something dreadful. Did he hurt you?"

"Yes," I said. "He sold the piano."

Her eyes widened, and she let go of my hand. "He sold the piano! That's it? After all you've put up with all these years, you left because he sold the piano!"

Put like that, I supposed it did sound ridiculous, but there was so much more to it that I just couldn't put into words. Especially not to someone like Tamsin. How could she, with her perfect life, ever understand?

Standing there, clutching that four-hundred pounds in my hand, it had at last been crystal clear to me that the relationship was over, and it was time to leave. I'd put the tin back, stuffed the money in my purse, and crept back to bed. The following morning, I'd got ready for work, as usual, kissed Seth goodbye, and walked out, knowing I wouldn't go back. Knowing he wouldn't shift off the sofa to see me off, it'd been easy to open the bedroom door and grab the ancient, battered suitcase that'd once belonged to my parents, which I'd packed after my shower, on my way out. Seth hadn't noticed a single bit of it.

I hadn't got much with me, only a few essentials. The worst thing was, I'd had to leave my books behind. Maybe one day, I'd have the courage to ask him to send them to me, although, by the time that day arrived, he'd probably have sold them all. "It was just the final straw," I said. "Anyway, it's done now. That life is finished."

"But what are you going to do with yourself? What about money?"

"I've got four-hundred pounds on me. Well, minus my train fare," I said. "And Granny's five-hundred pounds is in the bank. I'll be getting my wages paid into my account in a few days." And for the first time, it would be all mine.

How would Seth manage? He would have to sort himself out, wouldn't he? The kitchen cupboards were full of tinned goods, and there was some food in the fridge—however basic. He wouldn't starve. Though, he'd be forced to go to the job centre and grow up. I was doing him a favour, I told myself. He couldn't hide away in that flat doing nothing forever.

Besides, I was pretty certain Naomi and Isolde would take care of him.

"I booked the caravan to stay in, while I figure out what to do next."

"But that's just throwing money away," she said. "And you're going to need every penny. I don't suppose your wages are very high, and they won't last long. Then what?"

I didn't want her to burst my bubble. "I'll find another job," I said. "Look, I needed to get away, and that's that. It's just for one night. I won't get in the way, I promise. Besides, it will be nice to see Alice and Robyn again. I expect they've grown."

"I'd be very worried if they hadn't," she said sarcastically, "considering it's nearly three years since you last saw them." She stood up. "I'll put fresh bedding in the spare room," she said. "Goodness knows what Brad will think of it all."

"Where is Brad?" I said, then tutted. "Sorry. Of course, he's at work. I forget that some men do that."

"Huh. Some men do nothing *but* that," she muttered, opening the door into the hallway. "Help yourself to something to eat. You must be hungry, and there's plenty in the fridge."

There certainly was, and most of it was stuff I'd never seen before. Lots of fancy pots with weird pasta things in them, or couscous, or rice. No value vacuum-packed ham for Tamsin, but slices of real ham, beef and chicken, and three different varieties of cheese, and proper butter, and cream. The salad drawer was packed to the brim with lettuce, baby spinach, and watercress, cherry tomatoes, cucumbers, spring onions, and all manner of salad vegetables. Free range eggs, organic milk, soya milk, and almond milk. How much milk did a small family need?

I thought about the fridge at home. I'd have been embarrassed if Tamsin had ever looked inside it.

I realised that I was hungry, which surprised me. Surely, I should've been pining away and unable to eat? But no, there were definite rumblings going on in my stomach, and that cheese looked really tempting, particularly since I'd spotted a granary loaf in her bread bin.

By the time Tamsin came downstairs, I was tucking into a huge doorstop of a cheese sandwich and feeling much more contented with the world.

"Surprised you have something as high calorie as cheese in the house," I said, between mouthfuls.

She wrinkled her nose. "Brad loves cheese, and the children need a certain amount of calcium, although I watch their calorie intake, of course. I never eat the stuff."

"You ought to be careful," I warned her. "Your bones could end up snapping like twigs. You could do to eat a bit more, if you ask me. You're stick thin."

"Whereas you," she said pointedly, "are getting distinctly rounded."

"It's all the cheap mince and sausages," I said cheerfully. "Not to mention the frozen steak pies that Seth loves. A pound for four in the freezer shop."

"A pound for four! What sort of steak would they contain?" She sounded horrified.

"Best not to think about it too much," I advised.

She shook her head. "It's a different world. You need to take control of your body now. You'll never attract another man if you get any fatter."

"I don't want to attract another man," I said immediately. "Bloody hell, that's the last thing I want. As far as I'm concerned, the fatter I get, the better. Keep the buggers away."

"But you don't want to be alone for the rest of your life," she said, sounding appalled.

"That's just where you're wrong," I said. "I do want to be alone for the rest of my life. In fact, that's the plan."

It really was, too. I'd never let anyone make me feel not good enough again. With only myself to please, I could never let anyone down, could I? And if I didn't let anyone down, I would never experience that sickening lurch of disappointment in myself—that God-awful feeling of failure.

I shuddered. Nope. From then on, it would be just me. True love was a lie. Relationships were a let-down, and passion was a devil that blinded you to the truth and ruined your life. I would never be in its grip again. No more Heathcliffs for me.

#

The caravan was basically a tin hut on wheels, and if I'd been that farmer, I'd have been mortified with shame for daring to charge two hundred pounds a week for someone to live in it, particularly in early March, when the wind blew off the moors and rattled the thing so much I daren't even hold a cup of tea in my hands when it started. I spent the first week basically huddled under the duvet, with the gas fire on full, wearing a thick jumper over my pyjamas, and even, at times, gloves.

Tamsin's house had been a lot more comfortable, and it sometimes crossed my mind that maybe I should have thrown myself on her mercy and asked if I could stay there instead—if only for the central heating and the triple glazing.

Having said that, I didn't think she'd have had time for me. Alice and Robyn, it turned out, were so busy that Tamsin had no time for anything once they got home from school. They'd only been home five minutes before she'd had to rush around getting their equipment sorted for gym club. As she explained to me about their seemingly endless list of activities, I thought what spoilt little brats they sounded, then felt immediately guilty when they greeted me with excitement, obviously thrilled to see me, and seemed to see me as some super-cool auntie, whom they'd actually missed—unlike Brad, who'd rolled in from work at eight, had dinner, then disappeared into his office to 'make calls'. He'd barely so much as grunted when Tamsin explained why I was there, and hadn't seemed to care one way, or the other, how long I was staying, which didn't surprise me, given that he didn't seem to be in the house much anyway.

No wonder Tamsin filled her days with all those exercise classes, I thought. Some marriage. In her own way, my sister had been just as much a victim of the lie of true love as I'd been. She'd just had the foresight to fall for someone with cash and ambition. If you were going to be fooled, better to be fooled in a luxury house with lots of money in the bank, than a council flat with a dodgy boiler and orange kitchen units, with no idea of where your next loaf of Cheap 'n' Low thin white sliced bread would be coming from.

The following morning, she'd very kindly driven me to the caravan, which was on a farm about three miles from

Newarth, and her eyes had widened in horror when she saw it. "You can't stay here! You'll freeze to death."

I was worryingly aware that she could have been right, but I needed some time alone to think, and walk the moors, and visit Newarth, so I was willing to overlook the obvious drawbacks of my new temporary home.

"Call me," she'd said. As she'd climbed back into her Nissan Juke and shut the door, I'd thought of her heated car seats and envied her. "Keep me in the loop."

"I will," I promised, little realising that there'd be no signal and no internet access, and if I wanted to contact anyone I'd have to walk nearly as far as Newarth to do so. Not that walking to Newarth would be a hardship, but for the first few days, at least, I just wanted to hibernate.

Thankfully, Tamsin had taken me to a large supermarket near York, on our way to the caravan, and I'd stocked up on some basics, such as teabags and milk, and bread. I'd also stocked up on crisps and chocolate, much to her dismay, but I'd figured I deserved some comfort food. I'd also thrown a couple of thick paperback novels into the basket to keep me occupied, automatically hovering over the romance section of the bookshelves, until I'd realised what I was doing and snapped back to attention. No more romance for Miss Truelove! I hastily reached for the detective fiction, instead. Maybe I should change my name to Miss Marple?

After almost a week of alcoholic police inspectors, deranged serial killers, and Carroll's Caramel Choc Bloc, though, I was getting distinctly antsy. I was also wondering, for the first time in days, what was going on in the outside world. I couldn't help worrying about Seth. I hoped he was coping. Jilly had promised to call him, let him know what I'd done, as I hadn't the nerve to do it myself. I was too afraid he would talk me out of it, guilt-trip me into coming home. Jilly was made of sterner stuff, and wouldn't fall for his declarations of love for me. She'd never understood how I'd fallen for them myself.

"That's not love, Cara," she'd informed me, many times. "It's need. And there's nothing attractive about neediness in a man—or a woman, come to that."

Maybe I was doing Seth a favour, I told myself, and not for the first time. If he had to deal with life outside his little bubble, he might finally grow as a person. Who knew, having to pay the rent on the flat might even persuade him to get a job, although, thinking about it, I was pretty sure that, once he knew I was serious, he would be more likely to move in to Isolde's flat with Naomi. It was certainly big enough for three people, and Isolde would be more than happy to take care of him, no doubt.

I was curious, though, and so one day, I layered up with about three jumpers under my coat, pulled on my boots, and headed off towards Newarth.

I treated myself to a new book in the bookshop, having finished both novels already. I'd had quite enough of crime, and chose a fantasy novel instead. It was something new, and on the plus side, it was so big and heavy that, if it failed to entertain, it would make a good draft excluder. From there, I popped into the teashop and ordered a cup of tea and a toasted teacake, where I finally took out my phone to see what was happening on planet Earth.

I had about sixteen missed calls from Seth, which was a bit worrying, and three missed calls from Naomi, which was annoying, if not surprising. There was also a missed call from Mum and Dad. I had eight voicemail messages, which I dreaded listening to. However, fortified with teacake, and about to start on a cream scone, I dialled the number and waited, heart thudding.

As soon as I heard Seth's telephone number being read out, I deleted the message without listening to it. I couldn't bear it. I didn't want to be attacked by guilt.

The next four were also from him. Then there was one from Mum and Dad, saying they'd just heard from Tamsin that I'd left Seth, and they couldn't be happier, but they hoped I was okay in some caravan in the middle of nowhere, and if I needed anything, to get in touch, although they'd be flying off to Spain in a couple of days, so not to hang around for too long. The next one was from Naomi, and I deleted that, too, but there was also one from a number I didn't recognise.

It turned out to be Isolde's. She gave me a stern lecture on my disgraceful behaviour, and my inhumane treatment of Seth, and added that she would be taking care of him from then on, and she hoped that I would realise what I'd thrown away, and she thought I was extremely petty to take the piano money, which would seriously delay, if not completely derail, his chances of going into business with her.

I deleted that one, too, then turned my attention to the texts.

Tamsin had sent me a couple, saying she hoped I was okay, and if I wanted to get out of the caravan, she was sure Mum and Dad would let me live with them until I got sorted. Probably making sure I got the hint that her house was strictly off limits.

Redmond had texted me, too.

What on earth do you think you're doing, running off like that? You should have thrown him out instead. Tamsin says you've left all your possessions behind. My advice is to see a solicitor. Married, or not, you have rights. Oh, and you definitely shouldn't have left your job. Have you any idea how difficult it is for unskilled workers to find employment these days? Honestly, Cara, I do wish you'd spoken to me first. Take care. Redmond. x

Finally, there was a text from Seth. I decided to eat the cream scone first before opening it. It would take some courage to deal with his pleading, I thought.

When I finally opened the message, I realised I needn't have worried. His words didn't touch me, at all, although I did cringe at his terrible poetry.

Soft breaks the light. Hard breaks the heart.
I trudge on, feet of clay.
Night follows day.
Time has no meaning now we are apart.
Come home and give my life reason.
To leave your king was an act of treason.

The bathroom tap is dripping. What's the number of the council?

Seth, I decided, rather heartlessly, would just have to learn how to use the phonebook.

Chapter Five

Have gained two pounds this week! Time for Zumba!

Tamsin really did have a difficult life, I thought. How on earth did she cope with such anxieties?

Sitting on a bench, just off Main Street, duffle coat fastened up to the neck, I tapped my gloved fingers on my phone screen with a decided lack of accuracy. I'd just been to the cash machine to draw out another twenty pounds from my wages, and it occurred to me that, really, I had to stop living for the moment and start being the old, responsible Cara again. It had been lovely to escape, and I'd certainly needed the break to clarify things in my mind, and make absolutely sure that I'd done the right thing. Realising I was sure, though, I had to think of the future. It was all very well running away from home, but what next?

I didn't think Little Poppets Playschool was an option. Jilly would have had to find a replacement for me, and even if she managed to squeeze me in somehow, I wouldn't want to go back there. I was finally where I belonged—in Yorkshire—and I didn't want to go up to Oddborough ever again.

So, what to do?

Shoving my phone in my pocket, I decided to visit the café and have my usual tea and toasted teacake. The lady who worked behind the counter was getting used to me, it seemed, and she always had a cheery smile when I walked in. I sometimes saw a query in her eyes when she took my order, and I imagined she was curious to know who I was, and what I was doing, wandering around the village dressed like a fat Paddington Bear, my already rounded figure plumped up to even vaster proportions, thanks to the three jumpers I always wore under my coat.

Sure enough, the lady beamed at me when I pushed through the door, and said, "Tea and teacake, love?"

I nodded, and she turned away to start my order. I looked at the stack of newspapers on the table at the front, and decided to read the local one. There might be a job section in it. As dismal as the thought of returning to employment was, I knew I had to do something fast. It was either that, or throw myself on the mercy of Mum and Dad, and as much as I loved them, I felt too old to be living with my parents. Besides, I didn't want to leave the moors. I knew there wasn't much hope of finding a job in Newarth itself, but maybe there would be something in one of the other villages or towns? Even if it was just temporary.

I perused the situations vacant column with growing dismay. There were a couple of cleaning jobs, and a waitressing job that I could possibly apply for. There was also a bar job in a pub in Farthingdale. When the kindly café lady brought my order, I said, "You haven't got a pen and paper, have you?"

She rummaged in her apron pocket, tore off a piece of paper from a tiny jotter, and handed it to me, along with small plastic biro. Peering down at the opened newspaper, she said, "Job hunting?"

"Afraid so," I said, scribbling down the contact details

for the Farthingdale job, then scanning the column for the other possibilities I'd found.

"Bar staff? Wouldn't have you down for a barmaid," she said, looking at my strange attire and probably thinking I was as far removed from a vivacious, sexy barmaid as you could get.

"I've never done it before," I admitted. "Worth a try, though?"

She hesitated, as if wondering if it was any of her business. "You're not from 'round here, are you?"

"I was born here," I said. "And I lived here until I was seven. My great grandma lived here, until she died a few weeks ago."

"A few weeks ago? Do you mean Mrs Reed? Hutson Road?"

I nodded. "That's right. Did you know her?"

"Everyone knows everyone around here," she said, plonking herself down on the opposite chair. "Couldn't make the funeral service, but I was at the vigil the day before. Lots of the villagers went. I met your mum and dad, then. Didn't see you there, I don't think?"

"I couldn't get here before the funeral," I said, feeling regretful. The vigil had been the time when family and friends had gathered to pay respects to Granny Reed at the funeral parlour. Mum said it was an important part of the proceedings, and that a lot of Granny's neighbours had turned up, and they'd all gone for a drink and a chat afterwards. Granny had, apparently, been well thought of in Newarth.

"Drink your tea before it gets cold," the woman instructed. "Are you holidaying here, or have you moved back? I'm Rhoda, by the way."

"Cara," I said. "And I'm staying in a caravan a couple of miles away, on Southwick's Farm."

"That thing? In this weather?" She shivered. "Rather you than me."

"No, well, it was cheap and available, and I was in dire straits." I said. She raised an eyebrow, and I shook my head. "Long story. The plain fact is, I'd rather be in a caravan on the moors than in my old flat, and my old job, with—never mind."

"Ah." She patted my arm. "I get you. Well, I could ask around, if you like. See if there's anything going. Might be some jobs coming up in a few weeks, as the weather warms up and the tourists start arriving. I only know of one job going, at the moment, but I'm afraid they're insisting on qualifications."

"That pretty much rules me out," I said gloomily. "Unless they're happy with four average GCSEs and a diploma in childcare."

She stared at me as if I'd just said something amazing. "Childcare? You have a diploma in childcare?"

Well, I admit I hardly looked like Mary Poppins, but she didn't have to look quite so disbelieving. "Yes, I have. And I have experience working in a very popular nursery school, for your information." I didn't think it worth mentioning that it was only popular because it was free to anyone on benefits, and just about every resident of the local estate qualified, and couldn't wait to palm their toddlers off on professionals so they could get on with their dubious activities in peace.

"Sorry. I wasn't questioning you. Just that, well, the job I was talking about—they're looking for a nanny."

"A nanny? Are you serious?" I glanced down at the

newspaper. "It's not advertised in here. Are you sure? Is it 'round here? I don't want to move too far away."

"It's not been advertised at all, yet," she told me. "Although, when it does get advertised, it'll probably be in a national magazine, so if I were you, I'd apply pretty sharpish. It's live-in, too. Just the thing you need. I only know because Laura Fairweather comes in here sometimes—her sister lives two doors up, above the fish shop—and she mentioned it. Well, the kiddie's just arrived, and Laura isn't up to it, and she told him straight that she wasn't having it, so he told her to find someone and make sure they were qualified to do it, so there you go."

I really did try to keep up with that conversation but, to be honest, it was pretty difficult. "So, this Laura Fairweather has just had a baby, and she doesn't want to look after it?"

Rhoda laughed. "Laura Fairweather? She must be sixty, if she's a day. I'd be calling the tabloids if she'd just had a bairn. No, it's her employer. She's housekeeper at Moreland Hall, a couple of miles north of Hasedale, and she's been landed with the little girl. She's only four, so you can imagine, Laura can't keep up with her. She's desperate for someone, and she's not looking forward to interviewing, and all that palaver, so you could be in there, if you hurry up. He's left it all to her. Your teacake's looking a bit sorry for itself. Do you want a fresh one toasting?"

"What? Oh, no thanks. I think I ought to get myself to Moreland Hall and apply before she places that advertisement." Too right. If it went in a national magazine, I'd have no chance. No way could I compete with other nannies and nursery nurses, who'd probably worked in posh establishments that would put the Little Poppets Playschool to shame.

"No worries there, love. I'll give Laura a call and arrange an interview, right after I make you a fresh teacake. Reckon another cup of tea's in order, too, don't you?"

"Thanks ever so much," I said, feeling a bit dazed. Things were moving very fast. Surely, it was too good to be true?

Ten minutes later, I was eating a piping hot toasted teacake and listening in awe as Rhoda arranged my future over the phone with the mysterious Mrs Fairweather.

"All sorted," she announced, handing me a mug of steaming fresh tea. "She's that relieved. I told her you were a decent sort, and she's not to know that I've only known you five minutes, is she? Soon as I mentioned Mrs Reed, I heard her relax. Pillar of the community, Mrs Reed was. Well, until she lost her marbles, but fair's fair— she was as old as Methuselah by that time. I take it you can get references? I mean, you seem honest enough to me, but she'll want proof that you're actually qualified."

"I've got my diploma in the caravan," I said, "and I can get a reference." Jilly would give me a good reference, I had no doubt.

"Job's a good 'un," she said, folding her arms in satisfaction. "So, you've to go over there at three o'clock."

I gulped down my tea. "Three o'clock? You mean today?"

"Of course I mean today." She glanced at the clock on the wall. "You've got just over two hours. Have you got a car?"

"No, I haven't," I said, panicking slightly. "And I'm hardly dressed for a job interview, am I? How far away is this house?"

"About twenty to thirty minutes if you go by car," she said. "Tell you what, you get yourself to the caravan and get changed, and I'll send a taxi to pick you up at half two. I'll book it now for you."

As she headed back to the counter, my phone beeped. I glanced down and pulled a face as I saw Seth's name on the screen. Things were going so well, and I didn't want him to ruin it all. I shook my head as I read his text.

O! My love how can you treat me so?
I sit alone, sorrow etched on broken face,
The light has gone from this wretched place,
My heart is heavy, my spirit low.
Come home, sweet love, as soon you can.
Come home and save this lonely man.

Did you cancel my subscription to Quill Magazine? The latest issue hasn't arrived.

Honestly! I put my phone back in my pocket and finished my tea. I wasn't going to give Heathcliff a second thought.

Hearing Rhoda on the phone, I listened in, feeling a flutter of nerves at her words.

"Moreland Hall, and don't be late, 'cause she's got a job interview. That's right, Ned. Moreland Hall. You know, Mr Rochester's place."

My heart seemed to fly up into my mouth, and I gaped at her in horror. She put the phone down and turned to me, her smile dying as she looked at my stricken face. "What is it, love?"

71

"Who did you say the house belonged to?"

"Oh, didn't I tell you? That's who you'll be working for. Mr Rochester."

#

Trust me! Only I could contemplate swapping Heathcliff for bloody Mr Rochester. Well, I reminded myself, as I scrabbled around in the caravan, trying to find something suitable for a job interview, he was a father, which meant he was probably married, or, at the very least, romantically entangled with someone, so at least I'd have no trouble sticking to my resolution not to fall for any man ever again.

Half my clothes didn't fit me. Comfort eating, combined with lack of exercise for the last fortnight, had ensured that I'd packed more weight on. My size fourteen jeans were uncomfortably tight, and I could only hope that my one decent black skirt would still do up.

I frantically unrolled the only pair of tights in my suitcase and pulled them on, groaning as my nail caught and ripped a hole in them. Great, so I'd be turning up for the interview in laddered tights. I hunted around in my makeup bag and found an old bottle of nail varnish, which I dabbed hopefully on the edge of the hole, praying it would stop it from running any farther. My skirt took some squeezing into and did me no favours whatsoever. I decided against wearing my white shirt, which I'd planned to tuck into my skirt, and instead found a reasonably smart grey jumper, which was long enough to cover the waistband and my rounded stomach.

I decided, there and then, to cut out the Carroll's Caramel Choc Bloc.

As the taxi pulled up at the gate to the field, and the

driver beeped his horn, I hastily zipped up my boots, threw on my duffle coat, wishing I'd thought to bring my only decent jacket with me instead, and rushed out of the caravan. I was halfway across the field when I remembered the diploma, and had to wade back through the mud to get it, and by the time I finally got to the taxi, the soles of my boots were caked in thick mud, and I could only hope the driver didn't notice and refuse to take me.

Luckily, he didn't.

"So," he said, quite cheerfully, as we headed down the farm track, "we're off to Mr Rochester's place, eh?"

Even the sound of it was quite daunting. "Er, yes. Moreland Hall, isn't it?"

He shrugged. "Probably. It's always been called Rochester's place 'round here. Business, or pleasure?"

Bit cheeky, asking, in my opinion. "Definitely business," I said. *And no pleasure, whatsoever.* I was done with pleasure. Well, *that* kind of pleasure, at least. "I've got a job interview."

"Oh, right. What sort of job?"

Were all taxi drivers 'round there so nosy? Back in Oddborough, you'd be lucky to get a grunt from most of them. I supposed I just wasn't used to it, and he was being friendly, after all. Well, we *were* in Yorkshire. "Nanny," I said, not wanting to go into details. I didn't have any details to go into, to be honest.

"Ah, I see. Laura mentioned the bairn was staying there. Quite rare to have one of the family at home, these days. They tend to stay in London, as you can imagine."

Could I? I made a sort of mumbling noise, since I didn't know what to say, and he frowned at me through the rear-view mirror.

"You do know who they are, right? I mean, you do realise he's *the* Mr Rochester?"

He was? I seriously doubted that. "Is he?" I said politely, thinking he couldn't possibly be. Mr Rochester was fictional, wasn't he? Unless he was based on someone Charlotte Brontë had actually met? But even so...

"'Course, it was his great-great-grandfather who started it, back in the nineteenth century," the driver added, clearly enjoying showing off his knowledge. "But this one's certainly done his fair share."

"Oh, good," I said, wondering *what*, exactly, he'd done his fair share of. Attempted bigamy? Locking up mad women? It wasn't reassuring, either way.

"Laura will see you right," he said. "Don't you go worrying." Clearly, he thought my reluctance to chat was down to nerves.

He was right, in a way, but I had more to think about than just a job interview. I wasn't entirely sure what I was heading into, and I was beginning to think maybe I'd be better off if I *didn't* get the job.

We drove steadily on for nearly half an hour, the road cutting a swathe through the moors, which, at that time of year, looked bleak and desolate. Wondering how remote the house was, I was just about to ask, when the car pulled up outside a pair of wrought iron gates and the driver turned to me, smiling

"Far as I go," he said.

I stared at him. "As far as you go? What do you mean?"

He rolled his eyes. "The gates are shut, see? They always are. And it's a lot of palaver trying to get in touch

74

with the main house to open them."

"Then, how——?" I stared doubtfully at the wall, which was about nine feet high and backed by a whole forest of trees, by the look of it.

"There's a small gate in the wall for pedestrians, over there, look. Just press the buzzer, and someone will answer you eventually, but it's not worth me hanging around, is it? It's only a short walk up the drive."

"Oh, right," I said, unfastening my seat belt. "Well, if you're sure."

I paid him his fare and climbed out of the car, walking uncertainly to the side gate in the wall. I pressed the buzzer on the stone pillar and waited. The taxi driver beeped his horn and drove off, leaving me standing all alone in that strange place, miles from Newarth. It suddenly occurred to me that I should have asked him to wait, or at least booked him for the return journey. Typical of me not to think ahead.

"Hello?"

I jumped upon hearing the voice crackling through the speaker. "Crikey, you scared me to death! I mean, er, hello."

"Can I help?"

"Yes, I have an interview at three o'clock with a Mrs Fairweather. I'm Cara Truelove. I believe she——"

The speaker crackled and the gate clicked. Tentatively, I pushed it open and followed a narrow path through the trees, hearing the gate click again behind me.

The path led me to a driveway, and I walked nervously towards the house, which lay at the end of the tree-lined drive. Whoever lived there, they certainly loved woodland, I thought. As I got nearer to the house, though, the trees gave way to a beautiful lawn, and I stared in awe at the imposing stone property set out before me. It was huge, with what seemed like dozens of casement windows, and a slate roof and lots of chimneys. Straight ahead was a massive oak door, and steps leading up to it. Mr Rochester certainly liked to make an impression.

The door opened, and a woman stepped outside and stood on the top step. I'd half been expecting her to be wearing a Victorian dress and apron, with her hair in a bun, but the woman was wearing trousers and a bright red jumper, and had her steel-grey hair cropped short, in a rather Judi Dench fashion. To my relief, she beamed at me and waved as I approached. "Hello! You found us all right, then. I'm Laura Fairweather. Pleased to meet you, Cara."

Relaxing, I took the hand she offered with some relief. "Hello. Pleased to meet you, too."

"Come into the kitchen, you must be freezing. The fire's going, and it's lovely and warm in there. Would you like a hot drink? Tea? Coffee?"

"A cup of tea would be lovely," I said gratefully. I'd half expected to be asked to enter via the back door, so it was a pleasant surprise to find myself standing in a huge, double-height hallway. It was even more surprising to see how modern and bright it looked. The walls had been painted white, and there was a warm, wooden floor beneath a cheerful stripy runner, and some rather cosy antique pine furniture. A grand staircase stood straight in front of me, with two flights branching off from the landing, one leading left, and one right.

Mrs Fairweather smiled at me. "Not what you were

expecting?"

I shook my head. "Not really."

"I know. People always think it's going to be dark and gloomy in here, but the present Mr Rochester has done an awful lot of work to it. He hated coming here when he was young. It was practically gothic when I first started here, and he couldn't abide it. He's completely renovated the whole place. It's so luxurious now, I feel very lucky to live here."

I wasn't surprised, particularly when she led me into her own domain, which was the most gorgeous kitchen I'd ever seen. Tamsin would have been green with envy. Again, the walls were white and the floors wooden. At one end of the huge room was a beautiful fitted kitchen, complete with butler sink and large green range cooker. In the centre, stood an island with a modern hob built into its black Corian worktop. The white units around the side of the kitchen had thick wooden worktops. At the other end of the room, a flight of stairs led up to the first floor, and a large table and chairs stood in front of an inglenook fireplace, so tall it almost reached the ceiling, and within there was a wood-burning stove, which glowed brightly and threw out a heck of a lot of heat.

I defrosted immediately, and asked Mrs Fairweather if she minded if I removed my coat.

"Bless you, love," she said, reaching out a hand to take it from me. "You'll melt into a puddle, if you don't." She nodded towards the table. "Take a seat," she said. "I'll make that tea."

There was no waiting around for a kettle to boil in that house. Boiling water came straight out of a tap. Mrs Fairweather handed me a mug, which was reassuringly plain, and settled herself down opposite me. "Right, then. Let's get this over and done with," she said. "I'm the housekeeper here at Moreland Hall. It's my job to ensure the smooth running of this place. I do the cooking," she added, "and this is my kitchen, whatever his lordship likes to think." She winked at me. "I also see to the household budget, and I take charge of the indoor staff." She chuckled. "That sounds a heck of a lot grander than it is. When I say *indoor staff*, there's me, Mrs Jones and Mrs Turner. They come here three times a week and help me keep the place clean. Outside, there's Ken. He's the gardener and handyman. That's it for permanent staff. But soon there'll be you. That's if you get the job, of course." She gave me an encouraging smile. "Why don't you tell me a bit about yourself?"

"What would you like to know?"

I thought I'd have to be a bit selective. I told her about the nursery, leaving out the bit about the parents who frequently ignored our opening times and dropped their kids off early because they had appointments at the methadone clinic.

"I have my diploma," I finished, reaching into my bag and drawing it out. Thank God I'd had the foresight to pack that.

She took it from me and read it, nodding approvingly. "Would you mind if I kept this for now? Just until Mr Rochester has seen it." she said.

I felt a flutter of nerves, but nodded. "Of course. As long as I get it back."

"Oh, you will, never fear. And you'll be able to provide a reference?"

"The owner of Little Poppets Playschool will send

78

one to you. I'll give you her address."

She shook her head. "Email address would do. Mr Rochester likes to do things quickly, and he's a great one for technology. I'll ask her to email it to him, and I'll scan this diploma and email that to him, too."

I was quite impressed. "Is Mr Rochester not here?" I asked, scribbling down Jilly's email address on the piece of paper Mrs Fairweather pushed towards me.

She stood and walked across the room, from where she collected a brightly-coloured biscuit tin off the worktop. "He's in London. He rarely comes up to Yorkshire these days," she said, returning to her seat. "Have a biscuit?"

I thought about the straining zip on my skirt and shook my head. "Better not. But thank you. So, his daughter's here just with her mother?"

She stared at me blankly for a moment, as she crunched on a custard cream. "Oh, I see what you mean. No, no. Adele's not his daughter."

Adele! Was she having me on? Mr Rochester was caring for a child who wasn't his, and her name was Adele? Had I entered *The Twilight Zone*? I seemed destined to spend my life living inside Brontë novels.

"Don't tell me," I said. "Adele is the daughter of his French mistress. And I don't mean his teacher."

She looked baffled. Evidently, she wasn't much of a reader. "Adele is Mr Rochester's little sister," she said.

I hadn't been expecting that. "How old is she again?" I said.

"Four."

"Oh. Sorry, just that, I thought Mr Rochester would be older."

She grinned at me. "Than four? He is. He's nearly thirty-six. It's okay, my dear, I do see what you mean. There's quite an age gap."

She wasn't kidding. I wondered who was fooling whom, but thought it best to keep my opinions to myself. "Oh, right. So, is Adele's mother here?"

She looked disapproving. "No, she's staying in New York at the moment, visiting some friends. That's why he was a bit stuck, you see. Jodie—she was Adele's previous nanny—well, she had to leave suddenly, and there was no one to take care of Adele. I went down there for a while, but my place is here. Can't be doing with London. It was decided that Adele could spend the summer here, and it was thought that a local nanny would be preferable. Someone used to the city might not settle here, you see. Are you sure you wouldn't like a biscuit?"

I peered longingly into the tin. My hand hovered over a chocolate digestive, but as I reached forward, my waistband practically cut off my circulation until I was genuinely worried my button would pop and ping across the kitchen floor. Regretfully, I withdrew my hand. "No thanks."

She looked puzzled for a moment, then shrugged. "Okay. Well, would you like to have a look around the house and meet Adele?"

"I'd love to," I said, thinking it wasn't much of an interview. I wasn't going to point that out to her, though. Clearly, she was eager to hire someone, and I didn't want to do anything to make her think twice about choosing me. "I'll take off my boots," I added. "They're rather muddy, I'm afraid."

She seemed to approve of that, and gave me a smile

that radiated as much warmth as the wood-burning stove.

The house was gorgeous. I mean, really, it was stunning. Clearly, no expense had been spared. Considering the taxi driver had said the Rochesters weren't often there, they'd gone to a lot of trouble to make it very luxurious, in a cosy and welcoming sort of way. Every room had a beauty and elegance of its own. I particularly loved the huge conservatory, or garden room, as Mrs Fairweather called it. It wasn't like the plastic monstrosity that Mum and Dad had stuck on the back of their house, but was a tasteful stone and glass extension, with views across the most beautiful gardens.

"There are twelve bedrooms," Mrs Fairweather explained, as we made our way to the first floor. "Six of them are en-suite. Then there are three separate bathrooms. You'll never be caught short in this house," she said, her eyes twinkling.

I really liked her, and I had everything crossed that she liked me enough to recommend me to her employer for the job. I couldn't believe there was a chance I might live somewhere like that, and be paid to do so. Was I dreaming?

"This would be your room," she told me, opening a door into a room that was as big as both my old bedroom and living room combined. A soft cream carpet squished beneath my feet, a huge bay window looked out over the lawn and to the moors beyond, a king-size bed with a crisp white duvet cover and purple throw sat proud against one wall, and thick purple check curtains hung at the windows. Best of all, through an open door to the left of me, I spotted something I never thought I'd ever have in a million years. An en-suite bathroom! I *had* to have this job.

"Do you think it will do?" she said. "I know it's right at the end of the corridor, but it's next to Adele's room, and I think Mr Rochester would prefer that you were close."

"It's perfect," I assured her, trying to sound calm, even though inside I was mentally hopping up and down in excitement. I would have to take a photo of the place and send it to Tamsin. She'd be so envious. I knew I shouldn't be so mean, but I'd never had anything to show off about before. The job, the house, they could be my breakthrough!

"Wonderful," she said. "Well, I suppose the only thing left to do now is introduce you to Adele."

I felt a shadow pass over me. What if Adele didn't like me? What if I didn't like Adele? I remembered some of the aggressive little toddlers I'd dealt with at nursery and took a deep breath. I was up to the task. Once we'd established boundaries, we could make it work, I was sure of it.

Adele was apparently being entertained by Mrs Turner's teenage daughter. "We've had to rely on her a lot these past few days," Mrs Fairweather confided, as we headed back downstairs. "Really, it's all been very trying, I must say. Anyway, luckily for me, Susie works evenings at The Crown, so she's been able to come in every afternoon and take Adele off my hands for a few hours. I'm far too old for all this," she added, pushing open a door and ushering me into another stunning space.

In the corner of what appeared to be a sitting room, a little girl was curled up on a teenager's lap, seemingly absorbed in the story that was being narrated to her—in a rather bored tone, it had to be said. As she registered our arrival, Adele scrambled from the chair and ran over to us, her blue eyes wide with curiosity and a big smile on her face.

"Adele, sweetheart, this is Cara. Cara, this is Adele."

My heart just swelled as I took in the cute little tot, with her tousled brown hair and enquiring expression. She wore a red and black Minnie Mouse dress, with black and white stripy tights, and had a big floppy bow in her hair. Despite the horrendously garish outfit, she looked adorable, and she didn't greet me by kicking me in the shins or sticking her tongue out at me, which was definitely a bonus.

Instead, she held out her hand and quite solemnly said, "Hello, Cara."

Astonished, I carefully shook it and smiled down at her. "Hello, Adele. I'm very pleased to meet you."

The teenager, who I presumed was Susie, yawned and stretched. "Can I go now, Mrs Fairweather? I'm supposed to be meeting my mates in half an hour."

Mrs Fairweather nodded. "I suppose so. Thanks, Susie. I'll get your wages, if you'll come to the kitchen with me." She turned to me. "Will you be okay with her for five minutes?"

"Of course," I said. "Would you like me to finish reading you that story, Adele?"

Adele nodded, and Mrs Fairweather smiled. "There's a good girl. I'll be back in a jiffy."

She led Susie out of the room, and I settled myself in the comfortable armchair and lifted Adele onto my knee, then I picked up the book and continued the story of *The Gruffalo*, doing all the voices and making quite a decent job of it, if I did say so myself. Well, Adele seemed pretty impressed, anyway. She stared up at me, eyes wide, at first, then giggled in all the right places, and when I'd finished, she gave me a round of applause, so I must have done okay.

"Well, you're very good at that, I will say," Mrs Fairweather said from the doorway. I hadn't even noticed her return. "Come along, Adele. I need to get your tea ready." She held out her hand for the little girl. "Now, then, Cara," she said, as we headed back into the hallway towards the front door, "Do you think you could cope with the isolation of this house? You wouldn't crave the bright lights of the city?"

I pulled a face. "Hardly. This is the most perfect location. I'm definitely not a city girl."

"Thought as much. I've seen enough to be satisfied. What about you? Are you interested in the job?"

Was I! I could hardly wipe the smile from my face. "Absolutely," I said, trying to keep the eagerness from my voice. "But what about Mr Rochester? Doesn't he have the final say?"

"He'll check out your reference and the authenticity of the diploma, of course, but other than that, he'll leave it to me. He trusts my judgement, as well he should, after all these years. I know what it is he's looking for. He was rather, er, specific about certain matters, and I believe I'm a good judge of character. So, do you think you'd be able to start on Monday?"

"I think that would be fine," I said, thinking I must have died and gone to heaven. "What time do you want me?"

"Get here for around nine," she said, after considering

for a moment. "You can take the morning to unpack and settle in. Then you can take over the childcare after lunch, if that's all right with you."

I nodded. "Absolutely fine."

"Goodness, we haven't even discussed your wages," she said, as she opened the front door.

I hadn't even thought about the money. Living at Moreland Hall would be payment enough, as far as I was concerned.

Mrs Fairweather sounded almost apologetic as she told me what the hourly rate would be. "I know it doesn't sound much," she said, scooping Adele into her arms, "but it's more than the minimum wage, after all, and you'll have free board and lodgings."

"It sounds very fair to me," I said, fighting the urge to do a happy dance down the hall. "Honestly, I'm quite satisfied with it. I can't wait to start work."

She opened the door. "Nine o'clock on Monday, then," she said. "I'll look forward to seeing you. Say bye-bye to Cara, Adele."

Adele waved. "Bye-bye, Cara."

"Bye, Adele. See you soon. Goodbye, Mrs Fairweather, and thank you."

She tutted. "It's me who should be thanking you. My knees aren't up to this malarkey, my love. See you on Monday!"

I practically floated down the drive on a cloud of happiness. I couldn't believe it. Finally, my life was turning around, and things were going well for me.

It just showed you, I thought, what could happen once you put passion away and started to be sensible and level-headed about things.

It was only when I reached the gate that I remembered I'd forgotten to order a taxi.

Chapter Six

Yoga time!

Of course it is, Tamsin, I thought, smiling to myself. It'd been a huge relief to discover that I had both a phone and internet signal at Moreland Hall. As I lay on the extraordinarily comfortable double bed, I gave a sigh of contentment, as I scrolled through my Facebook timeline, catching up with what had been going on with everyone.

It had been a brilliant day. Even the weather had warmed up over the weekend, and it felt as if, finally, spring had put in an appearance. I'd arrived at nine, and had been welcomed like an old friend. Mrs Fairweather had asked if I'd had breakfast, and when I admitted I hadn't, she insisted on making me a full English. I did protest, honestly. I thought, at that rate, I'd have to buy some new clothes in a bigger size, and a plate full of bacon and eggs wasn't going to help, but I didn't want to appear rude on my first day, did I? The plan was to just eat half of it, but it smelt so delicious and tasted so good. How was I supposed to resist? I'd have to eat less for lunch, I decided.

By the time I'd troughed the lot, my jeans were digging into my stomach with such ferocity, I thought I was going to burst. Longing to undo the button, I struggled to my feet. "Is it okay if I go upstairs and unpack, Mrs Fairweather?"

She looked surprised. "Already? Wouldn't you like a nice cup of tea first?"

"I'll have one later, if that's okay. I'd really like to get settled in." *And get these flipping jeans off, so I can breathe again.*

"Oh, well, just as you like. Do you remember the way, or would you like me to show you?"

"It's fine. I know my room's at the end of the landing," I said, lifting the suitcase. "Should I go up these stairs?" I asked, nodding towards the staircase in the corner of the kitchen.

She shook her head. "That would lead you to the east wing. No one's used those rooms for ages. The family uses the west wing. Your room's at the end of the landing, with Adele's next to it, then Mrs Rochester's room—his mother, I mean. Then there's two guest rooms, and, finally, Mr Rochester has a suite of rooms at the beginning of the landing, nearest to the stairs. It's quicker for you to use the main stairs and go left."

"Where's Adele?" I asked, as I stepped into the hall.

"Helping Mrs Jones vacuum the drawing room," she called. "She's got a toy vacuum cleaner, bless her. Keeps her occupied for a while. Now, remember, when you get to the top of the stairs, take the left-hand landing," she said.

I nodded, vaguely hoping Adele hadn't been given heaps of toys designed to train her only in housework, and hauled my suitcase up the stairs. Passing the identical closed doors of various rooms, I noticed one door was much narrower than the others, and with curiosity getting the better of me, I opened it cautiously, finding a flight of narrow winding steps behind it. The entrance to the attics, I supposed. Given the size of the house, I reckoned they must've been enormous. Oh, well, I thought, and grinned to myself. As long as Mr Rochester didn't keep his secret mad wife up there ...

Entering my own room, I placed my suitcase on the bed with a sigh of relief, then threw myself down beside it. Staring round at my gorgeous new bedroom, I could hardly wipe the smile from my face.

After unpacking—my paltry belongings looked completely lost in the large wardrobe and chest of drawers—I changed into something a little more comfortable, then headed downstairs, where Mrs Fairweather told me to have a wander 'round the house and get to know the place a little before lunch.

"Would it be all right for me to have a walk in the grounds?" I asked, thinking they'd looked so magnificent from the garden room, I couldn't wait to explore.

She looked at me like I was a bit crazy. "What are you asking for? If you want to, of course you can. Come and go as you please."

"Thank you so much," I said and grabbed my duffle coat from the utility room, which was reached by a door under the stairs. From there, I headed out of the house into the garden, taking deep lungfuls of fresh air and thinking I was the luckiest person alive.

It took me a while to cover the grounds. I wandered for quite some time in the woods, where the last of the snowdrops peeped between the trees, and daffodils danced in the spring breeze. To the rear of the house, I explored the kitchen garden, where herbs and vegetables grew in raised beds, or in the greenhouse, then followed a path around the lawn, where I came upon a small lake, edged with reeds and weeping willows.

Most interesting of all, though, was the secret garden. At least, I assumed it was a garden, although I didn't suppose it was really a secret. I was quite sure everyone in the house knew about it, but it felt sort of secret, because it was hidden away behind a wall.

The wall itself was half hidden behind bushes and creepers, but when I spotted it, I followed it until I reached an old wooden door set in the brickwork. Unfortunately for me, it was locked. I wanted to go inside that walled garden so much, but it was probably for the family's use only. Besides, I was being romantic again. It was probably nothing more than a glorified vegetable patch.

I took my time walking back to the house, unable to stop thinking about Seth. Was he managing all right? Had he sorted out some benefits for himself? Was he still in the flat, or had he moved in with Isolde and Naomi?

I might've no longer been in love with him, but that didn't mean I didn't care what happened to him. I wasn't completely unfeeling, as much as I tried to be. In fact, I felt rather ashamed that I hadn't spoken to him. I shouldn't have left like that. I should have sat down with him and explained how I felt, told him I was leaving.

But then, I reasoned, *he would have talked you out of it. You know he would. He would have cried and told you how much he loved you, and even though you knew he didn't love you at all, just depended on you, you would have given in and stayed.*

Yes, I realised, I had to go without telling him, for my own sake.

It's funny, really. No matter how much your head tries to tell you that you did the sensible thing, your heart always betrays you. It floods you with all those awful feelings that make you believe you're a bad person. As I headed back to the house, I knew it would take me a long time to forgive myself for what I'd done. I needed to start work, keep busy.

"You were gone ages," Mrs Fairweather said, when I returned to the house. "I was about to send out a search party." She smiled at me. "Did you enjoy yourself?"

"The grounds are amazing," I said. "I love it here."

She nodded approvingly. "And why wouldn't you? Now, let's think about lunch, and then I'll hand Adele over to your care."

Looking after Adele proved astonishingly easy. After coping with a class full of three and four-year-olds, most of whom thought Jilly and I were basically theirs to command, the polite and pleasant little girl was a joy to work with. In fact, it didn't feel like work, at all. Like I was being paid to read stories, play with toys, and entertain her. The main priority, it appeared, was keeping her occupied, so Mrs Fairweather could get on with her own work without interference. I couldn't help wondering why they hadn't just enrolled her at a local nursery school, but Mrs Fairweather told me, over tea—or dinner, as she called it—that Mr Rochester had his reasons, though it wasn't for her to say what they were.

"Of course," she'd added, "she'll be going to primary school before we know it, and then it will all change."

I'd had a sinking feeling at that, realising that the job wouldn't be forever, after all. Of course it wouldn't. When Adele started school, she'd have no need of a nanny.

That evening, with Adele tucked up in bed, and Mrs Fairweather in her own little sitting room, watching television, I headed up to my room and lay on the bed,

91

While trying desperately not to worry about Seth, I decided it was time to relax, and tell Redmond and Tamsin of my good fortune. I hadn't mentioned it before, because I'd had a nagging fear that something would go wrong, and I'd have it all snatched from my grasp, but Mrs Fairweather had informed me casually that afternoon that my reference had reached Mr Rochester the day after my interview, and it was excellent, and he'd checked that my diploma was for a genuine, recognised qualification. Apparently, he'd been very impressed, so there seemed no danger of me being turfed out of Moreland Hall any time soon.

When I took out my mobile phone, I found there'd been another text from Seth.

Haunting laughter now surrounds me,
How cruel is another's joy.
No pleasure soothes this tortured boy.
Why can't you hear my desperate plea?
I need my love, my world, my life.
Return to me, my almost wife.

Don't you think this has gone far enough? I've had to sign on, for God's sake!

My sympathy drained away immediately. What a hardship for him, having to put his signature to a piece of paper once a week, or fortnight, or whatever it was. Terribly hard work.

That last line of the poem had annoyed me, too. *My almost wife!* Yes, and why was that? Because he'd refused to marry me, that was why. Marriage, he'd insisted, was a constraint, and he didn't even ask my opinion on the subject—although, to be fair, I'd no doubt have agreed to whatever he said, anyway. I was such a doormat in those early days. And, really, he'd done me a massive favour by not marrying me. No messy divorce for me to worry about. I was completely free.

Well, almost.

Feeling angry at myself for being so soft, I decided to text him back. It took me ages to determine exactly what to write, and I practically wrote an essay, at first, trying to explain myself to him. Then I thought, why bother? He wouldn't understand in a million years, and it would just lead to more questions, and a whole evening spent trying to make him accept things. Better to send just one short text, making it clear that I wasn't coming back.

In the end, I simply wrote a few brief sentences.

Seth, it's over. I'm sorry, but I've made a new life for myself now and I think you should do the same. I hope you have a good life. No hard feelings. Cara.

After reading Tamsin's yoga update on Facebook, I decided to message both my siblings and tell them of my good fortune. I was just about to do so when the phone pinged.

Seth!

And that's it, is it? No explanation? No apology? After all I've done for you! After all we've meant to each other! I don't understand this, Cara. You know we're meant to be together for all eternity, and you know I love you. Haven't I always told you, you're my world? I think this is just your hormones playing havoc with your common sense. I don't know. Maybe it's something to do with turning thirty. Hormones do strange things to women. Come home and we'll get you some help. There are medications you can take, you know. Isolde says there are patches which might be the answer. I'm willing to forgive and forget. Come home, my love. Your Heathcliff

I took a deep breath. My hormones! Typical! And trust Isolde to be feeding his stupid ideas. Bet she was praying I wouldn't come home, so she could have him all to herself. Well, she was welcome to him. I wasn't his love, and he wasn't my Heathcliff.

Even if he had been, I wouldn't have wanted him. Heathcliff was a psycho. I'd finally figured that much out, at least.

Wuthering Heights was a brilliant novel—a real masterpiece—but how I'd ever mistaken it for a love story was beyond me.

My fingers itched to send him a stinging reply, but I realised that would only be fanning the flames, so with enormous effort, I decided to ignore him. I'd said all I had to say.

Instead, I wrote a text, explaining about my new job and home, and sent it to Tamsin and Redmond.

Redmond replied within a few minutes.

Living in? With some strangers you know nothing about? How do you know this mansion house isn't owned by gangsters? Crime barons? You could be in real danger. You are so irresponsible, Cara. I do wish you'd talk things over with me before you do anything. Who is this man you're working for? Text me his name and I'll make enquiries. Redmond xx

Well, that hadn't helped my bad mood. Trust men to drain away every drop of joy from the day.

I was just wondering whether, or not, to answer when the phone rang. I almost dropped it in shock, then peered nervously at the screen. If it was Seth, there was no way I'd answer it, but luckily, it was Tamsin.

"Are you serious? You've got a job in a posh house?

94

How posh? Who are you working for? How the hell did you manage that?"

"Take a deep breath," I said, "and I'll begin."

I told her everything, right from searching the newspaper column in The Singing Kettle Café, to Redmond's and Seth's texts.

"Bloody men," she said. "Always spoil everything. Who do they think they are, anyway? Everything revolves around them and their needs, and sod us."

I was astonished to hear her speaking like that. "Are you all right, Tamsin?" I said worriedly. "I mean, everything's okay?"

"Oh, bloody perfect. Same old, same old." She sounded very bitter. "Got to go out in ten minutes to pick Alice up from dance class, and Robyn's throwing a tantrum because she doesn't want to come with me, because she's watching *Cinderella* for the twentieth time this week, but I can't leave her here, because bloody Brad's at work, doing overtime. Again. And I've spent all day cleaning the house from top to bottom, then trawling 'round the supermarket, doing a mammoth shop, because he's invited the boss and his wife 'round to dinner, without even warning me, or asking me if it was okay, or anything. Frankly, I'm sick to death of it all. Think you had the right idea about buggering off."

I didn't know what to say to all that. So much for Tamsin's perfect life. "I'm really sorry," I said.

"Oh, never mind," she said. "I shouldn't have vented like that. Just, sometimes, I feel so lonely and bored, and it's like my husband and children are living their busy and fulfilling lives, while I'm just here at everyone's beck and call. I don't feel like a mother, or a wife. I feel like a cook, cleaner, maid, waitress, chauffeur and nanny. Anyway, talking of nannies, how wonderful for you! I'm so pleased for you, Cara. You'll have to send me photos of that kitchen. I quite fancy updating ours, so it will give me some ideas. Oh, shit!"

"What is it?"

"Nothing. Just spilt my wine all over Robyn's *Pony Magazine*. She'll be furious." There was a big sigh. "I'd better go, sweetie. Keep me in the loop, okay?"

"I will. Promise."

Ending the call, I tapped on Facebook and read Tamsin's last status update.

Gosh, it's been a beautiful day! Had a lovely time, hitting the shops! Glass of prosecco now! Good times!

I put down the phone and rolled over onto my side to look out of the window. It just went to show. You never really knew what was going on in people's lives, whatever they might say in public.

#

I got an excited phone call from Redmond the following morning. I'd just settled Adele down for a nap, and I rushed out of the French windows so the ringtone wouldn't wake her up. I tried not to feel anxious as I accepted the call. It wasn't like Redmond to ring me. Last time he'd done that, Granny Reed had just died.

"Cara, you'll never believe this! I did some checking up on your Mr Rochester, as I said I would, and I'm stunned. You do realise, he's *the* Mr Rochester?"

"So I've been told," I said, "though that means little to me. The only Mr Rochester I know exists between the pages of *Jane Eyre*, and I doubt that's the one you're talking about."

"Don't be ridiculous," he snapped. "Ethan Kingston Rochester. Born 24th June, almost thirty-six years ago, in St Mary's hospital, London. Parents Jennifer Jane Rochester, formerly Kingston, society girl and social butterfly, and Thomas Edward Rochester, heir to the Rochester Department Store fortune."

He was clearly reading all that stuff from something, and as his voice droned on, I almost lost interest. Then I realised what he'd said, and my mouth dropped open.

"Rochester Department Store. You mean—you mean ..."

"Exactly," he said, a note of triumph in his voice. "Now do I have your attention? You're working for Ethan Rochester, who owns and runs the entire empire, since his father passed away six years ago."

Bloody hell! I'd never been in a Rochester's store, but I knew of them. Everyone knew of them. "They're pretty big, aren't they?"

"Big? According to Wikipedia, they own twelve stores which are worth in the region of five hundred million pounds."

I almost dropped to the floor in shock. Good God! Well, that explained the luxury house makeover, at least. A refit, even the size of the Rochester house, would be chicken feed to them. But how had someone like me ended up working for Ethan Rochester, of all people?

Hang on a minute!

"Did you say Thomas Rochester died six years ago?"

"Yes. Heart attack. Very sudden."

"And has Jennifer married again?"

There was a mumbling noise, and some shuffling of papers, and a few clicks. Eventually, he said, "No.

Grieving widow, apparently. They were married for over thirty years, and there was no scandal of any kind. No affairs on either side—well, that anyone knows about. Devoted couple. Shame. Why do you ask?"

"No reason." So much for Adele being Ethan Rochester's little sister. I'd guessed as much. Clearly, she was his daughter, but why keep that a secret?

"There's no mention of another child, though," he said curiously. "Whose kid are you looking after? Ethan and his wife have no children."

"He's married?" Mrs Fairweather hadn't mentioned any wife.

"Yes. Married his teenage sweetheart, Antonia Wilson-Smythe, from what it says here. He was only just twenty, and she was eighteen. They married in a Chelsea registry office, with just two friends as witnesses." He gave a low whistle. "She's not short of a few bob, either. Her dad's the owner of loads of prime property in London, and she's his only child. Jesus, those two are loaded. I hope they're paying you plenty."

Come to think of it, I was only getting just above the minimum wage. Mind you, I was living in luxurious surroundings, with no bills to pay and no food to buy. I could hardly complain. But he was married! I wondered why Mrs Fairweather hadn't spoken of Antonia. The cogs of my brain started whirring again. If Mr Rochester married Antonia when he was just twenty, that meant they'd been married for fifteen years, and since Adele was only four ....

So, Mr Rochester was a cheat. How disappointing.

Adele stirred, and I told Redmond I was grateful that he'd taken the time to check I wasn't living under the roof of a drugs baron, or an international arms dealer, but that I'd have to go as I had to get back to work.

"Me, too," he said, sounding less than enthusiastic. "And someone had to look out for you. You seem completely incapable of taking care of yourself."

He rang off before I could retort, although, thinking of it, I probably wouldn't have been able to come up with anything. My mind was too full of all the information I'd just received. Of course, if I'd had anything about me, I would have found all that out for myself. After all, I could get the internet on my phone.

Except, to be honest, I hadn't really been interested. Ethan Rochester was just my employer, nothing else, and as long as he continued to employ me and let me live at Moreland Hall, I hadn't been too curious about anything else. I was quite glad he wasn't around, though. I'd be far too nervous, having to talk to a multi-millionaire employer. I hoped he'd stay in London for a good long while.

#

The beeping of my phone awoke me the following morning.

Joined as common-law man and wife.
Your heart to my heart, your soul to my soul.
Torn away! Now just a gaping hole
Mutilated with traitor's knife.
Light of my life, return once more.
Mend the weeping wound you tore.

Naomi and Isolde came round last night. Isolde thinks you're insane. I defended you, of course. Mind you, at least she brought me a Chinese takeaway. I'm getting heartily sick of cheese sandwiches.

"Oh, bugger off, Seth," I mumbled, dropping the phone onto the bedside table and wrapping the pillow around my head. It was half-past five. I really couldn't be doing with his feeble attempts at poetry at that time of the morning.

Come seven o'clock, I finally staggered out of bed and made my way to the en-suite. A long, hot shower soon woke me up, and I realised I was hungry. I hoped Mrs Fairweather was doing one of her fry-ups.

Just as I was pulling on the skirt I still had to squeeze into, Tamsin called.

"Morning, Tamsin," I answered. You're up and about early."

"It's half-past seven," she said. "That's halfway through the day for me. You have no idea how much work it takes to get Brad off to the office and the girls ready for school." She gave a big sigh. "Anyway, how exciting is your news!"

"What news?" I said, puzzled.

"Ethan Rochester! Redmond called me last night to tell me all about it. Phew, talk about going from one extreme to the other. I mean, Feldane flats to Moreland Hall. Seth Blount to Ethan Rochester. It's quite funny, when you think about it."

"Huh. Trust Redmond," I grumbled. "Honestly, it's none of his business. He went hunting for information because he didn't think I could be trusted to make any kind of life for myself. He's done nothing but criticise me, since I left Seth. I thought he just wanted me to leave him, but it seems I'm incapable of taking care of myself, and should be asking my brother's advice and permission for everything."

She laughed. "Well, of course. He's trying to assert his masculinity. Can't do it with Susan, can he? She's practically cut his balls off."

"Has she? What do you mean?"

"Not literally, of course," she said hastily. "But you know what she's like. He has a hell of a life with her, doesn't he?"

"Does he?" It was all news to me. I wondered how come I didn't know, but, of course, I'd lost touch with my family over the years. I had no real idea what went on in their lives, I realised sadly.

"He's worn out, and she pushes and pushes him. Wants him to end up as dean, or something. She's absolutely determined that he's going to the top of the academic tree. She's always nagging him, and, of course, the worst thing is she refuses to have children."

"I didn't know Redmond wanted children," I said, astonished. "He never mentioned it."

"He wouldn't dare," she assured me. "I reckon, if he pushed for it, Susan would march him down to the vasectomy clinic quicker than you can say *snip*. She says children are an unnecessary distraction, an unwelcome expense, and lead to the inevitable ruin of a woman's figure."

"Well, it hasn't hurt your figure, has it?" I said. "You're thinner now than ever."

"Hmm." She sounded almost wistful, and I felt a sudden lurch of panic. What was going on? Was Tamsin struggling with food issues? Should I have been worried? "Anyway," she said, "the upshot of it is, Redmond has no life at all, and he's pretty bloody miserable. So he's asserting his masculinity with you, coming over all big brother, because it's definitely the woman who wears the trousers in that marriage."

I could hardly believe what I was hearing. My perfect brother and sister, with their perfect lives and perfect marriages, weren't having such a fabulous time, after all. The thought gave me no pleasure. I just wished I could make things better for them.

"You must take photos of the house," she continued. "I'm dying to see what the Rochester mansion looks like. I mean, I know the main home is in London, but even so. Will you send them to me?"

"Only if you absolutely swear not to put them on Facebook," I warned her. "I don't want to get sacked before I've even properly started."

"As if I would," she said indignantly. "What do you take me for?"

"A Facebook junkie," I replied, thinking of how often she posted. "Swear it."

"I solemnly swear," she promised.

"Okay. I'll send some later tonight. Got to go, Tamsin. Breakfast time."

"Yes, and I have to find Alice's swimming costume, so I'll speak to you later. Have a good day."

"You, too." I ended the call, feeling a warmth towards my siblings that I hadn't felt in years, but also a vague anxiety. What was going on with them both? Why would someone as seemingly in control as Redmond let Susan push him around like that?

My heart ached for him. He wanted children and couldn't have them because his partner didn't want them. I could relate to that. And as for Tamsin, there'd been something in her voice when I mentioned her figure that worried me. I knew she was an exercise addict, and that she ate healthily, but how far had that obsession gone? I felt a growing anger towards both Susan and Brad. My conversation with Tamsin just seemed like a confirmation of what love and passion did for you.

Both my siblings had married for love, and they were each stuck with selfish, ambitious spouses who'd pushed them into a life that was making them unhappy. I wished I could make them see that they would be better off putting love aside and concentrating on themselves. Although, of course, Tamsin had the girls to think of.

With a sigh, I made my way down to the kitchen, thinking how odd it was that, after all that time spent worrying about my own future, my family's futures had become my bigger concern.

Chapter Seven

It was hard to believe, but I'd already been at Moreland Hall for almost a month. Time flies when you're having fun.

Mum and Dad had jetted off to Spain and were having the time of their lives, if their texts were to be believed. I was happy for them. They'd worked hard for years, for little financial reward, and it was good to see them enjoying themselves for a change. At least I didn't have to worry about them.

Redmond was bothering me, though. He'd opened a Facebook account, which wasn't like him, at all. He didn't have many friends on there—just me, Tamsin, and five or six people who seemed to be work colleagues. Susan wasn't on his friends list, which was odd, because she definitely had an account—confirmed when, wonder of wonders, she sent me a friend request. I'd accepted it, rather unwillingly. What if she'd only sent it to check up on communications between myself and Redmond? Assuming, of course, she knew he'd joined Facebook. Odd that they weren't friends on there. I wondered if it was another way of Redmond asserting his independence and masculinity. Poor Redmond.

Tamsin, meanwhile, had thoroughly annoyed me by posting a picture of Moreland Hall, with the caption:

Sister's new workplace! Working for THE Mr Rochester, no

less! Go, Cara! #feelingproud

"What did I say to you?" I demanded, calling her as soon as I spotted the photo.

"You told me not to post any photos you sent me of the house," she said, "and I didn't. I downloaded that one from the internet. You didn't say anything about that."

"I didn't want anyone on Facebook to know where I was working," I said. "What if Seth finds out?"

"Why would he find out?" she said. "He's not even on Facebook."

"No, but his stupid sister and best friend Isolde are," I said crossly.

"Don't be daft. My account's not public. Only my friends can see what I post," she said confidently.

The next thing I knew, I was tagged in a post by Susan. Susan, of all people! She'd never even wanted me as a friend before, and suddenly I was being tagged in her posts. I clicked on the notification to find the same picture of Moreland Hall, and her show-off status:

*Moreland Hall, Yorkshire, home of Ethan Rochester of Rochester's Department Stores. New home of sister-in-law! That's some job, **Cara Truelove**. Congratulations! We'll visit soon. xx*

You bloody well won't visit soon, I thought angrily. What was she doing, sharing the picture like that? And since when did she ever care what I was doing, or where I lived? I'd have bet a million pounds that most of her friends hadn't even been aware of my existence until that moment. And *her* page *was* public.

Furious, I'd rung Redmond and demanded he tell her to remove the post, which she did, but only after a heated argument between the two of them, apparently. I should have felt guilty, but I was too annoyed to care whether those two fell out over it, or not. I then unfriended her again. At least she wouldn't be able to tag me in any more posts.

"This is all your fault," I told Tamsin. "If Seth finds out, I'll throttle you."

"Why would Seth find out? Are his sister and Susan friends?"

"No, but her page is public. What if Naomi's searched my name? Susan tagged me. It will be visible!"

"Why on earth would Naomi bother? I think you're being paranoid, Cara. And why would Seth go to that kind of trouble? He's far too idle to do anything about it all, anyway. Stop worrying."

I took a deep breath. She was right. I was being overanxious. Seth was probably too busy telling Isolde that she was his soulmate and writing terrible poetry to her, to even think about me.

Thankfully, the next text from him gave me hope that things were dying down on his part, at last.

Angry, desperate, tortured, broken,
This is how I feel inside.
As if my very soul has died.
The grief, the angst cannot be spoken.
What did I do to drive you away?
What is the crime, for which I must pay?

You know what, Cara? I had no idea you could be so cruel, so vindictive. There is no justification for this treatment. I'm beginning to see you in a different light.

Well, thank God for that. He might finally come to the same realisation as me. We weren't soulmates, and we weren't destined to be together forever. Hallelujah!

As the days passed, and I heard nothing more, I began to relax. It was time to put the past behind me, and get on with enjoying the present. And there was so much to enjoy. Adele was a delight, and she was quite bright, too. She loved picture books, and enjoyed being read to. She also, blessedly, liked going for walks around the grounds, and as the weather was warming up nicely, we were outside quite a lot. I'd even got permission from Mrs Fairweather to mess up her kitchen a couple of times, so Adele and I could make biscuits. That'd been great fun, if only to see the state of Adele when we'd finished, and to laugh at the expression on Mrs Fairweather's face when she saw the state of her worktops.

Though I was officially given the weekends off, life continued just the same on those days. After all, I was living in the house, and Mrs Fairweather was entitled to a rest, too. I did think it was a bit rich that people as wealthy as the Rochesters couldn't provide full-time care for Adele, and I also thought that it was quite disgusting that she'd been left all alone with people who were, when it boiled down to it, staff. Where was her family?

Mrs Fairweather explained, quite proudly, that she'd worked for the Rochesters for so long that they considered her family and probably felt as if they were just leaving Adele with an auntie. I didn't believe that for a second. It seemed to me that they were taking advantage of her. And why didn't they want to spend time with Adele, anyway? She was adorable.

"It's not that they don't want to spend time with her," Mrs Fairweather protested, loyal as ever. "Ethan is devoted to her. He's just very busy at the moment, but he'll be up here as soon as he can."

107

I smirked. "And what about her ... Mother? Surely, she's missing her."

Mrs Fairweather sighed. "She, er, has things to do, too. She'll be staying here shortly, though. Ethan has given instructions that she's to have his suite."

"His suite?"

"Yes. He has a suite of rooms at the beginning of the landing, but he's told me his mother is to take it when she visits, and he'll be using the room she usually has."

"That's a bit odd, isn't it? Why would he do that?"

She shook her head. "How would I know? None of my business."

And none of mine, either, clearly, judging by the way she said it. The Rochesters were a strange bunch, it seemed, but I shrugged it off. The rich were often eccentric. At least Adele had Mrs Fairweather, who clearly loved her, and she had me, too. I had to admit, I was already strongly attached to the little girl. It was the Rochesters' loss if they couldn't be bothered with her.

One Saturday afternoon, I decided to venture out onto the moors, and maybe explore Hasedale, a pretty moorland village just a mile or two from the house. Adele was napping, having spent the morning making potato prints. Mrs Fairweather was happy to keep an eye on her, so I pulled on my duffle coat and grabbed my bag, deciding that I would have to go farther afield the next week, to Helmston or Whitby perhaps, to buy some new clothes. The weather was getting too warm for a duffle coat, and I needed some new shoes. My boots were definitely not suitable for the milder weather, and trainers were hardly appropriate. Time to start spending some money on myself for a change. It was a strange prospect, admittedly. I'd got so used to going without stuff, it felt weird to even contemplate shopping just for myself. At least my skirt and jeans had grown more comfortable, as I'd been very strict about refusing biscuits and puddings— as difficult as that had proved—because I really didn't want to go up another dress size. Plus, with me walking more, it should be easier to keep the weight off, I thought. I certainly didn't fancy saying no to puddings forever. I didn't see how it was humanly possible. Unless you were Tamsin, of course.

I thought about Tamsin as I walked through Hasedale and passed a little bakery. Did she ever give in and buy something fattening, I wondered? Or was her obsession with dieting and exercise too strong? What was going on with her? Was it really just a health kick, or something more serious? If so, what could I do to help her?

Hasedale was a lovely village, and I passed a very pleasant hour, or so, wandering around and checking out the handful of shops, having a cup of tea in the teashop, and generally relaxing. Just as I decided it was time to head for home, the dark clouds rolled in, and the first drops of rain hit my head. Wonderful.

Within minutes, the rain was bouncing off the pavement, and I glanced around quickly for somewhere to shelter. I'd just passed an old-fashioned sweet shop, The Candy Cabin—a real, sweet treat of a building itself. It was a tiny stone cottage, with a large latticed window to the left of a small, extraordinarily narrow wooden door. It was if it had been built for fairies, I'd thought, then reminded myself that such notions were fanciful and out of keeping with the new sensible me. It would make a good shelter, though, and besides, I could always buy

Adele some sweets. That would be a good excuse to spend some time in there out of the rain.

I turned back, and just about got through the door without ducking, stepping down into a real sugar wonderland. Shelf after shelf of jars filled with the most appealing confectionary that brought back loads of happy childhood memories. The lady in the shop was even shorter than me, and so thin I doubted she'd ever tasted a single one of the products she sold, but she was lovely and welcoming, and after commenting on the dreadful turn the weather had taken, and assuring me it would pass as quickly as it had arrived, she let me browse for ages while I made my mind up.

After choosing a selection of the sort of sweets I'd loved as a child—white chocolate mice, pink candy shrimps and yellow foam bananas, chewy fruit sweets and red liquorice laces—I headed towards the door, scouting through the paper bag and wondering whether I should treat myself to one of the shrimps.

So engrossed in deciding whether, or not, to say hang the diet for the day and buy myself the same selection, I didn't notice someone trying to pass me to enter the shop—not until a deep voice said, "Excuse me, can I get by?"

I looked up, and there, looming over me, stood a tall, broad man, dressed all in black. If I hadn't sworn to renounce all such soppy notions and give up romantic fantasies for good, I'd have said he was a real-life Heathcliff. I mean, move over Seth, with your wiry, long hair and grey eyes and skinny frame—the man before me was in a different league altogether. He towered over me, his jet-black, rather shaggy hair dripping wet. Dark eyes pierced into mine, his strong mouth set firm. Silhouetted against a dark and brooding sky, he was, quite frankly, a bit intimidating, and I quite forgot to move out of the way and simply gaped.

He allowed me that luxury for all of five seconds, before he tutted. "Hello? I'm getting soaked out here," he said, as if speaking to a child.

"Oh, yes, sorry, of course," I said, all flustered, and stepped aside.

He ducked down and squeezed through the door, and I hovered near the window, looking out anxiously, fingers firmly crossed that the rain would stop. Behind me, I heard him asking the lady behind the counter if she had a decent box of chocolates. The shop felt far too small for both of us, and I heaved a sigh of relief as the rain finally fizzled out.

Without looking back, I called a brief thanks to the shopkeeper and rushed outside, just as the dark clouds began rolling away and the sunshine claimed its rightful place.

As I began the walk back to Hasedale, though, the fresh air brought me to my senses. He was just a man, for goodness sake. What had I been thinking, letting him daze me like that? He'd seemed pretty grumpy, true, but he hadn't been intimidating at all—not like I'd made him out to be. Just because he was tall, and broad, and dark and glowering.

Ugh, I really needed to get a grip.

Heading along the open road across the moors, I gave a big sigh of pleasure, and began to relax again. There was nothing quite as uplifting as sunshine after rain, when the light glinted on the puddles and everything felt fresh and clean and newly-laundered. I'd had a lovely afternoon. No way would I let anyone spoil it. Which reminded me, those pink shrimps were calling my name, and I'd forgotten to buy my own, so ...

One less shrimp in the bag wouldn't hurt Adele, surely. God, I wished I'd bought myself some. I was such a sugar addict, though, it was probably best to go cold turkey. Maybe I shouldn't even have one.

At the blast of a car horn, I jumped and shrieked all at the same time, and the bag of sweets left my hand, scattering the contents all over the road. A flashy red sports car screeched to a halt, and my heart sank when the dark-haired man from the shop yelled a string of expletives over his shoulder. How disgusting.

"Do you kiss your mother with that mouth?" I demanded. I'd heard someone say that on a programme once. Sometimes, being forced to watch endless television with Seth had its uses.

"Seriously? You're having a go at me? What the f— what the hell were you doing, wandering in the middle of the road like that?"

I cringed inside, seeing the way his black eyebrows knitted together, and the stony look in those dark eyes. Even so, he was the one in the wrong. He'd almost run me over with his mad driving, for goodness sake. "I'm sorry?" I began, "I think—"

"I should hope you are sorry," he cut in, looking me up and down in disgust. "Honestly, I've got used to idiots weaving across the roads in London, but up here, I foolishly expected people to behave with a bit more common sense."

I gave him my best glare and marched over to the car.

"Excuse me? I was walking at the side of the road. Not my fault that you were too close to the edge. Besides, you're driving far too fast. There are sheep and lambs wandering these roads. Are you blind?" I waved my hand pointedly, indicating the group of ewes and lambs grazing on the side of the fell, totally oblivious to the angry scene playing out below them. I cursed the fact that none appeared to be actually on the road, which was unusual for sheep in those parts, but typical of my luck.

His eyes flashed. "I saw you, all right. You were walking by the side of the road until just before I reached you, then you suddenly started veering into the middle, right in front of me. What the bloody hell were you doing?"

I blushed, attacked by doubt. Had I veered into the centre of the road? I supposed it was possible. I *had* been sort of focused on the bag of sweets, and hadn't really been concentrating on where I was walking. I could hardly confess to that, though, could I?

I drew myself up to my full five-feet-two-inches. "Well, that's your opinion," I said, with as much dignity as I could muster. "We'll just have to agree to differ. Anyway, there's no harm done, so I'll say nothing more. Good day."

"Good day!" He stared at me, clearly astonished. "That's it, is it? You just wander into the road, nearly cause me to crash, frighten the life out of me, and then you expect to just wander off, as if nothing's happened? I could have killed you. What do you think that would have done to my no-claims bonus?"

Wow, he was all heart. "What more do you want me to say?" I said. "Personally, I think it was you who wasn't

113

concentrating. It could just as easily have been your fault as mine."

"It most definitely wasn't my bloody fault," he said, sounding quite put out. "I drive very carefully, I'll have you know."

I eyed the red sports car with contempt. What a show-offy sort of car for him to drive. It screamed, *Look at me*! How distasteful. Deciding it was best just to get rid of him, I sighed and gritted my teeth. "All right, then. I'm very sorry you had a fright. Good day."

As I began to walk off, he exclaimed, "Bloody cheek!" The car started up, and I breathed a sigh of relief, only to jump again as it slowed down when he caught up with me. The driver kept pace with me, leaning over the passenger seat as I eyed him nervously. "You don't really think it was your fault, do you?"

Did it matter? I shrugged. "We'll never know," I said, my attention fixed firmly on the road ahead of me as I continued walking.

"But I do know," he said. "And so do you, don't you? Look, all you have to do is admit it, and we'll say no more."

"I most certainly won't admit it," I said. He looked as if he had a bob, or two, and how did I know I could trust him to keep his word? I didn't want him to sue me. He looked the type to have a very expensive solicitor, and I wasn't about to pay for any non-existent damages to that tacky car of his. I sneaked a sideways glance at him.

He shook his head. "Stubborn as a bloody mule," he said, and drove off, leaving me to stare after him, feeling a mixture of relief, regret and surprise.

I was even more regretful when I remembered the

sweets scattered on the edge of the road. I couldn't bear litter, and besides, it would be just my luck if some sheep swallowed them and got ill. I wasn't sure if sheep could digest candy shrimps and liquorice laces, but the way my day was going, I wasn't prepared to take the risk.

I headed back, picked them up, and shoved them in my pocket. They were only fit for the bin. I might as well have eaten them, after all. How frustrating was that?

Chapter Eight

Mrs Fairweather was all of a dither, when I arrived back at Moreland Hall. "Oh, thank goodness you're back. Honestly, what a palaver this has been. I need to get Mrs Rochester's room ready, pronto, and Adele's woken up, and nothing's prepared for dinner yet."

Dropping the sweets in the bin, I said, "Mrs Rochester? She's here?"

"No, no," she said, shaking her head. "She's still in London. No, *he's* here. Ethan. Just arrived out of the blue. No warning, at all. He hasn't even brought Michael with him."

"Michael?"

"Michael Lawson, his chauffeur." She looked me up and down. "Ethan wants to meet you. You'd better tidy yourself up and go and see him. He's in the sitting room with Adele."

I felt a strange thudding in my chest. How had I not realised? He'd gone on about idiots on the road in London, hadn't he? I'd like to think fate wouldn't be so unkind, but past experience had taught me fate had a particularly twisted sense of humour.

I had an awful feeling that Ethan Rochester and I had already met.

Trembling and feeling a bit sick, I hung up my coat, washed my hands, ran a comb through my hair, then entered the sitting room. My worst fears were immediately confirmed. The big, dark-haired man with the flashing eyes, who'd almost mown me down on the moors road, sat in the armchair, Adele perched on his knee.

Bugger. Bang goes the job.

At least I had the advantage of a short forewarning. His eyes widened in surprise and his mouth dropped open when he took me in. Only for a second, though. He quickly pulled himself together and then shook his head. "Well, well. We meet again."

"So we do," I agreed, thinking there was no point in trying to creep round him. I'd already well and truly blotted my copybook, so it was far too late for that.

"So, you're Adele's new nanny."

"I am." I took a deep breath then held out my hand. "Cara Truelove."

He gave me a grumpy look, as if even my name offended him. "Ah, yes. Truelove. Huh." He shook my hand, rather reluctantly, I thought. "And to think, I believed it didn't exist."

It was on the tip of my tongue to assure him that it didn't, but his face told me he wasn't in the mood for jokes, and I was already worried about my job security.

He dropped my hand and looked down at Adele. "And how do you like Miss Truelove, Adele?"

Adele beamed at me. "She's nice," she said shyly. "We bake biscuits, and she does funny voices when she reads to me."

"Does she indeed?"

"And we made potato prints today," Adele continued. "Would you like to see them?"

"Of course I would," he said.

She wriggled down from his lap and ran over to the sideboard, where we'd placed the pictures while tidying the room earlier. "Mrs F said mine can go up on the kitchen wall later," she told him, proudly handing him her painting.

He scanned it carefully, and I saw a look of genuine pleasure in his eyes. "Very good," he told her. "And quite right. It should be on the wall, so everyone can admire it." He glanced up at me. "Take a seat, Miss Truelove."

I swallowed and sank onto the sofa. The whole situation was ultra-embarrassing. Trust me to land myself in it, right from the first meeting. "Call me Cara," I said, hoping to ease some of the tension.

He hesitated a moment, then shook his head. "I think it best we keep things on a formal footing, don't you? Miss Truelove and Mr Rochester would be more appropriate in the circumstances."

Crikey, had I annoyed him that much? I was pretty sure that the family had referred to Jodie by her first name, and Mrs F definitely called her boss Ethan. Evidently, I was still in his bad books.

"I'm rich, Cara," Adele informed me with a wide grin. She rattled a piggy bank at me. "There's twenty-five pounds in there."

"Gosh," I said. "That's a lot of pocket money."

"It's not pocket money," she explained. "It's Ethan's fine."

"Fine?" I glanced across at Ethan, who looked distinctly uncomfortable.

"He says bad words when he gets grumpy," she continued, "so he promised me he would give me fifty pence for every swear word he says. He must have sweared loads of times, mustn't he?"

"Hmm," I said, thinking at least a tenner of that must have come from earlier on the moors.

Like he'd read my thoughts, he pulled a face. "Actually, Adele, I think I owe you a bit more now. I'll have to go to a cash machine later."

"More money!" Adele giggled. "Ethan bought me some sweets," she said, pointing to a bag on the coffee table. "Would you like one, Cara?"

Great minds think alike, I thought ruefully. "No thanks," I said.

"I think Miss Truelove has already had some," Mr Rochester said, giving me a knowing look.

"No, actually," I said. "Those sweets were for Adele."

"Have you bought me some sweets, too?" Adele said, sounding pleased.

I went red. "Well, no. Sorry. There was a bit of a mishap with them."

Mr Rochester smirked. "Got hungry on the way home?"

"Actually," I said, indignantly, "I dropped them in the road when your car nearly hit me."

"When you wandered into my path, you mean," he said. "I didn't notice them fall."

"Well, you wouldn't," I said. "You were probably too busy trying not to kill me."

He stared at me, saying nothing, and my heart thudded again. What on earth was I doing? I'd be sacked at the rate I was going.

"What I mean," I said, thinking I'd better do some damage limitation, "is you were a bit distracted, trying to avoid me when I walked into the middle of the road."

His mouth twitched, as if it wanted to smile but couldn't remember how. "Well saved," he said, and I breathed a sigh of relief. He might've been a bit bad-tempered, but at least he had the remnants of a sense of humour. "So, how are you settling at Moreland Hall? It must be very different from Oddborough. A bit isolated for you?"

Wow, he had a good memory. Fancy him remembering that I'd worked in Oddborough. "Not at all. I love the Yorkshire moors. I was born here, and lived here until I was seven. After that, I used to visit my granny every few weeks. She lived in Newarth, but she died recently."

"I'm sorry to hear that."

"Thanks. She was pretty old. In her nineties, I think, so it wasn't exactly unexpected. So, you see, I'm very happy to be living and working here. I feel really at home."

"Hmm." He watched me thoughtfully. "Mrs Fairweather speaks highly of you. She says you've fitted in nicely."

"Thanks," I said again. Maybe my job wasn't in jeopardy, after all.

"I don't come up north very often," he admitted, patting Adele on the head, as she climbed down from his knee before wandering over to the sideboard and fetching her colouring book and pencils. "I never liked it here when I was a child—the house, I mean. Far too gloomy and remote. It was completely different back then, and it used to terrify the life out of me."

I couldn't imagine him being terrified of anything, but I smiled politely. "You've done an amazing job with the

120

renovation."

"It was for my mother," he said. "She decided that she was going to make Moreland Hall her permanent home. One of her whims." He rolled his eyes. "It didn't last long. She'd lost interest before the paint even dried."

"It seems a pity," I said. "It's such a lovely house. What a shame it's empty so often."

"Perhaps." He glanced over at Adele, who was absorbed in her colouring, and his expression softened. "I wish I could spend more time here. London has lost its attraction lately, I must admit, whereas this place ..." His voice trailed off, and he seemed almost relieved when a light tap came on the door and Mrs Fairweather popped her head round.

"Sorry to interrupt. Just letting you know that your room's ready."

"Excellent." He stood. "Thanks, Mrs F. I'll go and unpack."

"Thank you so much for the chocolates, Ethan. Very kind of you," she said.

He'd bought her chocolates? Wow, she was honoured! I peered closer at her and noticed a faint flush of pink on her cheeks.

"Er, will Michael be joining us any time soon?" she enquired. "Only, he usually drives you up here. I was quite surprised to see you in your mother's car."

His mother's car! Thank goodness for that. The news instantly sent Mr Rochester up a notch in my estimation.

"Michael's staying on for the time being. He'll be bringing my mother up here, in a week, or so."

"Ah, that's good. It'll be nice to see him again. I mean, it will be nice to see them both again."

"Right, well, if you'll excuse me." He flashed a smile at Adele, who gave him a megawatt smile back, then he nodded at me and headed upstairs.

"What do you think, then?" Mrs Fairweather bustled into the room, her face bright with obvious curiosity. "Was he what you expected?"

"I can honestly say," I said, "he wasn't at all what I expected."

"He needs a haircut," she said disapprovingly. "Looking very unkempt, he is. Still, I'm sure you'll get on with him. He's very kind."

"Is he?"

"Oh, yes. Look how good he is to Adele, for a start. Practically brought her up. And giving up his suite for his mother, like that." She tutted. "You'll find he doesn't much take after her. More like his father. She's a bit of a flibbertigibbet."

"A what?" I said, laughing.

"Flighty piece," she said. "Mind, don't get me wrong. She's not a bad person, and you can't help but like her. Just, well, she's not like him. It takes all sorts, I suppose. Lucky for Adele her brother's more responsible."

"Isn't it?" I said, wondering if she really was that naive. He treated Adele as if she was his daughter. The fact that Adele called him Ethan and not Daddy made no difference. I wondered who her real mother was. Did Mr Rochester have any contact with her? Why had Adele ended up living with him and not her mother?

Adele put down her colouring pencils. "What's for dinner, Mrs F?"

Mrs Fairweather beamed at her. "Your brother's favourite—beef stew and dumplings." She winked at me.

"Always loved his comfort food. Not one for fancy cooking, thank goodness. And then there's rice pudding for afters. Is that okay with you, miss?"

Adele nodded. "I like your rice pudding."

"Good job you do," she said. "I'll get back to the kitchen, then, now that's all sorted. You'll be okay with Adele, Cara?"

"Of course." I hesitated, then whispered, "Does Mrs Rochester ever visit? I mean, his wife, not his mother."

She looked distinctly shifty. "Not often. Haven't seen her for a while. Some people find Yorkshire too remote. You know."

"So, she lives in London?" I persisted.

"She, er, travels around," she said. "Right, back to work for me."

As she left the room, I sank back onto the sofa and considered the matter. Clearly, Ethan Rochester's wife wasn't on the scene much, and I couldn't help wondering if Adele had anything to do with that. She couldn't be the little girl's mother, because why would they say Adele was his younger sister, if that was the case? Adele was obviously Rochester's guilty secret, but then, why stay married? His wife could have taken him for millions if she could prove adultery, and Adele was living proof, right there. It was all very odd.

I thought about the fictional Mr Rochester and his ward, Adele. Luckily for him, he'd had no rich wife who could kick up a fuss about her presence. Poor Bertha had had no say in anything he did, being locked away in an attic all those years, unaware of anything that was going on around her. Although, she'd been aware of some things, I supposed, or why else had she prowled the house, scaring Jane and setting fire to her husband's bed?

I shivered. At least my Mr Rochester wasn't keeping that sort of secret from me. I shook my head impatiently. Of course he wasn't! And he wasn't *my* Mr Rochester, either.

Honestly, Cara, you're the one who's going crazy.

I suspected sugar withdrawal was the culprit.

Chapter Nine

In spite of my initial expectations, I rarely saw Ethan Rochester over the next week. He spent a lot of time out walking, or shut away in his office. He made time for Adele every day, but, during those times, my presence clearly wasn't required, and I was free to do whatever I fancied. I wandered the grounds, or sat in the kitchen, while Mrs Fairweather baked, or went up to my room and watched television, or read, and caught up with the latest events in Tamsin's life.

Busy day today! School run, yoga, fab lunch with friends, collected children from school, fed children, dance class for DD1, swimming for DD2, dinner with Darling Husband! And relax...#TFIFriday

God, I felt knackered just reading that lot. On the Saturday morning, I rang Tamsin. "Are you awake?" I teased, when she answered, sounding a bit grumpy.

"Of course I am. It's almost eight o'clock," she pointed out.

"Yes, but after the day you had yesterday, I'm surprised you don't sleep for the whole weekend. So, you had a nice lunch with your pals, then?"

She tutted. "You must be joking. They're not really pals. They're the mothers of two of Alice's classmates, and they're the most boring people you can imagine. Louisa spent the entire time boasting about how her son is going to be the next Andy Murray, and Geraldine has already decided that poor little Fenella is going to win an Oscar before she's twenty-one. Poor children. They're pushed into doing all sorts."

"Hmm."

"What's that supposed to mean?" she demanded. "That was a very accusing *hmm*."

Crikey! Paranoid, or what? She was right, though. "Just that, well, Alice and Robyn seem to do an awful lot of out-of-school activities, too. Maybe you're pushing them a bit hard?"

She snorted. "You couldn't be more wrong. I pray every day that they'll get bored and decide to spend the evening lounging in front of the television like normal kids, but no such luck. They're always demanding to be taken somewhere, and I'm running myself ragged."

"Maybe you should be firmer with them?"

"I tried that. They threw a mighty tantrum, and in the end, it just wasn't worth the bother. I can only hope they grow out of it all. I wouldn't care, but they don't even seem to improve at the things they do. Robyn's hopeless at gymnastics, but it hasn't stopped her nagging at me to buy her a new leotard this week, and then there's Alice's sudden enthusiasm for ice skating. Yes, you heard me right. Ice skating. More money."

"Good job your husband has such a great job, then," I said. "Did you have a nice romantic dinner last night?"

There was quiet for a moment, then she said huskily, "It was okay. He spared me fifteen minutes before disappearing off to the study. I felt very privileged." There was a definite catch in her voice.

"Tamsin, are you okay?" I said, worried.

126

She sniffed. "Fine. Anyway, how are things with you?"

"Oh, nothing very interesting to report," I said, before adding mischievously, "except, Mr Rochester's here."

She gasped. "Wow! Really? What's he like?"

"I don't see much of him," I admitted, "but he's pleasant enough. He's very good with Adele, I'll give him that."

"Gosh. I Googled him, you know. Rather handsome. And much younger than I expected." She hesitated, then asked, "Any news from Seth?"

"Nothing," I said, relieved. "I think he's finally got the message. He's probably moved in with Naomi and Isolde and forgotten all about me."

"Thank God for that," she said. "Mum and Dad are having a fabulous time, aren't they? They won't want to come home at this rate. Have you heard from Redmond?"

"A couple of brief calls, just checking that I'm alive and well, and that I haven't been ravaged in my sleep. He sounded different. Odd."

"Really? In what way?"

I couldn't really explain it. There had been a note of excitement in Redmond's voice that I hadn't heard before. I supposed it could have been because I'd told him Ethan Rochester had graced me with his presence. Redmond was very impressed with the man and his business empire, I knew that much. I just hoped he hadn't mentioned it to Susan. She'd be wangling for an invitation to stay before anyone could say *gate-crash*. "Not sure, really," I said eventually. "Just, different."

"Oh. Well, I expect he's in line for promotion, or something else equally dull," she said with a sigh. "Have to go, Cara. The girls have drama club in half an hour. I'll

127

speak to you soon."

I put the phone away, noting with relief that there was still no word from Seth. I gazed out of the window. It was a beautiful April day, with blue skies and sunshine. Far too nice to be indoors. Since weekends were my official day off, and Adele had her *brother* home to help out, I decided to go for a wander through the grounds and maybe take a book with me to read. I picked up the fantasy novel/draught excluder and left the house, with a plan to make my own breakfast when I returned.

Outdoors was cool, but not unbearably cold. I explored the woods, noting in delight the wild garlic that covered the ground, a carpet for the clusters of nodding bluebells. I'd pulled on a jumper, rather than the duffle coat, and at first I wondered if I'd made the right choice, but as I walked, the chill disappeared and, as I emerged from the woodland and headed across the lawns, I raised my face to the sun, clutching the book to my chest and feeling a sudden contentment.

Right then, life was good. Okay, it wouldn't last forever. Adele would go to school, and I would have to find another job, another home. But that was for the future. Apart from my concerns about Tamsin and Redmond, I had nothing else worrying me, at all. It was a rare happy interlude in my life, and I was determined to make the most of it.

I found myself walking by the secret garden, drawn, perhaps, by the sight of the blue-purple wisteria that'd draped itself over the wall. Not expecting to find it unlocked, my hand, nevertheless, reached out to the door handle, and my heart leapt into my mouth when it opened.

I pushed inside into Eden. Okay, maybe that was a slight exaggeration. I mean, it was only April, not the height of summer, so it probably wasn't even at its best, but against the far wall, there was a line of cherry blossom trees in full bloom, cheerful pom-poms, the colour of strawberry ice cream, on every branch. The flowerbeds were a blaze of colour—bushy yellow wallflowers, delicate silver-blue crocuses, buttery daffodils and lemon meringue narcissus, baby blue grape hyacinths, flaming red tulips, fragrant, lacy-white lily-of-the-valley, and tiny, soft, creamy primroses. It looked as if nature had simply scattered itself across the ground, but I knew that a great deal of thought and planning must have gone into making the cottage garden look—and smell—so perfect.

Spotting an archway at the end of the garden, I followed the narrow winding path to take a closer look. Through the archway was another large square lawn, bordered by a high hedge. There was a bird table, a curved wooden bench, and, the immediate focus of my attention, a beautiful old sycamore tree.

My heart skipped when I saw a rope swing hanging from one of its sturdy branches, and I rushed over, dropped the book on the ground, and examined the swing carefully for signs of decay, but the rope looked strong, and the thick, wooden seat was secure. What was more, it was double width, meant for two people, so I wouldn't have to squeeze myself into it.

I glanced around, as if someone would suddenly rush over and tell me to get away, but, of course, there was no one in sight. I grabbed the ropes and lifted myself onto the seat, and spent a very pleasant ten minutes, or so, simply swinging back and forth, feeling blissfully happy, and rather guilty, all at the same time. I wasn't sure I was supposed to be in there, after all, but then again, if it was private, they should have kept the door locked, shouldn't they?

Shrugging off my doubts, I swung myself higher and higher, closing my eyes as the sun dazzled me and its warmth hit my face, and revelling in the sense of freedom—until the laughter bubbled up in me, and I found myself giggling out loud for the sheer joy of it all. I must have looked—and sounded—mad, but I didn't care. There was no one around to mock me, was there?

"Having a good time?"

I gave an involuntary gasp of horror and the swing juddered as I did my best to bring it to a halt. Ethan Rochester leaned against the tree, one eyebrow raised, arms folded, and an unmistakable look of amusement on his face.

"I'm so sorry," I managed, as the swing finally, after what felt like forever, stopped, and I leapt off.

He shrugged. "No need to apologise. You were having fun. It was nice to see it being used. It's been a long time." He strolled up to the swing and plonked himself down on it, tapping the seat beside him. "Please. Join me."

Was he serious? I stared at him in astonishment. "Pardon?"

"Join me. Come on, there's plenty of room. I promise not to squash you."

I could hardly refuse, could I? He *was* my boss, after all. Reluctantly, I climbed back on the swing, nerves jangling. My body pressed up against his, and, as he put his arm behind my back and took hold of the rope, I could barely suppress a shiver. He was quite a commanding presence. Maybe it was because he was such a powerful businessman that I felt totally awestruck. It certainly wasn't because he was tall, dark and handsome. I was well past all that nonsense.

A sudden stab of nerves raced through me as the swing began to rock back and forth. I grabbed the rope with one hand, but I couldn't reach the other rope without putting my arm around him, which hardly seemed appropriate. As the swing went higher, though, I thought, *sod it*. It was either that, or fall off. My arm went behind his back, and I gripped the rope for dear life.

He looked down at me, and I was sure I saw a gleam of mischief in his eyes, as if he found my discomfort amusing. "Don't worry," he said. "I won't let you fall."

I made a sort of squeaky noise, and I couldn't for the life of me say what I meant by it. "I'm sorry I was in the garden," I said eventually, when the quiet between us became deafening. "I just found the door unlocked, and I couldn't resist."

"It doesn't matter. It's not a secret. You haven't broken any laws, or anything."

"Oh," I said. "I could bring Adele in here, then. She might like the swing."

"As long as you're careful with her. Perhaps if you sat on here with her."

"Of course I'd be careful with her," I said indignantly. "I'm not completely irresponsible."

"Apart from your habit of wandering in the middle of the road," he said.

"You're never going to drop that, are you?"

"Probably not. It's always good to have something

over people," he mused. "Unless I find something a bit more interesting about you, of course."

"There's nothing interesting about me," I assured him.

"I beg to differ. There's something interesting about everyone, if you look hard enough."

"An admirable philosophy," I said, "but in my case, you couldn't be more wrong."

"Let me be the judge of that." He slowed the swing to a halt and turned to me, his arm still behind my back as he clung to the rope. "Tell me about yourself."

"There's nothing to tell. Honestly."

"You said you were born in Newarth and lived there until you were seven. Why did you move?"

"I didn't have much choice," I pointed out. "Most seven-year-olds don't."

"You're very prickly," he observed. "What are you hiding?"

"Nothing! If you must know, my dad got a better job, and we moved to Beverley in East Yorkshire. Do you know it?"

"Of course. I went to a wedding there once, at the Minster. Lovely town."

Surprised, I nodded. "Well, yes, it is. I missed the moors, though. I used to visit Granny Reed regularly, until I was sixteen, just so I got to come back up here every month, even though she made me play the piano."

"There's a piano at the house," he told me. "Would you like to play it?"

"Not really. And I doubt very much you'd like to hear it. Unless you're a particular fan of *The First Noel*. It's about as much as I ever mastered, despite her best efforts."

He laughed, a genuine, hearty laugh. I was so startled I almost let go of the swing rope entirely. "You sound as musically gifted as me. Ah, well, the piano lid will stay firmly shut, then. I don't think I can face a Christmas carol in April. It just seems all wrong."

"Exactly!" I said. "That's just what I told her, but she would insist. Mind you, she was a bit religious—in the way that the Queen's a bit posh. Pictures of the Holy Family everywhere, and she seemed to have a bit of a thing for the Pope."

"She sounds like quite a character. But you were clearly very fond of her."

"I was," I admitted wistfully. It was heart-breaking, the way things had turned out. I'd barely set eyes on her since I was sixteen. Was that my fault for moving in with Seth? Or her fault for being so judgemental? Maybe a bit of both, I supposed.

"So, what happened when you were sixteen?"

I stared at him, unnerved. "Nothing! Who says something happened then?"

"You did," he said. "You said you visited Granny Reed regularly until you were sixteen. So, what happened then?"

Drat him. He was far too observant for his own good. "We had a falling out," I admitted. "I didn't really see her after that."

Thankfully, he didn't ask me what we'd fallen out about. He just sighed and said, "Families, eh?"

"Yes," I agreed. "Families."

"Are your parents still alive?"

I wondered how much more he was going to probe into my private life. Was this the interview he'd missed out on? He was certainly more thorough than Mrs Fairweather had been. "Yes, they are. They're having an extended holiday in Spain, thanks to Granny Reed's inheritance."

He grinned. "Sounds like a plan."

"Definitely." I pulled a face. "She left me her piano."

He laughed again, and I found my face had shaped itself into a smile, without me even asking it to. "It could have been worse. My sister got her Rosary beads and a really unnerving picture of the Pope."

His laughter heightened again. Eventually, he said, "So, you have a sister."

"I do," I said, adding slyly, "as do you."

"Yes." He stopped laughing then, all right. "Adele was something of a surprise."

I'll bet she was! "There's quite an age gap," I said, rather daringly. "Must be, what, thirty-one years between you?"

"Thereabouts." He shrugged. "These things happen. It was unexpected, but I'm glad she arrived. She's a joy."

I couldn't argue with that. "She's adorable," I agreed, smiling up at him. "Impossible not to love her, really."

He stared down at me, as if considering me. Mrs F was quite right, I decided. He did need a haircut. It curled over his collar and looked quite casual for such an important businessman. "I'd better go," he said suddenly, then leapt from the swing without warning.

I just managed to grab the other rope and steady myself, and when I looked up, he was walking away.

"Stay as long as you like," he called over his shoulder. "I'll be with Adele all day today. I'm taking her to Scarborough, so feel free to make as much use of the swing as you wish."

I stared after him, thinking I'd never met anyone like him before. Strangely—and annoyingly—the swing seemed to have quite lost its charm since he'd stepped off. A day in Scarborough seemed much more appealing.

Chapter Ten

After staying a couple more days at Moreland Hall, during which time he rarely left Adele's side, Mr Rochester headed back to London.

"Never known him so reluctant to leave," mused Mrs Fairweather, as she returned to the kitchen after waving him off, like a fond mother bidding farewell to her favourite son. "Mind, he's had a bad time of it in London lately, what with one thing, and another."

"What sort of thing?" I asked.

She handed me a cup of tea and sat beside me at the table. "Not for me to say," she said.

"Of course. Sorry."

Quietly sipping my tea, I could tell that she was dying to tell me something, and sure enough, when I didn't push her, she spilled.

"He gets mithered left, right, and centre," she burst out suddenly. "If it's not one thing, it's another. I mean, as if running that empire isn't enough! And then he's got all his in-laws on his case, and that ridiculous woman and her antics, and all that business with Jodie, and now his mother's back home, which won't help. She's already giving him a headache. She wouldn't come up to see Adele, and she's asked him not to bring her down to London to see her because she has plans. Plans! What plans are so important that you don't want to see your own child?"

Reddening, she muttered, "And I shouldn't have said any of that. Not like me to be so indiscreet. Just that, ooh, it makes me that mad. He deserves better from all of them. And as for that child .... If it wasn't for him, God help her."

I didn't know what to make of any of that. It was obvious that Jennifer Rochester had no real maternal feelings for Adele, but then, why would she? Nothing had convinced me that she was truly the little girl's mother. Certain the whole thing was a cover-up, I couldn't get as worked up about her lack of parenting skills as Mrs F, because, in my opinion, it was Mr Rochester who should've been making more time for her.

The other things she'd mentioned were far more intriguing, though. What was the business with Jodie, the previous nanny? And why were his in-laws on his case? I assumed the *ridiculous woman* was Antonia.

"What's his wife been up to?" I said, unable to resist asking any longer. I had, I was rather ashamed to admit, Googled Antonia Rochester, to try finding out more about her. She seemed fairly reclusive. Not much came up—at least, not much recent stuff. There was a bit about her birth and early life, and then quite a lot about her surprise wedding. And she was mentioned by name in a few articles about her father, a wealthy landowner called Simon Wilson-Smythe, but other than that, there was nothing about her, or what she was up to, or even where she lived.

Where *did* she live? Was she in London? Did she share a home with her husband, or had they unofficially separated? It was quite intriguing. The most recent photo of her was taken at an airport five years previously. I'd expected her to be all tall, slender and gorgeous, but she seemed surprisingly normal, and had quite a friendly, open expression on her round, smiling face.

She raised an eyebrow. "His wife? Why do you mention her?"

"You said *that ridiculous woman and her antics*. I presumed you mean her?"

"You presume wrong, then," she said. "She's an entirely different kettle of fish."

"So, why are his in-laws on his case?"

She set her cup down on the table. "It's not for me to say, and I've said more than enough already. Now, shouldn't you be getting Adele up and dressed? I'm sure she's awake by now."

She'd made her point, so I didn't push her. I finished my tea and headed upstairs to see to Adele.

Adele and I had quickly formed a real bond, and the days and weeks flew by in her company. She was a well-behaved child, with a great sense of humour and an infectious giggle. Obviously, she had the occasional tantrum, but she was four, after all, and it came as quite a relief to find out that she wasn't *too* good. She'd soon become my little companion, and I was gratified to realise that she'd grown quite attached to me, too.

As April gave way to May, and the days passed, she and I had great fun, painting, baking, playing on the swing, and helping Ken in the garden. She loved pulling on her wellies and getting her little trowel out, crouching beside him as he planted and dug and weeded. She even had a little watering can, and made it her business to ensure that no flower ever went thirsty.

138

We caught the moorland bus one day and headed down to Pickering, catching the steam train and travelling the North Yorkshire Moors Railway line up to Whitby. Adele absolutely loved the whole experience, and by the time we'd caught the bus back to Hasedale, and got a taxi home to the Hall, she was happy but exhausted. After coaxing her into eating a sandwich, I'd quickly washed and changed her, then put her to bed, where she slept right through until almost nine the following morning.

One glorious day in mid-June, Adele and I decided to have a picnic. Mrs F kindly packed us a feast that would have satisfied four adults, never mind one adult and a child, and we headed into the secret garden, where I rolled out a blanket in the shade of the sycamore tree, and we sat down to tuck in to our outdoor banquet. Around us, daisies and buttercups peeped through the grass, freckles of white and yellow on a perfect green face.

"This is the life, eh, Adele?" I said, smiling at her as she chomped happily on an egg sandwich.

She nodded, grinning widely at me, which was rather off-putting, given the amount of half chewed food covering her teeth and tongue. Eventually, she managed to swallow her mouthful and said, "Jodie never did picnics. I'm glad she went and you came, Cara."

"Well, I'm very glad, too," I said. "Although, I expect Jodie misses you a lot."

"Not really," she said considering. "She wasn't really my friend. She was mostly on her phone."

"Oh, dear." Not so good, then.

"She liked Ethan, best." Her eyes twinkled with mischief. "She said he was gorgeous." She giggled and helped herself to a Scotch egg.

"Did she really?" I wasn't sure whether to continue that conversation. Dodgy territory. "Well, she shouldn't really have said that to you, should she?"

"She didn't. She was saying it to someone on the phone. Don't you think Ethan's gorgeous?"

Her face was alight with amusement, and I knew that, whichever way I answered, it would be in grave danger of being reported back to someone—possibly, God forbid, Ethan himself. I decided to change the subject. "He'll be back soon, I dare say. I expect you've missed him."

"Yes. I always miss him. Mummy's home from holidays, too. I spoke to her on the phone, and she says she'll come and see me soon. She can't come just now, but that's okay."

She sounded quite unperturbed by her mother's absence. I wasn't sure whether to feel glad, or angry about that. I supposed, for Adele's sake, it was best that way.

"Mummy didn't like Jodie," Adele informed me. "She said she was a bossy madam."

"Did she indeed?" I murmured. "Would you like a drink of squash?"

Adele nodded, and I poured her a cup of squash from the flask we'd brought with us. I ate a ham sandwich and tried not to dig for more information, as tempting as the thought was. It wasn't fair to use Adele in that way.

"Jodie told Mummy that she should spend more time with me, and Mummy got cross and said it was none of her business."

"Er, quite right," I said, thinking that Jodie had more courage—and more cheek—than I'd ever possess.

"Mummy said Jodie didn't understand, and she wasn't my natchell mother, anyway." Adele tilted her head to one

140

side and stared at me. "What does natchell mother mean? I asked Ethan, and he said it was a made-up word and didn't mean anything."

I nearly choked on my ham sandwich. What the hell could I say to that? So, Jennifer Rochester had admitted—to the nanny, of all people—that she wasn't Adele's real mother! Sadly, Adele had overheard. How did I get out of this tricky situation?

"I don't know what it means," I said, thinking the best bet was to take Ethan's lead. "Maybe you heard it wrong?"

She sighed. "Maybe. I like that word. Natchell. I like other words, too, but I'm not allowed to say them. Ethan heard me say one once and got very cross. Jodie said it was his own fault because he said it, too, and Ethan got even crosser, but then he said sorry, and after that he promised me fifty pence every time he said a bad word." She beamed at me. "Jodie said I should be glad when he has a bad day at work because I'll make a fortune."

Charming. Their London nanny sounded like a real piece of work, although, it had to be said, Jennifer Rochester impressed me even less. And then there was Ethan, who, it seemed, had to be Adele's real father. What a family. Poor Adele.

We finished up our picnic, chatting about food rather than nannies, thank goodness, before packing up. Mrs F seemed quite flustered when we arrived back at the house.

"Delicious picnic," I told her, smiling. "You look a bit harassed. Everything okay?"

"Well, Ethan's just rung me," she said, switching on a smile for Adele's benefit. "You'll be pleased to hear he's coming home in a few days, Adele. And not only that, but he's decided to have a party for his birthday. The house will be full of guests for the first time in years. Quite an event, and very little notice."

"A party!" Adele looked delighted, but Mrs F shook her head.

"Not your sort of party, my love, I'm sure." She glanced over at me, her eyes betraying some annoyance. "Honestly, he could have given me a bit more notice. Oh, well, we'll cope. We always do."

I had no doubt about it. I wasn't worried about the party. I was more worried by the fact that, in spite of all my misgivings about men in general, and Mr Rochester in particular, I couldn't deny that my heart had leapt when I'd heard that he was coming home again, at last. What on earth was that all about?

\#

"It will be good to have people in the house again," Mrs Fairweather said the next day, evidently torn about the party. "but I'm not keen on some of his friends. One, in particular."

"Oh? Who's that?" I enquired, reaching over and dipping my finger in the mixing bowl. She'd been baking some of her fabulous ginger cake, and always let me finish off the mixture afterwards. It tasted almost as good as the cake itself, and because it was unbaked, I sort of kidded myself that it didn't contain as many calories—obviously rubbish, but it was extraordinary what you tell yourself when you're trying to lose weight.

"Not for me to say," she said. "Mind you, I reckon you'll figure it out for yourself when you meet her."

"Her?" I felt a pang of something that I couldn't quite put a name to and shrugged it off. "What about his wife? Will she be coming up to celebrate his birthday?"

"I shouldn't think so for a moment." She closed the oven door and wiped her hands on her apron.

"It's a strange sort of marriage, isn't it?" I mused. "She never comes here, and he doesn't seem to spend much time with her in London."

"She—"

"Likes to travel," I finished for her. "So everyone keeps saying. But what sort of marriage is it, when they're never together? Was it always like this?"

"What Mr and Mrs Rochester do is entirely their business," she said, eyeing me sternly.

I arranged my features to look suitably chastened, and she seemed satisfied that I'd learned my lesson.

"Mind, he could be a bit less thoughtless—springing a visit on me one minute, then a party on me the next," she conceded.

"I suppose he could have warned you."

"Huh. I suppose he did, if you count casually dropping the fact that he's invited twelve guests to stay the night, to celebrate his thirty-sixth birthday, into a phone conversation as a warning. I've got to work out a menu yet, and I'll have to air all the rooms and put fresh bedding everywhere. By the way, did I tell you, you're invited?"

"Me? But I'm staff! Why would he invite me?"

She shrugged. "Why not? He's asked me, too. It's not the dark ages, you know."

"Really? Yet, I have to call him Mr Rochester, and he calls me Miss Truelove, even though he apparently called Jodie by her first name. It may not be the dark ages, but you can't deny, he's a bit formal with me, isn't he?"

"Yes, well, maybe he is, but then again ..." She

frowned, when my phone pinged and I stared at the screen in dismay. "What is it?"

I shook my head. "Nothing. I think I'll go up to my room, Mrs Fairweather. Just for an hour. I should catch up on my reading. Unless you want any help with anything, of course?"

"No, I'm fine, thanks. But what about your lunch? You didn't have breakfast. I can make you a sandwich, if you like."

Standing, I shoved my phone in my pocket and turned away. "No thanks. Not hungry. Catch you later."

Reaching my bedroom, I took out my phone and read the text in dismay. Seth! I'd been absolutely certain that he'd given up. What could have persuaded him to try again?

I wandered lonely as a cloud
Of sweet pink blossom, newly blown
From bare trees, which, like me did moan
And grieve their loss, and beg out loud
Come back to us, o! we implore,
And fill our empty arms once more.

You've broken my heart. Think carefully about what you're doing because I won't wait forever. Isolde has asked me to move in with her. I'm seriously considering it, you know. She makes a cracking lamb bhuna.

I was half tempted to reply with *Go for it*, but stuck to my plan of not responding. It was the only way he'd ever get the message. I checked on Facebook to see if Tamsin and Redmond had posted anything. There was nothing at all from Redmond, but Tamsin had posted a photograph of some gorgeous flowers in a crystal vase, with a cheerful update.

Beautiful flowers! Lucky girl!

Some people had commented, asking her if they'd forgotten her birthday, or was it her anniversary? Was it? I felt ashamed to admit I wasn't sure.

I decided to ring her, to check, since she hadn't responded to any questions.

She sounded awful on the phone. Really, really upset. My heart broke for her as she made a valiant effort to seem cheerful when, quite clearly, she wasn't.

"Are you okay, Tamsin? Did I forget your anniversary?"

"Wouldn't matter if you had," she said. "Brad wouldn't have remembered, either."

"Oh, no. Are things that bad?" I flopped onto the bed and stared unseeingly at the wall. "What's happened? Did Brad get you the flowers?"

She sniffed. "You must be joking. I bought them myself, from the market this morning, and arranged them for something to do. You know I love flowers. That status was just putting on a brave face. Truth is, I needed cheering up."

"Why did you need cheering up?"

There was a deafening silence, then she burst out, "Brad's left me. He told me last night he was going. He's moved into a hotel for a while."

My mouth dropped open in shock. "Left you? But why?"

"I have no idea. I'm guessing there's another woman. What else could there be?"

"But haven't you asked him?"

"No. I don't want to hear it. He said he needed some

space, time to think. That's basically code for *I'm shagging someone else*, isn't it? I'm not stupid."

"Oh, God. What did you say?"

"I told him to clear off, then. What else could I say? What do you want me to do? Beg? No chance. He's barely spent any time with me or the girls lately. I thought he was working overtime—putting in extra hours at the office. Bet he's been screwing some little tart all along. Well, she can have him, whoever she is. I won't beg for anyone, least of all a man who actually thinks it's okay to abandon his wife and children." She gave a big sob. "But what am I going to tell the girls? How do I explain it to them?"

"I don't know," I murmured. How awful. What could I do to help? I felt useless. "Do you want me to come and stay for a while? I could help you out." I wasn't sure how, but I wanted to do something.

"No, no. Don't be silly. You have work to do. The last thing I need is you getting the sack. I can't have something like that on my conscience, not when things are finally working out for you. I'll be fine. I'll sit the girls down and explain it all to them. There are going to have to be big changes, so they'll need to know."

"What big changes?"

"Well, all these after school activities, for a start. I may not be able to afford them now. I have no idea what—if anything—Brad will contribute, especially if he's got some slapper to pay for. I don't know. Maybe I'll have to take them out of private school. Send them back to the local primary. I may even have to sell the house. Oh, God!" A note of panic had entered her voice, as if she'd only just realised the possible repercussions of Brad's actions.

146

"Just calm down," I said, trying to soothe her. "You don't know what's going to happen yet. I'm sure Brad will be responsible. He's never kept you short of money before, has he?"

"He's never shagged another woman before, either," she pointed out.

I could hardly argue with that, and I felt a growing rage towards my brother-in-law. Men really were shits, when it came down to it. "Will you be okay?" A stupid question, because how could things ever be okay again?

"I will be," she said, sounding suddenly determined. "He's not going to ruin my life. If you can start over again, I'm damn sure I can."

I had to admire her. She was a lot braver than I'd have been in her situation. "If you need anything, any time, just call me, okay?" I knew, deep down, there was nothing I had that she could possibly want, and nothing much I could do to make things easier for her, but if there had been, if there was anything at all, I'd have done it.

I thought of Alice and Robyn with their whirlwind social lives and their posh private school. Surely, Brad wouldn't let them down over that, would he? He was a decent man, deep down. But then, I'd never have believed he'd have walked out on his family like that. It just showed, you couldn't trust anyone. Not really.

Mrs Fairweather gave me a very strange look, when I re-entered the kitchen, an hour or so later. She plonked a plate of sandwiches on the table and folded her arms. "Lunch. Eat."

I really wasn't hungry. In fact, I didn't feel I could face so much as a biscuit, not after hearing Tamsin's awful news. I felt quite miserable, and there was a part of me that also felt guilty, because my life was going so well, and her world, and the girls' world, had just come crashing down around their ears.

She didn't seem interested in my protests, however. "You've had no breakfast and no lunch. Get them eaten." She pushed me onto the chair and sat beside me. Her eyes looked suspiciously bright, and she patted my hand. "You know, if you've got anything worrying you, you can always tell me, don't you?"

It was really kind of her, but I didn't think Tamsin would appreciate me blabbing about her marital problems to someone she hadn't even met. "Thanks, Mrs Fairweather. I'm fine, honestly."

"Are you sure, Cara? Because I won't judge, you know, and they do say a problem shared is a problem halved."

Was I that transparent? Obviously, my worries were written all over my face. I gave her a half-hearted smile and picked up my sandwich. "Thank you. But I'll be okay."

She nodded, but watched me intently as I bit into my sandwich. I managed half and then admitted defeat. "Sorry. I'm just not hungry today."

She gave me an encouraging smile, but as I stood to leave, she said hastily, "Don't go just yet. I was wondering if you'd help me come up with a menu for the party."

"Me?" I blinked, as she rushed over to the kitchen drawer and took out a notebook and pen. "What do I know about organising a party? Especially one as posh as this one is sure to be."

She pushed the paper towards me. "Two heads are better than one," she told me. "And I really would value your input."

It seemed a very odd thing to say, but then, she seemed to be in a very odd mood. Sighing, I picked up the pen and poised it over the notepad. "Okay, Mrs F. Where do we start?"

Chapter Eleven

Mrs Fairweather was determined to give Mr Rochester a party to remember, and she'd drafted in Mrs Turner and Mrs Jones for extra duties of cleaning and airing the guest bedrooms, and giving the downstairs rooms an extra thorough scrubbing. She'd also hired waiting and bar staff, and was, despite her grumbles, clearly enjoying herself. Little wonder she seemed far from happy to get a message from Mr Rochester, informing her that he'd hired a party planner, who'd be arriving that day and would be responsible for choosing a theme for the event and decorating the downstairs rooms accordingly.

"And just what's wrong with my party planning skills?" she demanded, while I attempted to soothe her wounded pride by making her a strong cup of tea and patting her on the shoulder. "Just look at that text," she said, handing me her phone. "A professional party planner. If that's not a kick in the teeth for all my past efforts, I don't know what is."

Reading the text, I frowned. "But that's not what he's saying, at all! Look, he says he apologises for dropping the party on you with so little warning, and he knows you've already got more than enough to do and wants to take the burden from you. He's being thoughtful and kind, Mrs F. It's not an insult. It's a confirmation of how much you matter to him, if anything."

She eyed me suspiciously, then, as if seeing I was genuine, she sipped her tea and nodded. "Well, I suppose you're right. I don't suppose it will matter, just this once. As long as this party planner stays out of my kitchen!"

I'd hoped that would be the end of it, but I hadn't foreseen exactly who Mr Rochester would employ. At a buzz from the intercom, I rushed over to answer it, while Mrs F pulled a face and tutted.

"Hello?"

"Is Paolo."

"Paolo?"

"Paolo. Is Paolo."

"Er, are we expecting you?"

Mrs F scowled. "I don't like the sound of him."

I didn't see how she could possibly judge a man by the sound of his voice, but I decided to pick my battles.

"Is Paolo. Mr Rochester say you expect me? Am party planner."

"Ah, yes. Hang on."

I hung up the receiver and pressed the button that would order the main gates to swing open.

"Here we go, then," Mrs F sniffed. "Let's see what work of genius he comes up with."

"Give him a chance," I pleaded. "It's not his fault that he was employed, is it? He's only here to do his best for Mr Rochester."

She sighed. "I suppose so."

In the event, though, she had cause to be wary. I kept out of the way most of the day, taking Adele into the garden to play on the swing. We sat on the bench, and I read her a story, and we had another picnic on the grass under the tree. I decided that there were already far too

151

many cooks working on that particular broth, and I was better off out of it.

When I finally took Adele indoors to wash and change, I heard a commotion coming from the drawing room. After ushering Adele into the sitting room and settling her with some toys, I rushed over to find out what was going on.

"You're completely mad!" Mrs F stood, hands on hips, glaring at a small, slight young man, with fake-tanned skin the colour of a satsuma and startlingly white teeth. All he needed was a green wig, and he could've gone and worked for Willy Wonka. "You do realise who Mr Rochester is?"

"Of course. I meet him in London. He very kind. He very polite," Paolo snapped, his expression clearly showing that he didn't think Mrs F shared her employer's manners.

"Well, if you met him," she said, "you must surely understand that this is the last thing he'd want. It's a joke!"

"What's going on?" I said.

Paolo looked completely outraged, to the point I feared a walk-out. Behind him, two other men seemed equally indignant, and rather worried as they studied what I could only presume to be mood boards.

"Cara, you won't believe what he's got planned," Mrs F said. "*A Midsummer Night's Dream* as the theme. Seriously! Can you see Mr Rochester going for that? I mean, does he look like the king of the fairies?"

Biting my lip, I stifled a giggle. "It's very artistic, Mrs F," I said.

Paolo beamed at me. "You see? She understand! I think you," he said, glaring at her, "are prejudiced."

"Prejudiced? What do you mean by that?" she said

indignantly.

"You are afraid of men showing softer side," he said. "You are afraid that people think Mr Rochester is not real man."

It was Mrs F's turn to look outraged. "I sincerely hope you aren't saying what I think you're saying," she thundered. "I'll have you know that my favourite uncle is gay, and I have no problem with that, whatsoever."

"Then, what is your problem?" Paolo demanded. "Oberon is strong, determined, stubborn. He is masculine through and through."

"But he's a fairy!" Mrs F wailed. "Fairies are for children. Mr Rochester is a grown man, for goodness sake."

"Picture it," Paolo appealed to me. "A woodland scene. Branches and flowers adorn every surface. A fairy glade. A veesion in green."

"Forget it," said Mrs F. "I'm not having messy branches dragged in here, for a start. Besides, green's an unlucky colour."

"You are mad," Paolo shrieked. "You have no veesion."

His employees muttered to each other and shook their heads, evidently waiting for an explosion. I held my breath, while Mrs F folded her arms and glared at him, seeming unconcerned by his fury.

To my surprise, he unexpectedly relaxed and gave her a slow smile. "Okay. We do it your way. No fairies for Mr Rochester. I make this room masculine. Party for a real man's man. Yes?"

Mrs F smiled. "That's more like it. Now you understand. Well, now you've seen sense, I'll leave you to

153

it. Oh, and while we're at it, can you tell your cronies to keep out of my kitchen please. I don't like skulkers. If you want something, just ask."

Paolo gaped at her, while his two employees stared at each other and shook their heads.

As Mrs F swept out of the room, head held high, I rushed after her. "Well, that told them," I said, trying not to laugh.

"Really, have you ever heard the like?" she demanded. "Blooming fairies and muddy old branches in that nice drawing room? Where on earth did Ethan find him?"

"What was that about them keeping out of your kitchen?"

"Another one of his lot, in here, if you please, rooting for food. I mean, they should bring a packed lunch. I'm pretty sure he'd been in the fridge. I swear I heard him shut the door just as I walked in. Blooming rude, if you like."

"Have they eaten?" I asked.

"How should I know?" she said irritably. "That tangerine twit should take them out for lunch. I'm not having anyone in here, and that's that. Now, let's think about dinner, since we've put that lot straight. What do you fancy?"

"I don't really mind," I said. "I've had quite a big picnic lunch with Adele, so I'm not hungry."

She shook her head. "Don't be silly. You need to eat. You're wasting away, Cara."

To please her, I ate a hearty dinner with her that evening, after Paolo and his gang had left for the day. I didn't want to sit with her while she watched another riveting episode of some dreary drama series she was hooked on, though, so, despite her protests, I excused myself and went upstairs to my room.

Curled up on my bed, I read for a while, but didn't take much of the story in. I kept thinking about my family, wondering how they all were. Funny as it seemed, in spite of the geographical distance between us all, I hadn't felt so close to them for years.

Mum and Dad were still in Spain, and Dad had messaged me that morning to tell me that Auntie Sylvia had a fabulous lifestyle over there, and he'd quite made up his mind that he and mum wouldn't be wasting any more precious holiday time in a chalet in Skegness, which said a lot, since Dad was probably Skegness's biggest fan.

From his cheery text, I gathered he didn't know about Tamsin and Brad. I was quite glad she hadn't told them, because I didn't really want their holiday spoiled, but I was also incredibly proud of my sister for keeping it to herself. It must've been tough for her, especially since Alice and Robyn had since been told their father wasn't away on a business trip, as she'd initially told them, but had left the marital home for good. They'd, obviously, got very upset, she later told me, and all three of them had had a jolly good cry together.

Almost as if my thoughts had conjured her up, the phone rang with her name across the screen, and I answered the call.

"I was just thinking about you," I said. "Just remembering what you told me about how the girls took the news. I'm so glad they were there for you."

"It's odd," she said, "but they haven't been anywhere this week, except school, and they're happy to just stay in with me and watch television. It's like they don't want to leave me alone. I don't think we've ever spent so much time together—well, not since they were little, anyway. It's been nice, in a strange, surreal sort of way. We've talked so much. They're actually quite interesting people."

"That's great. And have you heard from Brad?"

"Not much. He's still at the hotel, as far as I know. Although, of course, that could all be a lie. I haven't checked. I guess I don't really want to know." She sighed. "He hasn't closed the joint account, anyway, and his salary still went in there this month. He hasn't said anything about taking my debit, or credit, cards away, so I suppose I can't say he isn't playing fair."

"Do you miss him?"

She laughed. "What's to miss? He was barely around, anyway." There was a sort of sniffling sound, and then she admitted, in a rather choked voice, "Of course I bloody miss him. Don't ask me why. How do you miss what you haven't had? But I always knew he'd be home, however late at night it was. And even when he seemed distracted, at least he was *there*. Bastard was probably daydreaming about his tart."

"I'm sorry, Tamsin," I said. "This must be so hard for you."

"There are worse things," she said, trying to sound cheerful. "At least you're sorted. And Redmond and Susan seem to be much happier."

"Do they?"

"Well, I presume so," she said. "At least, Redmond rang me the other day to offer his brotherly advice, and he was remarkably cheerful. Not like him, at all. Something's changed, clearly. Maybe she's stitched his balls back on for good behaviour."

156

We laughed and said goodnight, and I went into the en-suite and took a shower. I was just towelling myself dry when I heard it—a sound so faint I wasn't sure if I was imagining it.

I stared up at the ceiling with a frown, and head tilted to one side, I strained my ears, listening, but heard nothing else. Shrugging, I wrapped the towel around me and walked into the bedroom. I was just pulling on my pyjamas when I heard another sound. It didn't seem to be coming from directly above me, so it was hard to be certain what it was. A scraping sound, perhaps? Or a faint scratching?

I climbed into bed and pulled the duvet up to my chin. Something was up there in the attics. But what?

#

"Bats," Mrs F told me the following morning over breakfast, when I voiced my anxieties to her.

"Bats? Seriously?"

"More than likely. Little blighters. Still, better than rats, eh?"

"I suppose so."

I must have sounded doubtful, because she patted my arm and said, "Don't worry. We've had them before. They like to make themselves at home. And we can't do anything about it, you know, because they're protected. If they want to live there, that's their business, apparently."

"It didn't sound like bats to me," I said.

"Surprising how the mind plays tricks," she said. "Especially at night, when you're alone, and it's a big house like this one. You imagine all sorts. You don't want to worry too much about it. If it helps, they're not your average attics. Don't think they're dark, gloomy rooms,

157

with no light and creatures lurking in every corner. It's basically another floor up there, with lots of rooms off a central corridor."

"Is it?"

"Yes. Used to be the servants' quarters, a long, long time ago. Still some old beds and stuff up there, from when they lived there. And there's electric lighting, too, in a couple of the rooms, so it's not as scary as you'd think."

I nodded. "Okay. Well, maybe I was imagining things. Don't really like the thought of bats above me, but I suppose they're harmless."

"Nothing we can do about it, anyway, so no use worrying. Now, we had squirrels up there once. That wasn't so good. Had to catch them and hand them over to be put to sleep before they did any serious damage. Chew through wiring and wreak havoc, if you leave them."

"Put to sleep? Why would you do that?"

"Had to. It's an offence to let them go free. If they'd been red squirrels that would have been different, but these were grey ones, and there's enough of those running around already."

"Well," I said, "you live and learn."

"So, no more worrying about it, okay?" She gave me a reassuring smile. "Now, sit yourself down, because I'm about to dish up pancakes and syrup. Adele's favourite breakfast."

It was becoming increasingly clear to me that Mrs F was determined to fatten me up. Why, I couldn't imagine. It wasn't as if I needed help, was it? Thinking about it reminded me of Tamsin. I had a sneaking suspicion that her strict exercise programme and low-calorie diet was a way of taking back control in a life that, with Brad's workaholic behaviour, and the girls' demands, had seemed to be spiralling out of her control. Bearing that in mind, I had to wonder how she was coping with that? Given that her husband had walked out on her, was she eating at all? How did I find out? And how did I help her, anyway?

After doing my best to shovel down my breakfast, I shrugged off Mrs F's protests that I should stay at the table and let my meal digest, and left Adele enjoying her own pancakes, while I headed into the sitting room and switched on the laptop. Mr Rochester had provided it, saying he wanted Adele to learn how to use it as soon as possible, and that there were lots of things she could do on a computer that would be educational and fun. He was certainly keen on technology, as Mrs Fairweather had said. I was quite glad of the fact just then, though, as it meant I could do some research in peace. It was all very well Googling stuff on my phone, but it was a small screen, and took some reading. Much easier on a laptop.

I must have been very absorbed in reading the information I found, as I obviously didn't hear a car pull up outside, or the front door opening, or footsteps in the hall. It was only when the door to the sitting room opened and a voice enquired, "Hard at work already?" that I realised he was home.

Mr Rochester stood looking down on me, an odd expression on his face.

No use denying it—my heart thumped, and I felt an unmistakable joy as I smiled up at him. Without warning, he sat by my side, and I remembered what I'd been reading and hastily closed the laptop.

If he'd noticed the article about eating disorders, he didn't mention it. "How are things here?" he asked me. "Is

Adele behaving herself?"

I nodded. "Always. She's a little angel."

"Not like me," he confessed. "I was a wicked child. I drove my mother insane."

"Will she be visiting soon?" I asked. "I'm looking forward to meeting her. I expect she'll be here for your party?"

He sighed. "As it turns out, she won't be attending the party. She's going into hospital. I'm hoping she'll be out in a couple of days and will be able to come home, but she won't be up to socialising, I'm afraid."

"Oh, that's a shame," I said. "I hope she's all right."

"She will be." His dark eyes scanned me curiously. "And how are you, Miss Truelove? Still happy to be out here, so isolated from the rest of the world?"

I laughed. "It's not that bad. Adele and I went from Pickering to Whitby on the steam train recently, and she absolutely loved it. And I can walk to Hasedale, and from there I can get the Moors bus to a lot of different villages."

"Can I trust you to walk to Hasedale, though?" he teased. "I don't want you wandering in the middle of the road again. We wouldn't want anything to happen to you, would we?"

Wouldn't we? I felt a bit breathless, and was sure I was blushing. Those deep brown eyes gazed back at me, and I swallowed. "I'll be more careful next time. No sweets to distract me."

He looked away, seemingly thinking about something. I stared at his profile, noticing that he had a straight nose and a firm chin. Mrs F was quite right. I couldn't imagine him as King of the Fairies, no matter how I tried. He was masculinity personified.

When he turned back to me, I blinked, my heart thudding when I saw he was smiling again. "It's good to be home. It's funny, I always considered London my home, and this place just a bolthole that I could use once in a blue moon. It feels different now. I was looking forward to coming back."

"You must have missed Adele," I said. "And, of course, there's your party."

"Ah, yes. My party. That should be fun." He stood up. "I must get back to Adele. I promised her I'd only be a moment. I'll send her to you in a short while."

"Fine," I said. "I've got some activities planned for this morning, and I think she'll enjoy them."

With a curt nod of his head, he left the room.

I put the laptop on the sofa where he'd been sitting and leaned back, taking a deep breath. Oh, God, he was really having an effect on me. I mean, a bigger effect than even Seth had managed. That had been a childish crush, born when I'd had no experience of men and no idea what I was getting into.

This, however, was powerful in a way that really scared me, because this time I knew exactly what I was getting into, and given that Mr Rochester was a multi-millionaire businessman with a wife, it could only end in heartbreak.

Chapter Twelve

After a day spent entertaining Adele, I took her into the kitchen for her evening meal, to find Mr Rochester and Mrs F huddled together by the sink, looking quite serious. As soon as they saw me, they moved apart and smiled at me.

"Are we done for the day?" Mr Rochester asked, ruffling Adele's hair.

She nodded and announced that she was hungry, which launched Mrs F into a frenzy of activity, after she apologetically admitted that she hadn't yet got the little girl's tea ready and would see to it immediately. Adele usually ate around four, then had a light supper at six thirty, before bed around seven thirty. Her routine was pretty strict, according to Mrs F, because when she'd been in London, it had tended to be more chaotic, which she felt was bad for a child, so she'd long ago decided that, whenever Adele was in Yorkshire, she would give her the routine that was lacking at home, since Mrs Rochester senior was a bit hit-and-miss when it came to parenting.

I couldn't help wondering who actually had legal parental responsibility for Adele. After all, it was her *brother* who'd taken charge of employing me, and it was he who seemed to spend more time with her. What was keeping Jennifer Rochester in London? Though, of course, she *was* going to have an operation. Maybe her

162

health was bad.

"I wondered, Miss Truelove, if you'd like to join me for dinner this evening?" Mr Rochester enquired abruptly.

I blushed. No doubt about it. I could feel my face burning. "That's very kind of you, Mr Rochester."

Mrs F tutted. "All this Miss Truelove and Mr Rochester business—very formal, isn't it?"

"It's what Mr Rochester requires," I said, thinking I totally agreed with her, but who was I to voice an opinion?

He winced, looking faintly embarrassed. "Perhaps … I just think it's best that we set boundaries, that's all."

"Don't worry," I said. "It's fine by me."

"Cara knows her place," Mrs F told him. "Not like some."

She patted him on the shoulder, and he gave her a rueful smile. The deep bond between them was tangible. Maybe Mrs F was right, and Mr Rochester really did see her as family.

"So, you'll join me?" He raised an eyebrow, and when I nodded, he seemed pleased at my acceptance. "I'll get back to the office. I'll see you around seven thirty, Miss Truelove."

"You will," I confirmed. As soon as he'd left the kitchen, I turned to Mrs F. "Why has he invited me to dinner? It doesn't seem right, somehow."

"He probably just fancies some company," she said evasively. "Must be a bit boring for him, eating alone every night."

"Then, why hasn't he asked you?" I demanded, as she stir-fried chicken and vegetables on the hob.

"Because I'm going out tonight." She tutted at my

shocked expression. "Believe it, or not, young lady, I do have a life outside this house. I'm off to Newarth to see my sister. We're going to have a girls' night in, with plenty of wine and a couple of decent films, so if I were you, I'd stop questioning everything and just enjoy the fact that you'll be eating in the dining room tonight, and not here at the kitchen table. It will make a nice change for you."

"But it's a bit ... awkward."

"Why on earth will it be awkward?" She tossed some noodles into the stir-fry and glanced over at Adele. "Sit yourself down, love. Did you wash her hands?" she asked, turning back to me.

"Of course. It will be awkward because he's my boss. And it's weird, having dinner with the boss. What do I talk about?"

She gave me a strange look. "Goodness, talk about whatever you want to talk about. You talk to me when we're having dinner together. There's no difference."

I begged to differ; there was a great deal of difference. Mrs F didn't make my heart go thump, for a start, and she didn't make me almost forget my resolve to stay well away from men. I had to be careful. I didn't want my stupid emotions to run away with me again, did I? The only good thing about falling for a wealthy, married man would be that nothing ever could, or would, happen between us, even if I'd been silly and weak enough to want it to. As far as he was concerned, I was the nanny of his sister/daughter, and a member of staff. Way beneath him. And I was very relieved about that. Of course I was.

#

The dining room at Moreland Hall wasn't as intimidating as I'd feared. It was a big room, with a long table in the centre, red-painted walls, and a wooden floor, but there were lovely paintings of the Yorkshire Moors hung from the walls, making it seem much more informal, and some family photos on the sideboard that were of interest. They were mostly of Adele, but there were one or two of my employer with—I presumed—his parents, and one of his mother on her own. She was a bubbly-looking blonde, with a wide smile and her son's dark eyes. In spite of myself, I quite liked the look of her.

Discovering we'd be sitting together, rather than at either end of the table, unnerved me. I'd hoped for a large distance between us, but we may as well have been sitting at the kitchen table, for how close we were. Those same nerves led to me drinking far more wine than I was used to. My face felt quite hot, and I knew I'd be flushed. I knew I'd have to concentrate hard and take my lead from him. I didn't want to use the wrong knife and fork, after all, or make some other dreadful faux pas and show myself up.

I needn't have worried, though. It was a very informal meal, if uncomfortable. He barely spoke to me as we ate, and I wondered why he'd bothered to invite me, if he had no intention of making any attempt at conversation.

Sneaking the occasional glance at him as he ate, I was relieved to see that he didn't shovel his food down like Seth, and—bonus—he actually swallowed each mouthful before putting more in. Seth always ate as if he was terrified I was about to snatch his plate away at any moment. In contrast, Mr Rochester seemed deep in thought about something, so much so, I suspected food to be the last thing on his mind.

As I chewed some roast potato, I wondered what he

was thinking about. I noticed he needed a shave. A fine layer of stubble graced his chin, and as I traced its outline up towards his ears, wondering idly what it felt like, I had a moment's urge to reach out and touch it. From the corner of my eye, I watched him cut into a slice of roast beef. No wedding ring on his finger, I realised. Nice hands, though. Strong, capable hands with clean fingernails.

Feeling even hotter, I swallowed my potato without meaning to and ended up coughing.

Mr Rochester raised an eyebrow. "Are you all right?"

I nodded and coughed again. He handed me a glass of water, and I took a gulp, swallowing down the last of the stubborn potato and assuring him I was fine. That would teach me to daydream about what Mr Rochester's hands were capable of.

After dinner, I expected to be dismissed, but instead he opened another bottle of wine and seemed in no hurry to move. We discussed the Yorkshire Moors and the local attractions we'd visited, and he told me a bit about London when I confessed I'd never visited—something he found extraordinary. From his descriptions, I changed my mind about the place, and decided I'd love to visit one day, after all.

"It has a beauty of its own," he assured me. "It's not as bleak as you imagine. There are some beautiful old buildings, and so much history. Where I live, it's almost like a village. You'd be surprised."

"But it's not Yorkshire, is it?" I teased. "I mean, look at those paintings." I waved my hand at the pictures on the walls either side of us. "The artist has really captured the spirit of the moors. You can't deny that London can't compete with those views, not to mention the history. Look at that painting there! Whitby Abbey. More history than you can shake a stick at. And Rievaulx Abbey! Stunning. What about Helmston Castle and Scarborough Castle? Look at that beautiful painting of Farthingdale Moor!" I shook my head. "I don't see that London has anything to tempt me away from here."

"History? Oh, you should see the Tower of London! It's quite amazing," he said with sudden eagerness. He'd obviously quite forgotten he was on a mission to be aloof. "Then there's Hampton Court and Buckingham Palace, Westminster Abbey and St Paul's Cathedral. Not to mention all the various old pubs and streets that are off the tourists' maps." He smiled at me, which completely transformed his face. "If you love history, you'd love London. You should go. Perhaps one day, I'll take you."

Something in his tone made me quiver, and I stared down at my plate so he wouldn't see my scarlet face.

"I mean, Adele will need a nanny when she goes home for visits," he said abruptly, glaring at me as if I'd dared to assume anything else. "So—the paintings. You like them?"

Quick change of subject. Thankful, I looked up at them and nodded enthusiastically. "Absolutely. The artist seems to really understand the place, don't you think? Must be a local artist, surely?"

"Must be," he agreed.

"Don't you know?" I asked, surprised.

"I got them locally. I don't go into too much detail." He shrugged. "It was my mother who wanted me to put them in here. She shares your opinion of them."

"She has good taste."

He looked a bit doubtful about that. "Sometimes," he

conceded.

I glanced over at the photographs. "I assume that's her?" I said. "She has your eyes. Or, more accurately, you have hers."

"You think?" He followed my gaze. "I suppose so."

"Adele doesn't," I said carefully. "She has blue eyes." I looked pointedly at the photo of his father, who had eyes almost as dark as his wife and son.

He picked up a bottle of wine. "Another glass?"

Better not, I thought. I was already teetering on the edge of sobriety, and I didn't want to lose all my inhibitions. Bad enough I'd dropped a massive hint that I didn't believe Adele was his sister, so I didn't want to go too far. "Go on, then," I heard myself saying, despite all my mental protests, and he poured more liquid into my glass. "Were your parents together a long time?" I asked. Although I already knew the answer to that, I didn't want him to know my brother had already researched them, did I?

"Yes, they were." He went quiet for a moment, taking a sip of wine while seemingly deep in thought. "It was a shock to us all when my father died. It was quite sudden. He seemed to be in good health—then again, he worked too damn hard. We were always telling him. He lived for his work, and I think it killed him in the end. My mother's certain of it. She always warned him it would."

"It's hard living with a workaholic," I said, thinking of Brad and Tamsin. "She must have got quite lonely."

"I expect she did. They weren't very much alike." He leaned back in his chair and stared into his wine glass. "She was very sociable. Loved to party. Loved to spend money, too. Whereas he ..." He shook his head. "He was

168

the opposite. He couldn't be bothered with entertaining. He had few friends. He didn't really trust many people. He knew, you see, that most of them only stayed around him because of his wealth. They all wanted something from him. All of them. Even my mother."

"Oh." I didn't really know what to say to that.

"Don't misunderstand me," he said quickly. "She loved him, in her own way. However, I can't say for sure she would have married him, if he'd not been so rich. I know he doubted it, too. But they were happy enough. He let her spend his money and flit here, there and everywhere, and she made a home for him and gave him the child he needed, and somewhere relaxing to come home to when he finished working every day."

I thought about his words, as he took another sip of wine. "You said *needed.*"

"I'm sorry?"

"You said, *she gave him the child he needed.* Not wanted. Is that how it felt?"

Why had I asked that? It was a bit personal, after all. Yet, there was something about the way he'd said it that made me think it wasn't just a throwaway remark, and I couldn't help wanting to understand.

He seemed to hesitate a moment, then said, "It was important that he have an heir to take over the business. Sounds a bit mediaeval, doesn't it? But when you've got an empire like Rochester's Department Stores to handle, you have to make sure it's going to be taken care of after you've gone. It's our duty, apparently."

"Bit of a burden for you," I said. "What if you hadn't wanted to be a businessman? What if you'd wanted to do something completely different?"

169

He shrugged. "Who says I didn't?"

I gaped at him, unable to think of a reply. It hadn't occurred to me, actually. I just assumed that he loved the cut and thrust of corporate life. What else had he wanted to do?

He shook his head. "Sorry. Getting a bit deep here. Whatever I wanted to do, let's just say, I knew my duty, and leave it at that. I don't know. Maybe, deep down, I kind of envy my mother. She always did exactly what she wanted to do, and somehow, she managed to twist him round her little finger, so he allowed it."

"She sounds like quite a woman."

"She is." He smiled. "I love her to bits, whatever I say about her. She's one of a kind."

"I expect," I said slowly, "that you and your own wife will be thinking about children one day. After all, you'll need an heir, too. The Rochester empire must continue."

His face darkened, and I wished I'd kept my mouth shut. I'd clearly crossed a line. He reached over and poured another glass of wine, took a large gulp, and slammed the glass down.

"Sorry," I said. "None of my business."

"I can see you're curious," he said. "About Antonia, I mean. She has her own life, and she spends most of her time abroad."

"Is she abroad now?"

"Who knows?" he said. "She's an extraordinary woman. A real adventurer. Another one who knows her own mind and won't toe the line. At least, most of the time. Sadly, there's always a price to pay."

He sounded quite wistful, and I thought whatever their relationship was, complicated didn't seem to even begin to describe it. His eyes met mine, as he carefully said, "We married young. Very young. We were friends first and foremost. She's one of my favourite people in the world."

"That's nice." My hands trembled as I gripped my own glass, and I tried to push the jealousy aside.

"And bloody inconvenient." He said it so softly that I wasn't sure I'd heard him right. He swirled the remainder of the wine in his glass, then seemed to make an effort to lighten the mood. "So, tell me, Miss Truelove, have you ever been married?"

I could, at least, answer that honestly. "No, I haven't."

"And there's no one special in your life?"

I shook my head. "No one. I mean, obviously, I have family, and they mean the world to me, but I'm not in a relationship."

"Really? And do you have your sights set on someone?"

What sort of question was that? I frowned. "No. Why do you ask?"

He looked uncomfortable. "No reason. I suppose it's just that, most women I know seem obsessed with finding Mr Right."

"You hang out with the wrong women, then," I assured him. "Unless, of course, it's your irresistible charm unbalancing them."

Oh, heck, the wine had really gone to my head. Fancy saying that to him! As shock tugged at his face, I tried desperately to stifle a giggle.

"My irresistible charm?" He frowned. "You do remember that I'm a happily married man?"

"Crikey, don't worry. I was joking," I said. "You're

really not my type."

"I'm very relieved to hear it," he said, rather huffily. "It would make our working relationship extremely awkward, if you got the wrong idea."

"No chance of that," I promised him. "I'm staying well away from men from now on."

"Good for you."

"Yep. Good for me," I said, and took another slug of wine, just as he raised his own glass to his lips and drank deeply.

"Why are you staying away from men?" he said. "You're still a young woman—too young to make that decision. You don't mean it, surely?"

"I certainly do," I said decisively. "And if you don't mind me saying so, that's incredibly sexist of you. Not every woman wants a man, you know. We can, believe it or not, make lives for ourselves without them. I'm happier alone. I don't intend to get involved with anyone, ever again."

"Ever again?" His eyes narrowed. "So, there *was* someone?"

"There was," I mumbled, suddenly less defiant, "but that's well and truly over."

"Your choice, or his?" I stared at him, and he clapped his hand against his forehead. "I'm sorry. It's none of my business."

"It was my choice," I said quietly. "Though, he made it very easy for me."

We sat there, looking at each other for a few moments, neither of us saying a word. My stomach fluttering like a butterfly that had been trapped in a jar.

"I didn't mean to offend you," he said quietly. "And I

172

wasn't being sexist. It's not just women who want a home, a family, someone who's always going to be on your side, no matter what. Someone to talk to, laugh with, when the outside world gets a bit much."

"I suppose so," I murmured, thinking, was that what *he* wanted? If so, he didn't seem to be in luck. Antonia didn't strike me as the stay-at-home type. I couldn't see her being there to laugh and talk with him at the end of a weary day. I felt quite sad for him actually, so it was a bit of a shock when he unexpectedly leaned towards me, his expression serious.

"You are happy here, Miss Truelove? There's nothing troubling you?"

Me? I thought it was him who was troubled? I shook my head. "Nothing. I love working here, honestly."

His eyes bored into mine. "If you have any worries, any concerns at all, if you feel you need to confide in someone ..." I held my breath, only to let it out again as he said, "Mrs Fairweather is an excellent listener. I can vouch for that."

He gave me a faint smile, and I smiled back, not sure what on earth he was getting at, and cursing myself for the feeling of disappointment that had swept over me. Not that I had anything to confide in him about, of course, but... maybe I could make something up? "Thank you," I told him. "I'll bear that in mind."

Abruptly, he stood up. "I have a conference call first thing tomorrow morning. I need an early night, so I'd better head to my office now and finish up there. Will you be all right alone?"

"Of course." Why wouldn't I be?

He glanced at his watch. "Mrs Fairweather will be

back soon. Perhaps you could spend the rest of the evening with her?"

"I'll go to my room," I told him. "I have a book I'm halfway through, anyway."

He frowned. "I don't really like to think of you alone."

"But I'm fine. I like being alone. Well, some of the time."

The conversation had taken a rather surreal turn, I thought. Must have been all the wine. I brushed aside his concerns and left him to his work.

Lying on the bed a short while later, I thought about our evening together and tried to decide if I'd dreamt half of it. I wasn't used to drinking, and I had drunk a lot, after all.

As I drifted off to sleep, I could've sworn I heard a scraping noise coming from above me, but then again, that was probably just the alcohol. Or perhaps I was dreaming.

Chapter Thirteen

It was the day before the party, and Mr Rochester spent the entire time in his office.

"What on earth does he do in there all day?" I demanded, as Adele tucked into Mrs Fairweather's version of fast food—a homemade venison burger in a wholemeal roll, with lots of salad and a side order of sweet potato chips. No greasy hamburger with cheese and fries for that kid.

"Runs his empire." Mrs F rolled her eyes. "Just as his father ordered."

"From what he said to me," I told her in a low voice, mindful of Adele sitting at the table, "he wanted to do something else with his life. I assumed he was a businessman through and through, but it seems not."

"He's a mixture of both his parents," she said with a sigh, "and it doesn't sit easily with him. He wanted to please his father, though, and he made a promise, which he will keep. He always keeps his promises. Mind you, I think he goes too far."

"In what way?"

"Tries to do it all himself. He has plenty of people around him who are more than capable of taking some of the load from his shoulders, but he tries to control it all. He'll drive himself into an early grave, if he's not careful."

"How do you know that?" I said, curious as to how

she could possibly be so well-informed, living all the way out here.

She sniffed. "I've spent time in his London home. They only have a cleaner there, so I've gone down to the house, if they're hosting business dinners or other events, and, as I told you, I stayed there when they needed someone to mind Adele when—when they lost the nanny. Mrs Rochester—Jennifer—tells me things, sometimes. She worries about him. Frightens her that he may go the same way as his father, if he's not careful. And then, there's Michael." Her face went pink again, just at the mention of his name.

"Oh, yes. The chauffeur," I said.

"He's more than the chauffeur," she protested. "He's ferried Ethan around since he was a little boy, and he knows him inside out. Ethan confides in him. Like another father, really. And he's worried, too. Says it's all work and very little play. It's not right. I mean, he should have some fun in his life, don't you think?"

It was my turn to go pink. "Yes. I mean, of course he should. Everyone should. But it would probably help if his wife was at home more often, wouldn't it?"

She tutted and turned away. "We're expecting Mrs Rochester home later today—Jennifer, I mean. Michael called earlier. They should be here around six."

"Really?" I smiled. "Can't wait to meet her."

"She's not up to meeting people at the moment," Mrs F warned me. "She's been in hospital. Had an operation. She's here to recuperate, so don't get your hopes up."

"Is she really ill, then?" I asked, worried. A flibbertigibbet she may be, in Mrs F's words, but I knew her son loved her.

"Not for me to say what's wrong with Mrs Rochester," Mrs F said primly. "I'm sure if the family want us to know, they'll inform us in due course."

I had the strongest feeling that she knew perfectly well what was wrong with Jennifer Rochester, but she clearly wasn't going to share that information with me, so I didn't press her. I nodded meekly, and seeming satisfied, she turned back to the cupboard.

"Well, that's odd," she said. "I could have sworn I'd got a tin of tomato soup in here. I was going to have it for my lunch. Just fancied it with some hot, crusty bread. I don't know." She shook her head. "I think I'm going a bit daft."

"It's your age, Mrs F," I told her cheerily. "It's the start of a slippery slope."

"Cheeky madam," she said, laughing. "I've still got all my marbles, thank you very much."

#

Later that afternoon, I was heartened to see a Facebook status from Tamsin, which sounded much more like her old self.

Listening to classical music in the conservatory! So moving and so inspirational! Have had a lightbulb moment! Exciting times ahead!

"What exciting times are ahead?" I asked her over the phone, after leaving Adele in Mrs F's hands for her tea and heading upstairs to wash and change.

"That would be telling," she said. "Let's just say, I'm done with sitting around, crying and feeling sorry for myself. I'm taking back control, Cara."

"I'm really pleased to hear it," I assured her. "But in what way?"

177

"For a start, I'm not going to be a burden on Brad any longer. Oh, he's being very decent about everything. He hasn't mentioned the mortgage, or tried to stop me having any money, or anything like that. But I've been thinking about it all. What must his tart think of me? She must see me as some helpless woman, totally dependent on her ex. Well, I'm not having any little scrubber look down on me like that. I'm going to free myself from Brad, once and for all. I'm going to get a job, for starters."

"A job? Doing what?" Tamsin hadn't worked since Alice was born. The job market had changed drastically since then. "You might have to update your secretarial skills."

"I'm not going back to secretarial work," she said determinedly. "I'm not saying what I want to do yet, because I have some investigation to do first, but if it pays off, well, I'll be heading in a whole new direction."

"Wow," I said. "Well, that sounds fabulous."

"And then, once I'm working," she added, "I'm going to speak to Brad and the girls about selling the house. I don't want to stay here, where all these memories are, and I don't want to have a huge mortgage hanging round my neck, either. I'm thinking we may as well downsize."

"And what about the girls' school?" I asked. "Those fees must be enormous."

She sighed. "I know. I wish we'd never sent them there, but I can hardly ask them to leave now, can I? I'll just have to suck it up and wait until they've finished their education. But once they have, I'll be free of Brad forever, and I won't have to have any communication with him, at all."

"Is that what you want, Tamsin?" I said softly.

178

"Really?"

"Of course," she said, sounding far too hearty for my liking. "We're done. I'll never forgive him for cheating on me, Cara. I just can't, so there's no point in wishing for anything different, is there?"

"Are you eating okay?" I had to ask. It had been worrying me for ages.

She sounded surprised. "Eating okay? Of course I am. What an odd question."

"Just that, I know how you've been dieting so strictly, and exercising so much. I don't want you to fade away to nothing."

She tutted. "No danger of that, Cara, trust me. Anyway, how's it all going at Rochester Towers? Still enjoying yourself up there in the back of beyond?"

Too much, I thought, with a sudden clarity. "It's fine," I said. "Adele's lovely, and everyone's very kind here. I'm really happy. It's Mr Rochester's birthday party tomorrow, and I'm invited. It's going to be a very posh event."

"Ooh, get you. What are you wearing?"

I pulled a face. "My one and only dress."

"Not that black maxi dress with the pink roses?"

"Don't say it like that," I protested. "It's a perfectly nice dress."

"Nice isn't what you want for a posh birthday party, Cara," she pointed out. "This employer of yours is a multi-millionaire, and I'll bet he's invited loads of posh people. You can't wear a boring dress like that. What on earth are you thinking?"

"I'm thinking it's the only dress I have."

"Well, you'd just better get yourself to the shops and rectify the situation," she said firmly. "Seriously, you deserve this. Get a new dress. New shoes. Have your hair done. Buy some makeup. Live a little, for God's sake. You deserve it." We were both quiet for a moment, then she said, "No word from Seth?"

"Not for a few days. I'm praying he's moved on to Isolde now." I crossed my fingers. "And the best of British luck to her."

She laughed. "You're not wrong there. I'll love you and leave you, Cara. Have a great time at the party. Get a new dress! Don't snog anyone you shouldn't. Oh, what the hell, snog whoever you like. Bye, sweetie."

"Bye, Tamsin."

Snog anyone I like? If only! I stared out of the window at the lawn and thought I really would have to make sure that, tomorrow, I stayed well away from any alcohol. And I'd better stay well away from Ethan Rochester, too.

#

Michael, it turned out, was silver-haired and twinkly-eyed, and, without doubt, the object of Mrs F's affections. When I walked into the kitchen after putting Adele to bed, ready and eager for my dinner, I found her standing by the table, looking all coy and girly, while he sat there, hands cupped around a mug of coffee, enthralling her with tales from Old London Town.

She went very red when she spotted me. "Oh, Cara! Let me introduce you to Michael. Michael, this is Cara, Adele's nanny."

He beamed up at me and held out his hand. "Very pleased to meet you, Cara. I've heard good things about you."

"Have you?" I glanced at Mrs F and smiled. "Thank

180

you very much."

She looked down at Michael, whose eyes twinkled even more in response.

"Laura hasn't said a word," he told me.

I felt the fire spread from my chest, all the way up my neck, and across my cheekbones. *Mr Rochester* had said good things about me? "Oh," I said, or rather squeaked.

He watched me thoughtfully, until I felt like I was being barbecued.

"Ethan's having dinner in his suite with his mother," Mrs F said, changing the subject, to my everlasting gratitude, "so I thought the three of us could eat in here tonight, and then spend the evening in my sitting room. What do you say?"

I decided that three, in that case, would definitely be a crowd. "I'm happy to eat here," I told her, "but I think, if it's all right with you, I'll go to my room afterwards."

To my astonishment, she looked horrified at the very idea. I would have thought she'd be gagging to be alone with Michael. "Don't be silly," she insisted. "You don't want to be stuck up there on your own all evening. You can watch television with us, can't she, Michael?"

He looked a bit taken aback, and I had a feeling he was pretty surprised about her outburst himself. Clearly, he'd been expecting, or at least hoping for, some alone time with her. He obviously returned her affections, and there was no way I was going to play gooseberry.

"I'm perfectly happy to watch television in my own room," I said firmly. "Honestly, Mrs F. I'm quite tired, actually, and I fancy an early night, anyway. Now, what's for dinner?"

She seemed really put out by my reply, but Michael

twinkled his approval at me, and I thought I was probably doing her a favour, even if she didn't realise it. Perhaps she didn't trust herself with him, I thought, amused. I couldn't say I blamed her. I knew how it felt to be tempted, didn't I? But Mrs F had no reason to be cautious. If she liked him, and he liked her, what was the problem? She was far too sensible to be led astray, and he seemed like a nice, uncomplicated man. Not a pretentious, fake poet, nor a multimillionaire married man. No, I was definitely going to get out of their way later, however much she protested.

#

I must admit, heading up to my room after dinner, I was curious. Nearing the door to Ethan's suite as I stepped onto the landing, I was really tempted to put my ear to it and listen in. I was dying to meet Jennifer, but then again, I reminded myself, she was ill. She must have been. She hadn't even made an appearance, but had been whisked upstairs and given Ethan's suite, rather than her own room, and she hadn't even seen Adele. God, what if she was dying? It hadn't occurred to me before, but there was something Mr Rochester and Mrs F weren't telling me about her illness.

After a last, thoughtful look toward the door, I went on into my own room.

Though I tried to concentrate on the television, I couldn't settle. I realised I hadn't set eyes on Mr Rochester all day. Not once. It scared me how much I'd missed him. Then I remembered Michael's words.

Mrs F hasn't said a word. I've heard good things about you.

Only my employer could have said those things. But what had he said? Did he mean I was a good nanny, or something else?

You're being ridiculous, I chastised myself sternly. *Of course he meant I was a good nanny. What else could he mean?*

I didn't want him to mean anything else, anyway. I was off men, I reminded myself. No more Brontë heroes for me.

I jumped when the phone beeped on my bedside table. Picking it up showed Seth's name on the screen, and I experienced a sinking feeling in my stomach.

Betrayed! O cruel harlot!
I am Heathcliff, left alone to grieve.
You are Cathy, destined to leave.
Creation of Emily, not of Charlotte.
Was it foretold, down the ages?
In Wuthering Heights' gothic pages?

I think you should know I had to give up the flat. The council weren't very understanding about my rent arrears, so I hope you're happy now. You have no idea what you've driven me to. I don't know where we're going to live when you come back. You'd better hope Isolde is willing to forgive and forget, though I warn you, her spare room is tiny.

Not as tiny as his brain, clearly. I should have known he wouldn't sort out the rent. So, the flat had gone? It was no loss, though I did wonder, with a sudden panic, what had happened to my belongings. I'd barely brought anything with me, having had to leave some of my clothes, all my books, and some personal stuff like photos and old birthday cards behind. Maybe they were at Isolde's? Or maybe he'd burned them all, or taken them to the local tip.

Well, I told myself, they were just *things*. I had no use

183

for romantic novels anymore, anyway, and Tamsin, Redmond, and Mum and Dad would have plenty of photos that I could copy. I certainly didn't need any of Seth. I would be okay. Whatever happened, whatever he'd done, it didn't matter. He was no longer my concern.

After deleting all his messages, I lay back on my bed with a sigh of relief. Seth was the past. I had to look to the future. And that, despite my treacherous hormones, would be a strictly man-free zone.

Chapter Fourteen

What do you buy the man who has everything? And should you buy him anything, anyway, considering he's your employer and, as unbelievable as it seems, you only met him a few weeks before?

I'd struggled with what to do for ages, but decided, in the end, to just buy Mr Rochester a card. I didn't know him well enough to gauge what he would like, and I didn't want to ask Mrs F, so a card would have to suffice.

When he didn't show his face at breakfast the morning of his birthday, I presumed him to be with his mother, until Mrs F informed me he was out and about somewhere, having already eaten with her earlier, and that she reckoned he was probably psyching himself up for the party.

"Psyching himself up?" I said, surprised. "Is it going to be some sort of ordeal, or something? I'd have thought he'd be looking forward to it."

"Not if I know him," she said, handing me a cup of tea. "He was railroaded into it by his *friends*. They, no doubt, fancied a free weekend trip to the country to have a nosy round here. And he probably thought he should make the effort, since he does nothing but work when he's down there."

"Why did you say friends in that way?" I said, curious. "Don't you like them?"

"Not for me to say," she said, before saying exactly what she thought—namely that they were a bunch of hangers-on, only interested in having a good time and spending money. "Especially her," she finished. "You'll see what I mean when you see her."

"See who?"

"Not for me to say," she said again, leaving me exasperated beyond measure.

Adele was dying to see Mr Rochester. With a little help from me, she'd made him a lovely card, with a drawing of the two of them on the front, and a rather impressive attempt at her signature, plus several large kisses inside. She was very proud of her creation, and couldn't wait to give it to him.

Luckily, she didn't have to wait too long. She'd just finished breakfast when he entered the kitchen, and she practically dived off her chair and raced over to him, clutching the card in her hand.

He was suitably impressed, and seemed genuinely delighted with it, rewarding her with a loving cuddle. He then thanked me for my card, and when he leaned over and gave me a peck on the cheek, my face must've flamed with colour. I gazed at the ground for a few moments, not knowing how to respond.

Vaguely hearing Mrs F telling him that she'd made Jennifer a cup of tea, if he wanted to take it up to her, I risked a glance up at him, only to find that he was still watching me, even though he was answering Mrs F. Our eyes met, and I swallowed hard, unable to deal with the emotions assaulting me. To my relief, he turned away, and I offered a silent prayer. Oh, thank you, God, that he was attached, completely unavailable, and not my type at all.

How fortunate for me.

After a few moments of small talk with Mrs F, he took the cup from her hands and headed upstairs to take the tea to his mother. Once he'd gone, I finally took a deep breath and sank into the chair. It was going to be a long and difficult day. I really did have to get a grip.

The guests would be arriving from lunchtime onwards, so Mrs F was going to be kept busy, finishing up the food preparations. "I'm going to be rushed off my feet today," she said with a sigh. "It'll be nonstop."

"Why didn't Mr Rochester bring in professional caterers?" I said, thinking it was a bit unfair to land everything on her.

She gave me a look that would have slain a dragon. "And what do you think I am? Am I not a professional? Bad enough that that wretched Paolo ordered a cake from outside. As if I couldn't make a perfectly good one myself."

"Sorry, Mrs F," I said hastily. "I just meant, professional party caterers, that's all. It seems like a huge task for someone on their own, like you."

"He offered," she assured me, somewhat mollified. "Of course he did. I told him I wouldn't hear of it. This is my house, my kitchen, and I'm not having a bunch of college graduates come in here and start messing about with my appliances."

I grinned. "Of course not. What was I thinking?" I gave her a sly look. "Will Michael be helping you out, at all?"

Her face flushed. "He may pop in and give me a hand," she said, not looking at me. "Quite good in the kitchen, is Michael. Comes of all those years living alone, I suppose."

"He's not married, then? Not got a girlfriend?"

She tutted. "Divorced. Over ten years ago, now. She was a flighty bit, too. Do you know, in all the years they were married she never ironed his shirts? Not once! Imagine that. I mean, what was the point of getting married if she didn't want to look after him?"

I decided that a discussion on equal rights and the emancipation of women would be lost on her.

Luckily, she changed the subject. "Been thinking about what you said last night, about wishing you'd bought a new dress. Why don't you get yourself into Helmston today? There's some nice little clothes shops down Castle Street."

"Maybe so," I said, "but I doubt Adele would appreciate being dragged around them, while I try to find something that fits."

She shook her head. "No need to take Adele. I've got Susie coming in to take care of her. Rang her this morning. She's glad of the extra money, so it's no bother. You get yourself ready, and Michael will drop you off in town."

"Really?" I smiled at her, feeling a wave of gratitude. I'd been sure I'd left it too late, so it was a lovely surprise. "Won't Michael mind?"

She gave me a knowing look. "He won't mind, at all," she assured me.

Michael was duly summoned and instructed. Luckily, he seemed quite eager to take orders from Mrs F and agreed readily to her plan.

I headed into the hallway, intending to dash up to my room to get my bag, but I stopped dead when I saw Mr

Rochester on the landing. He'd obviously just left his mother's room and was starting to head downstairs, his mobile phone clutched to his ear, not even looking where he was going.

"I don't give a fuck," he snapped at some poor unfortunate person on the other end of the line. "Do what it takes. We can't lose York. It's our flagship store, for fuck's sake. If it comes to it, the Chapel Street branch is expendable."

He stopped and gripped the bannister, seemingly unaware that I was standing at the bottom of the stairs. "Listen to me, it's non-negotiable. What's Greg Carter doing? Right, and did he draft in Sarah-Jane? I don't give a shit about his pride. She's the best, and we need her on board. Tell him to get his head out of his arse and do as I say. I want results." He took a deep breath. "I don't need your approval! We have to move with the times, and you'll have to move, too, or move on. Simple as that."

He jammed his phone in his pocket and growled, but started as his gaze landed on me. "Er, business," he said, as if that explained everything.

"Obviously," I replied.

He glared at me, as if I'd done something awful, then muttered, "I apologise for the bad language. I didn't realise you were there."

"I reckon you owe Adele at least another one-pound-fifty," I informed him, keeping my voice light as I passed him. "Maybe you should just set up a direct debit."

I sailed past him, forcing myself not to deliberately brush against him as I did so, because the urge to touch him was overwhelming. I felt a pang of sympathy for him on noticing the tired look in his eyes. Wasn't like I blamed him for swearing. Clearly running a multi-million-pound empire was exhausting, and stressful. I couldn't have done it, that was for sure, and he hadn't even had a choice.

When Susie arrived to look after Adele, I was ready and waiting, and Michael grabbed his car keys and waved a cheery goodbye to Mrs F.

Helmston was a lovely market town, and as it was Saturday, the market was in full swing when we arrived. Unable to park in the centre of town, due to the stalls, Michael decided to drop me off in Castle Street and come back for me later on. "Just give me a call when you're ready," he said. "It doesn't take long to get here, so no worries."

The town was packed, due to the combination of decent weather and market day. I glanced at the entrance to Helmston Castle, half-tempted to pay my fee and have a wander round its elegant ruins, but I had a job to do, and I was a bit worried that I'd put all my eggs in one basket and my mission would be a dismal failure. If there was nothing in Helmston, there'd be no time to go elsewhere. I really needed to concentrate. Determined, I headed into the first clothes shop of many.

An hour later, I was in despair. I had money put aside for clothes, but that didn't just mean for a dress. I needed new shoes to go with any party dress, work shoes, a jacket. The prices in the clothes shops down Castle Street were too high. They were classy, expensive, not at all like the shops I usually bought my clothes from. I left each one empty-handed and red-faced. Maybe Helmston hadn't been such a good idea, after all.

I had a cup of tea and a toasted teacake in a little teashop near the castle, called, with a startling lack of imagination, Castle Teashop, and thought nostalgically of Newarth and The Singing Kettle and Rhoda, and wondered how she was getting on. I thought that I must write to her and thank her for all her help.

As my mind strayed to the party, my stomach churned over with nerves. I needed to find something to wear. I couldn't think why I'd imagined my dress would be okay. It was floor-length, lightweight jersey, with large pale pink roses on a black background, thin straps and a scoop neckline. Tamsin was right. It was hardly suitable.

I thought about the market, then dismissed the idea. A posh party called for a posh dress. I was hardly likely to find any such thing in a local market, was I? On the other hand, beggars couldn't be choosers.

Ten minutes later, I was in the middle of the market place, swamped by shoppers, and almost deafened by the loud and cheerful calls from the stallholders, as they tried to persuade people that their goods were exactly what was needed to improve their lives.

Almost immediately, I spotted a jacket that would be perfect for me, but I didn't dare buy it until I knew how much I would have to pay for a dress. It was stupid, I knew, to worry so much about an outfit for one little event when I'd needed a jacket and shoes for ages, but I couldn't help it. I wanted to feel, if not special, at least adequate for the party. I cast a despairing look around and then, just when I thought it was hopeless, I spotted it.

It hung from a rail just opposite me, and I knew, without even trying it on, that it was too big for me, but it was so lovely, I couldn't stop myself from wandering over to take a closer look. It was a simple sleeveless shift dress, with a high neck and a plain cream back, but the front was embellished with pale blue-green and silver sequins in a seashell design. It was eye-catching without being flashy, and I stared at it, wishing I could grow six inches or so.

"Lovely, isn't it?" The lady manning the stall smiled at me, her hands tucked into her money belt as she jingled coins between her fingers. "Suit you that would, with your shade of hair."

"I think it would," I said, smiling wryly. "Shame I'm not five foot eight instead of five foot two."

"You need the petite version," she said calmly, and rummaged on another rail while I stood there, heart in mouth. There was a petite version? Really?

"Here you go." She handed me a coat-hanger, from which hung the dress, wrapped in a polythene cover. I stared at it, then held it against myself to see how long it was. It came to well above my knee. The stallholder came to stand behind me, holding it in place against my shoulders so I could judge it better. "Reckon you're around a twelve. Am I right?"

"Well, yes," I said, blushing. "Or thereabouts." Thank God I'd resisted Mrs F's attempts to fatten me up. "What size is this?"

"A twelve," she said, giving me a withering look. "Wouldn't have passed you it otherwise, would I?"

"How much?" I asked, thinking it was bound to be out of my range.

"Forty-five quid," the stallholder told me. "And you won't find a better bargain here today, I can promise you that."

I thought she was probably right, and I nodded eagerly. "Done."

Taking hold of the carrier bag containing my precious

purchase, I rushed back to the other stall to purchase the jacket I'd seen earlier, then looked around for a shoe stall. I found some low black courts for work, and finally decided on a pair of high-heeled strappy silver sandals, which would match the silver sequins on the fabric of my new dress.

Weak with relief, I took out my phone, about to call Michael, when I had a change of heart. Instead, I jumped on the Moors bus and paid the fare to Hasedale. I would walk from there. It was a lovely day, and the fresh air and sunshine would do me good.

I got off the bus not far from the sweet shop where I'd first met Mr Rochester. I glanced in the window as I passed, thinking of that moment when he'd stood there in that tiny doorway, all dark and brooding, with the bruised skies just visible behind him and the rain pouring down on him, while I'd gaped like a moron. I grinned to myself. No wonder he'd got a bit narked with me and had been so eager to believe that I'd wandered aimlessly in the middle of the road. He must have thought I was completely gormless.

He was a strange man, I thought, as I left the main road and climbed Hase Fell, cutting across the moors towards Moreland Hall. His moods were as changeable as the weather, and he could be grumpy and aloof. Yet, somehow, I suspected that, beneath that harsh exterior, there was kindness, and a gentleness within. I'd seen evidence of his sense of humour, and he'd certainly shown an interest in my life. For some reason, though, he seemed determined to hide that side of himself from me. It was almost as if he was battling against his own good nature. Very odd.

Above me, the skies were blue and cloudless, but the wind blew off the moors, ensuring that I kept cool as I trudged up the hill. In high summer, those same moors would be clothed in rich purple, as the heather burst into flower, but there was no purple in sight at that moment. Instead, a patchwork in muted shades of brown and green spread as far as the eye could see.

As I neared the top of the fell, I stopped and turned, taking in the view of Hasedale, its huddle of stone cottages with their cheerful red roofs, and the little beck that cut through the village, snaking its way to freedom on the moors. I stood there, letting the wind ruffle my hair and cool my skin, blowing away the stresses and anxieties of the day, and closed my eyes against the sunlight for a moment, taking deep breaths of fresh, clean air.

Eventually, I turned and continued my climb, reaching the summit of the fell and striding across the moorland, where sheep grazed all around me. They took no notice of me, no doubt used to seeing walkers at all times of the day. I smiled fondly at the lambs, skipping around and revelling in the sunshine, but never straying too far from their mothers.

In the distance, I spotted a figure, sitting huddled on the ground, and as I grew closer, my heart began to beat faster. I recognised that man. Mr Rochester. What on earth was he doing out there on the moors? Shouldn't he be preparing to greet his guests?

He was hunched over what looked like a writing pad, and seemed to be scribbling something down. As I approached, something must've alerted him to my presence, because he hastily shoved the pad in the backpack nestling on the ground beside him, and then sat there, completely still, as I walked towards him.

"I didn't expect to find you here," I said, trying to sound casual. "Are you hiding?" I smiled at him, but he didn't smile back.

"Just refreshing my batteries before the party," he said.

"Oh. Right." I hesitated, then sat down beside him, determined that he wasn't going to fob me off again. "Do they need refreshing?"

He gave me a curious look. "What do you think?"

"I have no idea," I said. "I would have thought you'd be all excited, since your friends are arriving any time now."

"Huh." He shook his head, but didn't elaborate.

I felt that pang of sympathy again. He may have been loaded, but there was a sadness about Ethan Rochester that drew me to him. "Going by that phone conversation this morning, I'd guess you have more important things on your mind than a party," I ventured hesitantly.

"I'm sorry you heard that," he said. "I shouldn't swear so much. Adele's quite right. I am trying, though."

"I know you are. To be honest, by the sound of that phone call, you had every reason to swear."

He shrugged. "We may have to close a store. We have three in London, but realistically, the smallest one should go. It doesn't have the footfall that the others have. Then there's York ..." He shook his head. "It was the first Rochester's store. Some members of the board want to close it. I don't. I won't. I think we should renovate it, improve it. It has huge potential. Then," he added with a big sigh, "there's the online thing."

"Online?"

"Times have changed. We need to keep up with them. People like to shop from home these days, and we need to have a strong online presence. Some of the older board members don't approve. They worked for my father, and they think they know best. Want things done the traditional way. We can't afford to just sit back and let things continue to slide. The truth is, I'm going to have to shake things up on a huge scale. New blood. It's not going to be pretty. I guess that's why I've been putting it off for so long."

"I see. If it helps, I think you're right—about the online presence, I mean—and I'm sure your father would agree. He obviously believed that you were capable of making the right decisions, or he wouldn't have left the business to you. It meant so much to him, he'd have put someone in place to run it for you, otherwise, wouldn't he?"

When he didn't answer, I stood up, thinking he obviously wanted to be alone. "I'll leave you to it."

"You've been to Hasedale?"

I turned to face him, surprised at his sudden question. "Helmston,"

"Helmston?" He looked up at me, his hand shading his eyes. "Have you eaten?"

I really couldn't fathom him out. I wished he'd make up his mind whether he was friend, or foe. "Yes. I had a toasted teacake."

"That's not much. I've got a sandwich in my backpack if you're hungry."

I stared at him blankly. What on earth had got into him? "No thanks, I'm okay."

"I've arranged for Mrs Turner to have Adele tonight,"

he said unexpectedly. "Susie will be coming back to pick her up later. I thought it would be for the best, given that things may get quite noisy later on. Besides, you should have a night off. It's not fair otherwise."

"That's very thoughtful of you," I said. "Thank you. Although I wouldn't have minded looking after Adele—if the noise woke her up, I mean. She's no trouble, bless her."

He didn't reply. Instead, he turned his head and stared intently toward a ewe who'd wandered close by and was tugging at the grass, while her lamb watched us curiously.

"Swaledales." Mr Rochester nodded at them. "See the black faces and the curved horns? They're from the Dales originally, but there are quite a few of them 'round here. You'll see some Herdwicks and Cheviots, too, and plenty of Rough Fell sheep—they're quite big and chunky. Hill breeds, strong, hardy. They need to be tough to survive up here, you see? Sometimes they cross them with other breeds to make mules. There are lots of those around."

"Right," I said, puzzled.

"Hill sheep make excellent mothers, you know," he said. "It's one of their most endearing traits."

I watched him, wondering what on earth had got into him. "I didn't know you were an expert on sheep."

"I'm not," he said. "I just like to observe."

It was on the tip of my tongue to make a joke about men who had a thing for sheep, but I decided he wasn't in the mood to hear it. "Are you going back to the Hall?" I said uncertainly. "Only, I've been gone a while, and I think Susie will be waiting to get off home. I should get back."

He didn't look at me, merely shrugged. "You go. I'll

be along in a while."

I hesitated, wondering if he was okay to be left alone. He was in a most peculiar mood, that was certain. "Mr Rochester, are you sure you're all right?" I said quietly.

He finally turned to face me. "I just have some thinking to do, that's all." He smiled suddenly, and it was like sunshine after a storm. "Don't look so anxious. Everything's fine."

"Okay. Well, if you're sure …" I could hardly challenge him, so I turned and headed in the direction of Moreland Hall, leaving him behind, and thinking I'd never understand that man in a million years. And yet, I wanted to. Oh, I really wanted to.

Chapter Fifteen

I told Mrs F about my strange encounter with our boss as soon as I got back to the Hall.

"Do you think he's all right? He was most peculiar."

"Sounds like he's got a lot on his mind," she said.

I waited for her to elaborate, but she clearly wasn't in the mood. Or maybe it was just not for her to say. Sighing, I excused myself and took Adele out into the grounds, where we spent a pleasant half hour sitting by the lake, while I read to her from *The Wind in the Willows*, and she hunted for her very own Toad. She shrieked with excitement when she thought she'd found him, hiding under the drooping branches of a willow tree, and I didn't like to tell her that she'd actually found a common frog. We agreed to leave him alone to snooze in peace and headed back to the house.

Some of the guests had already arrived, judging by the cars parked in the drive. As I led Adele towards the kitchen, I wondered if the special female friend was among them. Why was she so special that Mrs F kept singling her out for mention? Was she romantically involved with Mr Rochester? Surely not. She hardly sounded the type of woman any man would fall for, let alone someone as intelligent as him. Then again, male hormones were notoriously fickle, something I knew all too well.

"She's here," Mrs F informed me, as soon as I returned. She ushered Adele over to the kitchen table and set down a plate of scrambled eggs on toast. "It'll have to do for now," she said, casting an apologetic look at me. "I'm rushed off my feet, and she'll be having some supper at Mrs Turner's later, anyway."

"Who's here?" I enquired, although my sinking heart proved I'd already guessed who she meant.

Mrs F tutted. "Her name's Briony Walsingham-Quinton. Huge chest, and a brain the size of a peanut. You won't be able to miss her, trust me."

"Sounds delightful," I said. "Her name's bigger than her IQ, by the sounds of it."

"Oh, don't you underestimate her," she said knowingly. "She may not know the capital of Italy, but she's sharp as a knife in other ways. Very good at getting what she wants, is that one. And I reckon she wants Ethan Rochester."

My stomach plummeted. "Really?" Well, hadn't I already guessed as much? "And does he want her?"

She sniffed. "He's married," she pointed out, as if that answered that question, which it didn't. Not really.

"Surely, she's not his type?" I said.

She eyed me curiously. "And what would you say was his type?"

How would I know? Around five-foot-two with green eyes and reddish-blonde hair? Fat chance. Someone with a double-barrelled name and big boobs would be more like it. I sighed. "I suppose you're right. He's a man. Any woman with a pulse."

"Do you really believe that?" She shook her head. "You may be surprised. But I do worry about him. He's very vulnerable. Lonely. And she's manipulative. I wouldn't put it past her to trap him."

"Trap him? How could she trap him?"

"Not for me to say," she said, giving me a look that clearly said that surely I could work it out for myself.

I felt sick. He wouldn't, would he? "But he's married," I protested, throwing her own words back at her, even though I knew the mysterious Antonia Rochester didn't appear to be much of a factor in his life. "Surely, he wouldn't ...?"

"Wouldn't what?" She hurried over to the oven to check on whatever was baking in there. "All I know is, he's looking for something that Antonia isn't giving him, and Briony would be only too happy to offer it, even though she'd be the worst possible choice for him. We can only hope," she added, pulling on her oven gloves, "that his self-control isn't lowered by all that champagne they'll be quaffing tonight. Maybe we ought to keep an eye on him, just in case?"

I launched into a rather satisfying fantasy, in which Briony fell down the stairs and twisted her ankle, and spent the entire weekend in her bedroom, while Mr Rochester caught sight of me in my new dress and couldn't take his eyes off me. As we danced together, I'd murmur, 'I wonder how Briony is?' Gently his lips would brush my ear as he'd whisper, 'Briony who?'

Ooh, that was a nice fantasy, but the banging of the oven door, and Mrs F's call to Adele to hurry up with her tea because she needed the table clearing, soon brought me back to real life, and I tutted to myself. Talk about an overactive imagination! All the same, I couldn't decide whether I was looking forward to finally meeting that

Briony woman, or dreading the very thought of it.

#

The house was full of people. It felt quite strange to see so many new faces and hear such a buzz of conversation everywhere I went. Usually the place was quiet, and always felt empty. The bedrooms in the east wing were finally being used, and the spare ones in the west wing were also taken, so for the first time in years, the house was as it would have been in Ethan's great-grandfather's day, when he'd employed plenty of servants and held regular house parties.

The bar staff were busy sorting out glasses and stacking drinks in one of the rooms. The downstairs rooms were all decorated with twinkling lights, and I was finally allowed to see the drawing room. I couldn't wait to see who'd won in the battle between Mrs F and Paolo.

As Paolo unlocked the door with a flourish, I gasped. "Good grief!"

He folded his arms and gave me a smug look. "Mrs Fairweather set the rules. I obey. She get what she want. Is just Mr Rochester's thing, yes?"

I wasn't quite sure what to say. "Er ..."

"He is man's man. I have that make very clear to me. No Oberon for Mr Rochester. I give him masculine theme, you agree?"

It was on the tip of my tongue to say that I thought he was rather taking the mickey, when I heard a shriek behind me and realised Mrs F had arrived.

"Is this your idea of revenge?" she said, glaring at Paolo. "You silly little man."

Paolo looked furious. "You say to me, no fairies for Mr Rochester. You say to me, no feminine side for Mr

Rochester. You say to me, he is manly, strong. I do as you ask, and you still insult me!"

"It's ridiculous," she snorted, not very tactfully. "He's a grown man, not a little boy. What's with the colour scheme? It's not a baby shower!"

"It is the masculine colour, is it not?" Paolo demanded. He seemed totally confused, and I couldn't help but smile. He'd definitely given her what she'd insisted upon, and it wasn't his fault that he'd taken her literally.

The room was wall to wall blue. Talk about overkill. There were symbols of masculinity everywhere. The bunting wasn't little flags, but stripy ties. There were party bags—party bags! As if he was about seven!—in the shape of shirts, with little bow ties on them. A large poster of a huge, military-style moustache hung on one wall, with the words *Happy Birthday Ethan* written beneath it. The cake was a three-tier extravaganza: the bottom tier a black jacket, complete with buttons; the second tier a white shirt collar and black tie; the top tier a bowler hat. Little cupcakes had been decorated with blue icing and black moustaches. Blue and white balloons bobbed everywhere, and one wall had been completely covered in old newspapers, some dating from the year Ethan was born, and some, to Mrs F's unmistakable horror, displaying the obvious charms of various topless models.

In one corner of the room, a sofa shaped like a racing car had been set facing a large flat screen television. A dartboard hung from one wall, a blackboard with a list of beers of the world chalked on it from another, and a pool table had been set up ready for play.

Did Mr Rochester drink beer? Did he play darts, or

pool? Judging by Mrs F's face, I thought not.

There was nothing about the party theme that seemed to have any bearing on his life. at all. On balance, it would probably have been wiser to allow Paolo to go with his *Midsummer Night's Dream* theme.

"Oh, my word! How kitsch!" A shrill voice behind me almost shattered my eardrums, and I turned around to see who I presumed to be Briony Walsingham-Quinton standing there, her hands clasped to her substantial bosom and her lip curled in a sneer. It had to be her. Mrs F had said she had a huge chest, and the intrusive woman certainly fitted the bill. They had to be fake, surely? Especially given the fact that she was the size of a stick insect everywhere else.

But, damn it, she was pretty. Exceptionally so. I'd been hoping she'd have a face like Shrek, but no such luck. Even without her ample assets, she would turn any man's head. She had long, dark, glossy hair that fell almost to her waist, and wore a tight shirt, tucked into a pencil skirt that revealed a slender, yet somehow curvy, figure. How sickening.

Paolo's dark, waxed eyebrows knitted together. "Kitsch? Kitsch? How dare you? This is Mr Rochester in a room. You see? I create masculine masterpiece." He glared pointedly at Mrs F. "Just as I was commanded."

"Well, this is different," said a young man, who'd just rushed up behind Briony and put his arm around her waist in a rather proprietary way. She didn't seem to mind, though, which was encouraging. "What is it? A birthday party, or a baby boy's Christening?"

Paolo reared up like an angry stallion. "This is party for grown man. Man's man," he added, scowling. "See?

All trappings of man's life. The pool table, the beers of the world, the racing car sofa."

"Where are the real page three models?" the young man demanded, looking approvingly at the awful, sexist newspaper cuttings.

To my disgust, Briony giggled, tapping him playfully on the arm. "Oh, Joel! You are terrible."

"Wait until Ethan sees this," Joel said with a grin. "He's going to love it. Not."

Paolo turned a cold stare on him. "Mr Rochester already sees, and approves. He is man of taste."

I didn't know which of us was most surprised. Probably Mrs F, judging by the dramatic way she clasped her chest and said, "Never!"

I couldn't have put it better myself. I'd have thought Adele's piggy bank would be bursting with fifty pence pieces after Mr Rochester saw that dreadful display.

"Just shows you, Mrs Fairweather," Briony said coolly. "Maybe you don't know Ethan as well as you suppose."

As I hooked my arm through Mrs F's, Briony turned her gaze on me, as if seeing me for the first time.

"I don't think we've been introduced?" she said coolly.

"Er, Cara Truelove," I said, taking the hand she offered with some reluctance and shaking it limply.

"Briony Walsingham-Quinton," she said. "I don't believe I've heard of you before. Are you a friend of Ethan's, or family?"

I was about to answer, but didn't get the chance. From behind me, Mr Rochester's voice replied, "Miss Truelove is Adele's nanny. Ah, you've all seen Paolo's theme, then? What do you think? Isn't it quite … astonishing?"

Paolo looked most gratified and shot Mrs F a smug look, while Briony giggled again and abandoned Joel to attach herself to my employer.

"Oh, darling, it's amazing. So much fun!"

"I thought you'd like it," he said, which just shows how little he knew her. He smiled at me, but I didn't smile back. I was still smarting from the *Adele's nanny* remark, even though he was perfectly right, and that was all I was, after all, so why I was annoyed about it, I couldn't imagine.

"You don't even play pool," Mrs F snapped, determined to get one over on Paolo.

"But it will be fun learning," Mr Rochester told her. "Joel here is very good. He can teach me."

"Ooh, and I'll learn, too." Briony fluttered her eyelashes. "We can learn together."

He looked surprisingly eager. "Great idea. Joel, you'll teach us, won't you?"

Joel beamed. "Be delighted."

"Excellent!" Briony simpered.

I couldn't believe Mr Rochester had fallen for it.

Mrs F and I exchanged glances, before she said, "Right, this won't get the baby his bonnet. I'm getting back to my kitchen."

"I'll come with you," I said, keen to get away from the gushing Briony and gullible Ethan Rochester.

"Aren't you both good." Briony smiled sweetly at us. "Ethan is so lucky to have such hard-working staff."

Mrs F pulled on my arm, and we headed back to the kitchen, saying nothing in reply to her clearly patronising comment.

"Told you," she said, as she closed the kitchen door

behind us and hurried to the cupboard, from where she grabbed a couple of therapeutic teabags. "Now you know what I mean."

"Okay," I said, "she's a bitch. I agree. But what's Ethan playing at? He can't possibly like that party theme! And why is he so nice to her? Why did he even invite her? Is he really that stupid?" He'd gone down in my estimation. I felt quite deflated suddenly. "I'd better take Adele off Michael's hands. I'll get her things packed and hand her over to Susie, then I'll get changed. Can't say I'm really looking forward to this party, though."

"If it's too awful, me and you and Michael will slip away early. We can have drinks and food in my sitting room. Be better than hobnobbing with that bunch." She sighed. "And we've got to put up with them all tomorrow, too. No doubt they'll be nursing hangovers, demanding cooked breakfasts, and being snappy and irritable. At least they'll be gone by teatime. Just grit your teeth and bear it, Cara."

"Lucky Mrs Rochester," I said. "Jennifer, I mean. Up there in her room, away from it all."

Although, for all I knew, she may have really wanted to attend. Maybe she approved of Briony. Perhaps she was hoping that her son would marry the woman—if he ever divorced his wife, of course.

Really, the man seemed incorrigible. It appeared he had women littered all over the place. Antonia, Briony, Adele's mother .... Could he really be as bad as he seemed?

Chapter Sixteen

I wasn't really looking forward to the party, but I was determined to pull out all the stops when it came to my appearance, nevertheless. There was no way I was going to let Briony Wotsit-Quaver, or whatever her name was, look down her nose at me.

As soon as I reached my room, I hurried over to the wardrobe and took out the dress, holding it against myself and admiring my reflection in the mirror. I'd tried it on as soon as I got home from Helmston, and I'd been thrilled with how well it fitted. I planned to curl my hair and take my time applying my makeup, so I'd look all glamorous and confident. Ethan Rochester wouldn't know what had hit him.

Hanging the dress on the wardrobe door, I peeled off my clothes and dropped them in the laundry basket, then headed into the en-suite to take a shower. I still got a thrill from having my very own bathroom. It seemed like the height of luxury to me, especially since the shower was one of those huge walk-in ones that could easily fit two people in the cubicle, and had a shower head the size of a planet.

I thought of the cheap shower over the bath, back at the flat in Oddborough, with the plastic shower curtain that was decorated with big orange fish, and I shuddered, not so much because of the shower, but at the memory of the mysterious hairs that always seemed to be embedded in the soap, and the scum that Seth left around the bath, having long ago decided that cleaning it out after himself was unnecessary, as clearly, there were mysterious bathroom fairies who did the job perfectly well for him.

My fault, I supposed, as I massaged shampoo into my hair and considered where things had started to go wrong for us. I'd grown tired of waiting for Seth to do his fair share, and had simply started to do it for him, which meant that, in the end, he saw everything on the domestic front as being my job. A bit like he saw everything on the money-making front as my job, too—or anything else that involved work, or thinking, really, except for writing poetry which was clearly his domain, however bad he was at it.

I wondered how he was coping at Isolde's place. I didn't believe for a second that he was staying in her tiny box room. She would have made it very clear to him that he was welcome to share with her, and I was pretty certain that Naomi would have encouraged their relationship. After all, if her best friend and brother got together, Naomi need never fear that she would have to get off her sorry backside and find a home for herself, or a job to pay for it. What a trio of losers, they were, I thought. How had I spent so long propping them up? They didn't even like me. Yet, there I was, the only one of them working, paying rent, so they could sit in comfort every day, while I was at the nursery, eating their way through my biscuits and having the cheek to sell my piano!

The piano. I felt a sudden sadness at the thought of it. I hoped whoever had bought it was taking care of it and treating it well. I remembered Granny Reed, sitting beside me on the piano stool, her bony fingers scuttling over the keys like spider legs. I could almost smell her lavender perfume, and the musky scent of that dusty old room. I blinked away the image. It was no use getting upset. What had happened had happened. I could only hope that she, somehow, knew that I had moved on with my life, and that I would never have sold the piano if I'd had any choice. Though, maybe it was a good thing that Seth had. Would I ever have finally snapped and made the decision to leave if he hadn't? I would never know.

I rinsed the shampoo off my hair and stepped out of the shower. With a giant, fluffy bath sheet wrapped around myself, I wandered back into the bedroom and sat on the bed, rubbing my hair with a towel.

The room seemed to darken quite suddenly. A glance out of the window revealed grey clouds had rolled in, dismissing the sunshine from duty. Beneath them, the trees waved quite frantically, almost as if they were trying to attract my attention.

I tutted. There I went again, letting my overactive imagination run away with me. *Concentrate on the party, Cara!*

My gaze fell on my new dress, and as time seemed to stand still, my mouth dropped open. Icy fingers ran up and down my spine, every one of my nerve endings jangled, and my heart thudded with fear.

The towel hung limply from my hand as I stared at the garment on the hanger, hardly able to make sense of what I was seeing. It was slashed, practically from top to bottom—not just once, but several times. Huge gashes severed the dress almost in half, beyond repair. I crept over to it, half afraid that someone would jump out of the wardrobe and attack me with the same knife. My fingers gathered the remnants, and I stared at the scraps of material, feeling a lump in my throat and blinking away tears.

Who would do that?

Why?

I could only think of Briony. She clearly looked down on me, but then again, why would she bother to destroy a cheap market dress belonging to a member of staff? I was no threat to her. Besides, she didn't even know which was my room. Another guest, perhaps? Someone who'd had too much to drink and had wandered into the bedroom by mistake?

What, carrying a knife?

Fair point.

My mind flickered over to Jennifer Rochester, lying in Ethan's room just along the landing. I had no idea what was wrong with her. She'd had some sort of procedure done, but what sort? No one had told me why she'd been in hospital. And why was she closeted away there in Ethan's suite, hiding away from everyone else in the house? Maybe she wasn't hiding. Maybe she was hidden. There was a big difference. What if she was mad? What if she was a lunatic who crept into people's rooms with a knife in her hand, sick with jealousy and rage when she saw evidence of another woman in the house?

God, calm down, Cara. You're being ridiculous.

But was I? What other explanation was there for the state of the dress?

\#

"Mrs Fairweather?" Tamsin's suggestion was ludicrous, of course.

I'd rung her for advice, not because I really expected

211

to get any, but because I needed to talk to someone. Anyone. And frankly, I wasn't sure who I could trust any more.

"Mrs F? Why would she cut my dress?"

"Jealousy, perhaps? Maybe she thinks you're getting too cosy with her precious Mr Rochester?" She giggled. "Are you?"

"You're being silly now," I told her. "And this isn't funny. Some lunatic with a knife is on the loose. What if it hadn't been my dress he cut up? What if it had been me?"

Oh, hell! I'd just realised that I must have been in the shower when he entered the room. It could have been like *Psycho*.

A sudden vision of Mr Rochester dressed as Norman Bates's mother entered my head, and I shivered. I was getting hysterical. But then again, I'd never actually seen Jennifer, had I? What if she didn't exist? What if she was a skeleton sitting in an armchair in his bedroom? What if he donned her clothes every night and prowled the house, muttering to himself and cutting up unwary people's dresses?

What had I got myself into?

"Maybe I should have listened more to Redmond," I said faintly.

"Christ, don't tell him, for God's sake!" Tamsin sounded appalled. "He'll have the police round there before you can say scissors. Look, tell your boss what's happened. Insist he makes enquiries, or you'll have to involve them yourself. I know I'm laughing, but it's not funny, is it? It's downright creepy."

"I know. It is."

"Bet you a pound to a penny it's a woman."

"Why do you say that?"

"Oh, come on! A dress! It's jealousy that's at the heart of this. You have to figure out who would be jealous. So, which women are there in the house that would be envious of you? How old's this girl you're looking after?"

I laughed. "Adele? You have to be kidding me. She's four years old, and she's a darling. She's hardly likely to be prowling around with a dagger. She's only allowed to use safety scissors when I'm with her."

"So, we're back to Mrs Fairweather."

"Mrs F would never do anything like that," I protested. "We get on really well, and she's the most sensible person I know."

"Well, what other women are around?"

"There are a couple of suspects," I admitted. I told her briefly about Briony and Jennifer.

"Ooh, well, they sound intriguing. I particularly like the sound of the mad mother locked away from everyone."

She would. She watched far too much American television. Then again .... I shivered anxiously. The mad woman in the attic. I'd heard noises coming from up there, I was sure of it, and I couldn't help but remember what Bertha Rochester had done to Jane Eyre's wedding veil.

"Briony might just be a jealous cow who's determined not to be outshone by any other female," Tamsin continued, sounding thoughtful.

"Believe me, no one could outshine her. She's tall, skinny, with huge breasts, and long dark glossy hair and a very pretty face. She's also got pots of money, by the look of her. I seriously doubt she's given me a second thought since I left the room earlier."

"Well, I really think you should do as I say and tell Ethan," Tamsin said. "Unless," she said, sounding eager, "you think he might be responsible?"

"Why on earth would he do something like that?" I said, ignoring the fact that, just moments before, I'd practically decided he was a psychopathic drag queen. "You're right, I should tell him."

"And in the meantime," Tamsin advised, "lock your bedroom door."

"There isn't a lock on my door."

"Well, shove something in front of it to keep any nutters out. Now, just as a matter of interest, what are you going to wear tonight instead of your new dress?"

I sighed. "That's the least of my problems. I think I'll give the whole event a miss."

"Don't be daft," she shrieked. "Get yourself dolled up and get down there. Show whoever did it that you're not one to be pushed around, or put off. Someone doesn't want you at that party, Cara. Don't give them the satisfaction."

"But I don't understand," I said. "I'm not special. There's no reason to keep me away from the party."

"Someone evidently thinks you're a threat," she mused. "The question is, who? And what is it they're feeling threatened by?"

We were both quiet for a moment, then she said, "Ooh, this is quite exciting, isn't it? Like *Midsomer Murders*, or something."

"Thanks," I said. "Glad the fact that your sister is being stalked by a homicidal maniac is of some entertainment value to you."

"Well, I will admit, it makes a change from worrying about my own life. Ta very much for that. Seriously, though, Cara, promise me you'll tell your boss. I'd feel a lot safer if you had him onside."

"I will," I said. "I promise."

"And get yourself tarted up for that party," she added sternly. "No one's going to put Cara in a corner."

#

I couldn't get Mr Rochester to myself for a moment, so I didn't have chance to tell him about the dress. It wasn't exactly something I wanted to announce to the whole room, and his friends seemed intent on keeping him close. I'd had to confide in Mrs F, because she knew about the new one, and I'd shown it to her. She'd raised an eyebrow when I'd made an appearance in my long black maxi dress, feeling ridiculously out of place.

"What happened to that nice mini dress?" she demanded immediately. "Don't tell me you chickened out. I told you, it's not too short, and the colouring suits you. Not like that one," she added, frowning at me. "If you don't mind me saying so, that black washes you out."

"Cheers," I said. "I don't have a choice. If I did, do you honestly think I'd be wearing this? Especially with these shoes?" I put on the new sandals because I needed a bit of height with the length of the dress, and flat shoes would have left me tripping over the hem, but it felt all wrong. The colour didn't match the dress, and I was only wearing them because I knew the bottom of the dress hid them from view.

I'd quickly filled her in on what had happened, and she was horrified. "Briony," she said from the off.

"Really?" I pulled a face. "Why would someone like

215

her do that? I'm insignificant. She can't feel threatened by me."

"It's not about that," she said. "She's a bitch. Simple as that. Probably took an instant dislike to you and decided to make life difficult for you. It probably wouldn't occur to her that you didn't have another party dress. She wouldn't have even needed a knife. Let's face it, those talons of hers would have done the job. You just wait 'til I tell Michael."

"Don't tell Michael!" It'd occurred to me that he was also an unknown quantity. After all, he'd not been at the house long, and he knew all about the dress, having been the one who'd taken me to Helmston. I knew I was being ridiculous, but I couldn't rule anyone out.

She waved a hand dismissively and disappeared into the crowd, and I headed over to the table to get some food. If there was no one to talk to, the best thing to do was eat. At least it would give me something to do. I reckoned I'd hang around for an hour, tops, then retreat to Mrs F's sitting room. My own bedroom seemed strangely unappealing at the moment.

Briony sidled up to me, wine glass in hand. "Enjoying yourself?" She looked beautiful in a tight-fitting red dress and bright red lipstick, her dark hair piled up on top of her head in a casual 'do that had no doubt taken ages to achieve.

"Yes thanks." I watched her warily, noting the way her gaze skimmed over my own dress, the look of smug satisfaction in her eyes, and the way her lips twitched.

"Don't you look, er, lovely." She casually swilled the wine in her glass. "Ethan's been telling us all what a little treasure you are. So much more sensible than the previous nanny." She smiled—a fake smile that didn't go anywhere near her eyes. "Do you know about the other nanny?"

"Not really," I said. "Only that her name was Jodie."

She nodded. "Oh, that one really got ideas above her station. Australian. No idea how to behave. Honestly, Ethan did the right thing by sacking her. There's a line," she said firmly, "and staff have to know where it is. I'm afraid Ethan had to learn that the hard way. He always was too kind and generous. He made the mistake of treating his servants like friends. It never works out, of course. They take advantage, you see. I warned him about the nanny, and I warned him about the housekeeper, too."

"There's nothing wrong with Mrs F," I said angrily. Had she really just called us servants? Who called staff servants those days? It was real life, not *Downton Abbey*. "She's a good and loyal woman."

"Hmm. She's been with the family a long time," Briony informed me, as if I didn't know, "and I'm afraid that leads to misunderstandings. In my experience, long-standing servants tend to believe—quite mistakenly—that they're practically part of the family. They start issuing advice, voicing opinions about matters in which they have no experience. It's very tiresome."

"How awful of them," I said, wondering what Briony's immaculately made-up face would look like after I'd pushed it into Ethan's birthday cake.

"She's a good cook," Briony conceded generously. "Basic, but good. And I'm sure she runs the household perfectly adequately. But she's not his mother, or his auntie. She'd do well to remember that, before dispensing her homespun wisdom every five minutes."

Hmm. Briony was rattled about something. Clearly,

she knew that Mrs F was not on her side, and she'd recognised that Mrs F's opinion counted for a lot with her precious Ethan, so she was on the attack. It struck me, as I saw the gleam of steel in her dark eyes, that Briony was exactly the sort of woman who refused to support other women because she saw them as her natural enemy. Granny Reed always said there were two types of women in the world: those who would do anything to support their sisters, and those who would do anything to tear them down. I could clearly see which type Briony was, and suddenly the idea of her in my bedroom with a knife didn't seem so implausible.

The real question was, what else was she capable of?

"Miss Truelove, you look lovely."

Noting with satisfaction a fleeting annoyance in Briony's expression, I turned toward Ethan. God, he looked gorgeous. He'd been wearing a dark charcoal suit, but he'd taken off the jacket to reveal a deep purple shirt under a waistcoat, which showed off his broad shoulders and chest and narrow waist. Sharp trousers emphasised his strong thighs, and his thick, dark hair was begging me to run my fingers through it.

I gulped, but then, remembering the dress, I blushed. I hardly thought lovely described my cobbled-together-at-the-last-minute outfit. "I'm so sorry I haven't had the chance to speak to you until now. I was rather, er, preoccupied."

Swamped would have been a better word. His London pals were all over him, in a rather nauseating way. The young man who'd put his arm on Briony's waist earlier had followed him over and stood at his side, hanging on his every word.

218

Mr Rochester turned his delicious smile on his bitchy guest. "I wonder, Briony, if you'd like Joel to teach you the rudiments of pool? The table appears to be free, at the moment."

"Oh, how lovely," she said, sounding as delighted as Brad had been at Tamsin's inheritance. "Let's make a start."

She hooked her arm through his, and I almost whooped with delight when he gently but firmly removed it. "Start without me," he told her. "I have some business to discuss with Miss Truelove first. I'll be over shortly, and then you can show me what you've learned."

"But it's your birthday party, darling," she cooed, giving me a look that could have curdled milk. "Surely, business can wait?"

"It's very important," he assured her. "Off you go, and I promise I won't be too long."

She hesitated, then shrugged and turned her saccharine smile on Joel instead. "Come on, then, Joel," she purred. "Show me what you can do with those balls." She giggled and nudged him. "That's your cue," she added, wrinkling her nose in a way I was sure she considered cute.

Joel, who was obviously as bright as a nineteen-forties living room with the blackout curtains closed, gazed at her with unmistakable adoration and practically dragged her across the room. Standing empty, the pool table had been abandoned, as people lost interest, having discovered that there was a games console attached to the forty-two inch television opposite the racing car sofa.

Mr Rochester heaved a big sigh—hopefully of relief— then turned to me, a frown creasing his forehead. "So," he said, "this dress."

"Oh. Who told you?"

"Michael had a quiet word. I'm so sorry, Cara. This is dreadful, and it must have been really scary. Are you all right?"

He'd called me Cara! He really was taking things seriously. "I'm fine. Now. Well, mostly. I was a bit shaken at the time," I admitted.

"I'm not surprised. I can't think who would have done such a thing. I know this lot are a bit tiresome, but they're not weirdos. At least, I don't think they are. I just can't imagine how this has happened. If it was someone's idea of a joke, it's not very funny."

"No," I said grimly. "It's not."

"I'll compensate you for the dress, of course," he said. "Just let me know how much it cost, and I'll make sure you get the money back."

God, no way did I want him to know it cost forty-five quid from a market stall! How humiliating would that be, given that Briony's dress probably cost ten times that, at least.

"It's okay," I said hurriedly. "It wasn't your fault, and I don't need compensation. I don't want your money, Mr Rochester. Mind you, I have to say, I'm glad Adele's safe at Mrs Turner's tonight."

His gaze lingered on me for what felt like forever. "You should have come straight to me," he said eventually. "I mean it, Cara. I hate to think of you feeling afraid in my home. It should never happen."

I'd never heard him speak so gently before, and it had a very disturbing effect on me. "No, well, I'll be pushing a chair against the bedroom door tonight." I shivered. To

220

be honest, the shiver was likely more to do with the way he was looking at me with such kindness in his eyes, and the way his hand rested lightly on my arm. How had I ever thought he could be a psycho killer?

As if he'd felt the tremor beneath his hand and mistaken its source, his brows lowered. "You're more scared than you're letting on. Look, take my mother's room tonight—we've swapped for the time being—and I'll sleep in yours. If anyone decides to come back and terrify you again, they're going to get a nasty shock. Keep it between ourselves, okay?"

"Don't be silly. I don't expect you to give up your room for me."

"I insist," he said. "Only my suite and my mother's room have locks on them. You can take my key, and then you'll be safe. I'd sleep easier if I knew no one could get in, although I'm sure nothing else will happen. Please, Cara?"

"Er, well, if you insist." I was going to sleep in the very bed Mr Rochester had been recently sleeping in! Wait 'til I told Tamsin that! Mind you, what a shame that he wouldn't be in there with me.

I didn't mean that, I thought quickly. *Really, I didn't.*

He nodded and smiled, then rummaged in his pocket. "Here. My key," he said. "Remember, I'm not in my own room, I'm in my mother's room, for the time being."

"I know. And thank you." And thank God, too, that I'd tidied my own room before heading downstairs. Imagine if I'd left it a tip! How embarrassing would that have been?

I felt a thrill of anticipation, wondering what his room would look like. Even if it was his mother's usually, it would still have his stamp on it, given that he'd been sleeping in it for a while. It all felt very intimate somehow.

He smiled. "Don't worry. Mrs Turner and Mrs Jones changed all the bedding in every room today in preparation for our guests."

"I wasn't worried," I said, then blushed fiercely. I really hadn't been, either, and if the thought of sleeping on someone's used sheets didn't bother me, then I really did have a problem. I was going to have to do something about my situation. I was in massive danger of developing a huge crush on Ethan Rochester, and I simply couldn't afford to do so. "You'd better go and keep your guest company," I told him, noticing the icy glares Briony was casting our way, as poor Joel tried valiantly to show her how to hold a cue properly. "I think I've taken up enough of your time."

"Not at all," he said. "You're my guest, too." He glanced over at Briony, who immediately switched on a Cheshire cat smile, and he sighed. "I suppose you're right. I must go and put this to bed once and for all."

Put what to bed? Briony? Not in my flipping bed, I hoped!

I tried to look unconcerned, as he patted me on the arm and said, "Let's hope Cupid works his magic. I'll see you later."

As he abandoned me for his glamorous lady friend, my fingers curled tightly around the piece of metal in my hand. I may have had the key to his room, but it seemed Briony really did have the key to his heart, after all.

Chapter Seventeen

Mrs F's face was a picture. I knew I shouldn't have found it funny, but she was so obviously jealous that I couldn't help it.

Over on the dance floor, Michael jigged around, looking ever-so-slightly self-conscious, while opposite him, a young brunette wiggled and writhed to the music, seeming quite oblivious to her dance partner.

"Just look at that," Mrs F said, when I made the mistake of orbiting too close to her. "She asked him to dance! Can you believe that? And he said yes. Can you believe *that?*"

"If it's any consolation," I said, "I really don't think he looks as if he's enjoying himself. Anyway, why didn't *you* ask him to dance?"

She flushed. "I can't. I don't know how to dance to all this modern stuff. It's not like the sort of thing I used to dance to, back in the day."

"And what day was that?" I teased, picturing a sedate tea dance in Scarborough, or something.

"The Newarth Town Hall disco." She sighed. "Those were the days. You should have seen it, love. That's where I met my husband. I was his *Coo-Ca-Choo*."

"I beg your pardon?" I said, baffled.

"Alvin Stardust," she explained. "All the other girls were besotted with the Osmonds, or David Cassidy, or

David Essex, but I fancied Alvin Stardust from the minute I saw him in all that black leather. And then, one night, Gerry turned up dressed just like him. My heart melted. You should have seen us rocking down to Slade and Sweet that night. What an experience."

"Crikey. I thought you'd be waltzing in the Spa, in between cups of Earl Grey and garibaldi biscuits."

"How blooming old do you think I am?" she said indignantly. Then her eyes went all dreamy again. "I was seventeen. It was nineteen seventy-three and I fell in love for the first time. We were married within a year."

"Oh, Mrs F, I'm so sorry. When—when did your husband die?"

Her eyes flashed. "Die? He never died! He cleared off with Belinda Wright, not eighteen months later. She was the spitting image of Suzi Quatro." She scowled. "All that black leather they both wore. I bet they stunk to high heaven. Terribly unhygienic, you know. My mother said to me, when they kissed it would be like rubbing two balloons together. Ugh."

"And you never married again?"

"After that experience, would you?" She shook her head. "Went to catering college and put it all behind me. I swore I'd never be fooled by any man again, and I never have." Her eyes strayed over toward where Michael looked increasingly flustered and uncomfortable on the dance floor. "Silly sod," she said. "Look at the state of him."

"Hmm. Michael doesn't strike me as the sort of man who'd run off with any woman in black leather. He's nothing like Alvin Stardust," I assured her, although I had no idea who Alvin Stardust was, and I wasn't much clearer about Suzi Quatro, come to that.

She shrugged and gulped down her vodka as if it was lemonade. Really, I thought, jealousy was a most unattractive quality.

My gaze fell on Mr Rochester, standing in a corner talking to Briony. Her eyes were like saucers as he leaned close, murmuring something to her. His hand tucked a strand of her hair behind her ear, and she thrust her chest towards him, practically pinning him to the wall.

Ugh! I noticed Joel scowling into his glass as he watched them, and thought he really should have more dignity. Draining my glass, I turned back to Mrs F, but she was still glaring at Michael. Honestly!

I hesitated a moment, then threaded my way through the crowd to the DJ. He listened as I practically bellowed in his ear, then he shook his head. "You must be joking, love. No one listens to that stuff anymore."

"Well, anything from that year would do," I said desperately. "You must have something?"

He considered for a moment, then nodded. "I think I do, as it happens. Leave it with me."

I returned to where Mrs F was sitting all alone, looking quite gloomy.

"He looks really embarrassed," I said, nodding towards Michael.

"He has every reason to," she said. "Silly fool."

"I'll bet he just got fed up with waiting for you to dance with him," I said. "You should have cut in. Don't let another woman push you around again."

She gaped at me. "Another woman? What, her?" She nodded towards the young brunette and smirked. "You must be joking. She probably asked him for a bet. Either

225

that, or she wanted a laugh."

"Or perhaps she felt sorry for him," I said. "Seeing as he's just been sitting here, waiting for an opportunity to actually get up and dance." I knew how he felt.

She looked as if she wanted to strangle me, but before she could speak, the music faded out and Michael turned towards us, looking highly relieved and a bit dazed.

At that moment, the next song began to play, and I couldn't stop smiling. Even I recognised that tune.

Mrs F's eyes widened. "David Bowie! Now you're talking!"

She slammed her glass down just as Michael staggered over to us. "Come on, Michael. You can't beat a bit of *Gene Jeanie*," she told him, and dragged him back onto the dance floor.

To my relief, he looked surprised, but delighted, and within seconds the two of them were dancing away as if it was nineteen seventy-three all over again. I clapped my hands in delight. I knew it!

"Oh, well played."

I swallowed and turned to face Mr Rochester, who'd come to stand beside me and was watching the two of them with a huge grin on his face. "Sorry?"

"Don't play the innocent," he said, winking at me in a rather attractive manner. "I saw the whole thing. You got the DJ to play this tune, didn't you?"

"I'm surprised you noticed that," I said before I could stop myself. "Thought you were too absorbed with Briony to see anything else."

His lips twitched. "She's very distracting," he said.

"Isn't she just," I muttered.

"Even so, I managed to tear my eyes away from her

long enough to see what you did. It was rather sweet of you."

I reddened. "They just needed a nudge," I said. "Anyone can see they're crazy about each other. They just need someone to push them along a bit."

"Cara Truelove," he said, eyes widening, "I thought you didn't believe in true love! Could there be a heart beneath that steely exterior, after all?"

"Steely exterior?" I said faintly. "Is that how you see me?"

His eyes softened, and he sounded quite sober when he said, "Not at all. As much as you try to convince me otherwise."

The bones in my legs seemed to dissolve. I wasn't quite sure how I managed to remain standing. I couldn't move. I couldn't even look away. I had to do something, fast. I needed him to break the connection, since I couldn't manage it. Maybe if I could annoy him ...

"This party," I managed to croak.

"What about it?" he said.

"It's bloody awful." There, that should do it. "The theme, I mean. This decor. It's hideous. What on earth were you thinking?"

To my astonishment and despair, he burst out laughing. "I know. Isn't it? Poor Paolo."

"You don't like it? But you said—"

"Between you and me," he said, leaning forward until his lips were practically nibbling my ear—not the effect I'd wanted, or expected, though I couldn't deny it felt amazingly good, "Paolo is the partner of one of my employees. He's just starting out in this business, and I took him on as a favour to Justin. I had a feeling it would

227

be bad, but I had no idea it would be this bad."

"Aren't you worried what people are thinking?"

"People think what they're encouraged to think," he said. "You watch and see. I've been praising this party theme all evening to my so-called friends. Whatever they thought of it at the beginning of the evening, they now all think it's wonderful, and *so* original. Bet you a pound to a penny that some of them will hire him for their parties."

"Really?"

"Guaranteed," he said confidently. "Paolo and Justin are nice guys. If I can give Paolo a shove up the ladder, it's the least I can do."

I stared up at him, thinking how wonderful he was, then reminded myself that I wasn't impressed by any man, let alone Ethan Rochester, who was a charmer, but a married charmer, which was the most dangerous kind of all.

"Darling, come and dance." Briony sidled up to him and hooked her arm through his, nearly causing him to spill his drink. "You've been terribly naughty this evening. We haven't danced once."

"You're quite right, we haven't. We must rectify the situation immediately."

As she turned and began to lead him away, Ethan winked at me and handed me his glass. I scowled after them, then slammed the glass down on the coffee table, feeling a sudden urge for something violently alcoholic myself.

As I glugged down another large glass of wine, I saw, out of the corner of my eye, Mrs F and Michael heading out of the room and smiled to myself. Looked like my plan had worked, after all.

"Would you like to dance?" A pleasant-looking young man with sandy coloured hair and blue eyes smiled at me. He was clearly sozzled, but at least he was still capable of standing up, and so what if he was so drunk he probably couldn't focus on me properly? A dance was a dance, and I was so ready to show ... everyone that I was having a good time. It didn't look as if anyone else was going to ask me, did it?

"I'd love to," I said, smiling pleasantly.

My knight in shining armour took my hand, and together we headed, somewhat haphazardly, onto the dance floor.

#

The party went on into the early hours, but I crept away before midnight. Watching Ethan Rochester, flirting openly and dancing closely with that awful woman, had made me sick to my stomach. It wasn't fun seeing him get steadily drunk, either. I'd no idea he was such a big drinker. Another black mark against him. He didn't so much as glance over at me, as I skulked in a corner, knocking back glass after glass of wine, contemplating my employer's disgraceful lack of self-control. It was too much. Besides, I had stuff to do while I could still think reasonably straight.

I tottered to my bedroom to gather my toothbrush, pyjamas, and a few things for the morning. I also took Mr Rochester's toothbrush to my room for him. I couldn't find any pyjamas lying around, and I didn't want to go rummaging through his drawers, so to speak—besides, for all I knew he slept stark naked.

Hmm. Ethan Rochester, stark naked in my bed. There was a thought. Not, I thought savagely, that he'd go

229

anywhere near my room that night. Briony had made her desires all too clear, and she seemed the sort of woman who always got what she wanted.

I had a quick wash in Jennifer's bathroom, brushed my teeth, pulled on my pyjamas, and crept into bed, glancing around me nervously. I'd locked the door, so I was safe, but even so. It felt odd to be in a different room, and knowing that a whole bunch of strangers were wandering the house, and that one of them was probably a knife-wielding maniac, I couldn't say I was expecting to sleep.

Fortunately, too much wine always made me sleepy, and before I knew it, my eyelids were drooping, and I snuggled down under the duvet, thinking I was far more tired than I'd realised.

I wasn't sure what woke me up. A rattle? A clicking noise? Something roused me from my sleep, and I blinked, not clear where I was. As awareness seeped into my brain, I froze with fear.

Someone was in the room.

I stared into the darkness, desperately trying to see. My heart was thudding and I felt sick with terror. Gradually, I became aware of shapes in the blackness. I could make out the window, and the dressing table, and the shape of the wardrobe on the far wall, and—dear God!

I screamed.

With a muffled, moaning sound, the monstrous form moved away from the bed and rushed out of the room, slamming the door behind itself.

How could anyone have got into the damn room? I'd locked it. I was sure I had. Hadn't I? I reached over, fumbling for the lamp, my hands shaking as I tried desperately to find the switch. Finally, my fingers found it, and I breathed a sigh of relief as I looked around the room, now flooded with light. Whoever it was had gone. Maybe that should be, *what*ever it was. It hadn't even looked human.

Fuelled by adrenaline and alcohol—a dangerous combination—I flew out onto the landing, but there was no sign of anyone, not even a gallant person coming to my aid upon hearing me scream. Huh. All too busy sleeping it off or ....

On a sudden impulse, I stormed over to my room and threw open the door without even knocking. I expected to find it empty. I was convinced that Mr Rochester would be in Briony's room, so it was quite a shock to see him lying fast asleep in my bed.

"Mr Rochester," I hissed, "wake up."

Nothing. So much for my protector. He'd probably worn himself out with all that dancing and flirting. Scowling, I marched over to the bed and shook him, not half as violently as I wanted to. He made a sort of muttering noise, but didn't even open his eyes. I spotted an empty glass on my bedside cabinet, and beside it, a large jug half-filled with water. Dare I? Really?

"Mr Rochester," I said again, in some desperation.

There was a bloated monster roaming the landing, and he was too drunk to do anything about it. I picked up the jug and hurled the water all over his face.

He shot bolt upright, blinking and shuddering. "What the fuck—" His eyes, wide with shock, focused on me, and he shook his head. Water dripped all over my pillow. "What the hell are you doing?"

"I'm sorry, but there was someone in my room."

He glared at me. "Did you lock the door?"

"Yes, but—"

"Then you were dreaming. Bloody hell, Cara! You nearly gave me a heart attack."

"What's going on?" Two of Mr Rochester's guests hovered in the doorway, including the man who'd danced with me several times before rushing outside to throw up—a rather unflattering event, it had to be said.

"What are you doing up?" I said, rather rudely, but I was suspicious of anyone wandering around.

"Heard a scream, and then Ethan seemed to be in distress."

"The scream was me, and that was ages ago," I said. "I could have been murdered by now."

"Murdered?" They looked at each other.

Mr Rochester threw back the duvet and climbed out of bed wearing black trunks—similar to the ones David Beckham wore in those adverts—and nothing else. I forgot all about the deranged killer and stared at his broad chest, noting the dark hairs that curled seductively on soft skin, as my heart thumped wildly. "Are you sure you locked the door?" he demanded, pulling on his trousers.

With a huge effort, I dragged my eyes away from him and busied myself taking off the wet pillowcases. "I may be a bit forgetful," I said, "but when there's a knife-wielding madman on the loose, I tend to remember to lock doors."

"You're certain? This is important, Cara."

I heard a zip being pulled up and gulped. "Of course I'm certain."

"And did you see who this person was?"

"I told you," said my drunken dance partner to his friend. "I knew I wasn't imagining it!"

"Imagining what?" demanded Mr Rochester sharply.

"That man."

His friend sighed. "He says he saw a man lurking at the end of the landing, earlier on, but take no notice. He's pissed."

"What did this man look like?" Mr Rochester asked.

My dance partner screwed up his face in concentration. "Not sure. It was dark. Tall, I think. Sinister. Ghostly."

"For God's sake," the first one said. "Get a grip, Tristan."

"Is that what you saw?" Mr Rochester asked me, his voice now sounding gentle. "A tall man?"

I shook my head. "It was too dark to see properly, but I don't think it was tall. It was a monster. All bloated and misshapen, and bald."

"Bald?"

"Absolutely." I bit my lip, considering. "I'm sure it was bald. It was totally gross." His mouth twitched, and I narrowed my eyes at him. "What's so funny?"

"Nothing, nothing. It's just that—"

Another piercing scream came from farther down the landing.

"Bloody hell," Mr Rochester said. "What now?"

His guests looked at him, as if to ask what type of horror show he had going on in his house, then ran out onto the landing, with Mr Rochester close behind. I decided that I was probably safer going with them than sitting there with an unlocked door, so I ran after them.

Briony stood by the door of her room, waving

something in her hand and wailing like a banshee.

"Briony, darling, what is it?" Joel—who evidently couldn't be bothered to come to my rescue, but had leapt into action upon hearing her cries—rushed to her side and tried valiantly to calm her down.

She didn't even seem to notice he was there. "Ethan, Ethan look!" She waved the paper in her hand at him, and he took it from the clutches of her bony fingers, while I stood there, trying to decide whether or not it was all some elaborate ruse on her part to throw us off the scent. Had she been responsible for my creepy visitor?

Mr Rochester stared at the paper, which I realised was a photograph. I peered closer, then glanced up at him. It was a picture of him and his wife. What was Briony doing with it? And why had it scared her so much? If someone as lovely as Antonia frightened her, she ought to try being awakened by a blobby bald monster. That was no fun, believe me.

Mr Rochester was studying the photo, so I studied it, too. I couldn't deny I was curious.

Apart from the airport picture from five years ago, I hadn't seen many pictures of Antonia, and I'd not seen one of the two of them together. I admit that seeing them posing in that photo, looking just like any other married couple, made me feel a bit funny.

My stomach churned suddenly. *I'm not jealous*, I thought fiercely. What was there to be jealous of? She was his wife, and it wasn't as if he'd ever kept that a secret. I was just the nanny, remember?

Even so, I stared down at the photo and felt a bit sick. They were standing with their arms around each other, laughing at whoever was behind the camera, and they seemed totally relaxed and at ease with each other. Judging by Mr Rochester's appearance, it was a fairly recent picture, too, so clearly, they had more contact than I'd realised.

"Paris," he murmured, and shook his head slightly.

They'd been in Paris together? The city of romance. So much for my belief that their marriage was dead. I stared harder at Antonia's face. There was a light of love in her eyes that was unmistakable. I wasn't imagining it. I kind of wished I was.

"It was on my pillow," Briony said, sounding rather hysterical. "I heard noises. They woke me up. I switched on the lamp, and there it was, right beside where my head had been. Someone came into my room and planted it there."

"Who would do such a thing?" Joel said, hugging her.

"I don't know," I said, tilting my head, as if trying to work it out. "But given there's a bald, deformed creature roaming the house with a knife, I'd say you got off lightly."

"What on earth is she talking about?" Briony said.

"She says she saw something in her room," said Tristan's cynical friend, in a tone that clearly said he thought I was imagining it all. "Probably a nightmare."

"Oh, for heaven's sake," Briony snapped. "Stop attention seeking." She seemed to finally notice my employer's half-undressed state, because she looked at me, then gave him a filthy look and said, "Hoping for a replay, Ethan?"

He scowled. "Can everyone just calm down and go back to bed?" He waved the photo in her face. "This is obviously someone's idea of a joke. I can't think what point they were trying to make."

"Can't you?" Her eyes gazed into his, her lips parted slightly, and she stood there all quivering, with an invitation practically oozing from her body.

"No," he said firmly. "I can't. Now get back to sleep and put all this nonsense behind you."

Joel squeezed Briony's shoulders. "Would you like me to sit with you a while? Make sure you're all right?"

Briony gave Ethan a long, hard look. Then she shrugged slightly and turned to Joel, giving him a seductive smile that seemed to send him all trembly, even as I watched. "Thank you, sweetie, that would be so kind of you."

Dazedly, he followed her into her bedroom, and they shut the door behind them, while Tristan and his friend grinned and nudged each other. Ethan turned to them and instructed them to get some sleep, and as they shuffled off, he said, "Cara, come with me."

"Where are we going?" I said, but he was already heading up the landing towards his old suite. He rapped on the door, then motioned to me as it opened. I walked towards him, feeling a mixture of curiosity and dread. What was I about to see?

"All right, Mother," he said wearily. "What exactly have you been up to?"

A strange vision met my eyes. A woman with a sort of face sling on her slightly swollen head was peering out at Ethan and looking rather guilty. She reminded me of the ghost of Jacob Marley. I wondered, if I removed her sling, would her jaw drop open like some fearsome ghoul?

Thinking that, I realised she must have been the strange apparition that had appeared in my room, and finally, a lot of things began to make sense.

"Jennifer Rochester?" I realised I'd said it out loud and blushed.

There was no mistaking the procedure that she had undergone. She'd had a face lift. The swelling and slight bruising, and the facial support sling, left no room for doubt. No wonder she'd hidden away up there and hadn't even seen Adele. She wouldn't want to alarm a four-year-old with her appearance.

"You'd better come in," she said stiffly, and we both followed her into the room, Mr Rochester closing the door firmly behind us.

I looked around, realising that it was, in fact, Ethan's own room. Well, his suite of rooms, to be accurate. I could understand why he'd given it to his mother, given that she was closeted away up there. Not only was there the bedroom and en-suite, but through an open door, I glimpsed a sofa and a television in another room. It was practically a self-contained flat, much like Mrs F's.

"I think you'd better tell us exactly what you've been up to tonight," Mr Rochester said, waving the photo in her face. "And don't try to deny it."

She gave a sort of twisted smile, which I didn't think was meant to be twisted. Her eyes, although puffy, were definitely twinkling, and in spite of the fact that she'd frightened me half to death earlier on, I thought she had a mischievous expression rather than demonic, which was reassuring.

"I'm not trying to deny it, darling," she said, gleefully. "It was terribly good fun. Although," she added, glancing apologetically in my direction, "I'm awfully sorry I scared you, Cara. I hadn't realised you were in Ethan's room. I only went in to warn him what I'd done to Briony before she started accusing anyone else."

"You frightened the life out of both of them," said her son sternly. "What did you think you were doing?"

Jennifer sighed and sank onto the end of the bed. "I was bored," she admitted. "Besides, I think that little madam needs reminding that you're a married man, don't you? I heard her tonight on the landing. Shameless little hussy."

On the landing? What had happened while I'd been fast asleep, oblivious to all the shenanigans that were taking place outside my door?

Ethan shook his head. "Don't you think I'm perfectly capable of looking after myself? I'm well aware I'm married. I know my responsibilities to Antonia, believe me." He sounded quite sad for a moment, and I glanced at him, puzzled. "I don't need you to look out for me, Mother," he added. "What you did was like something from an Agatha Christie novel."

"I know." Her eyes gleamed with amusement. "I did consider spearing the picture to the pillow with a dagger, but I thought that might be taking it too far."

"For God's sake!" He bit his lip, but I could hear the hint of laughter in his voice and felt suddenly quite indignant.

"Okay," I said, "so I get that you only put the photo on Briony's pillow to stop her flirting with Mr Rochester, and I understand that you didn't mean to frighten me to death earlier, but what about my dress?"

She frowned—or, at least, tried to. "Dress?"

Mr Rochester put his hand on my shoulder. "Oh, no, Cara. Not that. She wouldn't. Trust me."

"Why should I trust either of you?" I demanded. "I hardly know you, and she's clearly got a weird sense of humour." I probably shouldn't have said that, given he was my boss and she was his mother, but I was tired and I had an overflow of adrenaline sloshing around my system with nowhere to go. That was my excuse, anyway.

Jennifer tutted. "Weird sense of humour? How rude."

"Not as rude as slashing my new dress to bits," I protested, aware that Mr Rochester's eyes were fixed on my face and trying not to look at him, as irresistible as the magnetic pull from them was.

"My mother," he said firmly, "may be many things, but she's not vindictive, or cruel. She would never slash the dress, Cara. Obviously, you don't have to take my word for that, but I hope, by now, you realise you can trust me."

Could I? I wasn't sure about anything anymore. And how much did I know about him, anyway?

"What dress are you talking about?" Jennifer said, looking from one to the other of us.

"My new party dress," I mumbled. "And how did you know my name was Cara, anyway?" I added, as I realised she'd called me by my name when I entered the room.

"I told her your name, of course," said her son.

"He's told me all about you," she said. "Who else would you be? Not one of these hangers-on, that's for sure. Now, what about this dress?"

"Cara bought a new dress for the party and left it hanging on the wardrobe door while she went for a shower. When she went back into the bedroom, someone had been in and cut it to pieces. She was understandably scared."

239

"Oh, my dear." Jennifer stretched out her hand, and rather reluctantly, I took it. "How awful for you. No wonder you were scared! And then for me to appear like that in your room. I'm so sorry."

"She was very nervous, so I swapped rooms with her," Mr Rochester said. "I thought she'd be safe in my room with the door having a lock. I knew, of course, about you having your own key, but it never occurred to me that you'd go in there, tonight of all nights."

"Ah. I wondered what she was doing in your bed." Jennifer managed another stiff smile.

"Which brings me back to your irresponsible behaviour." Mr Rochester sounded like a stern teacher addressing a naughty pupil. "You're supposed to be resting, and keeping away from people, until your swelling goes down and the bruises have disappeared. Your idea, I might add, not mine. Yet, you're out prowling the corridors of this house where anyone could see you. If you're that unconcerned about your appearance, you could have come to the party, after all."

Jennifer looked guilty. "Sorry. Of course I'm concerned. I was just agitated, having heard that hussy practically issue an invitation to her bed, and sitting here, my mind was running riot. I wanted to warn her to keep her hands off, that's all."

"And as I've said, I can look after myself."

At least he hadn't taken Briony up on her invitation, I thought, though I couldn't help but wonder why. And what did he mean about his responsibilities to Antonia? She didn't show much responsibility towards him, leaving him alone all the time to go off on her travels. It was all a bit perplexing.

Jennifer squeezed my hand. "You look exhausted, Cara, and no wonder. Get yourself back to bed and lock the door. I promise faithfully that I won't leave this room tonight."

"I should hope not," Mr Rochester said. He gave me a concerned look. "You do look tired. I'll see you back to your room, make sure it's clear, then you can lock yourself in after I leave."

"There's no need ..." I began, but my voice trailed off as I realised I would rather prefer it if he checked things out for me. Any weirdo could have sneaked in and be lying in wait while I'd been chasing down monsters, after all. "If you like," I said feebly.

We said goodnight to Jennifer and headed back to my room, where Mr Rochester very nobly searched under my bed, in the en-suite, and even inside the wardrobe for me, just to make sure there was no one there.

My heart thudded the whole time he was in the room, and not due to the possibility of a monster under the bed. It occurred to me that Mr Rochester and I were alone, in a bedroom, practically naked. Well, not exactly. I mean, I was in pyjamas, obviously, but I'd become very aware that they were quite fitted, and I wasn't wearing a bra underneath. He, on the other hand, wore nothing but a pair of trousers, over those trunks.

Oh, those trunks! I remembered the sight of him throwing back the duvet and revealing that toned body, and my face burned. That image, and the broad chest and flat stomach still on display, proved difficult to ignore.

"No monsters in here now," he said, eventually, as he closed the wardrobe door.

"I'm relieved to hear it," I said, pulling a horrified face

as I realised how husky my voice sounded. Lust had clearly strangled my vocal chords.

He stared at me a moment, and I saw the expression in his eyes change, as if he'd just noticed what we were wearing, too. Thankfully, he turned away. "Lock the door after me, okay? I'm sure things will look better in the morning." Was it my imagination, or did his voice sound a little strained, too?

"Well, they could hardly look worse," I said, in an attempt at flippancy. I followed him to the door, key in hand. "Thanks for looking, though," I added, as he hovered in the doorway. "And I'm sorry I threw the water at you." I daren't look at him in case he could read the lustful thoughts that were chasing through my mind. "Goodnight, Mr Rochester."

To my amazement, he reached for my hand. My head shot up, and my eyes met his. It seemed like a million emotions attacked him all at once, and he just stood there, as if unable to put any of them into words. Slowly, he brought my hand to his lips and kissed it, then let it go. "Ethan," he said softly. "My name's Ethan. Goodnight, Cara." He turned and walked away.

I closed the door, then stood there, staring at it, my mouth open. What the hell had just happened?

After turning the key in the lock, I scuttled back to bed, pulling the duvet up to my chin as I lay there, staring up at the ceiling. I'd quite forgotten about monsters on the prowl. I was facing an entirely different kind of threat, more dangerous than anything else I'd ever known.

Chapter Eighteen

I slept in until almost nine the following morning, which was unheard of for me. I expected I'd be in a bit of bother with everyone because of it, but when I entered the kitchen, it was a scene of domestic harmony. Michael, Mrs F and Adele were sitting at the table eating breakfast, and they all beamed at me when I sat down, no trace of condemnation from any of them.

"I'm so sorry I overslept," I began, but Mrs F waved her hand at me.

"No need to apologise. Ethan told us what happened last night. What a performance! No wonder you overslept, although the wonder is you slept at all. Michael went over to Mrs Turner's and picked Adele up, to save you the job. We decided we're going to look after her today, so you can have the day to yourself."

"Won't you be busy looking after the guests?" I said, puzzled.

She tutted. "They can look after themselves. Ethan's up and out already, but the rest of them are still snoring their heads off, as far as I can tell. They probably won't surface until around lunchtime, so I'll do them all a cooked breakfast, and that will be that for the day. They can clear off before dinner, and I'm sure they can amuse themselves this afternoon."

All I really heard was, *Ethan's up and out already*. I didn't know where he found the energy, and what was he doing, anyway?

"His special guest has been asking for you," Mrs F added, giving a surreptitious nod towards Adele, as if to remind me not to mention Jennifer's name. "Seems you made quite an impression. Can you take her breakfast up to her? She asked me to ask you specially."

"Really?" I felt a bit dismayed at that, not sure I wanted to spend any time with a woman who did such crazy things in the middle of the night, not to mention hiding away from her own daughter—or granddaughter, if I was correct. Seemed I had no choice, though. "I'll make myself a cup of tea first, and then I'll go up. Good morning, Adele. Enjoying your cereal?"

She nodded, eyes shining. "Yes, thank you. Michael and Mrs F are taking me to the seaside this afternoon."

"Really? Aren't you a lucky girl?" I said, smiling at her.

"I know. I'm taking my bucket and spade," she added happily.

"Wonderful," I said. "Make sure you build a giant sandcastle and get Michael to take a picture for me."

"What about your breakfast?" Michael said. "I make a mean bacon sarnie, if you fancy one?"

"No, honestly. I'm not hungry." The wine from last night was still making me queasy. I shouldn't have drunk so much. Nerves, I supposed. I certainly couldn't face greasy bacon, or anything else, for that matter.

"You should eat," Mrs F said, sounding concerned. "You're fading away before my eyes."

I laughed. "Hardly! Don't worry, Mrs F, I'll be hungry at lunchtime, no doubt."

"Hmm. We'll see," she said.

I made a cup of tea, trying not to yawn. "What is—er—the guest having for breakfast?"

"There's a smoothie in the fridge for her." Mrs F rolled her eyes. "Some breakfast, but there you go."

I took the tall, lidded cup from the fridge, picked up my cup of tea, and told them I'd see them later, then I headed upstairs to face Jennifer.

Not wanting to disturb any of Ethan's guests, I crept along the landing. The last thing I needed was to come face to face with Briony Wotsit-Quaver, or the sycophantic Joel, or any other of Ethan's London friends. I couldn't imagine what he had in common with any of them. They really didn't strike me as his sort of people, at all. But then, as I'd pointed out correctly last night, how well did I really know him? Certainly not well enough to predict that he'd kiss my hand and tell me to call him Ethan.

I tapped lightly on Jennifer's door, and nearly fell into her room when she opened it immediately. Had she been waiting to pounce, or something?

"Morning, Cara," she said. "Thanks so much for bringing my smoothie. I'm feeling quite hungry today."

I checked the carpet to make sure I hadn't spilled any tea, then satisfied I hadn't, I studied her warily.

She didn't have the facial sling on, and her honey blonde hair seemed distinctly flattened and messy, something she was clearly aware of, as she patted it rather self-consciously and said, "I know I look a fright, but it will all be worth it in the end."

She motioned for me to follow her through to the living room part of the suite, which I did, looking around me curiously. It was quite a masculine sort of room—all

245

brown leather and oak furniture, and tartan fabrics, but there were French doors opening out onto a balcony, and Jennifer opened them so that I could feast myself on the amazing view of the lawns and lake. I sat in a large, comfy armchair, while she plonked herself on the sofa, feet curled under her, and slurped noisily on her smoothie.

"Ooh, I needed that." She closed her eyes for a moment.

I sipped my tea, wondering why she wanted my company all of a sudden. As the minutes ticked by and she said nothing, I began to feel distinctly uncomfortable. "You've taken your face sling off," I said, in a desperate bid to break the silence. "You don't look so scary this morning."

Why had I said that? Fancy implying that last night she'd looked hideous, which wasn't exactly true. Well, not really. Although she'd looked terrifying in the dark, looming over me like that, all swollen and bandaged, like something from a Hammer Horror film.

"Yes, I don't have to wear it all the time now. It's been just over a week. Things are settling down at last." She must have seen the doubtful look in my eye, because she managed a smile. "You think this is bad? You should have seen me the day after the procedure. I terrified the life out of myself. I expect you've guessed that I've had cosmetic surgery. Quite a lot of it, actually. I'm so happy with the results already. I was getting terribly jowly, and my eyes were so droopy. I feel quite like my old self again now, and I can't wait to show everyone my new look."

"Sounds painful," I said.

She nodded. "You're not wrong there. I thought I was going to die the day after the operation, but it passed. I stayed at the clinic for a week, so they could keep checking on me, and I had my stitches out, and then Michael brought me here to recover. I simply couldn't risk going back to the house in London. Too many people nosing around. This is out of the way—or so I thought. I couldn't believe Ethan decided to throw a birthday party the very weekend I arrived."

"Well, I suppose he couldn't exactly move his birthday," I pointed out, thinking that she really could have moved her op, instead.

"Oh, but he never has parties. He hates all that socialising. He's far more like Thomas than like me in that respect. No doubt he has his reasons. I just hope he knows what he's doing."

"You mean Briony?" I couldn't help myself, and she looked at me curiously.

"Do you know anything?"

I lowered my eyes. I shouldn't really get involved. It was Ethan's business, and I shouldn't discuss anything with his mother, anyway. "Only that it's obvious she wants him," I muttered.

"Huh. Wants his money, more like." She shrugged. "As he keeps telling me, he's old enough to take care of himself. We shall see. He hasn't done too well so far. What a mess. Talk about a tangled web. I think it's a good thing I'm here, given the situation he's landed himself in. Silly boy."

I was longing to know what she meant, but she offered no further information. I cast around, trying desperately to think of something else to talk about.

"Adele's going to the seaside today," I said. "Mrs F and Michael are taking her."

"How nice," she said.

"When were you planning on telling her you're here?" I asked. "Only, I'm sure she'd love to see you, and your face looks fine. I'm sure it won't scare her."

She sighed. "I know. I suppose I should meet up with her again. I'm just not awfully good at all that sort of thing."

"What sort of thing?" I said, surprised.

"Children." She sounded quite gloomy, and not at all like a doting mother. I gazed into my tea for a moment, wondering whether I had the courage to broach the subject of Adele's true parentage. I decided I had. It was now or never. "I think you should know," I said, carefully, "that Adele overheard a conversation you had with Jodie. She asked me about it."

She eyed me curiously. "What conversation? I rarely had any sort of conversation with that woman. She was hardly my favourite person."

If that was the case, I was a bit surprised that she'd confided such a massive fact to someone she didn't seem remotely keen on. It was all very awkward. Maybe I shouldn't have said anything, after all. I could feel my face heating up with embarrassment as she stared at me, waiting.

"She heard you telling her nanny that you weren't her natural mother. Of course," I added hastily, "she didn't understand what that meant. She simply asked me what natchell meant."

"And what did you tell her?"

"I—well, to be honest, I fudged it," I admitted. "I told her I didn't understand it myself and maybe she'd misheard. Sorry. I just didn't know what to say."

248

To my relief, her eyes twinkled with amusement. "I can see the thoughts running through your head, Cara. You're so transparent." Her face broke into a smile. "I didn't say I wasn't her natural mother. I said, I wasn't *a* natural mother—which I'm not, as I'm sure you've already realised."

My face burned even hotter. "I'm sorry. I wasn't saying—"

"Of course you weren't. You're far too polite. Don't worry, you're not the first person to doubt Adele's parentage. Many people assume she's Ethan's daughter, and I'm simply pretending that my granddaughter is my own child to save his reputation, given that Antonia clearly isn't her mother." She giggled. "And I can see by your face that you thought the same. Oh, dear."

"So—so Adele *is* your daughter?" I said faintly.

"She is. A rather unusual souvenir from my last holiday in Barbados. I was hoping for a mahogany carving from Pelican Village, but there you go."

"I'm sorry?"

"A holiday romance, darling. Not even that, really. A night of passion in a hotel, with a rather hunky chap who was on the last night of a somewhat raucous stag week. It was my first night there, so it was a brief encounter. That's a romantic way of saying one-night-stand. He was quite delicious, as I recall. We had a wonderful time in his hotel room, with Adele's album *21* playing in the background. That's why I called my daughter Adele. I'm pretty certain she was conceived to *Rolling in the Deep*."

"Gosh." There wasn't an awful lot I could say to that. Eventually, I asked, "Did you not tell her father? I mean, does he know about Adele?"

She shook her head. "Certainly not. It would have been terribly awkward, given it was his forthcoming wedding they were all celebrating. Besides, it was embarrassing. I mean, getting pregnant at that age! I was convinced all that was well behind me. I was menopausal—had been for ages, or so I thought. Just shows you. Anyway, even apart from all that, it wasn't an option." She gave me a mischievous look. "I never thought to ask his name. I'm almost sure it was something like David, or Damien, or Daniel. Or was it Rupert, or Robert? I really can't remember, and there's no point in worrying about it, is there?"

I supposed there wasn't. I sipped my tea and gazed out across the lawn, noting the sunlight glinting on the waters of the lake, and reflecting that I'd been very wrong in assuming that Ethan had fathered an illegitimate child. I couldn't help feeling guilty that I'd misjudged him.

"The fact is," Jennifer continued, after taking another mouthful of her smoothie and replacing her cup on the table, "Adele would probably be better off if Ethan *was* her father, and I her grandmother. He's practically brought her up himself, anyway. I never was very maternal. I was far too young to have a child. I got married when I was just nineteen, and before I was twenty, Ethan was in a crib in the nursery and I was a mother. I was woefully unprepared. I told Thomas, before they'd even wheeled me out of the delivery room, that he needn't think there'd be any more children. What a barbaric business childbirth is! And then, all the inconvenience and discomfort afterwards. Disgusting, really."

"Didn't he mind? About not having more children, I

mean?"

She tilted her head, as if considering the matter for the first time. "I don't think so," she said eventually. "He never said anything, anyway. Then again, he had an heir, which was all that really mattered, and he wanted me to be happy. That was important to him." Her face softened. "He was such a good man, you know. Kind. Considerate. He put up with a lot from me. I could have been a much better wife." She shook her head carefully. "Not that I was a bad wife, exactly," she said hastily. "I mean, I flitted and I flirted, but I was never unfaithful to him. And I was always discreet in my flirtations. I knew his reputation mattered to him, and I wouldn't want to damage that. Besides, it's so sordid, don't you think? All that infidelity business. Vile."

I nodded. "And painful."

She reached for her cup again, watching me thoughtfully. "You speak as one who knows?"

"I do." I didn't add any further information, and she sighed.

"I had the same experience with my father. The pain he caused my mother was unbearable to see. I could never have inflicted it on Thomas. Some people seem to see relationships as a game, but they're not. They're deadly serious. You see, that's the trouble with Briony. Well, one of the troubles with Briony. She really wouldn't understand, or care, about reputations, or discretion, or feelings, for that matter. All she cares about is money and celebrity. She would sell her soul for a cover spread in *All the Goss*. She's probably got the headlines all worked out already: *Briony and Ethan share their engagement happiness; Briony and Ethan's wedding day bliss; Briony's heart-breaking decision—Why I had to end my marriage.* Because it would end, you know. She'd always have her eye on the next rich man, and she would break Ethan's heart, which would break mine. My son doesn't need that sort of woman in his life."

My stomach did a funny little shudder. Must have been the tea sloshing around in there. "Well, it's his choice, I suppose," I murmured. "If she's the kind of woman he wants, there's not much you can do about it."

She looked at me with evident surprise. "Of course she's not the kind of woman he wants! He wants and needs someone steady, honest, faithful, kind."

"Maybe you should buy him a Labrador instead?" I suggested helpfully.

She giggled. "You are funny, Cara. You know what I mean. He's been hurled into this world of cut-throat business deals, sharp suits, and glamorous women, but he's not that sort of man really, is he? You must know that. He'd be happy to spend his days on the moors, and being with Adele." She hesitated. "He'd make an excellent father, you know. I've always thought so."

"Well, maybe he and Antonia—"

"Antonia?" She shook her head. "Let's not even go there. Something's going to have to be done about that situation. The clock is ticking, and it's not fair." She squinted slightly as the sun hit her face, and reached over to the coffee table for a pair of sunglasses, which she perched on her nose, conveniently hiding her expression as she said with deceptive calmness, "Have you ever considered having children, Cara?"

The tea did another slosh around in my stomach. Had I? I'd thought of little else for the last few years. I smiled, hoping the pain didn't show in my voice. "Of course, but the time was never right, and now I'm thirty—"

"Oh, tosh." She beamed at me. "I was fifty-two, for goodness sake. Thirty is nothing these days. Women are choosing to delay having their families until their forties. You're still young enough, and I'm sure it will happen for you. You would be so good at it. I've heard you're marvellous with Adele. It's a real gift, you know. I just don't appear to have it."

"Adele loves you," I assured her.

"Of course she does, much as one would love an older sister, or a favourite aunt. Not the same as a mother, though, is it? Thomas would have adored her, you know. How ironic. Still, things are what they are. We can't all be good at everything, can we?"

"No," I said. "We can't."

"I will see her, of course. Perhaps tomorrow? Or the day after?"

"Why don't you come out with us?" I suggested, on impulse. "We could take her somewhere nice for the day. It would be a lovely re-introduction to you, and I'm sure you could do with some fresh air and a change of scenery."

"Looking like this?" she said incredulously.

"A bit of makeup would cover that," I said. "Honestly, it's not too bad, at all, and I'm sure foundation would conceal the bit of bruising you have left. Oh, why not? It would be fun."

She considered the matter for a moment. "And you'll definitely come with us? Break the ice?"

I thought how sad it was that she felt she needed someone to be with her to break the ice with her four-year-old daughter. Was that the sort of mother she'd been to Ethan, too? I felt so sorry for all three of them. How much they'd missed out on. I thought of my own mother and felt a pang of homesickness that took me by surprise. I wondered how they were getting on in Spain. I hoped Dad was eating well and feeling better. "Of course I'll come with you," I said. "I'd love to."

"Excellent." She beamed at me. "And I'll mention it to Ethan. I'm sure a day out would do him good, too."

Hang on! I hadn't mentioned Ethan!

"So, that's all settled," she said, leaning back on the sofa and smiling. "I feel much better. That's Adele sorted. Now I just have to work on Ethan."

Clearly something was wrong, and it was worrying her. What sort of mess had he landed himself in?

Chapter Nineteen

I didn't see Ethan all morning, as he seemed to have vanished off the face of the earth. I remembered what Jennifer had said—he'd happily spend all day on the moors if he could. Doing what? And if that was the case, why did he spend so much time in London?

The rest of his guests stirred themselves throughout the course of the morning, stumbling downstairs and throwing themselves on the mercy of Mrs F, who cooked up full English breakfasts for each and every one of them who could face it, and provided tea and sympathy for those who couldn't. She was quite cheerful, and even friendly towards them all, not even complaining when one of them insisted he'd lost his breakfast and demanded a replacement.

"Lost it?" she chortled. "Well, I've heard it all now."

"But I did," he insisted. "Only put it down in the hallway for a minute while I went to call Alfie here, and some bugger made off with it." He scowled accusingly at another, rather portly man, who was tucking into a mound of sausages smothered in brown sauce. "And don't think I don't know who nicked it, either!"

"Get on with you." Mrs F laughed and handed him another plateful of food, and he beamed at her and wandered off, bad mood quite forgotten.

Briony was nowhere to be seen, which I was quite

glad about. Joel tucked into sausages and bacon with gusto and looked decidedly cheerful, and none the worse for wear, in spite of his previous night's alcoholic intake.

I was persuaded into eating a bacon sandwich by Michael, who seemed determined that I'd taste his cooking, for some reason. I had to admit, it hit the spot nicely. Fortified by my tasty butty and another mug of tea inside me, I bid them farewell as they took Adele off to Bridlington for the afternoon, and decided to go for a walk around the grounds with plans of escaping the London crowd with a book in my secret bolthole behind the wall.

I felt a bitter disappointment on discovering the gate locked. Though, maybe Ethan didn't want any of his guests to intrude upon the garden, a thought that cheered me up no end. Still, I didn't want to be disturbed by any of them, so after a moment's thought, I headed to the lake and crawled beneath the branches of an obliging weeping willow, where I leaned against the trunk and opened my book, knowing I was hidden from the outside world. Finally finding the page where I'd left off, I began to read.

I wasn't sure how long I'd been there when I became aware of a low murmur of voices. I froze, hoping no one would move the branches aside and discover me there, which was ridiculous really, because why would they? As I listened, praying I would remain out of sight, it dawned on me that the voices I could hear weren't exactly friendly.

My blood ran cold when I recognised Ethan's voice. "You're being ridiculous. There is no plot. I've told you, I don't know where she is at the moment."

"And I've told you, I don't believe you. Look, Ethan, I don't know what goes on between you and Antonia, and I don't particularly care. All I know is, her old man's in a bad way, and he wants to see her. Is that too much to ask?"

"Of course it's not, but what can I do? If I can't find her ..."

"But it's crazy! No one seems to know where she is. How is that even possible in this day and age?"

"If Antonia doesn't want to be found ..."

"And why wouldn't she want to be found? Has something happened between the two of you?"

"Not at all. You know Antonia. She likes to go off and do her own thing. Always has."

"Don't make out like you never see her. I know for a fact that you spent Christmas with her. I've made enquiries. You stayed in Paris together. Are you seriously telling me that six months later, you have no contact with her?"

"So we were together in Paris for Christmas. Why wouldn't we be? She's my wife, for God's sake. But then I had to return to London, and she wanted to go off on her travels again. She's like that, isn't she? She can't stay in one place for long. Never has."

"So, you won't help?"

"It's not that I *won't* help—"

"It's a bloody disgrace. Don't you think you owe Uncle Simon something, after the way you humiliated him?"

"Humiliated him! That was years ago! And what did he expect? It was like something out of the Tudor ages."

"That's not the point. There was an agreement. You made him look a fool. He gave you the benefit of the doubt, didn't he? And what happened? She abandoned

257

him completely. He's hardly seen her at all, since you two got married. You turned her against him, that's what you did. You isolated her. She was a real party girl until you got your claws into her, and after that, she practically vanished off the face of the earth. What did you do to her, eh?"

"Do you have any idea how paranoid you sound? For God's sake, Marcus, stop being an idiot. Antonia's very much her own woman, always has been. If Simon hasn't seen her, maybe he should look to himself for an explanation."

"Meaning what?"

"Never mind. Look, I understand Simon wants to see her before it's too late, and I'm genuinely sorry that he's ill, but I don't know where she is. If I hear from her, I'll let her know what's happening, and then it's up to her whether she contacts him, or not. It's totally her decision."

There were some vague mutterings, then the man, Marcus, said, "Whatever you say, there's no reason on earth that I can think of why she wouldn't want to see her father. I don't know what hold you've got over her, Rochester, but let me be very clear. If you can't find her, perhaps the police will."

There was quiet for a while, and I thought maybe they'd both moved away, so my heart leapt into my mouth when I heard Ethan say clearly, "Faith? How is she today? Oh, no, I'm sorry to hear that. Look, I wouldn't disturb you, but there's bad news, I'm afraid. Marcus just turned up at the house. It seems her father's taken a turn for the worse, and he wants to see her. Well, I know that, but if he doesn't see her, Marcus has threatened to get the police involved, and he means it. What are we going to do about it? Christ, Faith, this is such a mess. We have to sort this out, once and for all."

His voice grew fainter, and I realised he was walking away. Eventually, I couldn't hear him at all, and I sat there, feeling sick.

What was going on with Antonia Rochester, and why had Ethan just lied to her cousin?

#

You would never have known that anything untoward had happened. Ethan stood at the front door, bidding his guests a fond farewell, smiling and laughing, as they thanked him for his hospitality and teasing him about the unusual party theme. Any other time, I'd have found it amusing when several of his friends asked for Paolo's contact details. It was just as Ethan had predicted. Because he'd pretended he liked the theme, everyone else had taken to it, making Paolo a man in demand. I'd have said it was a kind gesture on Ethan's part, but after the phone conversation I'd overheard, I was no longer sure about anything.

Briony and Joel were arm in arm as they left the house. Briony barely glanced in Ethan's direction, merely waving her hand airily and heading down the steps towards her car. Joel, however, shook Ethan's hand eagerly.

"Good time?" Ethan drawled, raising an eyebrow in obvious amusement.

"You don't mind, do you?" Joel asked, sounding anxious. "I know you invited her here to seduce her—"

Ethan coughed. "Er, who told you that?"

"She did. It's all right, Ethan. I totally understand. She's amazing, isn't she? But the fact is, I've loved her for such a long time—"

"You don't say? You kept that quiet!"

It was obvious to me that Ethan was all too aware of the fact, and it dawned on me that he'd set them up deliberately. I remembered his remark about Cupid, and how he'd insisted that Joel teach Briony how to play pool. Had his flirting with her been an attempt to coax Joel into action? Despite everything, I felt quite warmly towards him for that. Joel was obviously mad about Briony, and Ethan had made it happen. What a shame, I reminded myself sternly, that he was also a liar and ... and—and what? I had no idea. I only knew that there was something extremely weird going on, and it concerned the mysterious Antonia Rochester, and whoever that Faith woman was.

"So, are we good?" Joel persisted.

Ethan smiled and held out his hand. "We're good, Joel. You're still my favourite cousin."

Joel grinned back at him. "Hey, I'm your only cousin! All the same, thanks, Ethan. Great party."

"You're welcome. Good luck with Briony. Hope it all works out well."

Joel practically floated over to Briony's car, where she made a great show of wrapping her arms around his neck and kissing him in a quite disgustingly graphic way. Sending a look of contempt Ethan's way, she climbed into her car and started the engine. Joel rushed over to his own car, gave a last cheery wave to us, then drove off following closely behind her.

As the last of the guests disappeared through the gates, Ethan heaved a sigh of relief and slumped against the doorframe. "Thank God that's over with."

"You didn't want this party, at all, did you?" I said, folding my arms and watching him curiously.

He shook his head. "That obvious? No, I hate all this sort of thing, but people had been nagging me to show them this place for ages, and when I realised it would be the perfect way to throw Joel and Briony together, it seemed like a great solution to multiple problems. Everyone's seen the house now, so they'll hopefully shut up about it. Joel has finally got the love of his life, God help him, and Briony—"

"Will finally leave you alone?" I raised an eyebrow, and he laughed.

"That's the plan. She'll be all right with Joel. He's far more suited to her than I am, and he's not short of a bob, or two. He'll be able to fund the lifestyle she so desperately wants, and he'll be far more accommodating towards her than I ever would have been."

"Was it ever on the cards?" I said. "You and Briony, I mean?"

"Of course not!" He looked at me, a hint of amusement in his eyes. "Did you think it was?"

"You were flirting with her all evening." Damn, why had I said that? He'd know I'd been watching them.

"All part of the plan," he said.

"To make Joel take action?"

"That, too," he said. He stared at me a moment, then shook his head. "Briony's really not my type."

"And, of course, you're a married man," I pointed out, watching him shrewdly.

His face stiffened. "Of course. Yes."

Huh! So much for the honourable Ethan Rochester. Sometimes, it seemed as if he'd completely forgotten he had a wife. I mean, okay, I sometimes forgot, too, but come on, it wasn't me who'd made the vows, was it?

As I turned to go back inside, he followed me in. "Your mother's going to brave the outside world," I told him coolly. "She's asked me to accompany her and Adele, perhaps tomorrow, or the day after. She feels ready to face everyone with a bit of makeup at last."

"I know. I saw her earlier. She asked me to go, too. Is that all right with you?"

"Why wouldn't it be?" I turned towards the stairs.

"Where are you going?" he asked. "We've got the house to ourselves now. Apart from my mother, I mean."

I faced him, my bemusement at his remark obviously showing, as he said, somewhat uncertainly, "I mean, if you're bored, we can do something? I don't know. Go for a walk, watch a film?" He moved towards me, his hand on my shoulder. "Cara, I—"

"No thanks," I said quickly, before I lost all sense of reason. "I won't interrupt you. Besides, don't you have another guest to see to?" It was a cheap shot, and he looked baffled.

"Sorry?"

"I heard someone else had arrived. Some man. Marcus, was it?"

"Who told you that?" His hand dropped to his side, as undeniable anxiety entered his eyes.

I shrugged. "Oh, I don't know. I heard it somewhere. Where is he?"

"Gone." He sounded bleak. "It was a brief visit. Business. It's done now." He looked totally defeated, and forgetting all my common sense, my heart melted.

"I see," I murmured, even though I didn't. I stared up

at him, and, without warning, he cupped my chin with his hand, tilting my face towards him, then he lowered his head and kissed me lightly on the lips.

I couldn't help it. Even though my mind screamed at me to push him away, my heart demanded more. I kissed him back, and he responded, his hands cradling my face as we stood there together, and suddenly I was in a different place, in a whole new awareness that scared the life out of me.

As if my fear communicated itself to him, he let me go and stepped back. "That wasn't—I shouldn't—I'm sorry, Cara."

He turned and strode into the sitting room, shutting the door firmly behind him.

He was sorry? Not half as sorry as I was.

I stood there, dazed, my fingers touching my bruised lips. God, I was an idiot. Ethan Rochester couldn't be trusted, and neither, quite clearly, could my foolish heart.

Chapter Twenty

Lying on my bed, my head felt on the verge of exploding. Not only did I have to puzzle out that kiss—oh, that kiss!—but I was also trying to work out why Ethan would keep a dying man from his daughter, and what reason he had for lying to Antonia's cousin when, clearly, he knew where she was.

I kept telling myself that none of it mattered. What was Ethan to me, anyway, except my employer? He'd clearly regretted kissing me, and I needed to forget it. Besides, he was married, and what went on between him and his wife, or their families, for that matter, was nothing to do with me. I had to put that moment of madness behind me, concentrate on my job, be professional.

I wondered if Adele was enjoying herself in Bridlington. I thought about Jennifer, lying in her room across the hall, apparently not even missing her little girl. How weird and unfair that someone like her could get pregnant so carelessly, when I'd been denied the chance to be a mother. Because I knew, no matter how much Jennifer insisted it was still possible, that I would never have a baby of my own. Seth had made sure of that by refusing to even consider it, while through all those years, my eggs had slowly deteriorated and my chances of conceiving grew fainter. It was all right saying plenty of women had babies in their thirties, but for that, they needed a man, and since I had no intention of becoming entangled with one of those ever again, I was pretty much stuck.

Needing to snap out of my miserable mood, I picked up my phone and tapped the Facebook icon.

Scrolling through my timeline, I pulled a face at all the boring rubbish and click bait posted on there, wondering why I even bothered with it anymore. I'd once used it to see what my siblings were up to, but since our relationships had improved—especially with Tamsin—I didn't feel uneasy about picking up the phone to call her any longer. Maybe social media had run its course for me.

Tamsin had posted earlier that day.

Chilled glass of prosecco while the girls are ice skating! Dinner and movie tonight! Looking forward to it!

Dinner and movie? Was Brad back? Hopeful, I clicked 'like' and commented:

Sounds great. So happy for you! Xx

Before I'd even put the phone down, it rang in my hand, Tamsin's name flashing up on screen.

"What's that supposed to mean?" she demanded, when I answered the call.

"What's what supposed to mean?"

"You're happy for me! Are you taking the mickey, or what?"

"Of course not! I assumed you were going out with Brad. Am I wrong?"

"Of course you're wrong," she snapped. "I've told you, Brad and I are over for good."

"Then, who—?"

"The girls, of course," she said. "I didn't specify I was going out, did I? I'm cooking a paella for dinner, and

265

we're watching a DVD of *Pete's Dragon*. It will be fun."

"Oh, well, I'm sorry," I said. "Just that it sounded as if you were going on a date."

"Yes, well." She was quiet for a moment. "Honestly, I was kind of hoping Brad would think so, too."

"Ah. I see."

"Stupid idea, right?"

"Understandable, Tamsin," I reassured her. "And I'm sure, if he sees it, he'll be overwhelmed with jealousy and rage."

She sighed. "No he won't. He'll see straight through me. I'll delete it."

I didn't know what to say. I'd been hoping Tamsin would cheer me up, but evidently not.

"Any news on the psycho knifeman?" she enquired.

"None. I think it must have been one of the guests," I said, though I was far from convinced. In fact, the more I thought about it, the more confused I became. There were far too many mysteries in Moreland Hall. What if they were all connected, somehow? But how?

"Hey, have you heard from Redmond?" she asked, suddenly sounding enthusiastic.

"No. Should I have done?"

"I was kind of hoping you had, since the wretch hasn't contacted me," she admitted. "You won't believe this. He's walked out on Susan."

"You're kidding!" She was right. I couldn't believe it. Solid, reliable Redmond, abandoning his wife! "Since when?"

"A couple of days ago, apparently. I only found out this morning, because Susan's been slagging him off all over Facebook. You're not friends with her on there, are you?"

"No," I shuddered. "Not after she tagged me in that post, just to impress her friends."

"Sounds about right. Well, apparently, they had a screaming row, and it got a bit heated, and he told her he was leaving her. She didn't believe it, but the next thing she knew, he'd packed a suitcase and gone. And the thing is, she has no idea where."

"I haven't heard a word from him," I said, feeling quite hurt.

"Don't take it personally. Neither have I. I don't think he's got a key to Mum and Dad's. either, so he can't have gone there."

"Have you got a key?" I asked, astonished.

"Well, yes," she admitted. "Only in case anything happens to them, and we need to get in. It's just because I live closest to them, that's all."

"Yeah. Sure." I could feel the hurt unfurling inside me, all over again.

"It is, Cara. Honestly. Don't do that thing again."

"What thing?" I said indignantly.

"That victim thing you do," she said. "You know. That whole *nobody loves me* thing. It's ever so annoying."

"Charming," I said. "Can I help it if I'm not made to feel welcome in my own family?"

"You were the one who left," she reminded me. "And you were the one who stayed away."

"You didn't exactly flock to visit."

"Can you blame us? Seth made it pretty clear that we weren't wanted, and you never rang, or got in touch to tell us any different. Anyway," she added, "I thought we'd got past all that? You're back in the fold now. You're just as much part of this family as I am, and that being the case, what do we do about Redmond?"

"What can we do?" I said. "Tie him up and force him to go home?"

"Hell, no!" I could hear the disgust in her voice. "I wouldn't wish that on the poor sod. I just mean, how do we make sure he's all right?"

"Oh, God," I said feeling sick, "you don't think he'd do anything stupid?"

"The thing is, he's had years of being bullied and worn down by that tyrant. Who's to say how low he's sunk? It must have been a pretty big argument for him to find the guts to leave her at last."

"Have you tried to call him?"

"Of course. Repeatedly. He's not picking up his phone. He's also deactivated his Facebook account. Gosh, I hope that bitch hasn't killed him and buried him under the patio." She giggled.

"Well, I'm glad you find it funny," I said.

"It was a joke," she said. "Honestly, Cara, where's your sense of humour? Even Susan wouldn't go that far."

I wasn't so sure. I wasn't sure about anyone's true character anymore. My judgement seemed off. I seemed to be surrounded by missing people. Not that you can be surrounded by missing people, because, after all, they're missing, but you know what I mean.

"Will you let me know if you hear from him?"

"Of course. And *you* let me know if *you* hear from him," she said, although I couldn't imagine he'd contact me before her. "I haven't told Mum and Dad. Thought I'd leave them to enjoy the rest of their holiday in peace. They'll be home soon, and then they're going to be attacked on all fronts. Bad enough Brad showing his true colours, but their little prince walking out on his wife will be a huge shock to them."

I had to agree it would. Better to leave them in blissful ignorance for the time being.

I said goodbye to Tamsin and lay down on the bed, but as soon as I had, the phone beeped again, and I lifted it up quickly, in the vain hope that maybe Redmond had got in touch, after all.

No such luck. "Oh, you've got to be kidding me." I groaned, seeing that I had a new text from Seth. That was all I needed.

I wait. Alone, unloved. A half-life.
The heart is stabbed with each lonely breath.
Forgotten. Condemned to a living death.
Your indifference cuts like a jagged knife.
One walks in sunlight, midst sweet-scented flowers.
One lies in shadows, and curses the hours.

I've told Isolde that I can't buy into the business with her, and she's cool with it. She's said we can have the box room, and she won't charge much rent. It's our best bet, really. The council won't help, I don't think. They seem to take a dim view of rent arrears. How much longer do we have to play this game, Cara? Time for home. Please. xx

Just leave me alone, Seth, I thought. I really can't give you what you want. The question was, what did he want? I'd honestly thought he'd have forgotten all about me by then, but it seemed he was more persistent than I'd ever imagined. But why? It couldn't be love, because he didn't love me. I was sure of that, if nothing else. Need? Perhaps. But he had Isolde ready and waiting to step into my shoes and take care of him, and she could do that in far more comfortable surroundings than I could ever manage, so what was stopping him? And Isolde must have been mad about him if she was willing to let me live in that flat with them. As if I'd ever want to do that! Maybe that was what she was counting on. No maybe about it, really. It was obvious. Isolde's motives were clear, but Seth's were very murky indeed.

I felt a pang of guilt at the way I'd left things. I should call him. Set him straight. Make it very clear to him that there was no way I was coming back. But I just couldn't do it. I couldn't bear the thought of speaking to him. I was finished with that part of my life, and I couldn't face going back to it, even if only for a moment, or two. Bad enough reading his texts. Having to speak to him would finish me off.

On a sudden impulse, I typed a quick message.

Seth, I'm really sorry that you're struggling with what's happened between us, but the fact is, I'm not coming back. Not ever. The relationship we had was never going to work. We are two different people, and we only make each other unhappy. We want different things, and there's no way to reconcile our needs. I wish you every happiness, but please don't text me again, as I won't reply. In fact, I think it best if I just block your number, and that way you can get on with your life and I'll get on with mine. Be happy, Seth. Cara. xx

I studied it for a moment, deleted the kisses as I didn't want to give him the wrong idea—knowing Seth, he would only focus on those rather than the words—and then pressed send. As soon as the *message sent* notification appeared, I went into my contacts list and blocked his number.

Heaving a huge sigh of relief, I lay down again, closed my eyes, and, without even meaning to, fell fast asleep.

#

I wasn't sure of the time when I opened my eyes. It wasn't dark, so that was something. I wondered if Mrs F, Michael and Adele were back, and strained my ears for the sound of voices. All was quiet, though, and I closed my eyes again for a moment.

I really would have to go downstairs and face Ethan at some point, though my stomach churned with nerves at the thought. Then I heard it, the same faint sound of something moving above me.

Bats? I didn't think so! I lay there, wondering whether to brave the attics alone. The thought of rats didn't really appeal to me, though, and what if they were running rampant up there?

Dare I ask Ethan to take a look? Would he think I'd gone insane?

At a dull thud, right above my head, I bolted up, terrified. That did it! Whatever was up there had to be chased away. Whatever my mixed feelings about Ethan, I would have to tell him.

I shot out onto the landing, just as Jennifer popped her head round her door, looking a bit puzzled.

"Did you hear it?" I demanded.

"Something's in the attics," she confirmed. "There was a distinct thud. Fetch Ethan."

I didn't need telling twice. I shot downstairs and practically collided with him, when he walked out of the sitting room just as I was about to run in.

"Are you all right?" He sounded anxious. "Has something else happened?"

271

What, apart from being kissed to within an inch of my life by you, you heartless wretch? "Your mother asked me to fetch you," I said coolly, thinking better to blame her than to admit I wanted his help, too. "There's something going on upstairs. In the attics, I mean. Something—or someone— is up there."

As I said it, I felt a sudden chill, and the image of Antonia Rochester came to mind. The conversation between her cousin and Ethan that I'd overheard in the garden replayed, over and over again. Where was Antonia? Why was Ethan lying to her cousin? Who was the mysterious Faith who was taking care of her?

I shivered, thinking about Bertha Rochester and Grace Poole, in spite of all my common sense, and as I peered up at the ceiling, my imagination ran riot.

Was Antonia being held up there?

I swallowed nervously. "Is someone living up there?"

Ethan frowned. "Up where? In the attics?" He shook his head. "Don't be ridiculous."

"But am I being ridiculous?" I persisted, because I wasn't sure anymore. Nothing seemed real, and no matter how much I told myself I was being irrational, I couldn't seem to help it. "You wouldn't be the first Mr Rochester to stick his mad wife in the attic, would you?"

He stared at me as if I'd gone completely off my rocker, which I probably had. What was I thinking, talking to him like that? We *were* in the twenty-first century, and things like that didn't happen in real life, anyway. Did they? "Are you ill, Cara?" he said slowly.

"Don't be so patronising!" I snapped. "There are noises in the attic. Mrs F said it's bats, but bats don't thud, and even your mother heard it just now. And where *is*

272

your wife, anyway?"

His expression darkened, and I realised that I shouldn't have spoken those thoughts out loud. It had nothing to do with me where his wife was. Of course it didn't. Besides, what exactly was I accusing him of?

"Are you seriously telling me that you think I've got my wife prisoner up there?"

Put like that, it sounded unlikely, I had to admit. "Well, no, not really," I squirmed. "I just—" I didn't know what else to say and looked at him in quiet desperation.

To my astonishment, he burst out laughing. "That wretched book. Have you any idea how many times I've been asked what I've done with my mad wife? I've never actually been accused of keeping Antonia in the attics, until now, though. At least, not to my face. I wonder how many people have assumed the worst?"

As the tension between us broke, I felt weak with relief, though a bit stupid. "There was a thud, though," I said feebly.

"Then, let's go and investigate," he said and held out his hand.

I looked at it, then took it, feeling a ripple of delight, in spite of myself, as his fingers folded around mine, and he led me up the stairs to where his mother hovered on the landing.

"So, Mother," he said, "I understand there was a noise from above."

"There was, you know," she said. "A distinct thud. Most unnerving. I do hope we haven't got rats, Ethan. I can't bear those nasty creatures."

"Rats with hob-nailed boots," I muttered.

"Cara and I are going to investigate," Ethan assured

her. "Would you like to come with us?"

She looked appalled. "You must be joking! Have a good look round, then report back to me when you're done."

"Yes, sir," Ethan saluted her, and headed us towards the attic door, his other hand still in mine.

Glancing over my shoulder, I saw Jennifer give me a thumbs-up sign before ducking back into her room. I wondered what that was about, but didn't have time to worry about it, since Ethan had let go of my hand and began making his way up the stairs.

"Come on, then," he said cheerfully, peering down at me. "You want to know, don't you?" He winked. "I promise, she's well restrained. I won't let her bite you."

I scowled. All right, I'd been a bit overwrought, but he didn't have to make fun of me. Although, given my recent hysteria and extremely rude accusations, I couldn't really blame him.

My stomach lurched when he murmured, "I'll be well restrained, too, Cara. Promise."

Was I glad about that, or sorry?

My heart was in my mouth as we reached the top of the stairs. What fiendish sight would greet my eyes? Well, not a lot, as it was quite dark on the landing, as it happened. However, as we moved forward, there was a sudden click, and I blinked as we were dazzled with light.

"Electric light switch," Ethan said cheerfully. "Always helps."

I felt so foolish. Whatever I'd been expecting, it hadn't been that. "Are you okay?" he asked.

He was probably wondering what kind of madness had possessed me. Maybe I was the lunatic who should be locked in an attic, rather than his wife. Not that any person with a mental illness should be locked in an attic, of course. I certainly wasn't condoning such behaviour, but still.

"I'm fine," I said. "I'm sorry for what I said down there. I didn't really think you'd locked your wife up in the attic."

"Didn't you?" He smiled at me. "I'm very relieved to hear it."

"Just that, it's not the first time I've heard noises up there," I added, in some small attempt at justification.

"What sort of noises?"

"Sort of scraping noises, and scratches. It definitely wasn't bats," I said defiantly. "I don't care what Mrs F says."

"No, it wouldn't have been bats," he said gravely. "They don't tend to scrape along the floor."

"I wasn't imagining it!" I snapped.

"I don't doubt you heard those noises, Cara. It was more than likely me."

"You? What would you be doing up here in the attics?" Crikey, did I really want to know? He could have been up to anything, and there I was, all alone with him. Of course, Jennifer knew I was up here, too, but then again, she could've been in on it.

In on what? There I went again, letting my imagination run away with me. I'd clearly read far too many books.

"Perhaps it's easier if I show you," he said, after a moment's hesitation. "Though, I have to say, it's a bit embarrassing."

Oh-oh! What was he about to show me? The image of Seth's stash of sordid magazines sprang into my mind, and

I pushed it away. Ethan wasn't Seth, and even if he did have sordid magazines of his own, he surely wouldn't want to show them to me. Would he?

I followed him, a bit reluctantly, as we made our way along a narrow corridor, and I stared around me in surprise. The attics were huge—a whole third floor full of rooms leading off the central passageway.

As we passed a dozen, or more, closed doors, he said, "These were the servants' rooms, back in the days of my great-grandfather. Shoved up here under the eaves, poor things. Thankfully, things are a bit more civilised now. I can imagine what Mrs Fairweather would say if I tried to make her live up here, can't you?"

I thought of Mrs F's cosy self-contained flat downstairs and grinned to myself. She'd soon tell him where to go if he tried.

We reached the end of the corridor, and Ethan opened a door and ushered me inside. "This is roughly above your room, I think," he said, "so whatever made that noise was probably in here."

I stepped inside, keeping close to him in case he decided to shove me in and lock the door behind me, but seeming to sense how worried I was, he took my hand again. It almost made the ordeal of standing in a dark room bearable.

There was a sudden click. "Let there be light," Ethan said.

My mouth dropped open when I saw easels, canvases in various stages of completion, pots of paint, jars of brushes, and shelves full of artistic paraphernalia. Studying some of the canvases, I recognised the style immediately.

"It's you!" I gasped. "You're the artist who painted

those Yorkshire landscapes in the dining room."

"Guilty as charged," he said, lowering his eyes as if embarrassed.

"Not guilty at all," I said, meaning it. "They're so good! I told you, didn't I? No wonder your mother made you put them on display. But why don't you have them all over the house? What a waste!"

He seemed uncertain. "Do you really like them?"

"They're wonderful. Honestly. I had no idea. Why didn't you tell me you painted them?"

"I don't talk about it much," he admitted. "Not many people know I paint. It's a frivolous waste of time—according to my father, anyway. I wanted to go to art school, you see," he said with a shrug. "I loved art, loved painting. It was what I wanted to do. But the die was already cast. I had a business to learn, and that was my destiny. Father said painting was a hobby, nothing more, and I had my duty to do, so I did it."

"That's terrible. You have a talent. A real talent. You shouldn't waste it."

"But it's not good enough. It's not a real job, is it? I have to carry on the family business, the stores. That's my job. I always knew that was my reason for coming into the world."

"If you don't mind me saying so," I said, "that's bloody terrible. Your father sounds awful." God, I'd done it again! I seemed to make a habit of overstepping the mark. "I mean," I added quickly, "I'm sure he was a very decent man, but he lacked understanding, didn't he?"

He grinned. "I know what you mean. He was, indeed, a very decent man, but he had a strong sense of duty, and he expected the same from me. Which is fair enough. We

277

have a lot of people relying on us. Art is all very well and good, but I have to think about all those employees whose jobs depend on me pulling my weight and concentrating on the stores. It's as simple as that."

So, he'd sacrificed his own wishes for the good of others. I quite forgot that I'd been angry with him earlier on, because my heart just melted, and for that moment, all thoughts of the missing wife vanished.

"Do you paint in London?" I asked, imagining a state of the art studio in his luxurious town house.

He shook his head. "London is where I work. It was always here that I painted. Even when the house was a gothic monstrosity and I hated it, I still used to wander over the moors, sketching. I could spend hours out there. Then I took over the business and there was never the time, really. But coming back here, I've rediscovered how much I love it all. I've been getting up early, going out to sketch, and working up here. Not as often as I'd like to, of course, but it's something."

I caught sight of some sketches on the table and exclaimed in delight. "The ewe and lamb! That's what you were doing on the moors!"

"Ah, yes. You almost caught me," he admitted.

"Have to say, I'm quite relieved. Thought maybe you had an unhealthy obsession with sheep."

He grinned. "They make very good subjects. They don't interfere, and they never demand that I capture their best side."

I picked up the drawing and shook my head. "It's brilliant. Oh, wow!" I put it down and snatched up another drawing that caught my eye. "That's Mrs F! You paint portraits, too!"

"I try," he said, pulling a face. "I'm not terribly good at it, but—"

"Why would you say that?" I demanded. "Stop being so modest. You've caught her expression perfectly. I love it." I sighed. "You know, this is such a shame. There's more to life than making money. You have such a talent, you should spend more time doing what you love. You need a better work-life balance. I mean, even when you're here, you spend a lot of time on the phone, or the computer. You don't switch off much, do you?" I looked around at all the evidence of his obvious gift. "This house should be somewhere that you completely escape to. Where the business and duty and responsibility is left behind. You should come here regularly and walk the moors and paint and spend time with your family."

"That sounds wonderful," he said wistfully. "But—"

"No buts," I said. "You have people around you who can run that business, I'm sure. And you're not exactly cut off from the world, are you? Not these days. You have broadband and a phone line. If there was an emergency, you could always be contacted. I just think that you should make the effort to come here regularly, and when you do, you're no longer Mr Rochester, of Rochester's Department Stores, but Ethan, son, big brother and artist. Doesn't that sound like a plan?"

He nodded, his lips curving gently. "It does," he agreed.

We stared at each other, and my heart thudded against my ribs. That wasn't good. I had to break the intensity of the moment somehow.

I cleared my throat. "Having said all that," I said briskly, "that doesn't explain the noises, does it?"

He blinked, then shrugged. "The scrapings would have been me, moving my easel around probably."

"At night?" I frowned. "You wouldn't have been painting at night?"

"No, but I did come up here a couple of times, just to look at what I'd done, or clear up. Mind you," he admitted, "it doesn't explain the thud you heard earlier."

He looked around, then walked across the room. "But that might," he said, nodding at a large canvas lying face down on the floor. "That was propped up against the bench yesterday," he said, lifting it up and checking it over. "Must have blown over."

"Blown over? How? The window's shut." I shivered.

"Maybe it wasn't balanced properly when I left it." He seemed more bothered about the state of the canvas than he was about the noises, and, looking at the beautiful painting as he stood it back against the wall, I wasn't surprised. It was of the cottage garden—a riot of colours on canvas.

"So, that's why the gate was locked that day!" I exclaimed. "You go in there to paint sometimes, and you didn't want to be found out."

"It's not that I didn't want to be found out," he said, laughing. "Mrs F, Michael and Mother know I paint, anyway. I just don't like being watched, that's all. It's easier to keep people out."

"But it's always open these days," I said. "Don't you paint in there now?"

"Sometimes. But I know how much you like the garden and the swing. It would be most unfair to keep you out of there."

I swallowed. He knew? "That's … very thoughtful of

you."

"Cara, would you let me paint you?" His words tumbled out in a rush, as if he was saying them quickly before he could change his mind.

"Why would you want to paint me?" I said, blushing furiously. "I'm hardly a fascinating subject."

"Oh, but you are," he insisted. "Those sea-green eyes, that rose-gold hair. Such beautiful colours."

"Rose gold?" I spluttered. "I've never had it described that way before."

"But that's what it is." He lifted a hand and stroked a strand of my hair between his fingers. "I would love to paint it. You have such an interesting face."

Interesting face! Was that artist-speak for pig-ugly? I scowled, and he laughed.

"Don't look like that! It's not an insult."

"Isn't it?" I said doubtfully.

"Far from it," he said softly, still holding my hair. I gulped, and he let go of the hair at last. "If you let me do some preliminary drawings tomorrow, that would be wonderful. I'd be so grateful."

"Not tomorrow," I said. "We're going out, remember? With your mother and Adele."

"So we are."

"I'm not sure where we're going," I added, desperate to make casual conversation. "But I expect we'll think of somewhere."

"I expect we will. I'm looking forward to it."

"And Adele will be so happy to see her mother again." Aware that I was starting to gabble, I backed out of the room. "So, now that's sorted out, shall we go back downstairs?"

The way he was looking at me, I felt I wasn't safe up there any longer. It wasn't him that was scaring me, though, but myself. My stomach was jigging up and down alarmingly, and there were tremors and tingles happening all over the place—places I'd quite forgotten could tremor and tingle. It was a bit disturbing, to be honest.

He nodded. "Of course. Unless you want to check on the other rooms, just to make sure that Antonia isn't in a padded cell somewhere up here?"

"Very funny," I said. "You can't blame me for wondering. Especially after what you said to—" I broke off, horrified. My face burned and I stared at him helplessly.

He frowned. "What I said to ...?"

"I'm sorry," I muttered. "I really am. I overheard you talking to someone called Marcus. You said you didn't know where Antonia was, but then you ..."

"Called Faith." He wasn't smiling or twinkly any more. He looked ashen. "I'm sorry you heard that, Cara."

Oh, God! What was he going to do? Kill me to shut me up? Lock me up there?

"Come on. Let's go downstairs."

Heaving a sigh of relief, I practically fell out of the room and rushed downstairs before he could change his mind. As we reached the landing, I took a deep breath and leaned against the wall, comforted by the knowledge that Jennifer was just a few doors away.

"I would tell you if I could," he said, looming up behind me and closing the door to the attic staircase. "Right now, I can't. I hope—I hope, one day, I can."

"It's none of my business," I said breathlessly. "Seriously. I shouldn't have said anything."

"You must have been thinking all sorts. No wonder you accused me of locking her up there." His mouth twitched, and for a moment he looked like his old self. "You're safe with me, Cara. You don't have to be afraid."

I looked into those dark eyes, and the reassurance I found in them made me wonder what on earth I'd been thinking. My imagination had always been too wild. Look how I'd cast Seth as Heathcliff, for goodness sake. And I was casting the hard-working, decent man before me as some sort of maniac who locked up his own wife. That was what I got for reading gothic romances. I felt thoroughly ashamed of myself, and rather embarrassed. "I know that," I said quietly, staring at the floor. "I'm sorry."

"Don't be sorry. It's me who should be sorry. What I did earlier—kissing you like that—was unforgiveable. It seems ridiculous to say it, given what I did, but please know that you *can* trust me. Will you? I know it's a big ask, but I swear, there's nothing sinister going on. Antonia's fine." He sighed. "Well, that's not strictly true, if I'm being totally honest with you, but it's nothing to do with me, I assure you." He smiled. "Not being very convincing here, am I? Come on. Let's go and reassure my mother that we're not overrun with vermin."

Chapter Twenty-One

'*I'm sorry, but I can't take your call at the moment. Please leave a message after the tone.*'

"Redmond, where the hell are you?" I hissed into the mobile phone, exasperated beyond measure that he wasn't picking up my call, yet again. I'd lost count of how many times I'd rung him. I was torn between thinking what a selfish swine he was, and praying that he was okay and was just downright thoughtless. "Ring me, or ring Tamsin. Just let one of us know you're all right. Please."

I pushed open the kitchen door and was immediately pounced upon by one very hyperactive little girl.

"Cara, Cara, guess where we're going?" Adele pulled on my hand, her face bright with excitement.

I smiled down at her. "Where?"

"Pleasure Planet!"

"Wow! Pleasure Planet!" I glanced across at Mrs F, who rolled her eyes and shook her head. "I haven't been there for a long time."

I really hadn't—not since a school trip when I was fifteen. Pleasure Planet was a theme park and zoo on the edge of the moors, and it was just the sort of place that Adele would love. There were plenty of rides for her to go on, and she could coo over the animals, too. I wasn't entirely sure what Jennifer would get out of it, though.

"Mrs Rochester's got a thing for meerkats," Mrs F

told me, "and there are quite a few of those there, apparently. Mind you, she'd best steer clear of the pandas. With all those bruises round her eyes, they might try to mate with her."

"Mrs F!" I couldn't help laughing, even though it was a bit unfair.

When Jennifer appeared, though, she looked remarkably normal. Her face had been very carefully made-up, and no one would ever have guessed she'd had a face lift not long ago, unless they knew and scrutinised her features for any swelling.

Ethan had shown her into the kitchen, after announcing to Adele that he had a surprise for her.

"What sort of surprise?"

"Someone's coming with us to Pleasure Planet," he told her. "Someone very special."

He then peered into the hallway and beckoned to Jennifer to come in, which she did, looking rather self-conscious. She had no reason to be, though. Firstly, she looked amazing, in white trousers and a pale pink fitted top, her blonde hair neatly styled. Secondly, and far more importantly, Adele seemed delighted to see her, hurling herself at Jennifer and squealing, "Mummy!" at the top of her voice.

I glanced across at Ethan and felt a warm, fuzzy feeling in my stomach when I saw the look of pleasure on his face.

"Come on, then," he said gruffly, "let's get off. Pleasure Planet awaits."

Michael entered the kitchen waving a phone charger in his hand. "Found this plugged into a socket in the parlour," he said. "Does it belong to any of you?"

We all shook our heads, and Michael tutted. "Must be one of your guests left it behind, Ethan. No doubt, they'll be in touch."

Hmm. Wonder which guest that would be, I thought cynically. Would Briony go so far as to deliberately leave something behind so she could return for it? I wouldn't put anything past her. Joel wouldn't hold her attention for long, I was sure. He wasn't in Ethan's league.

"Have a great time," Mrs F called, as we gathered up our belongings. "And don't stuff your faces with junk," she warned. "I'll have dinner on the table for when you get back. There's a thing, though. I was going to make you all a chocolate torte for afters, but I'm blowed if I can find the chocolate. I was sure I had some in the cupboard. Good quality stuff—none of your cheap rubbish. Oh, well, I must have used it for something else and forgotten."

"I doubt very much we'll be able to eat it, anyway," Ethan assured her. "I can't take my family to Pleasure Planet and not let them tuck into burgers and fries and candyfloss, and all the ice cream they can manage. It wouldn't be fair."

"Don't you dare," she warned him, laughing. "Enjoy yourselves!"

"And you," I said, winking at her, as Michael put his arm around her waist.

She flushed, but grinned at me, and Michael couldn't wipe the smile off his face. I had no doubt they would have a pretty good time with the house to themselves, too.

We did indeed enjoy ourselves, even though there was a tricky moment when we first arrived, and Jennifer discovered we'd have to queue like everyone else, despite the fact that the owner of Pleasure Planet was evidently a friend of the Rochester family.

"But you know Bill Adams so well, darling! Why on earth don't you call him? We could get VIP tickets and skip these wretched queues!"

"And where," Ethan said with a wry smile, "would be the fun in that? For one day, can I just forget about business and live my life like any other man?"

Jennifer looked a bit put out at the idea of that, but I thought it was admirable. How mortifying it would have been to sail past all those families queueing for rides, and wave wretched VIP passes at them. I'd have died of shame.

Adele loved the rides and wanted to go on everything—even the ones that were far too big for her. Ethan went on a couple of rides with her, which made Jennifer and I howl with laughter. Seeing his long legs curled up as he squeezed into a fire engine on a merry-go-round was too funny to ignore.

"I would have gone on the extreme rides, you know," Jennifer told me as we waited for the merry-go-round to finish, "if I hadn't had this operation. I can't risk it at the moment, sadly. Such a shame. I was quite a thrill-seeker in my youth. The scarier the rides, the better."

She snapped plenty of photographs, though, and then she took Adele's hand and wandered off to show her the meerkats.

"That's progress," Ethan murmured, as we watched them walking well in front of us, talking to each other in quite an animated fashion.

Adele seemed just as enamoured with the little

creatures as her mother, and the two of them strolled around the zoo, pointing at different animals and laughing together, which clearly delighted Ethan.

We stopped at a burger bar, having decided that we were all starving. I was trying to be good, and said I would have a salad, but Ethan begged me to have a burger with him. "We'll share it, if you like," he said. "I love the Triple Whammy Burger, but it's too much for one person. Will you eat the other half?"

I hesitated, but then decided that one day off the diet wouldn't hurt. "Okay," I said, feeling a thrill of delight when his face lit up, as if I'd just agreed to something wonderful. I wasn't so thrilled when he returned from the counter, and I discovered that not only did I have half of a Triple Whammy Burger to get through, but also a large portion of fries and a thick strawberry milkshake.

"You've got to be kidding me," I groaned.

"Are you seriously telling me you can't manage this piddling little meal?" he demanded, a clear challenge in his eyes.

I remembered the weeks in the caravan, and the vast quantities of crisps and Caramel Choc Bloc I'd managed to consume every day. Too right I could manage it.

"Watch me." I proceeded to prove that I was more than up to the challenge—a feat which he seemed strangely thrilled about. Honestly, anyone would have thought I'd done something remarkably clever, rather than simply proving what a gannet I could be.

Jennifer hooked her arm through mine, as Ethan went off to take Adele on a cable car ride around the park. "I understand Ethan told you his big secret last night," she said, smiling at me.

"Er, which big secret is that?" Let's face it, there were so many, I'd lost track.

"About his art," she said, sounding surprised. "He's awfully good, isn't he? He told me you liked his paintings. He was so sweet about it. Totally overwhelmed that you admired them. He's such a modest man."

"Too modest," I said. "He's really gifted. He should spend more time painting. It would do him the world of good."

"Oh, I couldn't agree more," she assured me. "And up here in Yorkshire seems to be the only place where he feels able to relax enough to paint. That's why I made sure the house was renovated."

I looked at her in surprise. "But Ethan said he did that for you! He said you'd decided to move up here permanently, but then changed your mind."

She laughed. "I know! He actually fell for that. As if I'd move to Yorkshire permanently. No, this area is where Ethan feels at home, not me. I just knew he hated the house, and I couldn't blame him. Dismal place. An absolute monstrosity, just as his great-grandfather had left it. I knew he would never get round to doing anything with it, because he never does anything to please himself, but tell him it's for me, and he'll pull out all the stops— which he did. Now that it's looking so beautiful and homely and welcoming, he's more inclined to stay, which means more painting."

"Ooh," I said admiringly, "you're good! And what about you?"

She patted my arm. "I prefer the Gloucestershire house and the New York apartment. I tend to split my time between the two places. Let's face it, as much as I love Adele, her place is with Ethan. He's far more suited to taking care of her than I am, and they both know it." She sighed. "He has to be in London sometimes for his work, and I know nothing and no one will persuade him otherwise. He's far too responsible, and too loyal to his father's memory. But I really do want him to make another life for himself up here, too. I just think it will take a bit more time, but it's happening. I can feel it."

I frowned. "It is?"

"Oh, yes, my dear. Most definitely. Ethan and I had a long talk this morning. We just have to unwind the tangled threads that are choking him, and then he can be free. It won't be long now."

"Right." I had no idea what she meant, but she didn't seem about to elaborate, so I concentrated on searching for Ethan and Adele instead, shading my eyes as I scanned the cable cars looking for a glimpse of them.

"There they are!" Jennifer laughed and waved, and my heart leapt as I spotted them both, waving frantically at us. I waved, too, unable to suppress the joy I was experiencing at the sight of them sitting there with their arms around each other, their faces showing their excitement.

Jennifer put her arm around my waist and rested her head on my shoulder, as if she'd known me for years. "Yes. Not long now," she murmured.

"That was fun!" Adele's little face was flushed when they joined us again, her dark hair damp with sweat. "Can we do it again?"

"How about," said Jennifer, crouching down and tenderly pushing Adele's wet fringe back from her forehead, "you and I have a go on the teacups?"

Adele frowned. "You want to go on the teacups?"

"I do. But only if you'll take me and hold my hand," Jennifer informed her.

Adele laughed. "Baby!" she squealed, but took her mother's hand and led her towards the next ride.

Ethan let out a big sigh. "God, I'm exhausted. This is hard work."

"Amateur," I teased. "You should try taking care of a whole class of three and four-year-olds."

"It would finish me off. I don't know how you do it, honestly. Now, that's a gift."

"Don't be silly," I said. "You're just out of shape. All those hours you spend sitting at a desk."

"Out of shape!" He looked outraged. "I'll have you know I work out regularly, and I'm in tip-top shape!"

Actually, I didn't doubt it, but there was no way I was going to let him know that. To my surprise, he grabbed my hand and began to lead me across the park.

"Where are we going?" I demanded.

"You'll see," he said. "Spotted it from the cable car. I'll show you who's out of shape."

A few minutes later, we reached our destination. "A test-your-strength machine." I looked at the fairground attraction before us and folded my arms. "Seriously?"

"I can't resist a challenge." He paid the money to an amused-looking man, who handed him the hammer.

"Bet you can't even get halfway," I said mischievously. "Now, there's a challenge for you."

There was a glint in his eyes. "You're a real tease, Cara. You know that?"

I tried not to show the effect his words had on me. "Go on, then. Stop talking and start proving yourself."

He shook his head slightly, then turned around and bashed the lump hammer down with a mighty crash. The little mouse shot up and reached midway between the seventy and eighty mark, before falling down to the base again. Ethan muttered a curse, then grudgingly handed me a fifty pence piece for Adele.

I tutted. "Three quarters of the way up," I said, shoving the coin in my pocket. "Hmm. Could do better."

A middle-aged couple stopped to watch. "You're right, love," the woman said. "My Arthur used to ring the bell every time when he was your age," she informed a mortified Ethan.

Her husband laughed and nudged her. "Don't put pressure on the poor chap," he said. "He's doing his best, I'm sure."

Ethan gaped at them, then turned around and swung the hammer again. Ninety!

"Ooh, so close," I said heartlessly. "Just not close enough."

"I'd give it up, if I was you." The woman giggled. "You'll do your back in."

"Ignore them, mate," Arthur advised. "Not everyone's cut out for it. I'm sure you can impress your girlfriend in other ways."

It was my turn to look mortified. As my face burned, Ethan looked at me long and hard, then he turned around, swung the hammer high above his head and crashed it down with such force, I thought he would break the machine. Or his back. One, or the other.

The bell pinged, and the woman clapped her hands and shrieked, "Ooh, well done, love."

"Knew you could," said Arthur, winking at Ethan and

leading his wife away.

The fairground man grinned and nodded. "Nice one, mate."

"What does he win?" I asked breathlessly, unable to take my eyes off my gallant hero.

"Reckon he's won the heart of a fair maiden," said the fairground man. "That's prize enough, don't you think?"

As Ethan watched me, as if awaiting my response, the expression in his eyes scared me to death. I turned and walked away as fast as I could.

"Hey, wait!" He caught up with me and grabbed my arm. "What is it? What's wrong?"

"Nothing's wrong," I said. "Adele and your mother will be wondering where we are."

He pulled me to a halt. "Who hurt you, little one?"

I glared at him. "What do you mean, who hurt me? And don't call me little one. Do you think because I'm just the nanny and I'm only five foot two, you can look down on me and make fun of me?"

"Who's making fun of you?" he said, clearly bewildered. "I'm sorry if you thought I was doing so. It wasn't my intention."

"Huh. Then don't call me *little one*." It wasn't that which had upset me, though, or that made me feel he was making fun of me. The whole flirting thing was clearly a joke, and I'd had enough. He obviously didn't understand the effect he had on me, or if he did, he didn't care. I was just the hired help. He probably thought giving me those intense looks was sport.

"*Little one* offends you?"

"It's patronising and rude."

He hung his head and stuck his hands in his pockets.

293

"I'm sorry, Cara. I didn't think."

"Well, maybe you would have done if you'd gone through a whole year at school with the boy you fancied calling you shrimp," I snapped.

He looked up at me. "You're probably right," he admitted. "Luckily for me, the boy I fancied always called me sexy, so I was never traumatised."

There was that familiar twinkle of amusement in his eyes again, and in spite of myself, I felt all my annoyance melting away. "Idiot," I said with a laugh.

His face lit up. "That's better. Am I forgiven?"

"I suppose so," I said, "but we still need to find your mother and Adele. They'll think we've abandoned them and gone home at this rate."

He nodded. "Quite right. Let's go and find them."

Out of the corner of my eye, I saw him hold out his hand, but I kept my face turned forwards. There was no way I would let him know that I'd seen his gesture, and I marched off, biting hard on my lip. I was in severe danger of losing all sense of right and wrong, and I simply couldn't do that again. He was a married man, and I was a sensible woman who'd been foolish enough to compromise myself too many times before. I could never let it happen again.

Chapter Twenty-Two

I was invited to have dinner with the family, as Mrs F and Michael were eating in her sitting room that evening. Adele ate with us, since we'd got home fairly late, and when we'd finished eating, Jennifer offered to put Adele to bed.

Ethan and I exchanged astonished glances, but Adele seemed delighted, and Jennifer explained that she was feeling quite tired herself, and would be going straight to bed afterwards. After we'd said goodnight to the two of them, Ethan and I looked at each other, suddenly awkward.

"I'll go up, too," I said. "Maybe an early night would do me good."

"Do you have to? I could use some company." Ethan seemed pensive for some reason. "Perhaps," he said slowly, "you'd like to walk in the garden?" He smiled, the gleam of mischief that he seemed unable to banish for long back in his eyes. "I could push you on the swing, if you like?"

I hesitated. I should have been keeping a safe distance between the two of us. He was dangerous in a way I could never have predicted, and I was losing control of the situation. Yet, for some reason, I heard myself say, "If you like."

We wandered through the grounds, making idle chat.

Ethan made the occasional observation about the gardens, pointing out new buds on the cusp of blooming, shrubs that needed cutting back, talking—as if to himself—about ideas he must discuss with Ken for new planting. Before I knew it, we were approaching the wall, and he opened the door, ushered me through, then followed me and closed the door behind us.

The garden was a living watercolour—a chaotic canvas of foxgloves, sweet peas, delphiniums, and roses. As we walked along the path, I breathed in the various scents, remembering the years of living in that grim council flat in Oddborough, with no garden and no flowers in sight. It was another world.

We walked under the archway, adorned with soft-cupped, sweetly-scented white roses, each flower tipped with a flush of palest pink. Ahead of us, the sycamore tree stood proud, the swing hanging from its bough—inviting and intimidating all at once.

He motioned to me to sit down, which I did, quite thankfully. My knees had begun to tremble. I took hold of the ropes, expecting him to start pushing me, but to my surprise he didn't. Instead, he sat beside me, forcing me to shuffle along the seat and release my hold on the left-hand rope. His thigh grazed mine, and the crisp cotton of his shirt sleeve brushed against my bare arm. As his fingers curled around the rope, I noticed the soft, fine hair on the back of his hand and forearm, and the clean, short squareness of his fingernails, his tasteful gold watch gleaming against the light tan of his wrist. The scent of him was a curious, but rather pleasant, pot pourri of fresh laundry, jasmine, patchouli and vanilla. Inhaling the smell, I closed my eyes for a moment, letting the mild evening sun gently caress my face. It was a moment as close to perfection as I had ever experienced.

"Thank you for today." His voice was soft, considered.

I opened my eyes and gave him a sideways look. "There's nothing to thank me for."

"But there is. It could have been awkward. My mother isn't always at ease with Adele, and she tends to run out of patience after ten minutes in her company. You made their reunion effortless. You have a very positive effect on my mother—on them both. I'm very grateful."

I knew my face was probably as pink as the roses in the cottage garden. "It's my job."

"And you're very good at it," he assured me, smiling again. "Did you always want to work with children?"

"Honestly?" I pulled a face. "I can't say I ever had a career plan, at all. I sort of fell into it. Childcare was recommended to me by the careers adviser, as something that even someone as academically challenged as me could manage."

He frowned. "That's ridiculous. Working with children certainly isn't a job that everyone could do. Besides, I find it impossible to believe that you're academically challenged, and equally difficult to believe that anyone would label you as such."

"Well, whatever you think, it's true," I said, trying to keep my voice light. "I never went to university. Never even did A-levels. Unlike my siblings."

"Having had a number of most illuminating chats with you, I'm quite sure you're more than capable of getting a degree. What stopped you?"

"That's really kind of you to say so, but—"

"I'm not being kind," he said sharply. "It's a fact." He sighed. "Sorry. Just that, you always do that—put yourself down. You should have more faith in yourself, as I have faith in you."

I trembled, not knowing how to respond to that, and unsure what to make of it.

"Tell me," he urged. "What happened to stop you from going to university?"

"Long and boring story," I assured him.

His eyes pierced into me. "Indulge me."

I looked away, unable to face that level of scrutiny any longer. "Okay. Well, at school, I was a bookworm who wanted to learn. I wasn't an academic genius like my brother, Redmond, but I was keen to discover new things, and there was nothing I loved more than spending my lunch hour in the school library, head in a book."

"Nothing wrong with that," he said. "So far, so good."

"Huh, you think? Except, I quickly discovered that, at my high school, bookworms were not popular, and were actually targets for bullies. I figured out that, unless I wanted to spend my days hiding in a toilet cubicle to escape the name-calling, or worse, I had to put aside the books and become the entertainment."

"Ah." He shook his head slightly. "Not good. So, that's what you did?"

"Yep. I turned myself into the class clown, and by making people laugh, I soon got the gangs on my side. I was no threat to them, which helped."

"Threat? In what way?" He sounded puzzled, and I hesitated, not sure I should expand on the subject.

"Just that, there was no way someone so small and insignificant, who wore no makeup and didn't bother with fashion, could compete for the boys." I blushed as his eyes widened. "I wasn't glamorous, like my sister, Tamsin, so I didn't see any point in trying. I survived high school," I said, hurrying on, "but it cost me. My chances of passing exams slipped farther away with every day, and I left school with a handful of very mediocre GCSEs."

"But you could have done more."

"A lot more."

"If you'd only been true to yourself."

He was perceptive, I'd give him that, and I nodded, feeling choked. "Redmond went to an all-boys school and didn't have that problem. He absolutely shone, and he flew through university, too. He's terribly clever. He lectures at a university now. Mum and Dad are so proud of him."

"And your sister? What does she do?"

What did Tamsin do? A few weeks ago, I'd have said Zumba, shopping, Pilates, flower arranging, and updating Facebook. If I was being honest then, though, I suspected I'd have to say, *panics a lot and cries more than she lets on*. The thought was depressing. "She's a mum," I said. "And before that, she excelled at college, worked abroad with a holiday company for a while, moved back home, got a job in an office and married the boss. Now she looks after my two nieces, and she's brilliant at that, too." I couldn't bring myself to mention Brad's betrayal. It felt disloyal to Tamsin, and my sister had had enough disloyalty shown to her lately. "So, you see," I finished, "my siblings have done really well. I'm definitely the last in the queue when they handed out brains in this family."

"You sell yourself short," he insisted. "We all have different gifts. You're wonderful with children, and you're

299

good with adults, too. You make people feel valued, wanted, cared for. You're a nurturing person, and there's absolutely nothing wrong with that."

"You don't exactly get paid a lot for nurturing people," I pointed out.

He tutted in disgust. "Money has nothing to do with anything," he said fervently.

Easy for you to say, mate, I thought, *you've got pots of the stuff.*

He gazed deep into my eyes. "I know what you're thinking."

Crikey, I hope not!

"You're thinking, easy for me to say money has nothing to do with anything. What would I know about it, given my financial status?"

Well, er, close enough. Oh, dear.

"You're quite right, of course. What would I know about needing money? But it doesn't stop me from knowing what makes a person happy. And, as someone who has always had plenty of money, I can tell you, it doesn't automatically equate to a sense of fulfilment."

He sounded so sad, my heart just melted. "You should ease off the business side of things. Why don't you delegate more? Let's face it, you're a fine one to talk. There you are, stuck running that business, when anyone can see you have a real talent for painting. You should do more of that. I told you, let someone else do the work sometimes. Your gift deserves to be nurtured."

"You're very kind," he said, smiling ruefully. "I'm just an amateur. Average, at best."

"Now who doesn't know their own worth?" I said, nudging him. "You have an amazing flair for painting, and you should be glad of it. Enjoy it. I mean, how much money do you need? You can't spend the rest of your life chasing the next deal."

"It's not about that," he said, staring at the ground. "My father made me promise that I wouldn't let the business fail, and it's not so easy in this day and age. We have to constantly watch the market, keep one step ahead of the game. Particularly now, when so many people shop online. Do you have any idea how many well-established stores have folded in the last few years? It's a cutthroat world out there."

"I can appreciate that." I thought sadly of our local branch of Woolworth's. How I'd missed that shop when it closed down. No more Saturday afternoons browsing the bookshelves, queueing at the record department, and mooching around the pic 'n' mix. Sad times. I wouldn't want Rochester's to disappear from the high street, even if I'd never set foot in one of their stores. I knew Tamsin shopped there and thought very highly of it. Besides, it was the principle of the thing. "But you must have other people around you who could take some of the burden from your shoulders, surely?"

He nodded. "Of course, but I feel I owe it to my father ..."

"You owe it to your father to do your best for the business *and* for yourself," I said. "If you're exhausted and stressed, you won't be able to think clearly. Therefore, it makes perfect sense to find a better work-life balance and spend more time doing the things you love, with the people you love. I'm sure your father would want you to be happy. Besides, didn't you say you were going to make big changes? You said you needed new blood. You need to go for it, if you ask me."

He lifted his head and watched me thoughtfully. "You're absolutely right," he admitted at last. "I need to put the shadow of my father behind me and make my own decisions. Time to surround myself with people who think the same as I do. I've known it for ages, really. There are some really excellent people I'd love to work with, and they'd definitely be able to share the burden." He sighed. "I suppose I never had much reason to stay at home before. I couldn't justify it to myself, but maybe now I can. There are people here who need me, and people I want to be with, spend time with. Perhaps it's time to rethink things."

"Adele would be happy about that," I told him, smiling.

"And what about you?" His voice was so quiet, I barely heard him.

"Sorry?"

"I said, what about you?" As his hand reached out and took mine, I thought I was going to slide off the swing and land on the ground with an embarrassing thump.

"Wh—what about me?"

"Would *you* be happy about that?"

I cleared my throat, trying at the same time to clear my mind of all the ridiculous thoughts racing through it— thoughts too far-fetched to possibly have any truth in them. "Happy about what? You mean, about you spending time with Adele?" *Of course that's what he meant. Idiot!* "Yes, that would be good for her, too, so obviously I'd be happy about that."

He stared down at my hand, softly squeezing my fingers. "But I didn't mean that. I meant, would you be

302

glad if I spent more time with the people who mattered to me? People like you, Cara."

Was he winding me up? My heart thudded so loudly, it had to be audible to him. "I'm just the nanny," I said feebly.

Standing up, he turned to face me and held the swing ropes in his hands, his expression becoming deadly serious. "You're not just the nanny to me," he said. "Don't you understand what I'm saying? Don't you realise how I feel?"

I giggled nervously. "Is Ken growing something dodgy in this garden? I think you're hallucinating."

I gasped when he pulled me to my feet and held me close. If I'd had trouble breathing before, I was positively suffocating then. I lifted my head to meet his gaze, and the shock hit me like a slap across the face. He studied me as if I was the most precious thing in the world, and I'd never been more terrified. I wanted to believe him. I wanted to forget all the things I'd learned over the last few months. I didn't have a clue what to say, how to react. How could I let myself fall for Mr Rochester, when I'd only just escaped the clutches of Heathcliff?

Except—except Mr Rochester wasn't like Heathcliff, was he? Heathcliff was a jealous, vicious, vindictive monster. Hadn't I realised, years ago, that *Wuthering Heights* wasn't a story of love, at all, but of revenge and obsession? And Ethan wasn't like Seth. Seth was a lazy, selfish, pretentious pothead. Why hadn't I faced up to the fact that Seth and I were not, and never had been, Cathy and Heathcliff? But what was I thinking? Ethan and I weren't Jane Eyre and Mr Rochester, either. This was real life, not fiction. I'd had enough of make-believe romances, hadn't I?

I wriggled free of his grasp and backed away, narrowly avoiding the swing and trying not to panic and run.

"What is it?" His voice matched his eyes—full of anxiety. "I'm sorry. I've behaved inappropriately, I know. I'm your employer, and this is completely unacceptable. Forgive me, Cara?"

"Look," I said desperately, "can we just forget this? Can you stop doing this, please?"

"Doing what?"

"Doing this weird act! You're saying things that make no sense to me. I'm just the nanny. You're a multi-millionaire businessman, with super-loaded friends, a lifestyle I can't even begin to imagine, not to mention a wife somewhere in the world—oh, God!" The wife! I'd almost forgotten about her. What was I doing, sitting on a swing, allowing myself to be sweet-talked by a married man? I was shameless. Though, not as shameless as he was.

He held out his hand, and when I took another step backwards, he threw up his hands in defeat. "Okay, okay. I won't touch you, I promise. But look, whatever I do for a living, whatever you do for a living, what does it matter? I'm just Ethan, and you're just Cara. We're two people who met and got on. We do get on, don't we?"

"Well, yes," I admitted. "But lots of people get on. I get on with Michael and Ken. I hardly want to start a romantic relationship with them, do I?"

"But it's more than that with us." He frowned. "Don't you feel it, too? Okay, look, tell me you don't know what the hell I'm talking about, and I'll leave you to it. I'll never bother you again. But you have to look me in the eye and tell me you don't feel something between us—some spark, some connection. I don't believe it. You and I—there's a bond. I felt it from the moment I almost ran you over on the moors road and we had that fiery exchange of words.

"I can't believe I'm saying this to you, and believe me, I know how corny it sounds, but I can't think of a better way to explain. An old Chinese proverb says that an invisible red thread connects those who are destined to meet, regardless of time, place or circumstance. It says the thread may stretch, or tangle, but it will never break. That's what I felt pulling me towards you. You and I, we're connected with that red thread. I know it. I've never felt this way before. When I kissed you yesterday, I knew—I knew for sure. And, yes, it scares me, too, Cara. It scares the life out of me. That's why I walked away. I'm sorry I did that, I really am, but it hit me harder than I hit that dratted machine this afternoon, and I just can't ignore it any longer."

"And did you say all this to your wife?" I demanded, sounding far harsher than I meant to. It was a struggle not to launch myself into his arms, but where would that get me? He was a married man, and besides, I'd heard all the same sort of stuff from Seth once. Many years ago. All that, *can't live without you*, stuff. *The bond*. The *I've never felt this way before* speech. Then he'd used it on Gina, and probably Isolde too, come to that. I wouldn't fall for all that again, just to be cast aside when the boredom set in, which it would, all too quickly. How could a man like Ethan Rochester be content with someone as ordinary as me, for heaven's sake? I may not have had a degree, but I wasn't stupid. Once bitten, twice shy, and all that.

He looked utterly wretched. "No. I can honestly say I never said all that to my wife," he said. "It's not what you think. This thing with Antonia ..."

"Your marriage?" I said pointedly.

"It's not a marriage. Not really. It's ... complicated."

"Of course it is." Wasn't it always?

"Trust me, please," he said, taking my hands in his and holding them against his chest. I remembered what that chest had looked like without his shirt and gulped. "I'm sorting this all out, once and for all. Things are in hand. Please, just be patient."

"I don't know what you're talking about," I said, growing ever more confused. "You're my boss, for goodness sake, and you're standing here, holding my hands, telling me all these things that I can't fathom, because why would someone like you ever look at someone like me? And I really don't understand what you—"

My sentence got cut off halfway through, as he pressed his mouth to mine and kissed me, pulling me closer to him and holding the back of my head so I couldn't have moved away if I'd wanted to. No, really, I couldn't. Well, not without a bit of effort, anyway and, to be honest, I wasn't exactly trying very hard. I felt as if all the blood in my body was pooling away to my feet. I had no energy, no strength to protest. And then, it was as if a fire was lit within me. All those cold ashes that had sat inside me, all dampened down and redundant, without so much as a smoulder for years, suddenly ignited again. Oh, they were doing more than smoulder, all right. I was aflame. The blood in my feet heated up like molten lava and coursed through my veins, heating my whole body as

306

I shamelessly returned his kiss with a passion that was, to be frank, quite disgraceful.

"Cara," he murmured, his lips brushing my cheek as he held me to him. I swore I could feel his heart pounding in his chest. He kissed me again, gently that time, and I melded against him, not wanting to fight it any longer. I'd thought yesterday's kiss amazing, but this—this was life-changing. I just wanted the moment to go on forever.

Of course, it couldn't. Regretfully, we moved apart, and he smiled uncertainly at me, his eyes betraying a sudden anxiety. "I'm sorry. I do know that this is inappropriate, of course I do. I don't make a habit of kissing members of staff, I assure you."

"That's not what Michael says," I said, teasing. I just wanted to lighten the mood, but his eyes darkened.

"He told you about Jodie?"

"Jodie?" I felt nauseous. "What about her?"

"Oh, God. You were joking. Of course you were." He stepped back, rubbing his forehead with his hand.

"Hang on," I said, my voice cold and steady, even though inside I was a churning mass of nerves. "Are you saying you had an affair with Adele's previous nanny?"

"What?" He looked at me as if I was mad. "Of course I didn't! But there was an incident ..."

"Is this the reason she was fired?" A tremble started within me. I wasn't sure I wanted to hear what he was about to tell me, but at the same time, a part of me was calmly telling myself that I needed to know. I vaguely remembered Briony hinting about some incident with the London nanny. Why hadn't I dug deeper? I'd got far too carried away. Hormones, I thought bleakly. You could always count on your hormones to overrule your common sense.

He took my hand again, staring down at it and squeezing it gently. "I swear to you, nothing happened. She, er, acted in a manner that wasn't invited, or welcome."

"Meaning?"

He took a deep breath. "Meaning, I got home late one night, went up to my room, switched on the light, and found her lying stark naked in my bed."

I gaped at him. "You're joking!"

"I'm so not." He bit his lip. "I really wish I was. That's why Mrs Fairweather had to come to London to take care of Adele, and why, rather than employ anyone else down there, we sent Adele to Yorkshire. With my mother in New York, it made more sense, because, to be honest, I didn't want to hire another nanny. I was hoping Mrs Fairweather would take care of her, but, of course, it was too much for her."

"Never mind all that." I gasped. "You found Jodie naked in your bed! What did you do?" Well, what would any red-blooded man do when it was offered to him on a plate?

"I told her to get dressed, and then I left the room and spent the night in one of the guest rooms." He grinned suddenly. "With a chair wedged under the door handle."

I saw the twinkle in his eye, and then I was laughing. He was telling the truth. Don't ask me how I knew, but I just did.

His face lit up, and he wrapped his arms around me. "Oh, Cara, you're so wonderful. Thank you for believing me."

308

We smiled at each other, and without even saying anything, we both turned to head back toward the house. I know he talked on the way in, but I couldn't recall anything he said. I was too busy battling with my conscience as it shrieked warnings at me. What was I doing, letting him kiss me like that? What had I promised myself? He was a married man who'd already admitted to a close encounter with a naked nanny. How could I believe anything he said? Why was I being so gullible?

It felt like Seth all over again, and I'd sworn to myself I would never fall for another man after that relationship. I had to get away, clear my head, think things through. I needed to put space between us. But how?

A sudden prickling sensation made me lift my face and stare at the house, and I shivered.

"What is it?" Ethan asked, concerned.

I shrugged. "I don't know. Just—just a feeling. Like someone was watching me."

He put his arm around my shoulder. "What if they were? Does it matter?"

I thought he was being a bit presumptuous. I hadn't made any promises, had I? Far from it. "I think you're being a little indiscreet," I told him.

He removed his arm and nodded. "I suppose you're right. We'll keep quiet about all this until things are clarified."

What things? And keep quiet about what? There was nothing to tell. He was making massive assumptions and being remarkably irresponsible, in my view. I had to slow things down, somehow.

As we entered the hall, my mobile phone rang. Ethan raised an eyebrow when I frowned down at the screen.

"It's my mother," I told him.

He nodded and smiled. "I'll get a shower, while you talk. I'll see you later."

"Mum! Where are you?" I said, watching wistfully as Ethan ran up the stairs, taking two steps at a time. "Are you calling from Spain?"

"No, I'm not." She didn't sound happy about it, either. In fact, she sounded distinctly peed off, and I snapped to attention. "Your dad and I got back this afternoon, Cara, and we can't believe what's going on with this family. Honestly, we leave you alone for five minutes, and all hell breaks loose. As if you moving in with a stranger isn't bad enough, we've just found out that Brad's abandoned Tamsin and the girls. Can you believe that? Brad! And to cap it all, we've just heard from Redmond."

"Oh, thank God," I said. "He hasn't contacted us. Tamsin and I were worried sick. Is he okay?"

"You mean, apart from the fact that he's gone stark staring mad?" She sounded grim. "Absolutely fine. He's as bad as Brad. He's walked out on Susan, and he's just informed us that he has no intention of going back. In fact, to quote him, hell will freeze over first. What on earth has happened to you all? It's like we got off the plane to find we'd landed in a parallel universe."

"I know it must be a shock to you both," I said. "We didn't want to worry you while you were on holiday."

"Yes, well, we're back now, fighting fit and ready to sort this mess out. So, first thing tomorrow, we're calling a meeting. Tamsin and the girls are coming, and I've told Redmond he'd better be here, or he'll live to regret it. I want you here, too. I want to know about this man you're working for, and I want to know that you're all right. I *will*

310

know the truth, so don't think you can fob me off, my girl."

"Mum, I can't just drop everything and come home," I protested, but even as I said it, the thought formed that maybe it could be the answer to a prayer. I needed to calm down and put all the passion I felt for Ethan behind me. I would be making a huge mistake if I went down that path again. Maybe, by going to Mum and Dad's, I'd get the space I desperately needed to see things more clearly, and strengthen my resolution to avoid romance in future. "Look, I'll do my best," I said.

"Make sure you do, because I shall expect you tomorrow. I'll call Tamsin and ask her to pick you up from York station and bring you here. She won't mind, I'm sure. Just let her know the train times, okay?"

"Okay." I wasn't going to argue with her anymore, because I'd made up my mind that, whatever Ethan said, I had to go. It might be the last chance I had to bring me to my senses, and I couldn't let that chance pass me by.

Chapter Twenty-Three

"Honestly, you'd think we were six years old, being summoned to the family home like this," Tamsin said, indignantly. In the backseat of her Juke, Robyn and Alice tutted and nudged each other, looking sulky and petulant.

I handed them both a bag of sweets, bought from the train station, and they took them hesitantly. Opening the bags, they peered suspiciously at the contents, as if I'd handed them a pistol and a round of ammunition.

"Is it okay, Mummy?" Robyn sounded doubtful.

Tamsin glanced at the rear-view mirror and frowned. "Oh, what the hell. Just this once," she said, causing her daughters to whoop with delight and pounce on the sweets like they were Fagin's orphans, normally fed on mouldy sausages.

"I think we're in for a bumpy ride," I said. "And I don't mean the road to Beverley. Mum sounded distraught. First, I leave Seth, then Brad—" I lowered my voice and murmured, "Brad leaves you, and now Redmond's gone all weird. He must be having a mid-life crisis, or something."

"Come to his senses, more like," Tamsin said. "You should see the comments Susan's put on Facebook. She's absolutely scathing about him, and of course, all her friends and cronies are crooning about what a little shit he is, and how she deserves so much better. Rubbish. She's brought it all on herself." She looked stricken. "Oh, God! Do you think that's what people are saying about me?"

"Of course not," I reassured her. "Besides, you never put anything bad about Brad on Facebook. You've never even mentioned the break-up."

She shuddered. "I don't want anything negative getting back to the girls. Not that I haven't thought it. If Susan thinks Redmond's a shit, she should think about what Brad's put me through." She eyed the girls in the mirror again, obviously checking that they hadn't heard anything they shouldn't, before she asked, "Did you have any trouble getting time off at such short notice?"

I shook my head. "No. Ethan was very understanding."

He had been, too—eventually. When I'd knocked on his bedroom door later the previous evening, he must've thought all his Christmases had come at once, judging by the light of surprise and delight in his eyes. That'd quickly dampened down, when I explained I'd come to ask if I could take a few days' holiday.

"You don't have to pay me," I'd added hastily. "I do realise I'm leaving you in the lurch a little, but I wouldn't ask if I didn't think it necessary."

He'd put his hands on my shoulders, fixing me with a serious gaze. "Cara, is this about what happened this afternoon? I thought—I mean, I believed that you—I didn't take advantage of you?"

In spite of my resolve, I felt myself weakening as I looked into his eyes and saw the concern there. "No," I heard myself say. "It's honestly because there are family problems at the moment, and Mum and Dad have asked us all to go home and spend a day, or two, with them, to

313

try to sort things out."

"And you didn't feel ... compromised?"

I laughed. "The way you speak! You're such a gentleman."

"I wasn't much of a gentleman this afternoon," he reminded me ruefully. "And I have to admit, I had distinctly ungentlemanly thoughts when you knocked on my bedroom door just now."

He held my gaze, and I saw the gleam in his eye and knew I could crumble so easily. How lovely would it be to just give in? To lose myself in his arms, pretend that things could work out, that if I would just surrender, there could be a real chance of a happy ending? Deep down, I knew that to give in to my highly inconvenient feelings would only bring heartbreak, and I had to force myself to remember that.

"I'd better go and pack," I mumbled, turning my head away from the disappointment in his face.

"You're leaving so soon?"

"Tomorrow morning."

"Let me drive you there. Or, if you'd prefer, I could ask Michael?"

"There's really no need," I said hastily. "My sister's picking me up from York train station. It's all arranged."

As I turned to leave, his voice came behind me, sounding rough as he asked, "How long will you be gone?"

"Oh, a day, or two," I said airily.

"I'll expect you back, then."

I glanced round, swallowing when I recognised the look in his eyes, his effort at trying to look business-like while failing dismally.

314

"A couple of days at the most," he said. "Adele will need you."

"I know," I said, even though I wasn't sure how long I'd be away. I just wanted to escape before I could throw caution to the wind and ruin my life forever. "Thank you for being so understanding. Goodnight, Ethan."

"Goodnight, Cara."

I hurried back to my room, but feeling a sudden prickling on the back of my neck again as I crossed the landing, I spun round. There was no one there, and Ethan's door remained shut. I stood still for a moment, taking deep breaths. I felt uneasy as goose-pimples broke out on my skin, and I rubbed my arms, wondering what had caused the sudden sensation of being watched, then I tutted. My imagination was running riot. I was overwrought, and no wonder, with everything that had happened lately.

Turning away, I entered my bedroom, determined to pack my things and get an early night.

Mrs F was the only person up and about when I left Moreland Hall the following morning, and she was shocked to see me leaving so early. "We thought it would be mid-morning. Ethan will want to know ..."

"My taxi's outside," I said quickly. "I can't keep it waiting. Catching the first train to York, Mrs F." I'd given her a brief hug, assured her I'd be back before she knew it, and asked her to give Adele a big kiss for me.

Her eyes were surprisingly bright as she said goodbye. "You will take care, won't you? Look after yourself. You know, I'm always at the other end of the phone, if you need to talk to anyone."

I hadn't a clue why she seemed so concerned. I was

only going home to my parents' house, for goodness sake, but I nodded reassuringly and promised I'd bear that in mind. I'd climbed thankfully into the taxi and challenged myself not to look round as it sped down the drive, putting Moreland Hall behind me in a matter of moments—at least, in the physical sense.

"Get you!" Tamsin's voice broke into my thoughts, and I blinked.

"Sorry? What?"

"Ethan! Whatever happened to calling him Mr Rochester?" She grinned. "Only kidding." Then her smile faded. "Hey, what are you looking at me like that for? Oh, my God!" Her eyes widened with excitement. "Cara Truelove! Are you shagging the boss?"

My face flamed, and I groped desperately for some answer that would appease her. To my relief, she burst out laughing, and I realised she was joking. Clearly, it didn't occur to Tamsin that Ethan Rochester would ever look twice at someone like me, and who could blame her?

#

As we got closer to Mum and Dad's house, I could sense the change in her mood. She was obviously gearing herself up for a fight.

"You don't have to worry," I whispered to her. "I'm sure everything will be fine."

"It's so unfair. Why am I even being summoned here? It's as if they think it's all my fault. I'll get the blame, you just wait and see. Brad was such a suck-up. Mum thought he was wonderful because he worked so hard and provided so well for us. As if that's all that matters!"

"No, but it helps." I thought about Seth. How was he getting on? Had he moved into Isolde's? Had he found himself a job? It seemed terribly unlikely, but if he wanted any financial help from the state, he would have to, at least, look for a position somewhere. Who would employ him, though? He didn't have the first clue how to do anything.

Not your problem, Cara, I reminded myself. I had enough to worry about.

We were soon negotiating the narrow roads of central Beverley, turning, with some trepidation, into Mum and Dad's street. Tamsin parked on the drive of our childhood home, just behind Dad's Volvo estate, which had to live outside permanently, as the garage was too full of the junk that had been accumulated over thirty-seven years of marriage.

Tamsin and I glanced at each other. She took a deep breath. "Here we go, then."

Mum ushered us into the spacious, nineteen-thirties semi-detached house. She looked tanned and healthy, her hair blonder—the streaks put in by the hairdresser lightened even further by the Mediterranean sun. Dad came forward to hug us, and as I pulled away from him, I studied him carefully.

"Oh, you look miles better," I said, relieved. The gaunt look had gone. He'd filled out again. The weeks in the sunshine had obviously done him the world of good.

He beamed at us. "I feel better," he said. "I think retirement is going to suit me, after all."

Mum had already put the kettle on, and she poured drinks of blackcurrant squash for Robyn and Alice, and fussed around them, and admired their clothes, and asked about school like a proper doting granny should.

"Is Redmond definitely coming?" Tamsin asked,

wincing as Dad handed her daughters a bag of crisps each. What with my bags of sweets and Mum's squash, she'd no doubt have them detoxing as soon as they got home.

"Oh, he'll come," Mum said. "Honestly, I can't believe what he's done." She waited, while Dad ushered the girls into the living room, assured them that they could watch whatever they liked on television, and handed them the remote to prove it, which was probably a bad idea. As he closed the door behind them, she continued, "Susan and I spoke on the phone yesterday. The poor woman's broken."

Tamsin snorted. "Broken! Don't let her fool you. You have no idea what Redmond's put up with. Oh! Talk of the devil."

We all turned at the back door opening, and Redmond sauntered in. No other word described it. He didn't quite swagger, but he certainly didn't walk in his usual manner. He had a look of rebellion on his face, a challenge in his eyes. He was obviously preparing for a fight, just like Tamsin. I sighed inwardly. It was going to be a tricky few days.

The kettle was refilled. Dad checked that the girls were engrossed in a film and had supplies of crisps and squash to keep them happy, then we all sat at the kitchen table and stared at each other.

"So," said Mum. "Who wants to start?"

My phone beeped. Everyone stared at me. Well, it couldn't be Seth, I knew that much.

"Well, go on, then," Dad said. "Read it, and then we can get on with this."

I pulled my phone from my bag and stared at the notification. Ethan!

Just texting you to say, hope you got to your parents' house safely, and that all goes well. Thinking of you. See you soon. Love Ethan xxx

My face flared and I swallowed. "Er, just someone at the house, checking I got here safely."

I typed a reply:

Got here safely. About to start war cabinet meeting. Fingers crossed. Cara.

Dad nodded. "Very kind of them, I'm sure. Well, while we're on the subject of that, we may as well start with you, Cara."

I was debating whether to add a kiss, and wondering if it would look too mean if I didn't, or give him the wrong idea if I did, but Dad's words startled me so much I just pressed send without thinking. Oh, well, that was that sorted, then.

"Me?" I squeaked. "What about me?"

"Who is this person you're living with? Is he reputable? Are you safe, under another man's roof?"

With everything that was going on in Tamsin's and Redmond's lives, I was astonished that the events in my life were even on the radar.

Redmond cleared his throat. "I assure you, Dad, I did plenty of checking up on your behalf, since you were away. Cara's working for Ethan Rochester, so I don't think we have anything to worry about."

Pompous git, I thought. Just trying to worm his way back into the parents' good books by making out he was taking care of me in their absence. Although, to be fair, I supposed he had. It evidently didn't wash with Dad.

"Who the hell's Ethan Rochester, when he's at home?"

Mum looked blank, too, and Tamsin and Redmond exchanged despairing glances.

"Rochester's Department Stores?" Tamsin sounded incredulous. "You must have heard of them! I think I took you there once, Mum, when you came to York for the weekend. Yes, I bought you that yellow Jenny Kingston handbag from there, remember?"

Mum frowned. "Oh, yes. Good grief, that was a dear do. I spent more in one day—hang on. You mean, Cara's boss owns that shop?"

Redmond nodded. "And eleven more like it," he confirmed. "Absolutely loaded."

"You're at Moreland Hall?" Dad whistled. "You know the place, Sally. That big pile over near Hasedale."

"Of course," she said, as light clearly dawned. "The Rochester place. I never clicked. Fancy our Cara living there."

"You know it?" I said, puzzled.

"Everyone from Newarth knows the Rochester place. I just never realised you were working for *those* Rochesters. Never made the connection, for some reason."

"Mind you," Dad said, "it's not surprising we didn't, really. House is nearly always empty, isn't it? The Rochesters rarely visited the area, back when I lived up there. Don't they usually stay somewhere in London?"

"He has a house in London," I began, but Redmond cut in, showing off.

"The house in Yorkshire belonged to his great grandfather, but they have others. Houses in London, Gloucestershire, and France, plus an apartment in New York."

"How do you know that?" I said, awed. Even I hadn't known about the French house.

"Honestly, Cara, have you never heard of Google?" he said, rolling his eyes.

"I don't give a monkey's how many houses or shops he owns," Dad said. "The point is, what sort of man is he? From what I remember, his father was a decent sort, but his mother's side was a different matter entirely. Jennifer Kingston—"

"Oh!" Tamsin yelped, then gave us an apologetic look. "Sorry, I just realised that their handbag range is named after her. I don't know how many Jenny Kingston bags I have. Fancy that!"

"Fancy," I murmured, while Dad shook his head.

"Her family were always in the papers," Dad continued. "She was a proper party girl before she got married, and her brother and father were notorious playboys. So, what I want to know is, does this Ethan Rochester take after his father's side, or his mother's? Are you safe under his roof? And how many other people are there with you?"

Was I safe under Ethan's roof? Well, there was a question. "If you're asking if he's a secret maniac with a basement full of torture implements, the answer's no," I said, carefully avoiding mention of the attic and remembering, with shame, my recent unhinged behaviour. "He's a decent man—the responsible sort. His mother's staying, at the moment, and she may have been a bit wild before she got married, but she settled down after the wedding, didn't she?" I crossed my fingers, hoping they wouldn't question Adele's parentage. I didn't think *that* little story would do Jennifer many favours. "Then there's

321

Mr Rochester's little sister, and Mrs F, who's the housekeeper, and Michael the chauffeur, and Ken the gardener ..." My voice trailed off as, out of the blue, I felt a pang of homesickness. It was as if I was talking about my other family, I realised. They'd all come to mean so much to me.

"Is the housekeeper pleasant to you?" Mum asked. "I've heard about these bossy women who think they can order young girls around. If she's giving you a hard time ..."

I laughed. "Giving me a hard time? She's lovely, Mum. She's always making sure I eat properly, and she keeps me close, so she can keep an eye on me and check I'm all right." She did, too, didn't she? In fact, sometimes, it was as if she couldn't bear to lose sight of me—as if she was afraid to leave me on my own. Or was it that she was afraid to be alone herself? But why?

Mum seemed mollified, at least. "Okay, well .... It's just, with everything you've put up with over the years from ... *him*, I don't want you to have any more hassle. You're sure you're okay? Things are working out for you?"

"Honestly, Mum. They are."

Dad smiled. "All right. It seems to be in order, which is a relief. You did the right thing," he said. "Leaving ... *him*, I mean. Life's too short to be so unhappy."

He put his arm around my mum, and they leaned together for a moment, almost as if they'd forgotten they had an audience.

Tamsin broke the silence. "Well, I'm glad you agree that life's too short," she said. "So, you'll understand why Redmond and I are now separated from Brad and Susan."

Mum gave her a flinty stare. "Hardly. I don't

understand any of that. Especially you, Redmond," she added, glaring at her little prince. "What are you playing at? You had everything going for you. Good job, wonderful wife, nice home. Why would you throw all that away? Is it the male menopause? I was reading an article about that the other day. It does happen, you know."

Redmond folded his arms and leaned back in his chair. "I've woken up," he said, beaming at us all. "Or rather, I was awakened."

Mum and Dad looked irritated, but light was beginning to dawn. "You've met someone else!" I gasped. Redmond, of all people! Dad raised an eyebrow, but Mum looked appalled.

"Oh, no! Please, Redmond, not that. Tell me you haven't become a love rat," she pleaded.

"You must stop reading those trashy tabloids," Tamsin advised her, before turning to our brother, her eyes wide. "Have you? Got another woman, I mean?"

Redmond didn't even look ashamed. "I have, and she's absolutely wonderful."

"Ooh," Tamsin said. "What's her name? What's she like?"

"You'll be able to see for yourself in half an hour." Redmond glanced at his watch. "I've invited her here to meet you all."

Mum looked horrified. "But you can't! You can't! Ring her up. Tell her she can't come!"

"Certainly not. Look, Mum, I appreciate that you don't want a divorce in the family, but the fact is, I love her, and I want you to love her, too, and I'm sure you will, once you meet her. If you'd just give her a chance—"

Dad shook his head. "It's not that, Redmond," he told

him, his voice serious. "Just that, well, your mum was only trying to do what's best for you, that's all."

"What do you mean?" Redmond gripped his mug of cold tea. "What have you done?"

"It's Susan," Mum whispered. "She's on her way here. I'm so sorry."

Chapter Twenty-Four

It was like waiting for someone to die. The silence was deafening as we all sat nervously at the table, glancing at a watch every so often, in Redmond's and Dad's case. Or the display on her mobile phone, in Tamsin's, or the clock on the cooker, in Mum's. And, in my own case, at the big, red clock on the wall, which was shaped like an apple with a bite out of it. I'd never liked that clock. It made me uncomfortable. I kept expecting the bitten part to turn brown, which, of course, it never did. Funny how, considering my dislike of the thing, I kept staring at it, almost daring it to go rotten. Tick, tick, tick. I wondered what Ethan was doing. I thought about the text and felt all warm inside.

"Well, this is another fine mess you've gotten me into," Dad joked. He was a huge Laurel and Hardy fan.

Mum tutted. "A pretty pickle, I must say."

"And whose fault's that?" demanded Redmond. "You had no right to invite Susan here. I can't believe you went behind my back like that."

Dad gave him a stern look. "Your mother was only trying to help. She thought bringing the two of you together here would make you sort things out. How was she to know you'd been playing away with some floosy?"

"Kitty is not a floosy!" Redmond said angrily.

"Kitty? Sounds like a real pussy cat." Tamsin giggled.

"Not surprising she got her claws into you."

"Stop being a bitch," Redmond snapped. "No wonder your husband left you."

Tamsin's face turned an alarming shade of purple. "How dare you? My husband left me because, like you, he couldn't keep it in his trousers. You're all the same. Lecherous, deceitful, lying ratbags."

"Maybe Brad couldn't cope with your pathetic lifestyle any longer." Redmond picked up her mobile, waving it in the air. "Ooh, Zumba today! Thrilling!" he trilled. "Off to yoga! Happy days!" He slammed the phone down and tutted in disgust. "You must be the most boring person in the world to live with. You're like a Barbie doll. There's nothing real to want to come home to. You're not a proper woman, and neither was Susan."

"Stop being so bloody horrible," I snapped, putting my arm around Tamsin, who looked like she'd been slapped across the face.

"That's enough, Redmond!" Dad glared at him, his expression thunderous. "Don't punish your sister because you're feeling guilty about abandoning your wife."

"I'm not feeling guilty," protested Redmond.

"Well, you damn well should be. Whoever this woman is who's made you cast Susan aside, I don't think she's someone we'd welcome into the house."

"You don't even like Susan!"

"Who says we don't like Susan?" Mum demanded. "I'm quite sure I've never said any such thing."

"I have," Tamsin admitted. She turned to Redmond, her face still shocked. "I said it loads because I was defending you. I know what she's like. I can't believe you turned on me like that."

326

He finally looked ashamed. "I'm sorry." He hung his head. "I just can't stand hearing anyone mock Kitty, especially when they've never even met her. If you'd just give her a chance, you'd see how wonderful she is. Really you would."

"Do you think," Tamsin said faintly, "that Brad feels as strongly about his bit on the side?"

I squeezed her hand, as Mum said, "Brad has a bit on the side? Oh, my God. It gets worse."

"Tell me you haven't invited him here, too," Tamsin pleaded.

Dad sighed. "She tried. Couldn't get hold of him. Probably ignored her calls. Just as well, by the look of it. Things are fraught enough 'round here, without adding more fuel to the flames."

"What happened between you and Brad, love?" Sounding a bit gentler, Mum laid her hand on Tamsin's arm. "You always seemed so happy, so in love. What went wrong?"

I felt a lump in my throat when Tamsin's eyes filled with tears, and she whimpered, "I don't know, Mum. I thought he loved me, but then he just—he just—" She crumbled completely, dissolving into noisy sobs, and Mum put her arm around her while Dad looked stricken.

Redmond's expression was one of guilt. As if noticing me watching him, he said, "It's not like that with me and Susan, honestly. I don't know what Brad's playing at. He always seemed to think the world of Tamsin, so I don't understand why he'd do what he's done, but with Susan ..." His voice trailed off, and he looked at us all, as if pleading for our blessing. "It was never right. It was always so difficult to please her, in every bloody way. And

Kitty's so different, so straightforward, so kind."

I understood. Kindness was very underrated, if you asked me, whereas passion—well, it might be fleetingly glorious, but it didn't guarantee happiness, did it? Of course, if you found someone who was kind *and* ignited a passion in you, you should ... *Should what, Cara? Never let go?*

I blinked and turned back to Redmond, smiling as he patted Tamsin awkwardly on the shoulder. He jumped at a knock on the door, and we all stared at each other in horror. Which of Redmond's women was going to turn up first?

Dad hurried into the hall, and we heard muffled voices, then he returned, trailing behind him a rather shy-looking young woman, with auburn curls and creamy skin, and a dusting of freckles across her nose.

She looked from one to the other of us, and her pale skin turned pink, then her gaze fell upon Redmond and she absolutely lit up like a Christmas tree. I glanced at Redmond and saw the same light in his eyes. He couldn't wipe the smile from his face.

My throat felt tight. I'd never seen my brother look at Susan like that. Not even on their wedding day, come to think of it. Without warning, the memory of Ethan's expression, as he told me how much I meant to him, overwhelmed me. I had a sudden longing for him, and I felt panicked as I wondered if I was strong enough to walk away from someone who provoked such an intense reaction in me.

"Kitty, sweetheart," Redmond said, stepping towards her and draping his arm over her shoulder as if he was claiming possession. "This is my mother, and that's Dad, and this is Tamsin and Cara. Everyone, meet Kitty."

We all nodded and murmured awkward greetings, then Dad said in a rather jovial voice, "Well, this is nice. Take a seat, Kitty, and I'll put the kettle on. Here, give me your coat."

Kitty glanced at Redmond, who nodded. Slowly, she unbuttoned her coat and handed it to Dad. We all stood there, gaping at her. She wore a bottle green dress, in a clinging jersey fabric, and there was no hiding the swelling around her middle. As she saw our incredulous stares, her face turned pink again and she hung her head, but Redmond, unbelievably, beamed at us all and said, "Surprise!"

Mum practically fell into her chair.

"You're not bloody wrong there," Tamsin said.

"Well," said Dad, "are there any more shocks you plan to spring on us today?"

Kitty looked mortified. "I thought you were going to tell them," she murmured to my brother. She had a soft, Scottish accent that was rather pleasant to the ear.

"I might have done, if they'd given me the chance," he said. "Unfortunately, they were too busy springing surprises of their own. And, darling, I should warn you—"

His voice trailed off at another, louder bang on the door.

Kitty raised an eyebrow. "What is it? You look as if you've seen a ghost."

"If she gets her hands on me, I might well *be* the sodding ghost," Redmond told her. "I'm sorry, sweetheart, but Mum invited Susan."

Kitty made a weird strangled sort of noise, while Mum

329

shook her head dazedly.

"Sit down, Kitty," I said, feeling sorry for her. "And congratulations. To you, too, Redmond," I added, smiling at him. "I know how much you've wanted a baby. It's wonderful news."

"Thank you, Cara," he said, while Kitty shot me a look of unmistakable gratitude.

"This is going to be fun." Tamsin mopped the tears from her face and sat up straight.

Dad rushed off to open the door to Susan, and we waited, eyeing each other nervously. My stomach was in knots, so goodness knows how Kitty and Redmond felt.

I sort of expected Susan to storm into the kitchen in a whirlwind of rage and righteous indignation, but she seemed to have decided to play the wounded wife card, and almost crept in behind Dad, looking suitably hunched and pathetic. She soon straightened up and found her old spark when she clapped eyes on Kitty, though.

"You!" She practically spat the word out, as Kitty stared up at her with a mixture of guilt, shame, and fear.

"Do you two know each other?" Mum eyed her warily, as Susan plopped herself down into the chair beside her, her eyes never leaving her rival's face.

"Of course," Susan snapped, no longer looking in the least bit pathetic. "She works in the newsagents at the bottom of our road. Oh, it all makes sense now. I couldn't fathom your sudden passion for Curly Wurlys. Now I understand, you cheating rat-bag!"

"Looks like she's got you by the Curly Wurlys, Redmond." Tamsin giggled.

Redmond glared at her, then turned his gaze upon his estranged wife. "It really is pointless you coming here,

Susan. I do appreciate that I should have confessed our relationship to you before I left, but then again, you weren't particularly in the mood to listen. I seem to recall you were too busy hurling my CD collection at me, at the time."

"It's hardly a loss to the music world," she snapped. "Bloody middle of the road rubbish! You never did have any taste, and now you've proved it. What the hell are you doing, walking out on me for ... *that*!"

Kitty's lip trembled, and Redmond immediately sat beside her and put his arm around her. "I love her. I'm sorry, Susan, but that's how it is. I intend to marry her as soon as I'm able."

Susan laughed. "Don't be ridiculous. You've had your fun, but now it's time to come home and start rebuilding our reputation. I'm a laughing stock, but I daresay people are mocking you even more. I don't know how you're going to show your face at work once this gets out."

"I'm not coming home, Susan," Redmond said firmly. "It's over. I want a divorce."

Susan's overplucked brows struggled to meet. "You're not serious? Look, you're obviously having some sort of breakdown. It's probably overwork. You have been putting in long hours at the university lately .... Oh, stupid me. Of course. You were shagging the Highland cow in the stock room, no doubt. Rolling around amid the toffee bon bons and the jelly babies. Terribly unhygienic."

Redmond cleared his throat, and Kitty's hand tightened on his arm. "Funny you should mention babies, Susan."

"You're kidding me. Tell me you're joking." Susan's eyes darted toward Kitty's stomach, and then her hand flew to her mouth. "Oh, my God. She's pregnant."

"She is." Redmond's voice was full of pride.

Susan seemed to gather herself together. The shock vanished from her eyes and her lip curled. "So, the Highland cow is in calf," she sneered. "Well, you've really gone and done it now, haven't you?"

I watched her curiously. There were no tears, no sign of despair, or heartbreak, at all. Whatever her motives for wanting Redmond, I seriously doubted love was one of them. My heart went out to Kitty and Redmond. I was glad for them. Glad they'd found each other. Susan wasn't right for my brother, but I had a strong feeling that Kitty was.

Susan tossed back her long, straight, dark hair and looked around at us all. "And you all approve of this, I suppose?"

Mum looked shell-shocked. "Well, I, er ..."

Dad put his hand on her shoulder. "We didn't approve of him walking out on you, Susan, no. Then again, having seen the way you two are together, and the way Redmond is with Kitty, I can clearly see that he's happier out of the marriage, and I would think you'd feel the same. Be honest, love, it hasn't exactly been moonlight and roses for a while, has it?"

I was astonished. It wasn't like my dad to be so brutally honest—and, believe me, that was brutally honest for him.

"Seems to me, all you two had in common was a desire to own a posh house and work all the hours God sends at those fancy jobs of yours," he continued. "It obviously wasn't enough to sustain a happy marriage. Maybe it's all worked out for the best."

332

Susan looked ready to explode. "So, that's the way the land lies, is it? You're on his side. I might have guessed." She tapped her fingers on the table and seemed to be considering for a moment, then in a much calmer voice, she said. "Well, if that's the way you want it, I'm happy to divorce you on the grounds of your adultery."

"Thanks," Redmond muttered.

"Of course, that will damage your reputation," she added.

He shrugged, pulling Kitty tighter to him. "I don't care."

"How sweet." She turned a fake smile on her love rival. "Just so we're clear, you won't benefit from this relationship, at all, in case that's what you're hoping."

"I'm sorry?" Kitty looked baffled.

Susan leaned back in her chair, worryingly relaxed. "I shall drag you through the courts for every last penny. I want the house. I want you to sign it over to me, and I'll fight tooth and nail to make sure I get it. I shall hire the best solicitor in town to take everything from you. And by the time I've finished telling everyone at the university what a rat you really are, your life won't be worth living. I know what that place is like. I know how reputations count. I should imagine they'll not take long to start nudging you out, and then what will you do? You'll be bankrupt, by the time I've finished with you. I shall make damn sure that neither you, nor your brat, make a penny out of this relationship."

Kitty and Redmond stared at each other, and I waited with bated breath to see what they would do. Mum looked ready to strangle Susan. I suspected her opinion of her had just been radically altered. Finally, she might see her daughter-in-law for what she truly was. But what about my brother? How would he raise a child like that?

"That's fine," he said quietly. "You can have the house in exchange for a quick divorce. I won't contest it, of course. Send the paperwork here for now, if that's okay with you, Mum?" When she nodded in bewildered agreement, he finished, "As for the university, do your worst. It really doesn't matter to me. I've already resigned."

I didn't know who was the most surprised of all of us. He'd resigned? And she could have the house? Was he mad?

"Oh, Redmond," Mum said, "you really are having a midlife crisis."

"There's more to life than money, Mum," Redmond told her. "And I hate that house, anyway. I always have. I just want a quiet life, to be with Kitty and raise our child together."

"Think carefully about this, son," Dad advised. "It's a massive decision. You're entitled to half of that house, after all."

"You've chucked your job?" Tamsin gasped. "With a baby on the way? Are you crazy?"

I had a feeling that Redmond knew exactly what he was doing, though, judging by the way he and Kitty gazed at each other and smiled.

Susan grabbed her handbag from the floor and stood up, glaring at him. "Fine. You want to throw your life down the toilet for this little tart, go ahead and do it. I shall visit my solicitor in the morning, and I'll make certain that you sign the house over to me. Good luck," she added, her eyes flashing sparks of venom at Kitty, and clearly not meaning what she said, at all. "You're going to have to sell an awful lot of Curly Wurlys to fund *that* little project." With one final distasteful glare toward Kitty's baby bump, she marched out of the house, slamming the front door behind her.

We all looked at Redmond and Kitty, who seemed remarkably unfazed.

"Okay, son," Dad said, "What have you got planned?"

"Tell me you're not going to become a drop-out," pleaded Mum. "I can see it now. You're going to join a commune, aren't you? You've gone all peace and love on us. It won't last, you know, and then you'll regret leaving the rat race and giving away your house. Oh!" She wailed in anguish. "That beautiful house. It was like something out of a magazine. How could you let her have it all to herself?"

Kitty gave her hand a reassuring pat. "Please dinnae fash yerself, Mrs Truelove. Wait 'til you see our new house. Oh, it's so beautiful, isn't it, Redmond?"

"You've found somewhere else?" Mum sounded hopeful.

Tamsin frowned. "How could you afford it? Unless you're renting. And what are you doing about your job?"

"Yes, come on," I said. "What have you got planned?"

Redmond beamed. "Kitty and I are moving back to her parents' home. They have a load of holiday lets, and they're giving us one at a very reasonable rent. They weren't going to charge us, but I insisted. It's a basic little cottage, but we can do it up, make it homely, and the views are outstanding. It's a real retreat. The perfect place to raise a child."

"I canna wait," Kitty said, coming to life before our

335

eyes, as her own eyes shone with excitement. "I've wanted to go home for ages, and now we are. Mum and Dad said I can help out with the letting business until the baby comes, then maybe go part-time afterwards."

"That's all very well," Mum said, "but what about Redmond? Surely, you're not going to clean holiday lets for a living? You're a genius! It's a criminal waste."

"Don't be daft," Redmond said. "I've already secured a job as an academic writer. I can work from home, and I'll earn good money. I can pick and choose the projects I want to work on, and the hours are completely flexible. It will be perfect for when the baby comes. I can help take care of it. I really want to be involved. Plus, I can get on with research for my next book. The peace and quiet of the location will make things so much easier."

"And we have a good broadband connection now," Kitty added, "so it won't be a problem."

We all looked at each other. "Er, where exactly is this holiday cottage?" Dad said. "Only, you're making it sound as remote as the Outer Hebrides, or somewhere."

Kitty cleared her throat, and her hands cupped her bump protectively. Redmond's face was flushed. "Er, funny you should say that, Dad. Have you heard of the Isle of Lewis, by any chance?"

Chapter Twenty-Five

Tamsin was in floods of tears again. I sat beside her on the bed, having heard her sobbing her heart out from across the landing. I felt completely helpless, and there was a growing anger inside me towards Brad. What the hell was he playing at, leaving her like that? And what about those two little girls?

Alice and Robyn had been taken to the park by Dad. "I could use some fresh air," he'd announced. "So, how about you two come with me to the park, and we can all have a go on that fabulous slide?"

"Can we feed the ducks, Grandad?" Robyn asked, and Dad had assured her they could. I'd also heard him promise, in a whisper, that he would buy them both the most enormous ice cream, complete with a big, fat, chocolate flake and sprinkles. They could hardly wait to leave the house.

Mum was still in shock over Redmond's departure. He and Kitty had driven off the previous evening, looking blissfully happy and seemingly desperate to get to Scotland and start living their brand-new life together. Mum was in despair, as if he was emigrating to Australia, or something.

"It's only the Western Isles, love," Dad put his arm around her on the doorstep, as we'd all waved the two of them off on their new adventure. "We can visit. Sounds like there's plenty of accommodation for us to choose from."

"But he had such a wonderful life," she said tearfully. "He had a stable marriage, a beautiful house, a great job. Now look at him."

"He'll have an even better life with Kitty," I assured her. "He'll finally be with someone who loves him, they'll have the baby he's longed for, and they'll be living on a beautiful Scottish island with Kitty's family to support them, and money coming in regularly from his new job. I don't know why you're so worried."

"It's a Scottish island," she said, eyes wide. "What if he turns to whisky and starts wearing a kilt?"

Tamsin had nodded. "You know, I'll bet that's exactly what will happen," she confirmed. "Bet he grows a really long beard, too, and keeps his Curly Wurlys in his sporran. How on earth will we live with the shame?"

We'd all looked at each other, and burst out laughing. "I suppose you're right," Mum said wearily. "I'll just miss him, that's all, and Lewis seems so far away. And then there's the baby—our grandchild. I would like to see something of it, but I doubt we will."

"Don't be daft, love," Dad said, squeezing her shoulders. "Kitty said we'd be welcome any time, and she seems to be the sort who means what she says. Personally, I'm feeling a lot easier about Redmond now. I knew he wasn't really happy. Seems things are working out beautifully for him. Two down, one to go."

They both looked at Tamsin, who went red and folded her arms. "Don't look at me like that," she said defiantly. "I'm quite sorted, thank you very much. In fact, hearing Susan carrying on like that brought me to my senses. I'm definitely going to file for a divorce as soon as I get home, and then I'm going to get on with my life."

"But what life will that be without Brad?" Mum said anxiously.

"Charming," Tamsin said. "You think I'm completely useless without a man in my life? Well, for your information, I'm going back to college to train as a florist. I intend to get a job doing what I love, and what I know I'm good at. I've already been accepted, and I start in September. So, you see, my life is on the up, too. I couldn't be happier."

She'd put on a brave face for the rest of the evening, but with her daughters out of the way, she'd completely crumbled. I sat there, listening to her sobs and wondering what the hell I could do to make things better.

"Have you spoken to Brad lately?" I said eventually, as her crying quietened down, and she reached for a tissue, sniffing disconsolately.

"Last week," she managed, rubbing her eyes. "He wanted to know when the car insurance was up for renewal."

"And what did you talk about?" I said gently.

Her red, teary eyes widened. "Talk about? Car insurance."

"And that's it? I mean, have you actually spoken to him about what's going on with your marriage? With him."

She shook her head.

"But why not? Why aren't you tackling this properly, Tamsin? You need to know what's happening."

"I can't," she whispered. "I just can't."

"But why?"

"Because I don't want to know," she burst out. Tears began to roll down her cheeks again. "I just can't hear him say the words, Cara. I can't. Once he says them, that's it. I mean, that's really it."

"What words?"

"That he doesn't love me anymore." She gasped. "That there's someone else who means as much to him as Kitty does to Redmond."

"Oh, Tamsin." I sighed and held her hand. "You really do still love him, don't you?"

"No!" She dabbed at her face with a tissue, then sobbed. "Yes. Of course I still love him. But I can't ever take him back after this, and anyway, he doesn't want me, does he? That much is obvious. I have to forget him and move on with my life, but it's so *hard* and I feel so pathetic for feeling this bad. I should be angry with him. I should have put him behind me and moved on by now. He doesn't deserve my love, does he? He doesn't deserve all these tears! But I just can't help it. How did you do it?"

"I'm sorry?" I said, startled.

"How did you move on after Seth? How did you find the strength to walk away?"

"It really wasn't difficult at all in the end," I confessed, realising it was true. "I think I cried all my tears while I was still with him. Then they just stopped. I had no more tears left for him—no feelings at all, really. It was easy to walk away once I'd made my mind up. Quite honestly," I admitted, accepting it at last, "I don't think I ever really loved him. It was an infatuation. I was very young, and I had no idea what love really was."

I really hadn't, had I? What Seth had stirred in me seemed so childish in hindsight, so immature.

340

I thought about Ethan, and the difference hit me with a bang.

Why, I wondered yet again, had it taken me so long to realise that Seth wasn't the one for me? Because, I finally admitted to myself, that would have meant facing up to the fact that I'd truly wasted fourteen years of my life on a fantasy. I'd thrown away my family, my home, my chances of a career, of a happy marriage, of motherhood, for ... that. I'd been fooled by passion, blinded by a stupid belief that some mythical true love could conquer all.

"Of course," I said heavily, "I eventually grew up and realised it wasn't enough, but by then, I'd made my bed, and I didn't think anyone else would want to lie in it with me except him, so I stayed. And in the end, I was so beaten down with it all that I couldn't imagine being happy, whether I was with him, or not. It was the piano that did it, of all things." I laughed suddenly, still astonished that something so simple had completely broken the spell. "I know it sounds crazy, but it was the final straw. Just woke me up and gave me the energy to take my life back in my own hands."

Tamsin nodded, staring at the wall. "I wonder what it was that woke Brad up?" she murmured.

"You have to talk to him," I said. "Properly, I mean. You have to find out what's going on in his mind."

She gave a mirthless laugh. "And when I discover that he's got some gorgeous girl knocked up and is about to move away with her, then what?"

"Brad's not Redmond," I reminded her, "and you're definitely not Susan. Be brave."

But as fresh tears welled up in her eyes, I had the awful feeling that she wouldn't muster the courage to contact her husband. She was broken. And I had no idea how to fix her.

#

The sun warmed my face, as I lay on my back on the lawn, eyes closed, feeling the heat on my skin and imagining the garden at Moreland Hall. I could picture the soft pink roses, smell their sweet fragrance, feel the velvet petals between my fingers. I imagined the swing, dangling invitingly from the lower bough of the sycamore tree, and the scent of fresh laundry and expensive aftershave. Ethan's eyes gazed into mine, a hint of mischief and a gleam of desire in those dark depths.

"What are you smiling at, Auntie Cara?"

I opened one eye, holding my hand to my face to shade out the sun.

Robyn stood over me, watching me curiously. Alice sat a few feet away, picking daisies to add to the daisy chain that was draped over her legs.

"Nothing," I said. "Just daydreaming."

Robyn plonked herself down on the grass beside me and gave a big sigh. "I wish Mummy would smile," she confided. "She never does anymore."

My heart contracted. "Well, it's been a difficult time for her lately. For all of you."

"When's Daddy coming home?" Her voice was small.

Alice glanced up at her. "He's not. I've told you, Robyn. Don't talk about it, or you'll upset Mummy."

"But why isn't he coming home?" Robyn pleaded. "I don't understand. Where's he living now? And when will we see him? It's been *ages*."

"Haven't you seen him since he left home?" I said, shocked.

They shook their heads. "I don't think he loves us anymore." Alice's voice wobbled and there was a hint of a tear in her eye, but she defiantly tossed her head and picked another daisy. She was so much like Tamsin, it hurt to look at her.

I sat up and shuffled over to sit beside her, holding out my hand to Robyn at the same time. We all sat together, and I put my arms around them. "Now, you listen to me," I told them. "I don't know what's going on between your mummy and daddy, any more than you do, but one thing I do know is that they both love you to bits. Your daddy must have a very good reason for staying away, but I absolutely know that he'll be thinking of you all the time, and I'll bet he's missing you so much that it won't be long before he makes some sort of arrangement to see you."

"But if he loves us, he wouldn't have left us, would he?" Robyn asked.

"Whatever has gone on with Mummy and Daddy, it has absolutely nothing to do with you. They adore you, you must know that?"

They both tutted, and Alice wrenched another daisy from the ground. "Suppose so," she muttered, her voice sounding suspiciously choked.

Robyn's eyes filled with tears. "But what if he doesn't love us?" she whispered. "What if he's fed up with us?"

"Why on earth would he be fed up with you?"

"He was never at home," she pointed out. "When he lived with us, I mean. Mummy used to get really sad. She pretended she didn't mind, but we knew she did."

"If he loved us, he'd have wanted to be with us," Alice said determinedly.

"But he was just very busy," I said, desperate to ease their pain. "It wasn't because he didn't want to be with you. He just had an awful lot to do." I stared at their little pinched faces and felt a lurch of grief for them. "Like you!" I exclaimed suddenly.

They looked up at me, clearly baffled. "What do you mean, like us?"

"Okay," I said eagerly, desperate to make them understand, "you love your mummy, right?"

They nodded. "Of course we do," Robyn said indignantly.

"Yet, you don't stay home much with her, do you? I mean, you have things to do, too. You're always here, there, and everywhere. All those activities you do. It's not because you don't want to be with your mummy, it's because you have busy lives. Just like Daddy. He wasn't out to avoid you all, he was just terribly busy."

They looked at each other. "It's not the same," Alice said.

"Yes, it is," I said.

Robyn shook her head. "It's not."

I sighed. "Well, I think it is," I said, feeling defeated.

"He's not going to come home, is he?" Robyn's bottom lip quivered.

I wanted to assure them that everything would be fine, that their father would be home before they knew it, and the issues between their parents would be resolved, but I couldn't. "I don't know," I admitted. "But whatever happens, you will see him regularly, I promise you that."

"Dahlia's going to love this," Alice said grumpily.

Robyn gave her a sympathetic look. "Just ignore her."

"Who's Dahlia?" I said. "And what's she going to

love?"

"The boss of my class." Alice pulled a face. "She told everyone that Daddy left, and they all think it's really funny. I told her he was away on a business trip and was coming back, and she said I was a liar. Now everyone will know she was right."

"How did Dahlia know he'd even left?" I said.

"Mummy told someone at Pilates class, and they told Dahlia's mummy. I hate her."

"I hate them all," Robyn said vehemently. "I hate that school."

My eyes widened. "What do you mean, you hate that school?"

"It's horrible. We've always hated it," Robyn confided. "But you won't tell Mummy, will you? We don't want to upset her even more."

"But why do you hate it?"

Alice considered the matter. "The girls there are all stuck up. They make fun of us, and they don't let us join in with anything. Not like our old friends. We really miss them."

"Don't you ever see them?"

Robyn nodded. "Yes, but only after school."

"Well, that's something," I said. "And you have to admit, you have a fabulous social life. What, with one club after another, I reckon you're going to be Olympic stars of the future, or prima ballerinas."

I laughed, but they didn't seem to see the funny side. "We're not very good at anything," Alice admitted. "But then again, we don't really try very hard."

"It's boring," Robyn added.

"What's boring?" I was bewildered. "Gymnastics?

345

Swimming? Ice skating? Ballet? Tap?"

"All of it," Robyn said, with some feeling.

"Not all of it," Alice corrected her. "I like dancing. It's quite good fun."

"Hang on a minute." I was totally confused. "If you don't like all those activities, why on earth do you make your mother drive you there every night?"

Alice seemed to give up on her daisy chain. She examined the string of flowers in her hand, then threw them on the ground beside her and heaved a big sigh. "Because," she said, as if explaining to a five-year-old, "Lucy goes to gymnastics, Katie goes to swimming, and Megan does ice skating."

"And Florence swims, too, and Juliet likes dance class."

"What does that matter? You're going to the classes to keep up with your classmates?"

Alice tutted. "They're not our classmates. At least, not anymore."

Light was beginning to dawn. "You mean, you go to the classes to catch up with your old schoolfriends? The ones from your previous school?"

They nodded. "Yes. We really miss them, but Mummy wants us to make new friends and play with the girls at our new school, and we don't like them half as much. They don't want to play with us, anyway. Mummy said we have to concentrate on making new friends, never mind our old ones, but she doesn't realise our old friends go to the classes." Alice sighed. "I did try to make new friends, you know. I went to Dahlia Robertson's house once for tea, and it was awful. It was when I first started at the school, and I think I was only invited so they could be nosy. Her mother was really stuck up, and she wanted me to tell her all about Daddy's job. What's it got to do with her? I fibbed and told her he was the Prime Minister, and she gave me a funny look and didn't ask me round again. Dahlia told everyone at school she wasn't allowed to talk to me anymore because I was a—a fantasy."

"A fantasist," I said absently. So, Alice and Robyn hated their new school, and all those activities that drove poor Tamsin mad and cost her so much money were just ways of getting to see their old friends? What a waste of time and money. There was a distinct lack of communication in their little family, and it made me wonder what other misunderstandings they were paying for. I stood up, brushing grass from the back of my skirt.

"Where are you going?" Robyn asked, squinting up at me as the sun shone in her face.

"I just have something to do," I told her. "How about you two go and wash up for tea, and see if Grandma wants any help? If you ask very nicely, she may even let you have strawberries for afters."

They looked quite pleased about that, especially when I added that I was pretty sure they'd be allowed cream with them, and headed into the kitchen to pester Mum. I dashed upstairs to the little back bedroom that had been mine since I was about nine, when Tamsin's makeup had taken over the bigger bedroom that we'd shared, causing me to throw a massive strop and insist that the 'box room' be cleared for me.

I couldn't remember why I had Brad's mobile number in my phonebook. I just knew it was there. It might have had something to do with Tamsin's birthday one year—some party that he'd arranged for her, back in the days when he actually cared, and he'd called me about it. I must have stored the number out of habit.

I jabbed at the phone screen and held the phone to my ear as I listened to the dial tone. Brad answered, just when I was on the point of giving up and throwing the phone across the room in despair.

"Cara? What is it? What's happened?" He sounded genuinely worried, which wasn't surprising, given that I'd never rung him before in my life. "Is it the kids? Tamsin?"

"Both of the above," I answered shortly. "You need to get your sorry arse to Mum and Dad's, Brad, and sort this mess out, once and for all. And, quite frankly, I'm not going to take no for an answer."

#

We'd eaten a really tasty tea of chips, quiche and salad, followed by strawberries and cream. Mum and I did the pots afterwards, and she confided in me that she was worried sick about Tamsin. "Did you notice? She never had a go at me for giving the kids chips," she said anxiously. "And all that cream they poured on their strawberries. She wouldn't have let them get away with that a few months ago. What are we going to do about her, Cara?"

"Don't worry, Mum. It's all in hand," I said confidently, hanging up the tea towel and closing the cupboard door. "Things will get sorted today, one way, or the other."

She eyed me suspiciously. "What have you done?"

"You'll see. Someone had to do something, and I guess it fell to me."

"Oh, hell." She wiped the taps with a dishcloth. "If this all goes wrong, it's on your head." She winked at me.

"Mind you, if it goes well, it was down to me."

"Okay," I said. "Seeing as you invited us all down to sort things, I guess I can give you that."

Mum glanced across at Dad, as he wiped the table. "Are you all right, Ray?"

"I'm fine, love. Right as rain," he assured her.

"Why wouldn't he be?" I said. "He's only wiping the table, not building one." I looked from one to the other of them. "Is there something you're not telling me?"

"Don't be so paranoid." Dad hooked his arm over my shoulder. "Like we said, I was a bit rundown and feeling a bit low about retiring. That holiday away has done me the power of good, and I'm fit as a fiddle now. Mind you, can I say the same about you?"

"What do you mean by that?"

"You've lost weight," he observed. "Quite a bit of weight."

"That's a good thing. I'd got very porky. I was barely fitting into my clothes."

He tutted. "Nothing wrong with having a bit of meat on the bone. Are you sure you're all right, love? Me and your mum couldn't believe you'd walked out on that man, at last. It must have taken some courage."

"It would have taken more to stay. I'm just sorry it took me so long."

"And what about now?" Mum's brow creased. "What's this new job like? Are you happy? Are you settled?"

"It will do for now," I said vaguely.

I didn't want to make them any more anxious than they already were. How could I tell them that the job wasn't permanent? Adele would be going to school before

349

I knew it, and I would be looking for another job and another home. Then there was the little matter of my growing attraction towards, and liking for, Ethan Rochester. That could come to no good. He was way, way out of my league and would grow tired of me very quickly.

Besides, I had to find my own way. I had to find something that I was actually good at, and make a new career for myself. A new life. And no man could distract me from that task, particularly one so obviously superior to me as Ethan. The problem was going to be keeping a clear head while I stayed at Moreland Hall. I had to remember that there was no future in it, and that falling for him would only bring me more unhappiness.

"What do you mean, for now?" Mum demanded. "What are you planning?"

A loud knock on the door saved me from having to answer. We all looked at each other, and Dad narrowed his eyes. "Expecting someone, Cara?"

I shrugged. "I had to do something. This is for the best, really it is."

He heaved a big sigh. "So much for the peace and quiet of retirement. I'd better go and answer the door, then."

"I'll go," I said. "One of you had better warn Tamsin."

"I'll take the kids upstairs," Mum said, but I put my hand on her arm. "Not yet, Mum. They need to see him. They've really missed him, and I daresay he's missed them, too."

She hesitated, but nodded, and hurried into the living room to warn my sister. Dad looked at me. "Here we go, then. Round two."

Brad was pale when I opened the door to him. He'd

lost weight, too, and there were dark shadows under his eyes. If he was living it up with some other woman, it didn't appear to have brought him much joy. "Hi, Cara."

His voice was different, humbler. My heart went out to him. "Come in, Brad."

Tamsin looked horror-struck when we walked into the living room, but any protest she may have made was drowned out by the delighted shrieks from Alice and Robyn, who hurled themselves at their father. I watched him crouch down to gather them to him, and when he lifted his face, there were tears in his eyes. I looked across at my sister, huddled in the chair, her arms wrapped around herself as if for protection. She chewed her lip and stared at her husband, fear in her face.

"Tamsin." He simply stared back at her, seeming unable to say anything else.

"I think we'll leave you to it," Mum said. She held out her arms to the girls. "Come on, lovelies. Let's leave Mummy and Daddy to talk for a while, shall we?"

"You won't go without telling us?" Robyn pleaded, reluctant to let go of Brad's hand.

He shook his head. "I promise," he managed, his voice choked.

Alice kissed him, and Robyn threw her arms around his neck and hugged him tightly, then they followed Mum out of the room.

"Talk to each other," I ordered. "And listen. Both of you."

Then I left them to it and headed into the kitchen to sit with Mum and Dad, as they tried valiantly to entertain two clearly anxious children.

It was about an hour later, when Tamsin popped her

head round the door. Her face was blotchy and swollen with crying, her lids heavy, and she looked frozen. "We're just going out for a walk," she told us. "We won't be too long. Will you be okay with the girls?"

"Of course," Dad said. "Get off with you."

"At least we can watch the telly now," Mum said, with forced brightness. "Come on, girls. Let's see what's on, shall we?"

Whatever was on, it didn't seem to hold their attention very well. In fact, they were extremely restless, and who could blame them? Whatever Brad and Tamsin were talking about, they were definitely being thorough about it. Was that a good thing, I wondered? Or were they taking their time because they had to sort out the divorce? Custody, access, the house, that sort of thing. I really hoped I'd done the right thing, forcing Tamsin to face up to the state of her marriage.

When they finally came home, the girls were just about falling asleep, and Mum was making fretful noises about getting them to bed.

I relaxed when I saw that they were holding hands, and Tamsin's face, although tear-streaked, was smiling. Brad looked like a new man.

"What happened?" Mum looked from one to the other. "Is it sorted?"

Tamsin glanced at Brad, and he pulled her to him and smiled down at her. "It is," he confirmed. "I'm coming home."

The girls shrieked with excitement and rushed over to him, and Tamsin smiled across at me and mouthed, 'Thank you.'

I winked at her, feeling so happy I could burst.

After the girls had gone to bed, Tamsin and Brad sat with us in the living room, Brad having accepted Mum and Dad's invitation to stay over so they could all go home together the next day. As we drank wine, they explained what they'd been talking about, and what they'd discovered.

"It was all my fault," Tamsin said, shaking her head.

Brad took her hand. "No it wasn't. It was both of us. We stopped listening, stopped talking. It takes two to ruin a marriage."

"And two to fix it," she said. "Or, in our case," she added, glancing across at me affectionately, "three."

"Thank you so much for calling me, Cara," Brad said. "I would never have had the nerve to come here, if you hadn't told me what you told me."

"I can't believe the girls feel like that about school," Tamsin said, still clearly shocked. "They never said a word. All that time and money, running around after them, and all the time, they just wanted to be with their old friends at their old school. Well, as soon as we get home, that's the first thing we'll sort out. I'll be glad to see the back of that dratted school, anyway."

"So, the children were only going to all those activities to meet up with their pals?" Dad shook his head, laughing. "You two have been a bit daft, haven't you?"

Brad nodded. "And not just about the girls," he admitted. "Talk about crossed wires. I was working all the hours God sends, worrying about Tamsin's spending habits. She seemed to live for the house and these wretched activities that the girls were doing. Then there were the classes she attended herself, and the constant demands for alterations and redecoration in the house. I felt as if the only thing I was there for was to make money. I worked myself into the ground, and I was just too exhausted to do anything else. And it made me resentful and angry. In the end, I thought, well, let her have the money. I may as well move out because, clearly, it's the bank account that matters, and she can have that, no matter what."

"Oh, Tamsin, how could you?" Mum said reproachfully.

"But I was only filling my time with classes and doing up the house because I missed Brad so much!" Tamsin exclaimed, somewhat defensively. "I hated the fact that he seemed to care far more about his job than he did about me and the children. I thought he preferred the office to home, and I felt so resentful and lonely. All that time," she added, gazing up at her husband, "and we were each missing the other, and longing for a normal life, and neither of us knew it."

Brad sighed. "If only one of us had the courage to say something."

"Well, it will all be different from now on," Tamsin said determinedly. "The kids can leave that wretched school, which will save us a fortune, and once they're back at their old place, they can pick one out-of-school activity, and the rest will be dropped. I shouldn't imagine they'll care, as they'll be back with their friends all day. Why they didn't just tell me they missed them, I can't imagine."

"Same reason you didn't tell Brad you missed him, I suppose," Dad pointed out.

She blushed. "Yeah. Fair point. Anyway, after that, we're putting the house on the market and finding somewhere smaller and cheaper, and Brad's going to cut down his hours, while I go to college and do my course, then we're going into business together."

"Into business?" I said astonished. "Doing what?"

"Once I qualify as a florist, Brad's going to set me up with my own little flower shop. He's going to do all the accounts and business stuff, and I'll be doing the flowers. We'll be worse off financially, no doubt, but with no school fees and a reduced mortgage, it should be do-able."

"And I shall put money aside in the meantime," Brad added. "It will be a couple of years before Tamsin qualifies, so we have time to plan and put things in place."

"Are you sure about this?" Dad looked worried. "New businesses are risky, especially in these uncertain times."

"I can always do freelance stuff," Brad said. "If we need extra income, I can make it. That's not a problem. I just want to support my wife and be with her. I've had a hell of a shock. I really thought we were over. I'm not about to let her go again."

"You won't get the chance," Tamsin promised him. "I'll superglue you to my side, if I have to. I can't go through all this again. I love you so much."

Mum, Dad and I pulled faces and made mocking noises as they kissed, but I knew my parents would be just as delighted about the outcome as I was. It seemed I'd done the right thing, after all. Which just left my own life to sort out.

Chapter Twenty-Six

It was no use denying it to myself. As I walked down the drive of Moreland Hall, bag in hand, I experienced a feeling of joy that I struggled to contain, and I was all too aware that, to me, it felt as if I was coming home.

Mrs F had sounded thrilled over the intercom. "You're back! I'm so pleased. Hurry up, and I'll make you a cup of tea."

Mrs F's wonderful, strong cups of tea. The answer to a million problems. I couldn't wait. Unable to wipe the smile off my face, I almost ran down the drive and hurried round the back way, letting myself in through the kitchen door.

I was pulled into a hug, then Mrs F stepped back and examined me. I'm not sure what she was expecting to find, but she seemed satisfied at any rate.

"You're looking well," she said, clearly reassured.

"I've only been away two days," I said, amused. "What did you expect? That I'd have rickets, or scurvy, or something?"

"You never know," she said sagely. "Now, sit yourself down, and I'll make you that drink."

"Where is everyone?" I kept my tone casual as I put the bag on the floor and sank into a chair.

"Mrs Rochester's taken Adele into York, shopping. Michael's driven them. I'm not entirely sure where Mr

Rochester is, but he's around somewhere."

"I'm sure he is." I took the mug of tea from her hand and sipped on it gratefully. "Oh, this is lovely, Mrs F. No one makes a cuppa like you do."

"Even your own mother?" she enquired.

"Even my own mother, but please, never tell her I said so."

She laughed and sat down next to me. "It is good to have you home, love. How are things with your family? Not that I'm prying, mind."

"Of course you're not," I said. "But you'll be pleased to know, I'm sure, that everything with the family is perfect. All our problems seem to have been fixed."

She beamed at me. "That's wonderful."

Wasn't it? Except—except I had an empty feeling inside me, and I wasn't sure why.

We sat at the table for half an hour, or so, making small talk and catching up, until she decided it was time for her to get on with making dinner. "They'll be back from York soon," she said, glancing at the clock and sounding panicky. "Can't believe how long I've sat here. Why don't you go and unpack, love?"

I nodded and carried my bag upstairs. As soon as I reached my room, though, I stopped and stood quite still, staring at the dressing table in amazement. There was a sketch on there—a pencil drawing of me. And it was incredible. I dropped my bag and sank onto the bed, holding the sheet of paper in my hands. I'd never seen anything like it. No photograph had ever made me look like that. It was—extraordinary. There was an expression on my face I couldn't even begin to describe. All I knew was, the artist had made me look beautiful. And the artist was Ethan.

My mouth felt dry. There seemed to be a huge brick sitting in my chest, squeezing my heart, blocking my throat. A half sob escaped my lips, and the image before me blurred.

I blinked furiously and walked over to the window, my eyes drawn to the lawn and the grounds beyond, and somehow, I knew, I just knew, where he was. All thoughts of being cautious vanished, and I jumped up and ran downstairs, throwing open the front door and running towards the place I had pictured in my mind's eye for the last couple of days.

Reaching the secret garden, I opened the door and hurried down the path, through the archway and into the garden beyond. He was sitting on the swing, not moving, just staring down at the ground. As I caught sight of him, I stopped dead and tried to catch my breath. I had to be sensible. I had to think straight. This was crazy.

"Cara!" He pushed to his feet, staring at me as if he couldn't quite believe I was actually there. "You're home."

Hands clenched into fists at my sides, I stood fighting a desperate battle within myself. It was me, or him. I knew it. I couldn't have both. If I chose him, I would lose myself again, and he would grow tired of me, and I would be alone once more. This time, it would be so much worse than it had been with Seth, because how could I bear to live without Ethan once I'd truly been part of his life? It was impossible. I felt sick, and almost collapsed as the blood seemed to drain from my body.

He was at my side in a moment, scooping me up and placing me on the bench. "You're not well." He sounded panicky.

"I'm fine." I took a deep breath. "I just haven't eaten today, that's all." It was a big fat lie. I'd eaten a huge lunch at Mum and Dad's, as well my own body weight in boiled sweets on the way to York station with Brad and Tamsin and the girls, but I had to think of something to say. I could hardly come out with the truth, could I?

He shook his head. "This has to stop, Cara," he said. "You must eat properly."

I looked at him in surprise. "What are you talking about? I eat all the time."

He bit his lip, as if considering whether to pursue the subject, then he burst out, "I know! Mrs Fairweather told me all about it. It's okay, I understand. We both do. We can get help for you."

I couldn't think of a response to that, since I didn't have the faintest idea what he was talking about. I simply gaped at him, wondering if he'd gone mad.

"The eating disorder," he said gently, taking my hand. "It's okay. We can help. Let us help. You don't have to go through this alone."

Realising my mouth had dried up, I swallowed hard. "What the heck are you talking about?" I managed eventually. "What bloody eating disorder?"

"*Your* eating disorder," he said. "Bulimia, is it? I've been doing some research, and there's a very good clinic—"

"Hold it right there." I stood and faced him, hands on hips, my strength suddenly returning. "Before you start booking me in for therapy, let me make one thing very clear. I do not have an eating disorder. Unless you count an addiction to Carroll's Caramel Choc Bloc an eating disorder, that is."

"It's all right. I can help. You don't have to pretend." He held out his hand, but I waved it away crossly.

"Stop saying you can help," I said. "I don't need any help. I don't have an eating disorder. Why on earth would you think I did?"

"You seriously want to do this?" he asked, his brows knitting together.

"Oh, believe me, I seriously do," I assured him.

He sighed and shook his head, then shrugged. "Okay. Firstly, Mrs F said you kept refusing food. She said you were always rejecting biscuits, puddings, that sort of thing, but that you also sometimes skipped lunch, or breakfast. And you always, always left something on your plate."

"And that's it, is it? By that definition, almost every woman in Britain's had an eating disorder, at some point, or other."

"Then there was that incident with the sweets."

"What incident with the sweets?"

"You said you dropped them in the road when I nearly hit you with my car, but did you? Or was it just that you binged on them and felt too ashamed to admit it?"

I almost laughed. "If you call a little bag of sweets a binge, you're an amateur," I assured him.

"I saw what you were looking at, that day on the laptop," he burst out. "I saw it, Cara! The information about eating disorders. You were clearly looking for help then, and I should have said something, done something. I spoke to Mrs F about it, and she voiced her concerns. She said you were getting thinner and thinner."

"Of course I was," I said incredulously. "That was the plan! I was a barrel when I arrived here. I'd been stuffing my face with chocolate and crisps for weeks, and I just

360

wanted to get back into my old clothes comfortably. Nothing sinister about it."

"So, how do you explain the missing food?"

I stared at him. "What missing food?"

"It's been happening for over a week now. Tinned food, stuff out of the fridge, chocolate, even one of the guests said his breakfast had been stolen."

"You're kidding, right?" I shook my head and sank down onto the bench beside him. "You think I've been pinching food?"

"No one's angry," he assured me quickly. "It's a symptom. We understand that. We're just worried about you. We didn't want you to rush off after every meal and throw it all back up again, so—"

"So, you made damn sure that I wasn't left alone after dinner," I said slowly, light finally dawning. "That's why Mrs F always wanted me to sit with her and watch television. Oh, God." And that was why, on the night she'd been going off to visit her sister, Ethan had stepped in and insisted I had dinner with him. I'd assumed he wanted my company, when all the time he'd been guarding me for Mrs F.

I was such an idiot.

I took a deep breath. "Okay, Ethan, cards on the table. I honestly have no idea who's been pinching food, if food truly has been going missing. Although, let's face it, it's been a bit hectic around here lately, and Mrs F has had a lot to deal with, what with the party preparations and her passion for Michael. It could be that she's simply lost track of what she had in stock. As for the website—yes, I was looking for information, but not for myself. I was checking up on my sister. I thought she might have bulimia, or anorexia. I was wrong. She was just bloody miserable because she thought her husband didn't love her any more. Turns out she was also wrong, but that's another story. As for the not eating puddings and biscuits bit—like I said, I'd piled weight on because I was bloody miserable, too, but went the opposite way to my sister. Coming here was a new start for me, and I was determined to pull myself together and eat sensibly, which I did mostly, until you challenged me to finish that Triple Whammy Burger and I couldn't resist. So, there you have it."

He watched me as if hardly daring to believe I wasn't lying. "And that's it? Honestly?"

I touched his arm—against my better judgement, I might add, but he looked so shell-shocked, I couldn't help it. "That's it. I swear to you. I do not have an eating disorder."

He put his head in his hands. "Thank God." He peered down at me, clearly embarrassed. "I've been an idiot, haven't I?"

"Not at all," I assured him. "You've been kind and caring and thoughtful, and I'm very lucky to have friends like you and Mrs Fairweather."

He smiled at me. "Can we forget this just happened?" he pleaded.

"I think we probably should," I agreed, "although, you'd better put Mrs F straight. No wonder she's been clucking round me like a mother hen, bless her."

"She thinks the world of you," he told me. "We both do."

I glanced away. I couldn't go down that road with him, however appealing it might seem.

362

"I have some news for you, anyway," he said abruptly, and I looked back, relieved at the change in his tone.

"Oh, and what's that?"

"I've enrolled Adele at the local primary school. She starts in the nursery class in September."

My heart plummeted into my shoes. "That—that's a change of heart," I managed. "Thought you didn't want her to go there?"

"It wasn't that I didn't want her to go there," he said. "I just didn't see the point because I wasn't sure where she'd be living. Now it's settled. Mother and I had a long talk, while you were away. She's told me she plans to split her time between New York and the house in the Cotswolds, which, to be honest, makes more sense. She has friends in both places, unlike here, where she really knows no one. She's asked me to take on responsibility for Adele, and I've agreed." His mouth twitched. "Let's face it, I always have taken responsibility for her, but we intend to make it official. My mother's just not cut out to take care of a four-year-old. I'd like to say it was down to her age, but she wasn't exactly cut out to look after me when I was that age, either. I love her, but she never really felt like a mother figure."

"I'm sorry, Ethan. You missed out on that," I said, thinking of my own lovely mum.

"Yes, I did. I'm not sure I realised how much, until recently. I want Adele to have better than that, and I think she will."

"That's good," I said, not at all sure how he planned to achieve his goal. Nursery school was all very well, but it was no substitute for the love of a mother. I tried to sound calm as I said, "I'll look for another job. I'd better

363

go online and find the nearest agency. I'm sure I'll find something, and I'll be out of your way in no time."

His whole demeanour changed. "Out of my way? My God, Cara! That's it, is it?"

"What do you want me to say?" I said, confused. "I'll stay on until September, of course. I won't leave Adele without a nanny."

"Is it that easy for you?" He loomed over me, his face a mixture of anger and pain. "You'll just walk away? You'll leave me without a backward glance?"

"Leave you? I don't understand."

"You do understand," he said bitterly. "You just won't face up to it. Did what I said to you here the other day mean nothing to you? We kissed! Did that mean nothing, either?" He rubbed the back of his head, staring at me with pain-filled eyes. "For fuck's sake, Cara, I thought we were past this." He dug into his pocket and handed me a plastic bag of fifty pence coins. "Keep these for Adele," he snapped. "I have a feeling I'm going to use them all."

"You're being ridiculous," I said.

"Am I indeed? Whereas you're being cruel! I told you how I feel, and I may as well have said nothing, because clearly, you're not interested. It's like you're playing some warped game with me. One minute you're kissing me back, the next you're cold and uncaring. What the hell do you want from me?"

Well, it wasn't going at all how I'd expected. "I only came to see you to thank you for the sketch," I muttered sulkily.

"You saw it?"

"I did." I half smiled at him, trying to appease him. "It's amazing. You did that from memory?"

364

"It was easy," he said, his voice harsh. "Your image is etched on my brain."

"You made me look beautiful."

"Cara, you *are* beautiful. I drew what I see, don't you understand that?" He reached for my hand. "Cara, I love you. Please tell me you feel the same way about me."

No, no, no! I knew it would only take one word, and I'd be lost forever—doomed to replay past mistakes like some hideous version of *Groundhog Day*. "Whatever you think you feel, it isn't real," I told him. "It won't last. Someone else will come along, and you'll forget all about me. Just trust me on this."

He stared at me in silence for a moment, his face pale. Then, slowly, he said, "Who broke your heart, Cara?"

I was about to deny that my heart had ever been broken. I intended to shrug it off, make light of his comment, but out of nowhere, tears sprang into my eyes, and my throat felt full and choked. "*I* did!" I burst out, without even meaning to. I threw the bag of coins on the ground. "I broke my own heart. And I can't do it again."

"You? I don't understand."

"*I* broke my heart!" I repeated, aware that my voice was becoming unattractively shrill, yet unable to shut myself up. The dam, it seemed, had burst. I'd had no idea that I even felt that way. "I'm responsible for all of it. I was so desperate for someone to accept me just as I was, and to be proud of me, that I didn't see what was happening. How unsuited we were. Me and Seth, I mean."

"Seth? Is he the man who made it easy for you to leave?"

"Yes. Eventually. You see, Seth may have taken advantage of that desperation, but it was me—I allowed it to happen. I didn't fight back. I didn't insist that he grow up. I just went out and got a job to support him—the first job I could get. And I turned a blind eye when he had an affair because, you know, maybe that was all I could expect. And I spent years just feeling more and more of a failure, and that put barriers between myself and the people who loved me. I didn't feel good enough for any of them, so I lost them. My parents, my brother and sister .... They all seemed to have perfect lives, whereas mine was a mess. How could I spend time with them and not give away how miserable I felt?"

I choked back a sob and, determined to make the situation clear to him, ploughed on. "So, I stayed away, and their lives went on without me, and I didn't get to know my nieces, and I didn't even know my brother and his wife were having problems, and when I saw my dad he looked so ill and tired .... How could I not know that? But I didn't, because I allowed myself to drift away from them, and I allowed myself to build a life with a man that was no good for me, and to hang out with people who meant nothing to me, and whose lifestyle I didn't approve of and didn't fit in with, and all the time I was thinking, there's something wrong with me, why don't I fit in? And the truth is, I was never meant to fit in, but it took me far too long to realise it. They weren't my people, you see. I shouldn't have been with them, and it only happened because I let myself down so badly. I wasn't true to myself, to my own values. I got what I deserved. The life I have now—this little life—is the one I created for myself.

"So, yes, I broke my own heart. And now it's up to me, and me alone, to mend it. I can't hand that responsibility over to anyone else. I'm on my own, and my happiness depends on me staying that way and making a new life for myself. A bigger, better life, while I still can."

I became aware that I was crying, but, even more astonishing, I realised that so was he. Tears ran down his cheeks, and it was all I could do not to wipe them away.

"You don't have to hand responsibility over to someone else," he said thickly. "Everyone must take responsibility for their own life, but that doesn't mean you can't be with another person. That you can't allow someone into your heart. What are you afraid of? That you'll make the same mistake again? That you won't have the courage to be your own person? That you'll be absorbed into the shadow of anyone you let in?"

"Yes! Exactly that! I *am* afraid of that. I'm not enough, do you understand that? I'm not enough, and if I allow another man too close to me, I will disappear. And I just can't do that again."

"Christ, Cara." He sank back onto the bench and stared at the ground. "What the hell happened to you?"

And so I told him. I sat down beside him on the bench and told him it all, about meeting Seth, about turning him, in my mind's eye, into something he wasn't. How I'd created some fictional life around a man who could never live up to it. How Heathcliff had turned out to be nothing but a dream—a wisp of a fantasy, born out of a longing to belong to someone who thought I was enough.

"You *are* enough!" His voice was hoarse as he turned to me and gripped my shoulders. "Listen to me," he said desperately, "you're more than enough. You're kind, loving, caring and funny, smart and loyal, interesting, and so beautiful. What more do you want to be?"

367

"I want ..." I shook my head. "I don't know what I want. To be proud of myself. To make my family proud of me."

"How could they not be proud of you?" he demanded. "It's impossible!"

"I don't have a good job like Redmond and Tamsin have. Had. And they've given my parents grandchildren. I didn't even get the chance to do that. I've done nothing to be proud of."

"You're mistaken, Cara. Your gift is in your nature. You're one of life's nurturers, and what's wrong with that?"

"There's got to be more to me than childcare," I pleaded. "I need a real job. I need to spread my wings. Don't I?" *Did I?* I wasn't even sure what I wanted any more.

"*I am no bird, and no net ensnares me,*" he murmured.

My eyes widened. He'd read *Jane Eyre?*

He stood up and began to pace. "A high-flying career doesn't define a person. You told me yourself that I should step away from my business and devote more time to my painting. You said I had a gift for it, and that I should nurture that gift."

"You should," I said weakly. "I meant it."

"And I mean this." He stopped in front of me and stared down at me with pleading eyes. "Your gift is with people. You said you never had a career in mind, that you just fell into childcare. But maybe that's where your talent has lain all along. What's wrong with caring for people? What's wrong with caring for children? What's wrong with spending your life making a home, making a family, loving that family with all your heart?"

"Have you never heard of feminism?" I half sobbed.

"Of course I have! I wear my feminist badge with pride, as, I might add, did my own father—as all the women he promoted on merit would testify. But feminism isn't just about building a career. It's about having the choice. If you wanted to do something—if you had a career in mind that you really wanted to pursue, I would support you all the way. You must know that. But for God's sake, don't assume that, if you don't want a career, if deep down inside, all you want is a home and family, you're somehow failing, or letting anyone down. Don't be afraid to admit that to anyone, least of all to yourself. It's your choice, and you're free to make it. Just, please, Cara, choose honestly. Be true to yourself."

It was as if a fog was lifting. As if light was breaking through the thick mists that had blinded me for so many years. I knew, with blinding clarity, what it was I wanted, more than anything in the world. It was what I'd always wanted, but I'd lied to myself. I'd persuaded myself it didn't matter, didn't count. Well, it mattered. In the end, it was all that mattered.

I thought, for a minute, that we were both crying again, until I realised that it was raining. His hair had glued to his head, and I knew mine must be the same, and that I must look a fright.

"Cara?"

His eyes burned into mine, and, not stopping to think, I launched myself into his arms. I sobbed, while he held me tightly and stroked my hair.

"I don't want to leave you," I told him desperately. "My heart would break."

"You don't have to leave," he said. "I won't *let* you

369

leave."

"But your wife? I can't betray her, and neither should you."

"We wouldn't be betraying her. It's not a real marriage. I mean, not in the way you think. I swear to you, I'm going to sort this out. I'll meet with her, and I'll end this, once and for all. I want to marry you, Cara. Will you marry me?"

It was madness. There was no other way to look at it, really. In the back of my mind, there was an uneasy awareness that he'd said he would contact Antonia, yet he'd told Marcus that he didn't know how to. And what did he mean, it wasn't a marriage? They'd been living apart for so long. Surely, if they'd wanted to end it, they could have done so before then?

Yet, I found myself nodding, and then I told him that, yes, I would marry him, and he laughed and kissed me, his hands cupping my face. Then we ran back towards the house with the rain pouring down on us, as if the gods were throwing giant buckets of water at us in disapproval.

"Go and get dried and changed," he urged me, as we entered the hallway. "I'm going to contact Antonia. Trust me, Cara, please. I swear to you that nothing will ever separate us again. I love you, and that will never change."

I nodded, believing him, and ran upstairs to my room. Overhead, a roll of thunder roared its warning, but I still took no notice. I was happy. For that brief, golden moment, I was truly happy.

Chapter Twenty-Seven

I'd slept in. It seemed impossible to me that I'd slept, at all, but somehow exhaustion had overcome me and I'd succumbed. After rubbing my eyes, I stared at the alarm clock on the bedside table in shock. Half-past nine! I'd never slept in so late—even after the party.

The day seemed so magical to start with. I climbed out of bed and headed into the bathroom. As I showered, my mind replayed the events of the previous evening, and I felt my stomach churned with nerves and excitement. Had I imagined it all? Had he been winding me up? What if, in the cold light of day, he regretted every word he'd said?

As I dressed, though, I'd been unable to wipe the smile from my face. He'd meant it—of course he had. I was going to marry Ethan Rochester. It seemed so ridiculously unlikely, that I actually laughed out loud. How could someone like him want to marry someone like me? Yet. it was true. It was really true!

I hugged myself, then hastily smoothed the sheets and plumped the pillows, and rushed round to the far side of the bed to straighten the duvet. From the corner of my eye, I spotted a piece of paper sticking out from under the bed, and my heart leapt. The sketch of me!

Remembering how beautiful Ethan had made me look, my whole body tingled with excitement and love, but when I bent down and pulled the paper out, everything seemed to stop.

The drawing was torn clean in half. I sat down with a thud and stared in horror at the two halves. Who had done it? Why?

Sitting staring at the torn paper, I became aware of a commotion downstairs and ran out onto the landing, wondering what was happening now and if I was ever to be happy.

Jennifer stood in the hallway, talking—rather loudly— to two women, who seemed quite distressed. Mrs F had Adele in her arms, and she shot me a rather anxious look, before hurrying into the kitchen, no doubt to get Adele out of the way.

Jennifer and the two women didn't seem to notice me as I walked slowly down the stairs, my eyes fixed on them. My heart beat so erratically I wasn't sure if it was going to stop altogether.

I knew one of those women. No mistaking her, it was Antonia Rochester—a very pregnant Antonia Rochester. I sank onto one of the steps and just stared, hardly able to believe what I was seeing, and trying to make sense of what I was hearing.

"He can't do this. He promised."

"Things have changed, Antonia. You must have known that one day they would."

"But not like this! Not now!"

"You do know," said the other woman coldly, "that her father's dying?"

"I do, and I'm terribly sorry. I know this must be very difficult for you."

"Difficult? You have no idea! He couldn't wait? He

couldn't just give me a few more months? A year, perhaps?"

"As he told you last night—"

"Where is he? I don't believe he's not here."

"He went to find you. He's probably knocking at your door in Devon right now. Why have you come up here, for heaven's sake?"

"To stop him! To make him think again! For God's sake!" Antonia dissolved into tears. "I can't do this, I really can't."

"Why don't you come into the sitting room, Antonia?" Jennifer's voice was gentle. "You're overwrought, and it's not good for you, or the baby."

"Babies." The other woman sounded furious. "And no, this isn't good for any of them, but whose fault's that? Ethan had better get his arse back here, pronto. How do you think the press would react if they knew he'd abandoned his pregnant wife just weeks before she gave birth to twins?"

Jennifer glared at her. "I don't appreciate your threats, Faith. I understand you're worried, but let's try to keep things civil, shall we? Besides, I should think publicity would be the last thing you'd want." As Antonia sobbed, she put her arms around her. "It will all be okay, Antonia. You're not thinking straight. This isn't as bad as you fear, I promise you."

"Not as bad as I think? How can it get any worse? How can he abandon me now, just when I need him most?"

Jennifer ushered her into the sitting room, and the other woman followed and closed the door behind them.

I sat there, staring through the gap in the bannister at

the closed door. I felt dead inside. All hope, all joy extinguished. I remembered the photo of the two of them—Antonia and Ethan, arms around each other in Paris. I remembered the look of love in Antonia's eyes. I remembered Ethan saying softly, 'Paris.' It had only been taken at Christmas—just under seven months ago. Seven months! Was that when Antonia's twins were conceived, then? I wasn't sure how pregnant she was, but it seemed likely.

He was going to be a father.

I stood up and walked slowly back upstairs. He was already a husband. That should have been enough to stop me. I'd let myself down once again.

I took my suitcase and threw my belongings into it. It didn't take long. I hadn't brought much, after all. I looked down at the few things inside and tears filled my eyes. The remnants of a life poorly lived. I looked around the room, remembering how happy I'd been just a few moments before. It seemed impossible that so much had changed in such a short time. I glanced at the drawing, torn in half. If ever there was a symbol of how I felt inside, that was it.

My fingers stilled as I fumbled with the lock. I remembered the way Ethan had held me the previous night. I remembered how we'd stood there, so desperate, so in love, while the rain had poured down on us. I remembered the look in his eyes, the pleading in his voice, the impassioned way he'd begged me to stay with him. Wasn't it enough? For God's sake, how could I leave him? How could I bear it? He loved me, I was sure of it, and I loved him. I loved him so much. So what if he was married? It wasn't a real marriage. They never saw each other. So what if she was having his babies? He could still be a father to them. I'd never stop him from seeing them. She hadn't cared about him when she'd been off travelling everywhere, leaving him alone to run a business and care for Adele. Why should she claim him all of a sudden, just because she'd decided she needed him? Couldn't I just accept the situation? Couldn't I just stay and love him and be happy? Who would know, or care? Who would judge me?

I closed my eyes as the answer came to me, unbidden and unwelcome. I'd judge myself.

I'd already let myself down so badly, and I couldn't do it again. If I allowed myself to make such a compromise, how could I look myself in the face ever again?

Deep down, I knew I would never forgive myself.

I pictured the looks on my parents' faces. They would try to understand, but they wouldn't be able to, not really. And how could I defend myself when, inside, I would know they were right? It might be old-fashioned, but I couldn't compromise my values any longer. I loved Ethan Rochester, but he wasn't mine to love. I had to leave.

I snapped the suitcase shut and left the bedroom, casting one last regretful look at it before closing the door on it forever. I made my way downstairs as quietly and as quickly as I could, and let myself out of the front door. The driveway seemed endless, but finally I followed the path through the woods, pressed the button on the wall, and walked through the side gate.

As the gate clicked shut behind me, I gripped my suitcase tightly, as it dawned on me that I'd left the sketch behind. Ethan would find it and probably think I'd torn it myself. I couldn't bear him to think I'd done that.

I glanced back through the gate, feeling as torn as the

drawing. What should I do? But it was too late. I knew I couldn't risk going back. I might never have the courage to leave again.

I took a deep breath and sent him a text message that simply said:

Antonia is here. I understand why it's been so difficult for you, but it's impossible for me. Whoever tore that sketch had more foresight than I had. I'm sorry. Be happy.

Then, much as I'd done with Seth, I blocked his number, blinked away the tears, and began to walk towards Hasedale, my head held high.

#

The smile on Mum's face died within seconds. I stood there on her doorstep, saying nothing, but something seemed to warn her of the state I was in. She ushered me inside, taking the suitcase from my hand and putting her arm around me, as I walked, half-dazed into the living room.

Dad was watching the television, and the minute I entered the room, shock entered his face. His hand reached for the remote and suddenly there was silence.

"What the hell? Cara, what's happened?"

I shivered, wondering vaguely how they knew. I'd not said a single word, but they'd already sussed that I was broken. That was parents for you, I supposed. The bond between parent and child—unbreakable. Not that I'd ever know. Ethan would, though. Soon, he'd have twins to care for, and he'd understand that bond in a way I never would.

A big, fat tear rolled down my cheek. I couldn't even be bothered to wipe it away.

I vaguely remember Mum pushing me into the chair,

and Dad rushing off to make me a cup of tea, and lots of cuddles and anxious expressions. In the end, Dad said, "You don't have to tell us anything just now, love. Whenever you're ready."

It turned out that I wasn't ready until the next morning. I'd slept in my old bed in the box room—although, to be honest, there wasn't much sleep involved. I'd mostly stared up at the ceiling, wondering if Ethan was thinking of me. More likely he'd thrown himself on Antonia's mercy, and they were excitedly choosing names for the babies. He'd make a wonderful father, I thought. As a husband, though, he sucked. Mind you, she wasn't much of a wife, either. Maybe they really did belong together. Maybe they were lying in bed together, right then, and he was stroking her bump and talking to his unborn children.

I think I did sleep a little. Well, I must have done, because one minute I was lying there in the darkness—imagining the cover of *All the Goss*, with Ethan's and Antonia's smiling faces as they cradled little Jonquil and Bunty in their arms, the headline screaming: *At Home with the Rochesters: Ethan and Antonia introduce their bundles of joy. We've never been so happy, says Ethan. We've made mistakes in the past, but it's all behind us now*—and the next minute, it was morning, and my room was flooded with sunlight, and I could hear Mum clattering in the kitchen below me, and Dad whistling in the garden.

I climbed out of bed, opened the curtains, and looked down on the lawn below. Dad was strolling down the path, swinging an empty pan in his hand. He'd obviously been to feed and water his pet rabbit, Dave. I smiled to myself, thinking how much I loved my parents, and how dear and familiar their house was. Nothing much had changed. Even after all the years since I'd left. Same noises, same routine. Comforting and familiar.

I took a deep breath. Okay, so I'd been badly let down by yet another man, but I wasn't the first woman it had happened to. I couldn't let it beat me. I'd been tempted, but I hadn't succumbed. I'd stayed true to myself. I'd changed the course of my life, and I hadn't compromised my values. I could finally be proud of myself. It was time for a new start.

"Bacon sandwich, love?" Mum's eyes were anxious, but she smiled brightly when I nodded and agreed that a bacon sandwich was just the way to start the day.

Dad put the pan on the draining board, washed his hands, then sat opposite me at the table. "You're looking a bit better this morning," he said. "How are you feeling?"

"Much better," I said defiantly. "I'm sorry I turned up like that out of the blue yesterday. And I'm sorry I didn't explain myself."

"You don't have to explain yourself," he said, shaking his head. "This is your home. Always will be. You can come here any time you like."

"Your dad's right," Mum handed me a plate with a doorstop of a bacon sandwich on it. "You don't have to tell us anything. It's your business."

Dad winked at me, and I grinned. It was clear to us both that she was dying to know, and so, over breakfast, I told them both what had been going on. Needless to say, they were completely enthralled as I poured the whole sorry story out to them. Dad quite forgot to eat his own sandwich.

"I don't believe it," he said finally, as I ended my

woeful tale and pushed my plate away.

"It's true," I said. "Honestly. I know it sounds unlikely, but he really did seem to love me."

"I can well believe that," he said indignantly. "Why the hell wouldn't he? I mean, I don't believe he lied to you like that. How dare he? What a swine."

"And twins." Mum shook her head. "Poor little mite. Fancy being pregnant with twins and having your husband do that to you."

"But to be fair," I said, because I couldn't bear them to think completely ill of him, "she was never around. She was always away travelling. He hardly saw her."

Mum sniffed. "Well, she obviously saw him at some point. Unless he posted a semen sample to her by Royal Mail."

"Sally!" Dad laughed, and Mum waved her hand at him dismissively.

"I don't care. What a rake, treating his wife like that, and treating our Cara like that, too. You're better off out of it, love. You can't trust people with loads of money. They're a weird bunch. Their morals are non-existent. All love rats and crack addicts."

Dad rolled his eyes. "If you say so, love. Mind you, Cara, she's right. You are better off out of it. I'm very proud of you for walking away."

"Me, too," Mum said. "Although, I'm always proud of you. You're such a good girl."

"What?" I stared at her in astonishment. "Proud of me? What on earth for?"

Dad frowned. "What do you mean what for? We've always been proud of you. Always."

"Always?" I shook my head. "Yeah, right. Even at

379

school?"

They looked at each other, clearly puzzled. "Of course at school. We always looked forward to parents' evenings, didn't we, Ray?" said Mum.

"What for? I never got the glowing reports that Redmond and Tamsin got," I said.

"You've got a short memory," said Dad. "Redmond may have got good marks and done well at sports, but the teachers were pretty scathing about him at times, weren't they, Sally?"

Mum rolled her eyes. "Oh, yes. He was always contradicting them, insisting he knew best. He used to tell them the lessons were boring and cause an awful lot of fuss in class. Mind you, he was so clever, I expect he found the other children slowed him down."

"Which is pretty much what he told his teachers on a regular basis." Dad laughed. "Then there was Tamsin."

"Ooh, we had fun and games with her, didn't we?" Mum agreed. "*Tamsin is, unfortunately, rather bossy,*" she said, as if reciting from something. "*She would do well to remember that she is a pupil, not a member of staff.*"

"I remember that report," Dad said. "Too cocky by half, she was. Always thought she knew better than anyone. She was a bit unkind to that little lass with the sticking out teeth, too. Remember?"

"I do. We had to go in to school a few times about her attitude, didn't we? Not that she physically bullied anyone," she explained hastily. "But, it has to be said, she could be quite thoughtless and nasty sometimes. Some of the kids were scared stiff of her."

I couldn't believe it. Tamsin! But she was so pretty, so popular.

"You, on the other hand," said Dad, smiling fondly at me, "were adored by all your teachers. Polite, kind-hearted, hard-working. Never a single complaint. We used to feel very smug when we left your classroom, I can tell you."

I blinked away tears. How had I never known that?

"You were always the one who looked after the unpopular kids, too," Mum said thoughtfully. "You always made sure they weren't alone. I remember your form teacher saying you were worth your weight in gold, and that you were like a little mother hen, taking care of her chicks. Mind you, you've always been motherly," she continued blithely, having no idea the effect her words were having on me. "We always said you'll make a brilliant mum one day, and you will."

"But," I managed, "it was Tamsin who played with the dolls. Not me."

Mum laughed. "Tamsin liked to dress up her dolls and boss them around. You didn't play with them, true, but you looked after that pet guinea pig of yours as if it was a real baby. You didn't just shove it in its hutch and forget about it, like Redmond did with his rabbit. Don't you remember? It was you who used to feed and water it, and clean it out. He lost interest after a week. And you were the one who all the local mums wanted to babysit their children. You used to make a fortune. I remember Mandy at the end of the street saying to me that you had the patience of a saint with her kids. Oh, yes, we were always very proud of you, love."

"Until I met Seth and left home," I said, choked. "Then I let you down badly."

Dad shook his head. "You didn't let us down," he said

seriously. "Yes, you made a mistake, but by God, you more than paid for it. Point is, you got on with it. No complaining. No whingeing. You got yourself a job, put a roof over your head, and kept going. You supported not only yourself, but that useless lump, too. You never gave in. You never became like him. You were always Cara, no matter what. How could we not be proud of you for that?"

"We'd never want you any other way," Mum said, squeezing my hand. "You always had your head screwed on tight, and your heart in the right place. What more could we possibly want, or ask for?"

"If it wasn't for you," Dad added, "we might never have found out how Robyn and Alice really felt, and Brad and Tamsin might still be separated. They didn't tell me and your mum. They couldn't even tell their own parents. But you got through to them. They trusted you enough to be honest with you. That says a lot, Cara."

Isn't it funny how you can get your own life so completely wrong? I'd seen myself through a tinted lens, somehow, unable to see the bright bits that Mum and Dad remembered so clearly. My vision of myself and the life I'd lived had been very different to the one they had. For the first time, I began to believe that I wasn't the waste of space I thought I was. And for the first time, I began to understand how someone like Ethan Rochester could love me.

What a pity it had all come too late.

Chapter Twenty-Eight

Sitting in the garden, Dad and I shared the hammock that Mum had bought him for his birthday—even though, as he reminded me with a twinkle in his eye, it was her who'd always wanted one.

"You're so lucky," I said with a sigh, leaning my head on his shoulder as we rocked gently back and forth. "You and Mum, I mean. You have such a happy marriage, and such a simple life."

He laughed at that. "You think?"

"Well," I said, surprised, "don't you?"

"No one's marriage is that perfect, love," he assured me. "And no one's life is untouched by pain and loss and fear. No one's." He turned to face me. "This Ethan chap—what made you fall for him?"

"Does it matter?" I said. "It's over now. No point in going over it all."

"But I've been thinking about it," he admitted. "About him. He said his marriage wasn't a real marriage. What do you think he meant by that?"

I shrugged. "I suppose, because they rarely saw one another. As Mum said, though, it didn't stop them conceiving twins, did it?"

"Hmm. It all seems very odd to me. But you believed him? I mean, at the time. You believed he was genuine, and that he loved you?"

"I didn't want to," I said. "That was what made it so different from Seth. With him, I desperately wanted to believe that he loved me, and that blinded me to reality for so long. But with Ethan ... I really fought it every step of the way. I couldn't allow myself to believe he meant what he said. Somehow, though, he got through my defences. I couldn't help it."

He sighed. "Life's a very funny game, isn't it? And love's even funnier."

"But you struck lucky," I said. "You're happy."

"Oh, yes. Now."

I narrowed my eyes. "Now? Are you saying you and Mum have had problems?"

He took my hand and squeezed it, then he looked at me, and I was horrified to see tears in his eyes. "Now, Cara, I'm going to tell you something that Redmond and Tamsin don't know, and your Mum would be furious if she knew I was telling you this, but I want to now. It's time. Don't you get scared, love, but, well, I've had cancer."

"What?" My throat tightened, and I felt sick with fear. "When? What sort of cancer? Have you had treatment? Are you going to be all right?"

"Shush, now, your mum'll hear you." He leaned back in the hammock and seemed to consider for a moment. "It was months ago when we found out. I needed an operation and chemotherapy. That's why I took voluntary redundancy. It was a godsend, really. Came at just the right time. I didn't have to worry about being on sick, or taking time off work, or how we were going to manage financially. Always a silver lining, you see? Anyway, I was lucky. They'd found it early, and after a pretty gruelling course of treatment, I got the all clear."

"I knew you looked ill," I said, wondering why I hadn't pressed for more information at the funeral. "Mum said it was because you were stressed about retiring, but I could see how much weight you'd lost and how tired you were. I'm so sorry, Dad."

"Sorry for what?" he said. "You didn't know. I didn't want you to know. I made your mum promise that we wouldn't tell anyone. Anyway, when the treatment finally ended, that windfall from Granny Reed paid for a nice long holiday, and I had a very lovely recuperation period in the sunshine. Timing again, see? Someone's been looking after me." He smiled up at the sky, and I thought, only Dad could go through so much and still see the bright side.

"But you're all right now?" I said anxiously.

"Oh, yes. I mean, I have to have regular check-ups, but the doctors seem very confident, and I feel wonderful. Better than I have in ages."

"Thank God," I murmured.

"Yes, even I've begun to thank Him," he said, grinning mischievously. "Whether God's an old man with a beard, or a genius of a computer programmer, I'm very grateful. You see, Cara, no one's life is completely straightforward, no matter how it looks on the surface. You may think they're having a wonderful time of it, but beneath the public facade, things may be very different."

"Like Tamsin with her cheerful Facebook statuses," I said. "In private, her heart was breaking."

"Exactly," he said. "What I mean is, however it looks to the rest of us, who knows what's really going in Ethan Rochester's life? People don't do things for no reason. I'm

385

not saying you should take his word for it, necessarily, but what I am saying is, maybe you should look a bit deeper. He said he would tell you all about it when he sorted things out with his wife, but he never got the chance, did he? After everything you went through with Seth, he must be a pretty special man to win your heart the way he has."

"He's very special," I admitted. "I never thought someone like him could love someone like me."

"Maybe that's been your trouble all along, Cara," Dad said. "Maybe it's not other people you don't trust, after all. Maybe it's yourself. You have to start believing that you're good enough for others to want to be with you. When you've figured that out, you may see things very differently. If I were you," he added gently, "I wouldn't give up on this chap of yours just yet."

I didn't know how to answer him. Part of me was holding on to every word he said, clinging to the hope that he was right, that there was something I didn't know that would change everything. But the other part of me was afraid. Afraid to believe in Ethan's feelings. Afraid to accept that such love was truly possible. "We'll see, Dad," I said, patting his hand. "We'll see."

#

You could have knocked me down with a feather. The last person I expected to find in Mum and Dad's kitchen when I entered it that afternoon was Michael, but there he was, large as life, and looking quite embarrassed about it.

I'd only been to the local shop for some milk. Honestly, who could have predicted that I'd get home to find Ethan's chauffeur sitting at the table, sipping tea from Mum's *Emmerdale* mug?

"So, there you are," he said, his eyes twinkling. "I was

beginning to think you'd done a bunk. Again."

"Sorry, love," said Dad. "He was quite insistent that he saw you."

Mum was eyeing him suspiciously. "I won't have you upsetting our Cara," she said. "Your precious boss has already done that, thank you very much. If you've come here to make things worse, you can sling your hook right now."

Michael looked offended. "I'd never upset you, now, would I? Be fair."

I dropped into the chair opposite him and stared at him in bewilderment. "What on earth are you doing here? I mean, why—how—?"

"You're not as clever as you suppose," he said. "You provided Ethan with a reference from your previous employer, remember? Ethan contacted her and explained that he needed to get in touch with you regarding unpaid wages. She gave him this address."

That explained that. Jilly knew my parents' address, all right. She'd come to an anniversary party there with me one year, when I'd been invited and hadn't wanted to bring Seth. I hadn't seen my parents for ages and hadn't wanted to turn up alone. I'd expected to be mostly ignored, and Jilly had offered to come with me so I'd at least have someone to talk to. As it turned out, I'd had a lovely time. Everyone had been so delighted to see me, and they couldn't wait to catch up.

I blinked away tears at the memory. "Okay, so you've tracked me down. But why? There's nothing to say, Michael. I heard everything."

"I'm under orders to give you these," Michael said, reaching under the table and handing me a bunch of flowers.

Mum tutted. "What a cheapskate," she said. "All that money, and he can't even send her a proper bouquet."

Michael looked steadily at me, and I knew exactly what he was thinking.

"You don't understand, Mum," I murmured. Taking the handtied offering, I inhaled the beautiful scent of blush-tipped creamy roses and palest pink sweet peas, my mind flooding with happy memories. "They're beautiful."

"He cut them himself this morning," Michael told me. He leaned forward, his voice serious. "What are you playing at, Cara? He's tried ringing you and texting you, but he can't get through. Guessed you'd blocked his number. He's at his wits end."

"Not here, though, is he?" Mum demanded. "If he's that bothered, where is he?"

Michael glanced up at her, then back to me. "He's at the hospital."

"Hospital?" My hand flew to my mouth. "Is he all right?"

"He's fine, love." He patted my hand. "It's Antonia. She's gone into labour."

The world seemed to spin. I heard Dad say, "Well, that's put the cat among the pigeons."

Mum put her hands on her hips. "Well, that's charming, I must say. So, his wife's in labour, and he's sending flowers to another woman. What a lovely man he is."

"Ethan Rochester is one of the most decent, honourable men I know," Michael said, glaring at her. Clearly, he'd had enough her attacks on Ethan's character. "You only know one side of the story, and that's a bit cock-eyed, if you don't mind me saying so. Sorry, Cara," he added, "but it's a fact. If you hadn't run off like that, you'd have found out the truth."

"She knows the truth," Mum said. "She heard—"

"We know what she heard," Michael said. He looked at me, an appeal in his eyes. "Laura remembered, you see. When we discovered you'd gone, she remembered that you'd been on the stairs. We realised you'd heard and misunderstood."

"Maybe we should leave you to it," Dad said, and grasped my mum's arm, leading her into the living room, in spite of her obvious objection. "Just hear him out, love," he pleaded with me, before he shut the door behind them—though, not before Mum threw Michael a very threatening glance over her shoulder.

Michael shook his head. "Feisty, your mum, isn't she?"

"Is Antonia okay?" I said anxiously. "The babies— they're not due yet, are they?"

"No." He sighed. "It's a bit worrying, I won't lie. That's why Ethan's with her. He's been going mad, waiting for your old boss to give him this address. He was all set to come here today, bring you the flowers, plead his case. Then he got the call from Faith, and—well, you know Ethan. He was devastated. About both of you, I mean. Blames himself for it all. Worried sick about you, worried sick about her. Torn, he was. Torn. I told him to get himself to the hospital, because if anything happened, he'd never forgive himself. He made me swear that I'd not come back without you." He patted my hand. "You've led us a proper merry dance, haven't you? But you must know by now that Ethan wouldn't do anything to hurt you. Not deliberately. He's a good lad. Come home, Cara. Let him explain."

I buried my head in my hands. "I don't know what to think anymore. There are so many secrets and lies in that house, and you can't deny that he's a married man, and that his wife is pregnant. And that woman said, quite clearly, that he was abandoning his wife just weeks before she gave birth to twins. Do you deny that?"

He sipped his tea slowly, as if considering what to say next. Finally, he put the cup down and said, "Look, love, I can't get into all this with you. From what Laura told me, yes, Faith did say those words, but there's more to it than you know. Ethan's not a liar, or a cheat."

"He told Antonia's cousin he didn't know where she was, but he knew the whole time. He lied then."

He shrugged. "Things are never that straightforward. What do you want me to say? I could sit here and argue with you all day, but it strikes me that there's only one thing you need to decide. The way I see it, you either trust the lad, or you don't. If you don't, then there's no point in going back. Of course, he'll be distraught if I go back without you, and, in all likelihood, he'll be down to fetch you himself as soon as he can leave the hospital, but personally, I see no point in taking you back to Moreland if you've no trust in him. That's no basis for any kind of relationship. I know Ethan inside out. I'd trust him with my life. Question is, would you? Because that's what he's asking, you know. It's not just a fling to him. He's asking for the rest of your life, and he's willing to give you the rest of his. Do you want it, or not?"

I could have been making the biggest mistake of my life. I could've been throwing away all my integrity, all my common sense. I could've been heading back down the same road I'd taken with Seth, compromising myself yet again.

Yet, as I looked into Michael's face while he watched me steadily, through totally honest, kind blue eyes, I knew the answer.

"I trust him," I said finally. "I'm coming home."

Chapter Twenty-Nine

The drive to Moreland Hall seemed to take ages. Michael was a professional driver, and had no intention of breaking any speed limits, however much I urged him, although the journey was a lot quicker than it would have been if I'd had to get the train and a taxi, or bus, again.

I noticed him checking his phone, as he'd stood patiently by the car, waiting for me as I'd tearfully hugged Mum and Dad.

"Don't you take any nonsense from that Rochester fella," Mum said. "If he gives you any trouble, you come straight home, do you hear me? I don't want you putting up with any more rubbish from men."

"I won't," I promised.

Dad hugged me. "Just give him a chance and make up your own mind," he whispered.

"Take care of yourself, Dad," I murmured, holding him tightly. "I love you so much."

He winked at me, then let me go. I'd climbed into the car and they'd waved to me, as Michael started the engine. "Love you, Cara," they shouted. "Ring us. Let us know how it goes."

I'd nodded, smiling tearfully as the car headed down the road. We'd turned the corner and they were gone from my view.

"Mrs Rochester's just messaged me," Michael

informed me. "Babies have arrived. Identical boys. They're poorly, but not thought to be critical. Ethan's on his way home."

"Is Antonia okay?" I said anxiously.

He nodded. "A bit shocked and exhausted, obviously, but fine otherwise." He surveyed me through the rearview mirror. "Reckon Ethan will be in shock, an' all. What a traumatic few days you've all had, eh?"

He could say that again, I thought. I'd have given anything for a quiet life. "Can you go a bit faster, Michael?" I begged.

"No." He didn't appear willing to negotiate, so I settled back in my seat and tried not to fidget.

After what seemed like hours, but was actually barely ninety minutes, he cleared his throat and said, "Not long now. You should catch sight of the house any minute."

I leaned forward, eager to see the first sight of Moreland Hall. I was so excited and nervous that, at first, I thought my eyes were playing tricks.

"Michael," I said slowly, "is that—is that—"

"Christ almighty," he gasped. "Smoke. The Hall's on fire!"

He seemed to forget all about speed limits and his professional integrity as we raced towards the house, too terrified to even speak.

The gates were standing open, which just seemed to emphasise the severity of the situation. Smoke billowed from the roof, and flames leapt from the shattered window of Ethan's art room.

"Adele!" I jumped out of the car and raced over to where Jennifer was holding her daughter, Mrs F standing by their side and looking grey with worry. Thank God they were safe, at least.

"I've rung the fire brigade," Mrs F said, her voice choked with fear. "But Ethan—Ethan ..."

I looked at her in horror. "You're not saying he's up there?"

"He ran back in. I couldn't stop him. He said he saw someone at one of the attic windows, just before ..." She looked up at the shattered studio window, clearly traumatised.

"I'm going in," Michael said, but Mrs F grabbed his arm.

"You're doing no such thing! With your asthma? Ethan told us to get Adele out and stay out. The fire brigade should be here by now. Where are they?"

Adele was crying, and Jennifer clutched her tightly. Tears were running down her own face as she stared up at the burning attic. "My son. My baby."

My hands flew to my mouth at a loud crash, and we all jumped when several tiles fell to the floor, clattering on the drive.

Michael looked helpless. "I have to try," he said.

"It's dangerous standing so close to the house," I said. "Michael, get them all to the end of the drive."

"What are you doing?" Mrs F said, as I turned away.

"Just go!" I yelled.

Michael's hand shot out to grab me, but I dodged it and ran into the house.

The downstairs was already beginning to fill with smoke as I rushed into the kitchen. I managed to find a towel, which I soaked in water and wrapped around my face. Before I could think about it too much, or talk myself out of it, I ran up the stairs, my eyes burning with the thick smoke that was blocking the landing.

The attic door stood open, and I stared at the black, smoke-filled cavern in terror. Yet, I knew I had no choice. Ethan was up there. I couldn't lose him. I would never leave him again.

The heat was unbearable as I stumbled along the central corridor, my eyes stinging and streaming as acrid smoke choked me. I thought of Ethan's artwork and his cleaning materials. No wonder the window to his studio had blown out. But what was he doing up there, anyway? No one could have been up there. Jennifer, Adele and Mrs F were safe. He must have imagined it. Unless .... Unless there really had been someone up there all that time. All those noises I'd heard. Bats, Mrs F had said. Ethan moving the easel, he'd insisted. What if they'd both been wrong?

I sobbed. "Ethan! Ethan!"

My voice sounded choked and muffled. How would he ever hear me? My eyes hurt badly. I could barely breathe. The roaring of the flames made it impossible to hear anyone moving around. What if he wasn't moving? What if he was unconscious? How would I ever find him? I couldn't even tell where his studio was.

Through the blinding smoke, a dark shape loomed. Some weird, misshapen form stumbled towards me, and I reached out my hands, groping for contact. The towel dropped to the floor, lost somewhere in the smoke.

Ethan's face was black, his clothes filthy, his eyes red-rimmed and streaming. I saw the shock on his face as he registered my presence, and I heard him say something, but his voice was too hoarse to be properly audible. I looked down at the crumpled figure he was dragging with him. I couldn't tell if it was a man, or a woman. It was too difficult to see anything properly.

"Out, out." Ethan's eyes pleaded with me. I wasn't going to leave him. No way. I put my arm around the unconscious figure, and, somehow, I managed to help drag him to the stairs.

We half fell down them, collapsing on the landing.

Ethan's breathing was laboured. He looked about to pass out any moment. "Get out," he wheezed eventually.

"No way," I said, with huge difficulty. I wanted to say so much more, but it was impossible. I felt as if a giant hand was choking me, wrapping its merciless fingers around my windpipe and squeezing tight. I thought, *we're going to die here. We really are. This is it.*

Ethan's eyes seemed to flare into life again. He made a superhuman effort and headed for the staircase, his determination making me redouble my own efforts. Together, we dragged the unconscious person down the stairs.

The smoke thinned, and I saw a light ahead of me. I hoped it wasn't heaven. I guessed from the way my eyes and throat were burning that I hadn't actually died yet, so it was a safe bet that the light was the outside world.

We moved forward, down the hall and out onto the steps. I was dimly aware of other shapes pushing past me, and felt a massive relief that the fire brigade had arrived. Michael and Mrs F rushed over to us, helping us, and then someone in a uniform took the figure away from us, and I almost fell against Mrs F, coughing and spluttering, while beside me, Ethan sank to the ground.

I didn't really remember how I ended up sitting in an ambulance, but someone had put an oxygen mask on me and was telling me, in soothing tones, to take nice deep breaths. As it became easier to breathe again, I looked around me in a panic. "Ethan?"

"He's just outside having some oxygen, love. Don't worry, he'll be right as rain."

"What about the other person?"

The paramedic's eyes softened, and she rubbed my back gently. "Just keep taking nice deep breaths, love. There's a good girl."

#

Ethan came to find me, in spite of Jennifer hanging on his arm, begging him to rest. "How are you doing?"

I made my way to the ambulance exit and stepped down onto firm ground. "I'm okay," I said. "But what about you?"

"I'll be fine," he assured me, although his voice sounded hoarse. He glared at me through red-rimmed eyes. "What the hell did you think you were doing? That's the most stupid thing I've ever seen."

"I beg your pardon?" I said indignantly.

"What were you playing at? Fancy running into a burning building!"

"You mean, like you did?" I demanded.

"That's different!" He coughed, shaking his head at the same time. "You could have been killed."

"So could you," I pointed out.

We stared at each other, then he put his arms around me, and his forehead pressed against my own. "You came back," he whispered.

"I did. And whatever happens, I'm never leaving you again."

If I'd needed something to convince me of how much

I loved him before, I'd had my proof. When I thought I was going to lose him in that fire, I'd felt as if my own life was over, too. I had no idea what was going on with Antonia, but at that moment, it really hadn't seemed to matter.

"And what you heard ..."

"It doesn't matter right now," I said, aware that neither of us were up to a deep and meaningful conversation. Besides, there was a more pressing matter to discuss. "Who was the person in the fire? And are they going to be okay?"

He looked towards a second ambulance, his face anxious. "I have no idea who he is," he confessed. "But he doesn't look good."

"What on earth was he doing in the attic?" I said, bewildered.

"I haven't a clue. Thank God I spotted him, though. If I hadn't gone up there ..." His voice trailed off, and he stared up toward the roof. The flames had been extinguished, but the Hall looked in a sorry state. Smoke still billowed from the windows and the hole in the roof, and I could only imagine how bad it looked inside.

"Your lovely house," I murmured. "I'm so sorry."

"Houses can be repaired," he said firmly. "All that matters is that we made it, and, hopefully, our mysterious visitor will make it, too."

"Quite right," said Jennifer tearfully. "I was so scared when I realised you were in there, Ethan, and then when Cara followed you .... Honestly, you two are both mad. You were made for each other."

Ethan winked at me, and I grinned.

"You look like you should be singing *Chim Chim Cher-*

ee," I told him. "You need a shower."

"We both do," he said, trying to sound seductive. Unfortunately, another bout of coughing put paid to that effort. "Serves me right," he said finally, then took my hand. "I need to check on our mystery man, Cara. Wait here, if you like. I'm not sure how he'll look, so—"

"I'm coming, too," I said firmly. "I want to know he's okay, and I want to know who he is."

The paramedic in the second ambulance was writing something down when we approached. On the trolley to his side, a figure lay with an oxygen mask on his face.

"We're just about to get off to the hospital," the paramedic said.

"Is he—I mean, will he—"

"He came round long enough to speak to me," the paramedic assured us, "and the signs are good. Do either of you want to go with him to the hospital?"

"I'll go," Ethan said. "Someone needs to find out who he is. He must have someone, somewhere, who's worried about him."

The paramedic raised an eyebrow. "Don't you know who he is?" he said, puzzled.

We shook our heads. "Not a clue."

"Hmm. All I got out of him was his name's Seth," the paramedic informed us. He put down his clipboard and nodded to Ethan. "Okay, get in if you're coming. We need to get off."

Ethan and I stared at each other in shock. "Seth!" I glanced over at the figure, lying still on the trolley. "What the hell was he doing up there?"

"You'd better go with him," Ethan said, squeezing my arm. "It's okay," he added, clearly seeing the look of anxiety in my eyes, "I'll follow you. Go on, Cara. If he comes round again, he'll need you."

I could only nod in bewildered silence, before the paramedic closed the ambulance doors, and we headed off to the hospital.

Chapter Thirty

Seth, it transpired, had initially passed out, not due to smoke inhalation, but because, in his own words, he was 'as drunk as a skunk'.

It was the following day before he was well enough to talk to us, and Ethan and I sat by his bedside, in stunned silence, as he recounted his tale of woe.

"I'm so sorry, Cara." He looked genuinely mortified. "I can't explain it. It was like some madness descended. I was so scared when you left. I'd never been alone before. I didn't know what to do. I just had to be with you. I only felt safe when you were nearby."

Sitting beside him on the bed, Isolde squirmed uncomfortably. "It's true," she said sullenly. "He was inconsolable when you left, and nothing me and Naomi said could persuade him that he'd be just fine on his own. He'd somehow got it fixed in his mind that, without you, he wouldn't be able to cope. Crazy."

"You could say that," I said.

Ethan leaned towards me and whispered, "Understandable, in my opinion."

"Don't encourage him," I whispered back, squeezing his hand.

Seth had quickly discovered my whereabouts, thanks—as I'd feared—to Susan tagging me in that wretched photograph of Moreland Hall on Facebook.

Isolde had spotted it and tipped him off, little realising the effect it would have on him.

"So, what took you so long to go to the Hall?" I asked. "Susan put that post up ages ago."

"I thought you'd come back," he said. "I was convinced you'd come to your senses and return home. I couldn't believe it when you ignored my poems. They took me hours to write, you know."

"It was very difficult," I said solemnly, "but I knew I had to try."

"Naomi and I kept reassuring him that things would be okay, but after a few weeks, he was getting worse, not better." Isolde shook her head, clearly bewildered. "Then he just disappeared. He was supposed to be moving in with us, but when we went to the flat, he'd gone."

"I needed to talk to you, make you understand you were making a big mistake," Seth explained.

The problem he'd faced was, how to get in? The gates were electronic, he didn't know the keycode, and it was impossible to climb that high wall.

It'd been Paolo's timely arrival that had enabled him to sneak in. Paolo, he said, had pulled up in his van, and he and his buffoons had got out to press the intercom. They'd been so busy chattering among themselves, peering through the gate and congratulating each other on landing such a lucrative contract, that no one noticed when he'd followed the van through the gates, shot off into the woodland, and sneaked slowly and stealthily into the house through the back door.

"I couldn't believe it was that easy to get in," he admitted.

"Neither can I," Ethan said grimly. "Security will have

to be reviewed, that's for sure."

Seth looked embarrassed. "Thing is, once I got in, I had no intention of leaving, in case I couldn't get back in again. I hadn't brought much with me, though. My phone, my charger—which I seem to have lost somewhere—"

Ethan and I exchanged knowing glances at that. So, it wasn't Briony's charger, after all.

"I didn't have so much as a change of clothes," Seth admitted. "All I had on me was a couple of joints, and I daren't even smoke them, in case the smell gave me away. Cara's like a bloodhound when it comes to dope," he informed an amused Ethan. "I knew I needed some food, if nothing else, so I helped myself to some stuff from the fridge. I nearly had a heart attack when your granny spotted me, and lectured me on being in her kitchen uninvited."

Ethan looked puzzled. "My granny?"

"He means Mrs F," I said, thinking how furious she'd be to be mistaken for Ethan's grandmother.

"Anyway, whoever she was," Seth continued, "she seemed to think I was with that little foreign chap, so I let her think it, then I buggered off upstairs."

He didn't have a plan, he said. It'd been sheer luck that led to him discovering the attics, but once he had, he'd realised there was a place he could hide out easily. He'd chosen one of the old servants' bedrooms, complete with iron bed, closed the door behind himself, and hidden well away. He was, if not exactly comfortable, hardly slumming it.

"He texted me," Isolde admitted. "Told me where he was. I said it was daft, and what did he hope to achieve by it?"

"Well, quite," said Ethan. "What *did* you hope to achieve by it?"

"I wasn't thinking straight," Seth moaned. "In the back of my mind, I was just waiting for Cara to see sense and come home. I can't tell you what was going on because it's all a blur. I was off my head."

Ethan leaned back in his chair and folded his arms. "How ironic," he said. "I appear to have had a madman in my attic." He winked at me. "There's a twist we never saw coming."

"So, you're the one who stole all that food," I said. "Do you know everyone thought it was me? They thought I had an eating disorder."

"Well," Seth said uncomfortably, "you do tend to scoff a lot. It's an understandable mistake."

Of all the cheek!

"Sorry I nicked your food, mate," he said to Ethan. "It was pretty easy to get it. No one was around at night, and the house was often empty, anyway. Your granny, or whoever she is, was the only real fly in the ointment, but I soon got used to her routine. I even swiped one of the guests breakfasts one morning." He actually had the nerve to chuckle to himself. Served him right, when it brought on a coughing fit.

Isolde patted his arm. "Be careful, Seth. Don't overdo it."

As something else occurred to me, I looked at him coldly. "You slashed my dress, didn't you?"

Ethan glared at him. "Did you? Why on earth would you do that?"

Seth reddened. "Do you know how hard it's been, watching you two grow so close? I never expected that, did I? I could see you, from the attic window. I watched you walking across the lawn together. Sometimes, I even risked standing on the landing so I could hear you talking. That was a bit dodgy," he admitted. "One of your party guests spotted me once, but luckily he was too drunk to realise what he'd seen."

"So, you were spying on me," I said, shivering.

"I couldn't stand it," he confessed. "I could see what was happening, from the moment I saw you together, and that dress—it was disgusting. What were you doing, flaunting yourself like that for him? You never wore anything like that for me."

"It was for me, not him. Anyway, we never went anywhere," I pointed out. "It's hardly the sort of thing you wear to nip to Asda, is it?"

He looked shamefaced at that. "I guess not."

"And the sketch?" I said. "Was that you, too?"

"It just finished me," he admitted. "Sorry I ripped your picture, mate," he said to Ethan. "Just, I saw the way you'd captured something in her. I could see the way you felt about her, and I couldn't stand it."

"A bit like the picture Isolde drew of you," I said.

His eyes widened. "What do you mean?"

Isolde went scarlet.

"Are you seriously telling me you don't know?" I shook my head in wonder. "You really don't, do you? Isolde, don't you think it's time you told him?"

"Told me what?" he said, looking baffled.

After a brief silence, Ethan said gently, "I don't know either of you, but it's perfectly obvious to me that this girl loves you."

Seth tutted. "Loves me?" He glanced across at her,

where she sat, head down, plucking at the bedspread, and frowned. "But—but she's just Isolde."

Isolde's head shot up. "Thanks."

He looked stunned. "You mean, you mean it's true?"

Isolde hesitated, then she burst out, "Of course it's bloody true, you idiot. Why do you think I've been cooking for you and taking care of you since she left?"

"Exactly," I said. "She even offered to let you move in with her."

"But she said you could move in, too!" Seth exclaimed.

"Because she was so desperate to please you," I said, exasperated. "Don't you see? Isolde has always loved you. She'd do anything for you, even put up with me."

He stared at Isolde as if he couldn't take it in for a moment, then his mouth curved into a smile. "I never knew," he murmured.

"I didn't know how to tell you," she muttered. "I just kept trying to show you instead."

"And you know now," Ethan said. "So, if I were you, I'd do something about it. When someone loves you, really loves you, you should hang onto them for dear life. It's a precious thing, love."

He smiled at me, and I smiled back. "You and me, Seth, it's not real," I said, turning back to my dumbfounded ex. "You know that, don't you?"

He nodded. "I know. I think I've known for a long time, but I was just scared. I'm sorry, Cara. I think—I think I lost my mind for a while. I can't tell you how much I regret what I did. What happened." He hung his head. "I'm sorry I burned your house down, mate," he told Ethan. "And thanks—for coming in to get me, I mean. I'd never have made it without you."

"Yes, thank you so much," Isolde said, her eyes filling with tears. "I can't imagine ..." She broke off, and Seth reached for her hand. She stared at him for a moment, then they smiled at each other, and I felt a huge burden lift from my shoulders.

"It was an accident," Ethan said. "You were stupid and irresponsible, but I accept that you didn't mean to start a fire."

"I'd had those joints in my backpack all those days and never touched them," Seth said wistfully. "Then, just as I'd finally accepted it was time to move on, I had to light one. I thought, it's my last night in the attic. Why not? I hadn't dared smoke it before, in case you smelled it. You always said it had a horrible smell. I couldn't risk it. I can't believe I fell asleep."

"Well, two bottles of wine all to yourself can make you drowsy," Isolde said, shaking her head.

The fire brigade had said that a discarded match had set light to some rubbish in the corner of the room. Seth had apparently dumped all his food wrappers there, and having lit his joint, he'd blown out the match and thrown it over onto the pile. Sadly for him, the match hadn't gone out.

"You're lucky to be alive."

"I know. I know that." He barely whispered the words. "I don't even remember anything about it. I was so drunk. Sorry I pinched your wine, mate," he said, adding another apology to the list. "I must have woken up, seen the flames, tried to get out. If you hadn't seen me moving in front of the window—"

It didn't bear thinking about, really. The fire had

spread quickly, and once it reached the studio, the materials in there had exploded. Ethan had found Seth lying in the corridor, not far from that room. If he hadn't spotted him, Seth would have died up there. It made me sick, imagining an alternative outcome. Whatever he'd done, I couldn't have coped with that.

"I'm not a bad man, Cara," Seth said earnestly. "I never meant to hurt you, or make you unhappy."

"I know that," I said, "and you're quite right. You're not a bad man. You're just bad for me, as I'm bad for you. Your way isn't the wrong way, and neither is mine. The trouble is, we wanted different things. We simply weren't compatible."

"But there were some good times?" He sounded anxious.

I smiled. "There were," I said. "We were very young, and it was all very romantic for a time. Besides, you made me feel loved for a while. I thank you for that. Now you can make Isolde feel that way."

He glanced at Isolde and smiled.

"You're going to be all right, Seth," I told him.

He leaned back on his pillow and closed his eyes, still holding Isolde's hand. "I think you're right, Cara," he said softly. "I think we're all going to be all right."

Chapter Thirty-One

We left the hospital, Ethan and I, and drove quietly back to Moreland Hall. Jennifer, Adele, and Mrs F had been driven back to London by Michael. The Hall was hardly somewhere they could stay, given that it was still being examined, and the smoke damage was horrendous, not to mention the actual fire damage upstairs.

Ethan and I had checked into a hotel, as he needed to be around for the investigation and was determined to stay close by to oversee repairs, while I was equally determined to stay with him, wherever he was. As the car pulled up outside the house, we climbed out and stood staring up at the blackened roof and shattered windows.

"I'm so sorry," I said. "If it hadn't been for me, Seth would never have—"

"It's just a house," he said firmly. "It's the people that make it a home, and we're all safe, thank God." He took my hand. "You came back."

"I know I did." I smiled. "You don't get rid of me that easily."

He turned to face me. "But why? What made you change your mind?"

"Because," I said, "whatever I heard, however bad things look—and I've got to say, Mr Rochester, they look pretty bad—I trust you."

His face lit up. "You do?"

"I do. I believe you love me, and I know for a fact that I love you. The simple fact is, I can't live without you, so you'd just better have a bloody good explanation for everything that's happened, mister."

"I have." He hooked his arm over my shoulders. "Let's go to our place, shall we? It's time I told you everything."

The secret garden was as magical as ever—perhaps more so. With the house so blackened and damaged, it felt like a miracle that, in there, the roses still bloomed, and the air was still scented with their beautiful perfume. We wandered through the archway and settled ourselves on the swing.

"So," Ethan said, "where do you want me to start?"

"How about," I said slowly, "you tell me about these twins you've allegedly fathered with your wife?"

"It's not true," he said. "They're not mine."

"But Faith said ..." I shook my head. "How are they, anyway? I feel awful. I haven't really had chance to ask."

"They're going to be okay. They were quite a good weight, considering they were six weeks early, and the doctors seem very optimistic."

"And Antonia?"

"Absolutely shattered, scared to death, but over the moon." He grinned. "Faith was with her for the birth. I waited outside, pacing up and down like some Victorian father-to-be." He looked stricken. "But I'm not," he added hastily. "A father-to-be, I mean. Or a father, come to that." He took a deep breath. "Let me start at the beginning."

"I think you should."

"Antonia and I have been friends since childhood. She

was a good pal. One of the boys. I had no romantic feelings towards her, but we always got on, and she understood my situation, as I understood hers. When she turned eighteen, she got a pretty nasty shock. It seemed her father had, more or less, promised her in marriage to the son of a business associate. It wasn't about her, or what she wanted. The two of them had apparently cooked up the deal when Antonia was little more than thirteen."

"What? But that's mediaeval." I gaped. "No one does that in real life, surely?"

"You don't know Simon," Ethan said grimly. "Oh, he couldn't force her, of course, but he's always been exceptionally good at making Antonia feel guilty. She adores him, and she's always wanted to please him, even when she was a little girl. That time, though, he'd made a huge mistake. He had no idea. She came to me for help. She didn't want to hurt him, or fall out with him, but she simply couldn't marry that man, and she was desperately afraid that he'd convince her to do so. So, we decided, there and then, to stop that from happening, and to solve my own problems at the same time."

"What problems were you having?" I asked.

"The same problem that keeps cropping up, even now," he said with a sigh. "There were girls. Girls like Jodie Palmerston and Briony. Girls who saw me as a walking cash register, and were determined to get a ring on their finger, one way, or the other."

"I'm sure there were plenty of girls who just wanted to be with you, whether you had money, or not," I protested. "I hate to say it, but you are rather gorgeous, you know."

He grinned at me. "Really? I wondered if you fancied me. You've never actually said."

I blushed. "I know, I just assumed it was obvious." I nudged him. "Oh, okay. You're sex on a stick, and I fancy you like mad."

"Thank you," he said. "That's very reassuring."

I laughed. "Go on, then. About these girls."

"Oh, yeah. Well, anyway, the point is, I didn't trust them. I'd seen it with my own father. I'd watched women flirt with him for years—to no effect, I might add. My father adored my mother, and besides, he knew perfectly well what they were after. He always warned me to be careful. Said some women had no self-respect, and would go all out to trap me. He said, not all women were like that, and that I had to wait until I found someone who would love me, even if I went bankrupt tomorrow."

"That's me," I said. "I don't care if you have money, or not. You do believe that, don't you?"

"If I didn't, I wouldn't have let myself fall for you so utterly and completely," he said. "But you have to remember, I was just a kid back then, and I didn't know how to tell the difference. I didn't want to end up with a broken heart and a stack of maxed-out credit cards, so it seemed to Antonia and me that the best thing to do to help both of us was to get married. To each other, I mean. That way, her father couldn't force her to marry his associate's son, and women wouldn't be able to get their hands on me. So, that's what we did." He sighed, and I reached for his hand, studying it while I tried to make sense of their marriage of convenience.

"So, it was never about love?" I said eventually. "You and Antonia, you got married to protect yourselves. That's what you meant when you said it wasn't a real marriage?"

"We were friends," he said. "Good friends, but

412

nothing more."

"And—and was the marriage ever consummated?"

He squeezed my hand reassuringly. "Never. I'm not Antonia's type, for one thing."

"Don't be so naive," I said. "You're every woman's type. I can't imagine how she could keep her hands off you."

"Now who's being naive?" he said, raising an eyebrow. "When I said, I'm not her type, I mean I'm the wrong gender. Faith," he added, "is much more her type."

"Faith!" I let out a long breath. "Ah, I see. But surely, if she'd told her father the reason she couldn't marry a man, he'd have understood?"

"Like I said earlier, you don't know Simon." Ethan's eyes glinted with contempt. "It's hard to believe that men like him still walk the earth, but it's true. He would despise her, if he knew the truth, no doubt about it."

"In this day and age?"

"Honestly. And it would break her heart. She struggled for a long time to accept herself the way she was. She really doesn't need to have her already low self-esteem completely crushed by that man. Antonia and I made vows when we got married. Not the ones we said in the registry office, but to each other in private. We promised that we wouldn't reveal the nature of our relationship to anyone until we both felt the time was right. I vowed to protect her. You rather put a spanner in the works."

"She's not ready to come out?"

"She's terrified. Scared stiff that he won't have anything more to do with her."

"But surely her relationship is more important than

413

her inheritance?"

"It's not about money," he assured me. "Antonia's wealthy in her own right, due to an inheritance from her grandfather. She doesn't actually need what she'll get from her father. The simple fact is, as bigoted as he is, she loves him. She doesn't want to disappoint him. She doesn't want to see that look of disgust in his eye."

Oh, I could relate to that. There was absolutely nothing worse than believing you'd made your parents ashamed of you, however unfair that might be. "Poor Antonia," I murmured.

"So, her solution was to go off travelling. She and Faith have seen the world. It was all so easy at first. We'd meet up now and then, and attend some family function, or other, to keep the gossip at bay. We'd spin the story that I had to be in London for work, and she loved to travel, and we'd put on a show of togetherness to convince everyone that, as unconventional as our marriage was, it worked for us. Then she'd go back to Faith, and no one was any the wiser. Simon wasn't happy about our marriage at first. In fact, he was furious. But I think my fortune eased his pain somewhat, and he accepted it eventually. Things ticked along nicely for ages, but it's all changed now. Things are tricky."

"Because of me?" I whispered.

"You're the reason I wanted to break my promise," he admitted. "But things got tricky even before then."

"Christmas? In Paris?"

He shook his head. "Devon, last July. It got messy."

"What happened?"

"She invited me to spend her birthday with them. I thought, perhaps she wanted to ask if we could end the

414

marriage. I knew she and Faith were keen to get married, themselves, and I thought, maybe they'd found the courage to be honest. I went over there, expecting to be told that the need for pretence was over. Instead .... Well, let's just say I got a shock. Faith and Antonia had decided they wanted a baby. More than that. They were desperate for one. Time, they felt, was running out for them. Faith couldn't have children, so it would have to be Antonia who carried the baby, and their idea was that I should father it."

"You're kidding!" I bit my lip. Of course he wasn't kidding! I already knew that part, didn't I? "So, it's true? The twins are—"

"No, no." He shook his head and gripped my hand even tighter. "Please believe me. No matter what you heard, the twins aren't mine. Faith was just panicking. Making idle threats. The babies were fathered by an anonymous donor at an expensive clinic. Antonia and Faith spent Antonia's entire birthday weekend trying to persuade me to be their donor, but I refused. I could see too many problems. For one thing, I couldn't bear not to be part of any child of mine's life, and I knew that wasn't in their plans. Faith wouldn't have stood it, for a start, so I told them they'd have to find some other way. We argued quite seriously, and parted on bad terms. Then, out of the blue, they invited me to spend Christmas with them in Paris. I wanted to make it up with them, so I went. They'd wanted to patch things up, too, but they also had some news they couldn't wait to share. After our row, they'd gone back to Plan B, which was the clinic, and Antonia had been lucky. She got pregnant the first time they tried, and it was twins. She was thrilled to bits, but, boy she's been ill. Sick all the way through it. She ended up in hospital at one point, it was so bad. I should think she's terribly relieved it's all over."

"So, what happened after that?" I said.

"Obviously, she knew that everyone would assume I'm the father, and I could hardly deny it without causing problems for her, could I? It was all such a mess that, in the end, I told my mother everything. She was appalled. Said I'd got myself into a real tangle, and I needed to force Antonia to come clean. But how could I do that to her, especially with how sick she'd been? She was hiding away, keeping the pregnancy secret as long as she could to avoid questions. Her own family don't know even now. She was so fragile, I just couldn't put any more pressure on her. Then I met you, Cara."

He put his arm around me. "I tried so hard to resist falling in love with you. It was the last thing I wanted, or expected. I didn't know who to trust, and I've always kept women at arm's length, for that reason. Being married made things so much easier, although it didn't put them all off. Jodie, for a start, and Briony, of course. I can't pretend I've been a saint, but I've always avoided relationships. When I met you, though, everything felt different.

"Before long, I knew I would have to make a choice. I knew it was either break my promise to Antonia, or lose you. I desperately wanted to tell you the truth, because I knew I couldn't get involved with you with all this hanging over my head. I told Antonia about you, but she didn't want to know. She insisted that you were probably a gold digger, just like all the others. She was too unwell for me to press her, so I left it for a while.

"Then Marcus came and told me about her father. I rang Faith, as you know, and told her Antonia needed to make her peace with him before it was too late. I talked to Antonia the other night, and I tried—I really tried—to convince her that she should tell him about her and Faith before it was too late. I explained that I had to be free to end the marriage, because I needed to be with you, but she got really upset and slammed the phone down on me. I was so worried about her, that I travelled down to see her, to talk things through with her. Unfortunately for me, she'd decided to come up to Yorkshire to confront me, which is why you heard what you heard. I'm so sorry, Cara. I never meant for you to find out that way. You must have hated me."

"Hating you would have been easy," I said. "It was loving you that made it so difficult." I leaned over and kissed him softly. "I'm sorry I left you without giving you the chance to explain."

"I understand," he said. "I'm just glad you changed your mind."

"And I'm sorry my ex-boyfriend tried to burn your house down."

"Hmm. Well, we've both got skeletons in the closet," he said, smiling.

"So, what about Antonia? What has she decided to do?"

"She's going to see her father, as soon as she's well enough. Tell him about his grandsons. He's not got long, and she'll continue spinning the lie. He'll assume they're my children, and she'll let him assume. When he's gone, she'll go through a tough time of it. Guilt, regret .... I can see it happening, but I just can't make her understand.

Still, at least she'll finally be able to live an honest life with the woman she loves." He stood up and faced me, his expression nervous. "I'm sorry, Cara, I really am, but I don't think she'll ever tell her father the truth, and I can't force her to do it. I don't want her to stress about anything, not when she's just given birth and she's got those two little boys to worry about. I can't annul the marriage just yet. I know what I said, but—"

I smiled. "Of course you can't annul it yet! She's got enough to deal with. Anyway, what does it matter? We have the rest of our lives together. We can wait a bit longer."

"As long as it takes?"

"Forever, if necessary. I'm going nowhere, Mr Rochester. I'll never leave you again."

"Promise?"

I stood up and kissed him gently on the forehead. He closed his eyes, but not before I'd seen the relief in them.

"As soon as we're able, we'll be married," he promised me.

"I'll hold you to that."

"No need." He wrapped his arms around me, and it was like coming home. "I know a good thing when I see it. This Mr Rochester has finally found his Truelove."

Chapter Thirty-Two

One year later. Paddington, London.

Michael opened the door of the Daimler for me, smiling broadly. I guess my emotions were written all over my face. "It went well, then, Mrs Rochester?"

"Brilliantly," I said, as I climbed into the backseat. "Ethan won't be a moment, then we'll have something to show you." I straightened the hem of my Stella McCartney dress, dropped my Jenny Kingston bag on the floor, and kicked off my Louboutin shoes, sighing with relief. I couldn't wait to change into my comfy jeans, pull my hair into a ponytail, and get back to normal.

"Excellent. I can't wait." He closed the door after me, then took his own seat at the front.

"Have you heard from Mrs F?" I asked, as he adjusted the rear-view mirror. I noticed the amused expression in his reflection, and tutted at my mistake. "Sorry, Michael. I can't get used to her new name. I mean, have you heard from Mrs Lawson?"

He grinned. "Of course. My good lady wife has only just put down the phone, as it happens. She sends her love. She can't wait to see you."

"And everything's okay?"

"Marvellous. She says the house looks wonderful, better than ever, and Mr Rochester's new art studio is amazing. He's going to love it."

"And Adele?"

"Currently installed in her new playroom and having afternoon tea with some of her schoolfriends."

Smiling, I took out my phone, delighted to see a message from Tamsin.

Redmond's invited us all to Baby Freddie's christening. Hope you're up for a trip to Lewis? We've just been to an ice cream parlour. I'm completely stuffed. Fabulous ice creams, though, worth every calorie. Brad sends his love and the kids are dying to see you. How's it going? Mum and Dad said today's the big day. Any news yet?

A trip to Lewis. I was desperate to see my gorgeous, red-haired nephew again, and I knew my husband would be keen to go with me. He'd really taken to my family, even Redmond, in spite of the pompous man-to-man chat he'd insisted on having with Ethan at our wedding. At least Kitty had tactfully cut it short in a very loving and gentle way. Adele would enjoy the trip, too. Alice and Robyn had quite taken her under their wings at the wedding, and I knew she'd be glad to see them again.

As the car door opened and Ethan jumped in beside me, my smile spread even wider, if that were possible. "You got it?"

"Of course. It's perfect, darling. Look."

I peered at the photograph he held in his hand, hardly able to believe what I was seeing. "Oh, gosh," I said, "how can such a grainy picture be so wonderful?"

He laughed. "It is a bit grainy," he admitted. "Nevertheless, it's the best photograph I've ever seen. I'm going to frame it. Look, Michael," he said, leaning forward and waving the picture in an amused Michael's face.

"Wonderful," Michael said, gruffly. "I'm very happy for you both."

I suspected he was being kind. It was very difficult to make it out clearly, to be honest. Those things usually were, weren't they?

As Ethan and Michael cooed over the picture, I picked up my phone and sent a text to Tamsin, Mum, Dad and Redmond.

Just left St Mary's hospital. First scan. All well. Baby Rochester is thriving. I'm very happy xx

Ethan leaned back and put his arm around me, as Michael started the car. "I'm very happy, too," he murmured, nodding at my phone. "In fact, I've never been happier in my life."

"Home, sir?" Michael enquired.

"Home, Michael," Ethan confirmed, then kissed the top of my head, as I curled up against him, and we began the long journey, back to our house on the moors.

Acknowledgements

My thanks, first and foremost, must go to you, the reader who has purchased this book. I'm grateful to everyone who has ever taken the time to read any of my stories, and I hope you have enjoyed *Resisting Mr Rochester*.

I'd like to say a big thank you to my husband, Steve, who drove me to the Brontë Parsonage Museum in Haworth, one rainy day, so that I could soak up the atmosphere and draw inspiration from the house. At least, that's what I told him. I just really love that place! Walking around the very house, where the Brontë sisters wrote their most famous works, is an awesome experience. I confess, as I gazed at Charlotte's belongings, and the quotations from *Jane Eyre* on the walls, I was in tears more than once. Thanks, Steve, not only for taking me, but for plodding patiently around the Parsonage, waiting for me to recover my composure, understanding my rather pathetic fangirl attitude, and not complaining when I spent yet more money in the gift shop. Thanks, also, for the endless cups of Yorkshire tea you always provide me with as I write. Your patience is very much appreciated.

Thanks, as always, to J B Editing Services for their sterling work with my manuscript. Any mistakes that remain are mine. Also, a huge thanks to Berni Stevens, who designed the gorgeous cover, and remained patient while I made up my mind what it was, exactly, that I wanted.

Finally, thanks to Alex Weston and Julie Heslington, who read an early draft of *Resisting Mr Rochester*. Their amazing suggestions and insights enabled me to pull the novel into shape. They both have a wonderful knack of seeing right into the core of my writing and knowing just how to improve it. Thank you both!

Other books by Sharon Booth

There Must Be an Angel (Kearton Bay 1)

When Eliza Jarvis discovers her property show presenter husband, Harry, has been expanding his portfolio with tabloid darling Melody Bird, her perfect life crumbles around her ears.

Before you can say Pensioner Barbie she's in a stolen car, heading to the North Yorkshire coastal village of Kearton Bay in search of the father she never knew, with only her three-year-old daughter and a family-sized bag of Maltesers for company.

Ignoring the pleas of her uncle, Joe Hollingsworth, Eliza determines to find the man who abandoned her mother and discover the reason he left them to their fate. All she has to go on is his name – Raphael – but in such a small place there can't be more than one angel, can there?

Gabriel Bailey may have the name of an angel but he's not feeling very blessed. In fact, the way his life's been going he doesn't see how things can get much worse. Then Eliza arrives with her flash car and designer clothes, reminding him of things he'd rather forget, and he realises that if he's to have any kind of peace she's one person he must avoid at all costs.

But with the help of beautiful Wiccan landlady, Rhiannon, and quirky pink-haired café owner, Rose, Eliza is soon on the trail of her missing angel, and her investigations lead her straight into Gabriel's path. As her search takes her deeper into the heart of his family, Eliza begins to realise that she's in danger of hurting those she cares about deeply. Is her quest worth it?

And is the angel she's seeking really the one she's meant to find?

A Kiss from a Rose (Kearton Bay 2)

One kiss can change your life…

Rose Maclean's new beginning in Kearton Bay didn't go quite as expected, but now she has a new career and things finally seem to be improving.

But Rose's life never runs smoothly for long. With money tight, space in her tiny flat at a premium, and her eldest daughter, Fuschia, behaving even more strangely than usual, the last thing she needs is to spend more time with her mother. Mrs Maclean is straight-talking and hard to please, but when she becomes the unexpected victim of a crime, Rose has no choice but to take her into her already cramped home.

Reduced to sleeping on the sofa, dealing with her mother's barbed comments, and worrying endlessly about her teenage daughters, Rose is desperately in need of something good to happen.

Flynn Pennington-Rhys is the quiet man of Kearton Bay. He lives alone in a large, elegant house, and works as a GP in the village. Thoughtful, reliable, but a bit of a loner, Flynn is the last person Rose expected to fall for. Then a drunken kiss at a wedding sets them on a path that neither could have predicted.

But Flynn has his own issues to deal with, and when events take an unexpected turn, it seems Rose may not be able to rely on him, after all.

Will the quiet man come through for her? Will her daughters ever sort themselves out? And will Rose ever get her bedroom back from her mother, or is she destined to spend the rest of her life on the sofa?

Once Upon a Long Ago (Kearton Bay 3)

Lexi Bailey doesn't do love. Having seen the war zone that was her parents' marriage, she has no interest in venturing into a relationship, and thinks romance is for fairy tales. As far as she's concerned, there's no such thing as happy ever after, and she's not looking for a handsome prince.

For Will Boden-Kean, that's probably a good thing. He hardly qualifies as a handsome prince, after all. He may be the son of a baronet, and live in a stately home, but he's not known for his good looks. What he is known for, among the residents of Kearton Bay, is his kind heart, his determination to fund Kearton Hall — and his unrequited love for Lexi.

While Lexi gazes at the portrait of the Third Earl Kearton, and dreams of finding the treasure that is reputed to be hidden somewhere in the house, Will is working hard to ensure that his home survives. When he goes against Lexi's wishes and employs the most unpopular man in the village, she begins to wonder if he's under a spell. Will would never upset her. What could possibly have happened to him?

As plans take shape for a grand ball, Lexi's life is in turmoil. With a secret from Will's past revealed, a witch who is far too beautiful for Lexi's peace of mind, and a new enchantress on the scene, things are changing rapidly at Kearton Hall. Add to that a big, bad wolf of a work colleague, a stepmother in denial, and a father who is most definitely up to no good, and it's no wonder she decides to make a new start somewhere else.

Is it too late to find her happy ending? Will Lexi make it to the ball? Will Buttons save the day? And where on earth did that handsome prince come from?

This Other Eden (Skimmerdale 1)

Eden wants to keep her job, and, as that means spending the summer caring for three young children in the wilds of the Yorkshire Dales, she has no choice but to go along with it. Her consolation prize is that their father is unexpectedly gorgeous. Sadly for Eden, she's not quite herself any longer...

Honey wants to spend the summer with her married politician lover. The only problem is, there are quite a few people determined to put obstacles in her path. But what Honey wants, Honey usually gets...

Cain wants a knighthood and is willing to sacrifice almost anything for it. If his daughter is putting that goal in jeopardy, it's time to get tough...

Lavinia wants to keep her marriage intact, and if that means turning a blind eye to her husband's philandering, she'll do it. But that doesn't mean she can't have someone else spying for her...

Eliot wants to care for his children, and to be left in peace to heal. When he gets an unexpected guest, he wonders if it's time to start living again. But is this sheep farmer having the wool pulled over his eyes?

Cake baking, jam making, gymkhana games and sheep showing. Blackmail, deception, spying and cheating. Laughter, forgiveness, redemption and falling in love. A lot can happen during one summer in Skimmerdale...

Other novels you may enjoy from Fabrian Books

A Highland Practice by Jo Bartlett

Dr Evie Daniels has recently lost her mother. Unable to save the person she loved most in the world, she considers giving up medicine altogether; especially when her fiancé is unable to understand her grief. Instead she decides to leave her life in London and fulfil her promise to her mother to see as much of the world as possible. Her first stop is to escape to the wilds of the Scottish Highlands and a job as a locum in the remote town of Balloch Pass. It's only ever meant to be the first step on her journey, though, a temporary job she has no intention of sticking with. There's a whole world to see and a promise to fulfil, after all.

But she doesn't expect to be working with someone like Dr Alasdair James – a hometown hero – whose own life changes beyond all recognition when his best friend dies and leaves him guardian to two young children. With enough drama in their personal and professional lives to fill a medical encyclopaedia, they soon develop a close friendship. Can it ever go beyond that when Evie's determined to see the world and Alasdair has commitments at home he just can't break? Or are they destined to be forever in the wrong place at the wrong time?

Air Guitar and Caviar by Jackie Ladbury

Busker Dylan spends his days pulling pints in the local pub and singing on the high street, waiting for fame to call. That suits him fine, until beautiful, but frosty, air stewardess, Scarlett, tosses some coins into his hat but ignores his killer smile and his offer of pizza.

He sets out to get the girl, but Scarlett isn't in the right frame of mind to date anyone, let alone a penniless, if charming, busker boy.

Dylan's desperate for his big break, but will it bring him the happiness he longs for? And with Scarlett's past threatening to ruin her future, will Dylan be left to make sweet music all on his own?

Beltane by Alys West

When Zoe Rose stays at Anam Cara – a guest house in Glastonbury, a town steeped in magic and myth – she dreams of a handsome stranger. The next day she meets him.

Tall with untidy brown hair and grey eyes, Finn is funny and intelligent but doesn't open up easily. Instantly drawn to him, Zoe doesn't initially recognise him as the man from her dream. When Finn finds out where Zoe is staying he warns her not to trust Maeve, the healer who owns Anam Cara.

His enigmatic comments fuel Zoe's growing unease about what's happening at Anam Cara. What power does Maeve have over the minds of the other guests? Is it coincidence that they become ill after she's given them healing? Why does the stone table in the garden provoke memories of blood and terror? And how did the Green Man, carved on a tree in the garden, disappear during a thunderstorm?

Finn's torn between wanting to protect Zoe from his world and a strong desire to be with her. And the more time they spend together the harder it is for him to keep his secrets from her. As they uncover the dark, supernatural secrets of Anam Cara, they grow closer and Zoe's forced to accept that her dreams reveal the future and Finn is not all he seems.

For Finn is a druid, connected by magic to the earth, and the old scores between Finn and Maeve are about to put Zoe's life in danger.